A GENTLE TOUCH

He watched the sleek falcon move to Vivian's arm. She seemed to have a rare calming effect on the bird. "Who taught you to gentle a falcon to your hand?"

"One learns quickly when dealing with a wild creature what to do and not to do. She has never harmed me."

Rorke watched, fascinated, as the falcon cocked her lovely head this way and that to catch the soft nuances of Vivian's words. He reached out and stroked the falcon's downy breast; it recalled the satin texture of Vivian's skin.

A faint frown wrinkled Vivian's forehead. "She has never taken a stranger's hand before today," she said, "nor tolerated another's touch."

"And what of her mistress?" he asked, reaching to stroke the back of a finger along the curve of Vivian's lower lip. His voice had gone low in his throat, as though he sought to gentle her with touch and words.

Strange feelings, remembered vaguely from a summer day long ago, spiraled through her. How was it possible that such a hard, brutal hand could be so gentle?

He felt the tension that quivered through her. The heat of innocent sensuality glistened at her parted lips. A raw desire, naked and powerful, clenched inside him, a taut low fist at his belly, as he imagined her slender hand stroking him as she stroked the falcon . . .

MERLIN'S LEGACY:
DAUGHTER OF FIRE

Quinn Taylor Evans

Zebra Books
Kensington Publishing Corp.
http://www.zebrabooks.com

ZEBRA BOOKS are published by

Kensington Publishing Corp.
850 Third Avenue
New York, NY 10022

First Printing: January, 1996
10 9 8 7 6 5 4

Printed in the United States of America

Legend

"Merlin is dead!"

The rumor swept the land and men, both highborn and low, wept with grief. "The enchanter, the sorcerer, the kingmaker is dead."

And from remote fortress castle, from fields tending their flocks, from boats with lines cast into gleaming dark waters, and blazing forges, men looked toward the hollow hills for the glow of the sorcerer's funeral pyre. But instead, they saw a bright blue star high in the midnight sky like a brilliant jewel suspended between heaven and earth.

A sign, some said, as the star streaked the sky, a fiery beacon that lights a path, a dragon's eye that sees beyond the mists of time. And even as word of Merlin's death reached the farthest shores of the realm, another story was whispered around the fires and at water's edge, like a promise on the cold night wind.

"Not dead, but asleep . . . asleep in the mist."

Prologue

"Element of fire, spirit of light, essence of life, awaken the night. Fire of the soul, flame of life, as light reveals truth burn golden bright."

High in the tower of the crumbling abbey the ancient words whispered across cold, damp walls.

A single candle glowed, the flame steadily growing stronger with each word. At her perch in the corner of the tower, a small falcon flared her wings, golden eyes fastened on the flame.

Vivian leaned over the candle, its golden light bathing across pale, taut features, delicate auburn brows, high cheekbones and gleaming like molten fire in the flaming torrent of unbound hair that cascaded down her back. Dark lashes lay against her cheeks as with eyes closed she repeated the ancient words.

Brilliant blue color blended with bright gold in spinning, shifting patterns across stone walls as the flame reflected off the large blue crystal she held suspended before the candle. It created a tapestry of light that glittered and winked as if the walls and ceiling had suddenly become the night sky filled with stars.

Then, as if it obeyed her command, the light suddenly swallowed itself, the glittering patterns of light at the ceiling coalescing into a single point of light until all that remained was the flame that now burned inside the crystal.

"Reveal to me a time that is not yet time, on a day that is not yet a day," she whispered.

The flame pulsed and quivered with each word, like a heart beating in silent, still air. It had been over five hundred years since a vision last appeared in the ancient blue crystal. As Vivian opened her eyes, a scene slowly revealed itself. She saw two great armies joined in a fierce battle of fire, death, and destruction, and bodies lying on a vast, dark plain. Her heart ached as she saw the Saxon Stag consumed by the Serpent, knowing with a certainty the army of King Harold would fall before the army of William the Conqueror. Knowing, too, that she was powerless to prevent it. For what she saw was the future that was already written.

Tears of anguish slipped down her cheeks. She didn't want to see any more of the death and destruction, and squeezed her eyes tightly shut, trying to block out the tragic images as she saw her world ending.

But a power stronger than her own compelled her to look once more into the crystal. For such was the curse as well as the blessing of the gift she'd been born with. Once a vision revealed itself, she must see all of it no matter how painful or terrifying. And as the vision continued to unfold at the heart of the crystal, she knew the fate of her people was in her hands.

The flames of death and destruction she had first seen slowly burned to ashes, and the smoke of battle cleared as another prophecy revealed itself. From amidst the dying flames and ash, a magnificent creature raised its head—a creature born in the fire and blood of destruction.

It was sleek and powerful, and at the same time fierce and terrifying. A great predatory bird with feathers of yellow, orange, and red flame as wings slowly unfurled in a blaze of fiery grace amidst a gathering darkness, and words whispered to her from the heart of the crystal.

"Beware the faith that has no heart, and the sword that has no soul."

As if the creature knew she watched, its head turned. The

blood of war stained its beak, eyes burning into hers. And a new and far different emotion swept over her, unlike anything she had ever experienced.

The creature rising from the ash and flames like the mythical phoenix took on the features of a man, and a wild, savage passion reached out from the heart of the crystal.

One

"Soldiers!"

The cry of alarm rang out in the chill morning air from the yard below and was heard high in the abbey tower.

At her perch, the falcon's plaintive warning cries joined the alarm, glossy wings poised for sudden flight. The cat, Nicodemas, sleeping contentedly by the brazier, suddenly jumped to the floor and fled under the table.

Beware, Vivian!

The warning whispered along the walls of the herbal, the words urgent amidst the bubble and hiss of concoctions simmering at the brazier.

Vivian ran to the narrow window at the east wall of the tower and caught a glimpse of young Tom, the smithy's son from the village, in the yard below.

He ran past the pigsty, where the sow suckled her new litter of piglets. Skinny legs pumped furiously as Tom crossed the stream and ran down the cart road, spreading the alarm.

In the distance, Vivian saw the mounted soldiers emerging from the forest on the old Roman road. Their battle armor was deadly gray beneath the bleak late autumn sky, and the banner they carried as they rode toward the abbey was a serpent on a field of black seething overhead on the bitter cold wind.

Fear clutched at Vivian's heart for she had seen the serpent in the vision that appeared in the crystal. Ever since that day, the villagers of Amesbury had waited with dread, for many men and boys from the village had gone to fight with King Harold at Hastings. Now the prophecy of the crystal had been fulfilled. England was lost.

The villagers would already have been warned by Tom, who spent his mornings hunting in the forest. Therefore, her first concern was for her guardians, the monk, Poladouras, and her old nurse, Megwin. For they might not have heard the boy's warning of the soldiers who now rode toward the abbey.

Earlier that morning, she and Meg had gone to the garden to gather the last of the herbs before the first winter snow fell. Vivian had returned to the herbal to brew the medicinal concoctions needed for the villagers through the coming winter. Meg had remained behind to finish the gathering.

Poladouras had spent most of the morning with her in the herbal, for the light there was better for studying his ancient journals. Long ago the roof timbers of the uppermost part of the tower had rotted away from neglect, since his fellow monks had abandoned Amesbury for the newer abbey at St. Anne's in Croydon.

The gap in the roof let in light during the day and provided a window on the sky at night for the scholarly monk to chart the stars. Only a short while earlier, he had returned to the chapel below for one of the ancient manuscripts that he was constantly studying.

As if the crystal sensed her fear, it shimmered and glittered about her neck with a sudden fiery light amidst the firefall of red hair that swirled loose about her shoulders as she ran for the stone steps leading to the chapel below. She must warn Poladouras and Meg.

That fear tightened around her heart and hastened her descent faster than was wise without a candle or torch to light the way along the steep downward spiral of stone steps. But Vivian had crawled these steps since she was a babe, after she and Meg first came to live with Poladouras.

They had been pilgrims led by another falcon on an uncertain journey, and taken in by the reclusive, kindhearted monk in the midst of the worst storm that anyone at Amesbury could remember. When winter ended they remained at the abbey.

As she grew and learned the healing ways from old Meg, mornings were spent in the herbal brewing the ancient healing concoctions. Afternoons were spent at Poladouras' knee learning languages, mathematics, and sciences that he acquired a knowledge of on his travels to the Eastern empires.

Life was quiet at the abbey, their few needs provided by the small garden Meg and Vivian planted, and the food and wool provided by the villagers out of gratitude for Poladouras' spiritual guidance and Vivian's healing tonics.

The villagers were simple people who barely eked out an existence. While to the east, the village of Croydon, situated on the main road to London, was far more prosperous. Because they had nothing of value, Vivian had been certain the villagers of Amesbury had little to fear from the Norman invaders.

Amesbury Abbey had fallen into neglect and ruin over the years since it was abandoned by the monks. Only Poladouras had remained, ostracized by his fellow brethren for his learned ways.

The outer walls were little more than a pile of loose stones, the mortar between long ago crumbling away and exposing gaps that let in the rain and cold.

Now, all that remained of Amesbury Abbey was the dingy, soot-filled kitchen, a handful of niche chambers once occupied by the monks, the tower that she used for her herbal, and the small chapel where Poladouras read of an evening before a brazier and old Meg worked at her spinning wheel.

Why then, she thought frantically, were Norman soldiers now riding toward the abbey? What did they want?

Beware, my child!

Again she heard the urgent words, as if the stones of the tower whispered the warning to her.

She reached the bottom landing and immediately saw Poladouras hobbling toward her. The meager light from the nearby brazier, which had been lit for warmth, played across her pale, taut features, and reflected in eyes as blue as the ancient crystal that hung about her neck.

"Young Tom . . . !" she said breathlessly and heard the fear in her own voice.

"Aye," the kindly monk nodded gravely. "Norman soldiers. Just as you have foreseen."

There was no surprise in his voice, for the monk learned long ago to trust her visions. "King Harold's army has fallen then," he said grimly, his voice breaking. " 'Tis a tragic time for all England."

"Meg?" she asked anxiously.

"I am here," the old woman called out.

With the bond that connected them from the first moment the old woman held the newborn child in her arms, old Meg's gaze turned toward the steps. She crossed the chapel with surprising spryness for one so bent and crippled by the painful stiffness in her joints. Her thin hand, which had eased so much childhood pain and fear, was surprisingly strong as it closed over Vivian's arm.

"You must leave!" she said urgently. "Flee now, child, by way of the hills, while there is still time."

"Aye, you must go," Poladouras said adamantly, adding his voice to Meg's with a sudden harshness she'd never heard before. Vivian was stunned by their vehemence.

"I will not leave!" Then she saw the look that passed between her beloved guardians and knew it had already been decided.

Poladouras' expression softened. "Dear child," he said, pleading with her, "the days ahead will be dark enough for us all. More than anyone else you must know that you must not fall into Norman hands. We will be safe enough. Now go, quickly!" he implored. "Before it is too late!"

But it was already too late.

Sagging oak doors, which barely kept out the wind and cold, suddenly crashed back against the stone wall. The bitter cold wind that had carried the ominous warning of an early winter storm for two days, swirled through the opening, smothering out candles that had been lit against the midmorning gloom as the weather steadily closed in.

The only light came from the guttering fire in the brazier and the gray gloom at the doorway as the acrid stench of smoldering tallow gusted through the sanctuary. The light cast a pall of shadows over the room as Norman soldiers swarmed inside the abbey with drawn swords. Meg pulled Vivian into the shadows behind the altar.

"Say nothing!" she warned vehemently as Poladouras turned to face the Norman invaders.

The monk stood before the altar, stooped and round-shouldered as though far older than his years. He leaned more heavily than usual on the stout walking stick as though the simple effort of standing required all his strength. The crucifix he always wore gleamed against the coarse wool of his cassock for all to see, and the expression on his round, kindly face was one of surprise. But the hand that gripped the head of the stout walking stick was white-knuckled, his gentle eyes gleaming with a fierce, defiant light, and Vivian's heart constricted with fear for she sensed the dangerous game he played.

Vivian could easily have broken the old woman's grasp at her arm, but another voice added its urgency to Meg's warning.

Do not! All is at stake!

"Stand away!" A command was harshly ordered in French and the soldiers parted to let one among them pass through.

Poladouras frowned. " 'Tis not necessary to break down the chapel doors. What is the meaning of this? Who are you? Why do you bring weapons into God's house?"

"This is now William of Normandy's house," the soldier who came forward among his men informed him contemptuously in heavily accented English. "As is now all of England."

The Norman soldier was dressed in heavy chain mail armor, with leather leggings and gauntlets. His helm had been removed, the mail link coif molding hard, cold features. His tunic was green and hung to his knees. The hem was badly stained. With a jolt of alarm, Vivian realized the stains were blood.

"We have come for the healer whose reputation is well-known," the Norman soldier announced, gloved hand resting at the handle of the broadsword belted at his waist.

Poladouras' expression was that of mild surprise. Then he shrugged and shook his head, and Vivian was stunned at the lie that fell so easily from his lips.

"I know not of whom you speak, milord. There is no one else here. Only myself, a humble monk."

The Norman soldier's eyes narrowed and Vivian sensed the danger in the flat, dark gaze that fastened on Poladouras.

"A Saxon said the healer could be found here. He was most certain of it, for he carried a wound he claimed the healer had treated. According to him, the healer's talents are well-known."

Again Poladouras shrugged. "He is mistaken. Amesbury is far too poor for someone of such reputation."

"The man's hand had been severely burned," the Norman explained. "Although it was almost healed when we met," the Norman informed him. His mouth curved with a cruel smirk. "I know not the man's name but he spoke of the healer, before he died under my blade."

In the shadow of the altar, Vivian gasped, for she knew he spoke of young Tom's father. The smith had burned his hand badly only days before he and the other men left for Hastings.

Sensing her anguish, Meg's hand clamped even more tightly over Vivian's arm. "There is naught you can do for him now, child!" she whispered.

Poladouras dismissed the Norman's claim, betraying no outward sign that he knew the man the Norman spoke of. "A simple mistake," he insisted, "for there is no healer at Amesbury."

But the Norman soldier was not convinced of it. His eyes narrowed dangerously as he ordered his men, "Search the chapel! Bring me the healer!"

Poladouras hobbled forward as though to stop them. "This

is sacrilege! I must protest! You may not enter this sacred place with your bloodied weapons!"

The Norman drew his sword and held it threateningly against Poladouras' chest. "Cease your pious whining, old man. Or you will die where you stand."

Vivian struggled to free herself, but Meg fiercely held on. "Say nothing!" she warned. "You have heard the Voice! These Norman pigs must not find you!"

The soldiers quickly moved through the chapel. A chair was smashed beneath one soldier's boot. Another swept a basin of broth for the midday meal from the table, its contents soaking into the dirt floor. The rest of the meager food—a loaf of stale bread, mold-crusted cheese, and hard-cooked eggs—was seized and stuffed into greedy mouths. The table was shattered beneath a war ax. Casks of Poladouras' favorite ale, delivered the day before from the village, were split open, their pungent contents puddling on the floor. A fleece blanket that Poladouras used to keep warm on long winter nights as he sat reading was sliced to shreds, the pieces stomped into the ale-soaked dirt on the floor. Another blanket was tossed onto the fire at the brazier, the acrid smell of burning fleece fouling the air already redolent with the stench of tallow, spilt ale, and smoke.

Poladouras' precious journals and manuscripts were discovered and joined the pile of debris on the dirt floor. Astrology charts, painstakingly made, were torn from the walls and tossed onto the smoldering fire. Flames caught and greedily consumed the parchment and a lifetime's worth of work.

Vivian's throat ached with tears at the loss, her heart breaking that it was because of her. Her slender hands clenched into fists of helpless rage as Meg continued to whisper her desperate warnings. If Vivian had had a weapon, she would gladly have turned it on them and not cared the blood that was spilled.

"Please," the monk beseeched them, hobbling from one to the other on swollen, gout-ridden legs. "The books are of no importance to you," he reasoned. "Do not destroy them."

"You are correct, monk," the Norman assured him in a contemptuous voice, "they are not important. But you may save your precious books," he suggested, "by giving me the healer!"

"I have already told you," Poladouras insisted, even as the soldiers spread to other parts of the abbey and he knew it was only a matter of time before Vivian and Meg were discovered. "I know not of whom you speak. Surely not even William of Normandy would dare to defile a chapel!"

A terrified scream came from the passage that led to the kitchen, and Vivian immediately thought of Pegeen, the village woman who often brought food to the abbey. But it was not the stout Saxon woman's scream she heard. It was the young girl, Mally, whose terrified mewlings were like that of a wounded animal.

The girl had come to her earlier that morning for an herbal tisane to ease her dying mother's discomfort. No doubt she had been caught by the soldiers on the village road. She was dragged by one of the soldiers into the chapel, sobbing hysterically.

"Ho, Vachel!" the soldier called out in French, grinning viciously. "See what I have found not far from the abbey. A sweet little reward for our trouble."

Her captor held Mally by the neck of her gown, dragging her to the middle of the chapel, where he hauled her to her feet and pulled the girl back against him, the blade of a knife pressed against her throat.

Mally's dark hair was tangled, eyes wild with fear. Her bottom lip was split and bleeding. The bodice of her gown gaped open over young breasts where dark bruises discolored tender flesh. Blood stained her skirt.

"I cannot bear to have others suffer because of me." Vivian's heart constricted, a sob choking her throat.

"You must bear it!" Meg hissed vehemently. "The girl's fate must not be yours!"

Tears of helpless rage burned at Vivian's eyes. Her slender hands clenched over the folds of her skirt, nails scraping against the hard length of something forgotten until that moment, in the pocket of her gown.

She thrust her hand into the pocket and felt the cool length of blade she'd used that morning to cut herbs in the garden. She'd dropped it into her pocket as she returned to the herbal.

Raising his walking stick overhead and waving it about as though it was a weapon, Poladouras hobbled toward the Norman soldiers and bravely faced them down.

"This is consecrated ground!" he chastised them. "The girl is no more than a child. How dare you bring your death and destruction into this Holy place! For the sake of your mortal souls, release the girl and leave at once before you are damned for all eternity!"

The shouting and lewd comments among the Norman soldiers abruptly ceased. For several moments there was only the guttering sound of the smoldering fire at the brazier and Vivian sensed the uneasiness among Vachel's men at having God's wrath called down on them.

Vachel no doubt sensed it too, and sensed as well that his men wavered. An expression of cold fury twisted his cruel features.

"Damn you! old fool," he cursed, raising his sword and viciously striking Poladouras against the side of the head with the hilt.

The blow staggered Poladouras to his knees, and Vachel's flat dark eyes gleamed with pleasure as he raised the sword to strike again.

"Nay!" Vivian cried out fiercely as she lunged from her hiding place and ran to protect the monk from another blow.

An agony of despair filled old Meg's heart that she had not been able to protect the child who had been entrusted to her care so many years ago. Still, she thought quickly, there might be a way to trick these simpleminded fools.

"I am the one you seek," she told the Norman soldiers as she emerged from behind the altar and slowly walked toward them. "I am the healer."

"No!" Vivian cried out as Meg was immediately seized by two of Vachel's men and thrust to the dirt at his feet.

Vachel reached down, cruelly seizing Meg by the throat and jerking her chin up. The silvery nimbus of her long, white hair fell back from her face. His gaze narrowed, features contorting with the beginnings of a dangerous rage at the pale, sightless eyes that stared back at him. He cursed.

"The old hag is blind!" He brutally cuffed Meg against the side of the head and sent her sprawling into the dirt.

As she fell, Meg cried a desperate warning to Vivian, "Flee, *mo chroi*. Save yourself!" Then, with amazing agility, she flung herself at Vachel, wrapping her thin arms about his legs.

He kicked her brutally, lifting Meg's fragile, wispy body with the toe of his boot, and flinging her aside as if she were no more than a bothersome mongrel.

"Do not touch her!" Vivian cried out. With a fierce protective instinct, she lunged for Vachel's throat with the knife.

On a shouted warning from one of his men, he deflected her attack with his arm. Instead of his throat, the blade opened a ribbon of flesh at his cheek. He yelped, like one of Poladouras' stray hounds, his fingers probing his injured cheek. His flat, dark eyes gleamed dangerously.

"Saxon bitch!" he snarled, raising his fist. The blow caught Vivian on the shoulder and would have sent her to the floor except for his other fist twisted in the length of her hair.

A tingling sensation spread the length of her arm from her bruised shoulder to numb fingertips. The knife fell to the floor of the chapel.

Vachel pulled her toward him, her hair twisted about his fist like a thick satin rope that he slowly drew in. Her head was forced back, anchored by his fist at her hair.

"There are ways to tame a cat with sharp claws." He smiled— a cold, vicious expression—lips pulled back over teeth set in the wreath of matted and crusted beard. He brought the sword up and pressed the blade against her throat.

"Now, I will show the bloodthirsty vixen who is her new

master," he vowed. He angled the sword lower and with a flick of his wrist cut through the bodice of her kirtle to tender flesh below, carving a gleaming dark crescent in the pale skin at her breast. Droplets of blood beaded at the wound and Vachel's smile deepened as his gaze fastened on the glistening mark.

"I pay back threefold, demoiselle," he vowed against her cheek. "My brand on you is but the first." She was turned and dragged back against him, her back pressed against the wall of his chest, the mat of his beard sticky with his own blood, pressed against the side of her face as he held her. The links of chain mail that covered his arm bit through the soft wool of her gown to scrape the flesh at her breasts.

"I will tame you," he vowed. "And then I will ride you like the Saxon bitch you are! When I am through you will crawl at my feet! You will beg to call me master and do my bidding."

Vivian refused to cry out or cower. Instead she held herself rigid against him, her chin lifted proudly, eyes glittering with hatred. Vachel jerked viciously on the thick silk of her hair bound about his hand.

"Do you understand?" he demanded viciously, in heavily accented English. "Are you Saxons too ignorant to comprehend the simplest command given by your new masters?"

"Je vous comprends," Vivian answered in perfect, flawless French, her own voice filled with contempt, and watched with satisfaction the stunned expression at those cruel eyes.

Then she asked defiantly, *"Me comprenez-vous?* Do you understand *me?"*

Her features were taut, color high at her cheeks. Her voice was filled with all the loathing and hatred she felt as she said, "Confess your sins, Vachel, and pray for forgiveness. For I vow, by the ancient ones, for what you have done you are already dead."

His soldiers' laughter joined his. "Tell me, demoiselle," Vachel asked, his coarse beard scraping at her cheek. "How have I died? Have you perchance slain me and I am a ghost who now holds you prisoner?" He threw back his head and laughed all the harder. "Have you used some magical sword to strike me down?"

Once more he brought the sword up and laid it against her cheek. "If I am dead," Vachel speculated, his breath hot and foul against her skin, "how is it possible that I now hold this blade against *your* lovely throat?"

Vivian recoiled with revulsion, inwardly cringing at the terrifying threat of the blade, outwardly refusing to let him see even a trace of that fear.

"Please! I beseech you," Poladouras implored as he struggled painfully to his feet. "Do not harm her. She is but a foolish girl. She meant no harm, but sought only to protect the old woman as any child would protect her mother."

But Vachel seemed not to hear as he pressed the sword more firmly against soft, supple flesh, his eyes glinting with cruel pleasure.

Suddenly, the sagging doors of the abbey were flung back with a crash that shuddered through the walls of the chapel. A score more of Norman knights and an equal number of armed soldiers stood just inside the entrance to the chapel.

"Cease, Vachel! Or die!"

Vachel's expression flattened with disbelief, then contorted with rage as he spun around, dragging Vivian with him.

"Rorke FitzWarren! You blackhearted son of Lucifer!" he hissed.

Vivian felt the sudden uncertainty of Vachel's hand at her hair, saw the uneasy tic of muscle at his cheek above the heavy growth of beard, and smelled the unmistakable tang of his fear.

The Norman knight stood framed by a leaden sky at the gaping entrance to the chapel, then slowly walked forward, battle sword drawn. His men moved similarly, insinuating themselves amongst Vachel's men and she sensed the cold, threatening rage that seethed between the two men and their soldiers.

Rorke FitzWarren filled the chapel with a dangerous, powerful presence; heavy muscles—no doubt hardened by many battles—were molded by the cumbersome chain mail with an ease of familiarity as if both armor and battle were longtime companions.

The thick mail coif was pushed carelessly back and lay in heavy folds across wide shoulders. His hair was a rich dark sable color, glossy as a falcon's wing, and worn long to his shoulders rather than the bowl-shaped style Vachel and his men favored.

In the guttering light from the brazier, Vivian saw strong, sharply angled features at the slope of a wide forehead, the ridge of long nose, the flat plane of high cheekbones, and set of his jaw that might have been either strength of character or stubbornness or perhaps both, beneath the shadow of several days' growth of beard.

By contrast his mouth was well curved, with a startling sensuality, even now as his lips thinned and flattened with contempt at the wanton destruction he saw before him. Eyes that reflected the bleak day in their cold, gray depths, looked about him with disgust. But beneath the icy aloofness she saw a furious anger.

Some inexplicable awareness shimmered through her, like an invisible hand caressing her startled senses—of danger, mind-numbing terror, and stunned fascination.

As Rorke FitzWarren raised his sword and leveled the lethal tip against Vachel's throat, the guttering light of the brazier played across the crest of his tunic.

Golden threads shimmered and glowed, catching the meager light from the dying fire. As if the threads became the flame itself, the lean, hunting bird woven into the fabric seemed to rise from the red-and-gold flames like a magnificent creature born in fire and blood.

Fear sharpened and spiraled through her, stronger than any fear she had of Vachel. For it was the same creature she had seen in the crystal, the mythical phoenix rising from the ash and flame of destruction.

Then the man whose features she had first seen that day in the heart of the blue crystal looked at her, and that wild, savage passion burned deep into her soul.

Two

If a flame could take human form, it would be the beautiful creature standing before Rorke FitzWarren.

Her skin was pale golden light, the tangled mass of her hair that spilled to her waist like all the colors of fire at the hearth, with brilliant red and deepest burgundy, blended with soft amber. But it was her eyes that drew his attention and held him captive.

They were like the shimmering heart of a resting flame when soft yellow color goes completely clear, and then magically transforms to intense blue.

He had seen the fire of countless war camps in dozens of foreign places he would rather forget, on the battlefield where good men fought for just causes and died and others fought for greed of wealth and lived, and at the funeral pyres of the fallen. So long had he been at war, that when he thought of fire, he thought of death.

Until that moment he had never thought of fire as something pure and alive. The beautiful Saxon was alive with the fire of indomitable pride, defiance, and passionate anger, as if fire found life within her and any who touched her would surely be burned. But it would be an exquisite torture.

Even now, he felt the fascination stir into a longing of desire to touch that pale skin, to feel the fiery silk of her hair between his fingers, to lose himself in those angry, defiant eyes and discover if the fire burned within.

Within those wintry gray eyes of the phoenix, Vivian felt as if she had looked within herself and glimpsed all the deepest, darkest shadows that haunted her visions and dreams.

Rorke FitzWarren was her enemy, a creature born in fire and blood in a vision not seen for five hundred years. He was death and destruction.

And yet she could not look away, for she knew she was staring at the future that was not yet written. It was reaching out to her, dark, unknown, and terrifying, like the bold Norman knight who stood with sword drawn, and eyes like winter's dawn.

"Damn you!" Vachel spat at Rorke FitzWarren. "I was sent to find the healer. Why are you here?" he demanded.

FitzWarren's expression became even more predatory, his gaze like arctic ice. "I wanted to make certain you encountered no *difficulty*." Then he demanded, "Release her."

"The Saxon bitch came at me with a blade," Vachel snarled, his hand tightening in Vivian's hair. "I might have been killed."

"Aye," Rorke FitzWarren commented. His frosty gaze lowered to the front of her bodice, where Vachel's blade had drawn blood.

"I can well see the grave danger you were in," he said cynically, then repeated, "Release her."

At her back, Vivian felt his subtle shift of muscles as Vachel's shoulders pressed at her back and knew he had no intention of letting her go. He shifted his stance and moved to raise his broadsword. But he was immediately confronted by the gleaming length of FitzWarren's blade. It sliced dangerously below Vachel's chin as it pressed against the vulnerable flesh at the neck opening of chain mail armor.

Vachel's eyes widened, and he paled. Then color swept furiously up his neck and across his cheeks as he inhaled on a harsh, guttural curse. Vivian felt him stiffen and the curse froze in his throat. She saw the cause of it in the ribbon of blood that slipped down the length of Rorke FitzWarren's blade.

"Release her, or die," FitzWarren said with such brutal calm that Vivian shivered. Vachel suddenly stood very still.

She sensed his fury and the silent battle he waged with it,

and the fear. It matched her own, for that lethal blade gleamed beside her cheek, so close that the crimson of Vachel's blood blurred against the glimmer of Rorke FitzWarren's steel blade.

Terrified that he might waver and lose control of the sword, her gaze swept back to FitzWarren. She needn't have had any fear. For he was so cold of purpose and perfectly controlled that she was certain no heart beat within him. And she began to doubt that he was the creature of fire and blood she had seen in crystal. At that moment she believed Rorke FitzWarren would kill Vachel.

"I have often thought," FitzWarren told him, "that the best soldier is one who has experienced both ends of the blade." The tip of the blade was only a hairbreadth from the rapidly pounding pulse it pressed against.

"The experience of one makes for a better appreciation of the other. It is a wise man who understands this." He shrugged, a gesture that seemed improbably casual beneath the weight of the chain mail hauberk he wore. "And a fool of one who does not." He paused only slightly in the casual exchange.

"Tell me, Vachel, are you wise? Or are you a fool?"

Since gaining his own knighthood, Rorke had known countless men like Vachel. Vachel was a mercenary, a professional soldier like so many others who sold their services to the highest bidder.

Rorke's cause was far different. He was a bastard by birth whose only recourse had been knighthood. He had chosen knighthood as a means to gain what he had been denied by birth—the duchy of Anjou—which he had vowed to take—by blood if necessary—from the father he loathed and despised.

He and William of Normandy shared many things—their bastard birth, their ambition, and war. They first met on the battlefield against the Moors who defended a huge cache of gold at San Cristabol.

William's army was surrounded on three sides and might have perished if Rorke and his men had not joined the battle. William's horse was cut from under him. When the beast fell William was pinned underneath and would have been slain had Rorke not saved his life.

Afterward, when William asked how he might repay him, Rorke calmly demanded half the gold at San Cristabol. Under any other circumstances William might have been inclined to refuse, but with Rorke's men protecting his left flank, conceding half the gold seemed better than forfeiting all. He had been with William ever since, but it was often a topic of discussion as to who served whom.

When William made the decision to take Britain and again needed a formidable army, he had struck a bargain with Rorke for the duchy of Anjou. Better, he thought, to have an ally at his back—for Anjou bordered Normandy—when facing down the French king, who was a constant threat.

But Vachel had no such ambitions of land, honor, or power. The money he was paid by William's brother, the bishop, meant little to him. What mattered most was the kill. He was the consummate hunter—dangerous, with a bloodlust that gave no quarter.

Above the tip of FitzWarren's sword Vachel's face contorted in rage. He cursed and then winced as more blood slipped down the length of Rorke FitzWarren's broadsword. He lowered his sword and Vivian felt the grip of the fist at her hair ease. He released her, and she quickly stepped away from him.

Rorke nodded. "It is a wise man who knows his limitations. And, so you will know exactly what it feels like to have your flesh split beneath the sword and your blood running freely." To emphasize the point he wished to make, FitzWarren angled the tip of the blade by degrees first in one direction then the other with an effortless flick of his wrist, carving a small crescent at the base of Vachel's throat, and Vivian was stunned to realize that it greatly resembled the mark Vachel had made with his own blade.

"So that you will know how it feels," FitzWarren told Vachel. Vachel's breath hissed out through his teeth. His face was now deathly pale. He swore again, this time in pain, his breath wheezing from his taut throat.

"This will not be forgotten!" he promised as his terrified gaze remained fixed on that gleaming length of blade and his blood that streaked the length of steel. He swallowed convulsively, the tang of his own fear permeating the air.

"Curse you to the fires of hell, FitzWarren!"

FitzWarren shrugged, a heavily muscled shoulder moving easily beneath the weight of heavy chain mail. "There are many others who have already wished for it." Then in the same unemotional voice that only seemed to heighten the threat of danger, like the sigh of the serpent before it strikes, he ordered Vachel, "Surrender your sword, or I will be forced to kill you."

Vachel hesitated. Then, one by one, his fingers slowly uncurled from about the handle of his broadsword. A dangerous expression twisted his features as the sword dropped to the dirt at his feet with a dull thud. His hard, dark eyes showed no surrender but instead gleamed with a cold, deadly light, and Vivian knew not which man was the more dangerous.

"Why are you here?" Vachel hissed from between clenched teeth, even as the tip of FitzWarren's blade still rested against the flesh at his throat. "*I* was sent to find the healer! There is no need for you or that cursed barbarian who follows you about like a shadow."

There was a shift of movement among FitzWarren's men, and Vivian saw a warrior with a strangely curved blade move silently closer to stand at his side. Rorke FitzWarren's only response was the subtle angle of his head, as if he sensed rather than saw the other man's movement.

The warrior wore long robes bound at the waist, then flowing down over leather leggings past his knees. His head was bound with a white cloth that hung past his shoulders, and made a stark contrast against dark golden skin. Brows as black as night slashed sharp angles above rigid features only barely discernible in the dimly lit hall, giving him the watchful, dangerous look of a panther.

Vivian watched him with a stunned fascination, for he reminded her of the stories Poladouras had told her of the dark-eyed Persians of the Byzantine Empire to the east. But his eyes were as blue as summer sky.

A second knight stepped to FitzWarren's right with sword drawn as though he might challenge the strangely dressed, blue-eyed warrior for the privilege. The second warrior swept his helm from his head, the shaggy mane of dark russet hair falling to his shoulders and the eager look of the hunt glinting in eyes the color of liquid amber.

Vivian saw that he was younger than FitzWarren and the strangely dressed warrior, but no less formidable in size. Careful calculation of every movement made FitzWarren dangerous. She knew this younger knight would strike first and then calculate the consequences afterward, like a swift and deadly snake.

"Would you like me to separate the head of the bishop's dog from his mangy shoulders? So we are no longer bothered by his irritating yelping?" he asked with a tone that suggested it would be a great pleasure to do so.

Vachel sneered at sight of the young knight. "I see you've brought the young bastard with you as well." The depth of his hatred fouled the air, even in a place as sacred and consecrated as the abbey. "I wasn't aware that fetching a healer from the Saxon countryside warranted the *royal* presence."

Vivian watched with growing curiosity as the young warrior reacted violently and would have struck Vachel down with his sword had Rorke FitzWarren not intervened.

" 'Tis not worth it, Stephen," he told the younger knight. And then she heard him add with lowered voice, "The day will come. But not here, not now. Far more urgent business is at hand." The young warrior lowered his blade but did not resheathe it.

FitzWarren's gaze swept the destruction in the abbey, Poladouras' bruised countenance beneath the bloodied wound at the side of his head, Meg's equally bloodied and crumpled form in the rushes at the floor, the hysterical, weeping servant girl, and then rested on Vivian. Again she felt that subtle violation, as if he saw far more in that cold-as-ice gaze that burned through her.

With Vachel and his men under the swords of his men, Rorke FitzWarren slowly inspected the damage to the chapel.

"It would seem, Vachel," he said, his tone at first contemptuous and then cynical, "that there is much need of me here. It is obvious these Saxons are very dangerous. A harmless monk, an old woman, a frightened child, and a young woman."

His gaze came back to Vivian, and again she experienced the sensation that he had somehow touched her. Then he crouched down on bent legs to retrieve one of Poladouras' ancient manuscripts from the dirt floor, turning the fragile, torn pages with unexpected care.

"No doubt the monk threw a book at you. This one, perhaps," he suggested. He stood and, with surprising gentleness that was almost reverence, laid the manuscript on a small table that had somehow escaped the destruction. And Vivian frowned at yet another unexpected aspect of the Norman knight.

"Perhaps," FitzWarren went on to suggest, "the old woman overpowered you and made you fear for your lives."

He stood over Meg, crumpled into the dirt at his feet, and commanded her, "Look at me, old woman." The ease with which he slipped into the Saxon language startled Vivian.

Meg squared her thin shoulders. "You do not frighten me, warrior," she hissed, refusing to obey as she stared stubbornly down at the dirt floor.

Vivian heard the hatred that burned in the thready voice, and knew that FitzWarren had heard it as well, for hatred was an emotion that crossed all barriers of language. Her breath caught at the sound of ancient Celtic curses Meg muttered.

Be silent, you dear old fool! she thought as she glanced at the knight. Meg would pay dearly if he even so much as guessed at the insults and curses she hurled at him, and Vivian doubted the old woman's fragile bones would endure further abuse.

Then Vivian ceased breathing altogether as he stripped off

heavy mail-covered gloves and crouched low before old Meg with a lithe, almost-graceful ease of movement in spite of the heavy layers of battle armor he wore. At that moment she was certain he understood the vile things Meg had said. Then he stunned them both as he seized a handful of flowing white hair and gently forced Meg's head up.

Meg screeched several more vile profanities as she clawed and scratched at FitzWarren's hand, clamped over her hair. Undaunted, he angled her head back, her wrinkled face marred by bruises Vachel had inflicted. Meg threw her hands up as if to protect herself from another blow, making grotesque gestures with her fingers.

Only Vivian understood the ancient signs the woman made with her hands, calling on every evil creature she could summon from the Darkness, every possible disease she knew of, and a few even Vivian didn't understand.

She was stunned when Rorke FitzWarren didn't strike the old woman. Instead, he clamped his other hand over her thin wrists and drew them away from her face.

"Do not think to hex me or conjure up some spell, old woman!" FitzWarren warned her. "For I do not believe in such things."

"You will believe!" Meg warned ominously. "When your eyes fall out of your head and your manhood shrivels no bigger than a worm!"

He ignored her threats as he turned to Mally. He slipped fingers beneath the girl's trembling chin and angled her face up so that she too was forced to look at him. She whimpered, tears streaming down her bruised and dirt-smudged face, her gaze carefully averted.

"I will not hurt you," he said with such surprising gentleness Mally looked at him from beneath her pale lashes with guarded wariness.

"Though God knows you have enough reason to fear me," he added, speaking once more in French and unaware that any but his own men understood. "And even more reason to doubt what I say."

Vivian was stunned by his unexpected concern for the girl, and watched him with new curiosity. Then he told Mally in English, "Look at me."

Eventually, she looked up, blue eyes wide with fear in the darker miasma of bruises marring features that might have been pretty if not for the raw, scraped skin and swelling that cruelly distorted her appearance. She looked more like a pathetic kitten that had been trampled underfoot and barely escaped with its life. Anger flashed across FitzWarren's implacable features.

"Let her go," he ordered the soldier who held her prisoner. Terrified and bewildered, Mally slipped into the shadows at the wall.

FitzWarren's voice was like winter's death, cold, bitter, and unforgiving as he told Vachel, "If it were left to you, you would kill all Saxons, *including* the healer!"

Vivian's gaze fastened on Vachel. Until that moment she assumed he sought a healer for a healer's purpose—to tend to someone who'd been injured. What could Rorke FitzWarren possibly mean by his accusation? Why would Vachel want her dead?

As if he heard her silent thoughts, Rorke FitzWarren slowly turned to her. When he stood before her, those gray eyes assessed her with a far different expression. His gaze lingered on the cut fabric of her kirtle and the bloodied mark on pale flesh beneath. His mouth flattened into a hard line.

"My apologies, demoiselle. The king would be offended to learn you have been so sorely abused."

Her auburn brow lifted slightly as she answered him in French, her words dripping with all the loathing, hatred, and contempt she felt for all Normans.

"You no doubt speak of King Harold," she said defiantly. "And you are right, milord. He would never tolerate such abuses of his loyal subjects, nor would he tolerate foreign tyrants on English soil."

He looked at her with new curiosity in discovering she spoke French as well as he.

"I speak of William of Normandy," Rorke informed her. "Your *new* king."

"William is not my king," Vivian said adamantly. "Saxon England will never bow before a Norman overlord. The road from battlefield to throne is long and often filled with danger." Denying with all her heart what she already knew to be true, that all of England was already lost. But she couldn't bear to bow before this Norman knight who brought death and destruction upon her people.

"Aye, the road 'tis long and dangerous," he acknowledged gravely. "But I assure you, William of Normandy *will* be king of England."

Something glittered at the dirt floor and caught Rorke's eye. He crouched low and, with that same economy of movement, retrieved the gleaming object. Vivian's breath stilled in her lungs as his fingers closed over her knife.

He stood then, slowly turning the blade over between those long, scarred fingers that had wielded a broadsword and drawn Vachel's blood with a powerful ease, and then gently calmed a terrified young girl. Again, Vivian found herself confused by the contradictions of Rorke FitzWarren.

He drew the flat of the blade down between thumb and forefinger and Vivian frowned as he then touched his tongue to the tip of his finger. He looked at her speculatively.

"Oil of rosemary." He watched for her reaction. When there was none and she remained defiantly silent, he commented, "I have been told it is most effective against gout." That wintry gray gaze glanced to Poladouras and his gout-swollen legs. "And often found among a healer's medicines."

Vivian's stunned gaze met his. Her breath quickened apace with her heart as the vision of the phoenix once more shimmered before her—a creature born in fire and blood.

Rorke brought his hand up and immediately saw the wariness that shifted behind those brilliant blue eyes, the sudden tensing of every muscle in the slender body as if she braced for a blow. Instead, he reached out and brushed back the fall of flame-colored hair that sculpted her face, partially concealing her features and draping her shoulder like a mantle of molten fire.

He felt heat in the silken warmth of her skin and saw it in the flame that leapt in the depths of those blue eyes. He heard it in the sudden, startled whisper of her breath against his hand like a warm caress that made him instinctively feel the need to pull away lest he be burned, at the same time his hand opened to feel more of her.

The contact was brief, his hard, callused fingers grazing over Vivian's cheek, somehow touching her in a far deeper way, in some hidden place, like a vision in the heart of a blue crystal not seen for five hundred years.

Then his gaze lowered to the gaping fabric seeped through with blood at her breast. Vivian's hands trembled with far more than fear as she pulled the remnants of her torn bodice together. With fear and hatred in her heart, she told him what he had already guessed.

"I am the healer you seek."

His cool gray eyes fastened on her, measuring her with an intensity that she found impossible to sense anything about, as if his thoughts and emotions were closed to her.

Then he slowly turned the blade around and handed it back to her. She stared at him with a new wariness, unable to fathom his intentions in returning the knife to her.

"Do not think to use it against me," he warned, as if he knew her thoughts. "You have no cause to fear me. I need you alive and unharmed." Then, as he turned to his men, he told her in a voice that disguised neither his urgency nor his resolve, "Far too much time has already been wasted." His gaze angled past her to Vachel, who still had not moved, with FitzWarren's men surrounding him.

"Make ready to leave at once, demoiselle. Gather your healing herbs and powders, for time is of the essence if the duke of Normandy is to live."

Vivian was stunned. Never had she considered their journey was of such import. Then anger replaced her first surprise as she defiantly told him, "I will never use my skills to heal the Norman butcher who is the cause of Saxon pain and suffering!"

Rorke FitzWarren slowly turned around, the sputtering light from the brazier playing across sharply angled features, catching at the threads of the fierce creature woven at the front of his tunic, and for a moment it seemed that man and creature became one. Just as she had seen in the vision in the flame at the heart of the blue crystal. His expression was fierce, predatory, dangerous, his eyes as cold as winter's death. By stark contrast, his words were low and carefully measured.

"You will, demoiselle," he assured her, and then vowed, "or all of Amesbury will pay the price. The choice is yours."

Those brilliant blue eyes burned with all the hatred he knew she must feel at that moment. She was trapped, without any real choice, and he knew that as well. For he had seen her loyalty toward the monk and old woman. She would gladly have given her life for any one of them. But with the lives of all the villagers at stake he had given her an impossible choice. Just as he'd intended.

The agony of that choice was plain for all to see in the painful, heartrending look he saw shimmering in eyes like the heart of a flame as she glanced at the monk and old woman, her decision already made. But her indomitable spirit would not give her leave to show him any obeisance or acknowledgment of yielding to his power over her.

Instead, she whirled around and slowly walked to the stone steps that no doubt led to the tower he had seen as he and his men approached the abbey. At a nod, he sent Tarek al Sharif to follow her and make certain she did as he commanded.

The strangely dressed warrior with that deadly curved blade joined Vivian at the stone steps to the tower.

"Does he send you to guard me and make certain I do not escape?" she asked, putting a scathing tone in her own language, certain this golden-skinned barbarian could not possibly understand. But he understood very well.

He smiled at her gently and politely introduced himself—Tarek al Sharif—and in his name she realized the truth of her earlier sense of him. He was Persian from the Byzantine Empire. She wondered, how did such a man come to fight at the side of William of Normandy?

"Allow me to assist you, mistress," he said in accented English. No weapon filled his hand. Instead, he reached out to gently guide her up the steps though she hardly needed his help. And in his touch she sensed compassion. "So that nothing may be forgotten," he explained as they reached the herbal.

Though Tarek al Sharif said nothing, Vivian felt his silent contemplation as she quickly gathered everything that she would take with her.

At his questioning look when she left a portion of each powder and herb in the vials and clay pots, she informed him, "The villagers will have need of these while I am gone."

Vivian was again stunned when he did not object; nor did he order her to include them with the medicine she prepared to take with her, but instead nodded as he helped her carefully put the packets and vials of precious medicines into a large leather pouch.

Rorke FitzWarren and his men waited astride their horses in the yard outside the abbey, the breaths of their mounts pluming in the frosty morning like the breath of ancient dragons. Vachel and his men, also astride their horses, waited apart from the other knights and mounted soldiers. She felt Vachel's contemptuous gaze on her and again wondered if what Rorke FitzWarren had said was true. Had Vachel come to kill her?

Farewells were hastily said, there was no time for more. Poladouras gently laid his hand against her cheek. "God goes with you, my child. He will return you to our care." He dared say no more as Rorke FitzWarren glanced impatiently at them. But old Meg had no fear of the Norman warriors, nor could she see his impatience.

"You have the crystal?" Meg asked urgently.

"Aye," Vivian assured her as her hand instinctively pressed against the crystal where it hung from her neck and lay nestled at her breasts. She felt the calming reassurance of the power of the flame that burned at the heart of the crystal.

"Be strong, *mo chroi*," Meg told her, speaking in the ancient Celt language they shared. "Remember, they cannot harm you," she whispered, trying to impart with a few words all that she wanted to say. "You must escape at the first opportunity."

"Nay!" Vivian said vehemently with a glance to Rorke FitzWarren and remembering his promise to her. "I cannot risk the lives of others." Then she hugged Meg fiercely and they bade their last farewells. Meg and Poladouras followed her from the abbey.

She wore a thick shawl, pulling it high over her head and knotting it about her shoulders to cover the gaping bodice of her gown, for there had been no time to don another. The pouch of medicines she tucked under her arm as she stepped out into the chill morning air.

As Vivian crossed the abbey yard, she saw the full extent of damage the soldiers had inflicted at Amesbury Abbey—another of Poladouras' mongrels lying trampled in the yard, sheep from the field scattered everywhere; a young lamb bleating plaintively for its mother, also trampled in the yard under the hooves of warhorses, her thick wool matted with blood; and the prostrate shepherd, who must have run in from the field at the first sight of the soldiers. With a cry of protest, Vivian ran to him.

"Conal!"

He lay on his side, bleeding heavily from a deep wound at his head. He moaned as she slipped an arm beneath him and carefully wedged his shoulders off the ground to cradle his head at her arm.

"Soldiers!" he whispered in delirium, the words thick with

pain as he struggled to sound the alarm, unaware they were all past any hope of escape. "You must flee!"

"Aye, Conal. Do not talk now," Vivian coaxed as she blotted the blood from the wound with the edge of her shawl. The knot of anger at the cruelty of the Norman barbarians tightened, leaving no doubt as to the fate of the villagers if she refused to go with the soldiers.

The rain that had threatened all morning began to fall. The outline of mounted soldiers, horses, and armed knights was an ominous shadow in the gathering gloom.

"Leave him," Rorke FitzWarren ordered harshly, his large warhorse suddenly looming over her. The animal moved restlessly in the gathering downpour, and would have easily trampled her had it not been for that powerful hand clamped over the reins.

Brilliant blue eyes locked with winter's gray in stubborn refusal. "He is badly injured," Vivian protested. "I must close the wound." Then she added, her voice filled with all the contempt she felt for Rorke FitzWarren, "Surely, milord, even you are capable of understanding this."

Eyes cold as ice narrowed, and his lips thinned. Droplets of water soaked Rorke FitzWarren's long, dark hair, making it darker still and making him seem as Vachel had cursed him—like Lucifer himself. She shivered at the resemblance to such evil.

"I understand very well, demoiselle," he informed her. "Leave him where he lies, or you may be assured of his imminent death."

"You would not kill an injured man!" Vivian protested in disbelief.

Rorke FitzWarren's sword sang a deadly cold sound from its sheath. "The choice is yours, demoiselle."

Their gazes locked. Yes, she thought, just as the choice between the well-being of the villagers and their deaths was also hers.

"Forgive me, Conal," she whispered, stroking his face with a gentle hand. "Meg will see to your wounds."

His hand closed over hers with a determined strength. "I will find you," he whispered. "They will pay for what they have done with their blood." Then he groaned and his head slumped against her shoulder. Mercifully, he had lost consciousness.

Vivian's heart ached at the wounds he had suffered, for they were childhood friends and she cared for him deeply.

Conal had wanted desperately to go with the other men to Hastings, but an old injury from childhood that left him partially crippled had prevented it. Instead, he remained at Amesbury to tend the sheep and watch over the village.

She eased her arm from beneath his shoulders as Meg found her way near and crouched beside him.

"Now, mistress," Rorke ordered her. He understood her pain and anger, and experienced a self-loathing for what these people had suffered, but there was a much more urgent need elsewhere.

Meg heard the anger in the Norman knight's voice, and assured Vivian, "I will see to his wounds. Go now, *mo chroi.* And remember what I have said."

Vivian slowly stood and defiantly faced Rorke FitzWarren, hatred burning in her eyes as she felt, at the bottom of her pocket, the reassuring shape of the knife he had unwisely returned to her.

"Hate me if you will, mistress," Rorke FitzWarren told her, "but we will delay no longer." He reached down, his arm encircling her waist as he leaned from the saddle. His gloved hand flattened across her belly, fingers digging in with surprising gentleness below her ribs.

She was easily lifted and settled crosswise in the saddle before him, her legs dangling to one side. The pouch of herbs and powders was secured and hung at the other side. Then he called sharp orders to his men and the yard turned to a sea of mud beneath the churning hooves of the warhorses.

She left the abbey, perhaps never to return again, for it was part of the future she could not yet see, and her eyes filled with tears for those she loved.

Plaintive cries sounded in the chill air, and Vivian's gaze was drawn skyward. High overhead, her small falcon soared on the winds of the gathering storm, calling mournfully as it followed them.

Three

The light rain that had begun to fall as they left Amesbury became a downpour. It stung at her skin and eyes. Riders became hardly more than dark, huddled shapes in the gathering gloom as water soaked through layers of heavy chain mail armor and thick leather underpadding. The horses' heads hung low in misery.

They were forced to slow their pace as the old Roman road became treacherous underfoot, horses slipping dangerously in the mud.

Rorke FitzWarren's captive sat before him with hands clamped over the pommel of the saddle, chin lifted, and spine rigid, holding herself as far away from him as possible in something more than stubborn Saxon defiance. She was not what he had expected to find at the abbey.

The very notion that she lived in an abbey suggested a cloistered, reclusive life of humility, obedience, and subservience. Healers were either wrinkled old crones or stout peasant midwives who had acquired some knowledge of healing ways.

But the girl who sat before Rorke was neither old, wrinkled, nor stout. Nor was she humble or subservient.

Beneath her worn and mended garments, she was slender and fine-boned. In spite of the bruises of Vachel's abuse, her skin was like the finest, pale satin, and her hair beneath the shawl drawn against the driving rain was like a brilliant red-and-gold firefall. And her eyes.

Those blue eyes had burned with a fierce, angry fire as she defied Vachel, then reflected the deeper blue of sadness and anguish at leaving those she loved. Now, they were like a resting blue flame as she stared fixedly ahead, revealing nothing of her true emotions.

She was a surprising combination of vulnerability and strength, innocence and beguiling beauty, like a fine, rare flame that drew the hand to its fiery heat. How had such a beautiful, unusual creature come to be at the abbey? Rorke wondered.

The thin wool of Vivian's shawl and kirtle were soaked and lay plastered against her skin. Beneath her the leather saddle had become slippery, adding to her misery as she shivered violently from the cold and practically became unseated. He steadied her with a hand at her hip.

Unaccustomed to a man's hand, she was stunned by that simple warm touch, felt through layers of cold, wet garments. She stiffened and would have pulled away, but his hand prevented it.

"Be still," he said, his hand shifting to her other hip, his arm angling across her breast and anchoring her against him. "Or you will unseat us both. And I have no desire to find myself in the mud." She quit squirming, but she could not seem to quit shivering.

"You are cold."

"I have been cold before," she informed him, trying to wedge distance between them. He settled her more firmly against him, the weight of his mail-clad arm intimate possession that made her go still in the saddle before him.

She felt the sudden shift of his weight in the saddle behind her, the clenching of powerful leg muscles clasped about hers, and wide, powerful shoulders framing hers as he settled his heavy mantle about them, enclosing them in a fur-lined cocoon.

A wild, new fear settled and grew inside Vivian at this sudden closeness. It made her feel trapped and vulnerable in ways she'd never experienced before.

She longed to fight her way out of the layers of mantle that created a terrifying intimacy in the shared heat of their bodies.

Rorke discovered there were dangers far more hazardous than finding himself suddenly unseated from his horse, danger in the slender, shapely thighs clasped within his and the soft curve of her bottom snugged against him.

Wrapped in the thick folds of his mantle, her fragrance washed over him. She smelled of wind, rain, and the sweet promise of spring as her warmth began to mingle with his. Her hair was like heavy satin at her shoulder. Her pale skin begged a man's hand.

Desire knifed through him and his flesh hardened, pressing painfully against the constraints of battle armor. He cursed softly.

He could not remember hardening so easily or painfully with a maid since his first time at the age of fourteen. And certainly not with one so unwilling, who was also his enemy. Nor was he ruled by his flesh as some soldiers were, seeking conquest of any soft, warm flesh, willing or not.

He took his pleasure with women, but only those who came willing and asked nothing of him but a few coins. Conquests he preferred to take on the battlefield, for only there might he conquer the demons that raged as strong as physical desire.

Still, this simple Saxon healer, with eyes like the heart of a flame and hair like the molten fire of a sunset, had made him feel what others did not.

Were it not for those layers of chain mail and leather, his reaction to her would have made itself known, and he could well imagine her frantic efforts to flee then from the sword pressing at her back.

" 'Tis not necessary to share your mantle with me, milord," she said, pushing at the cloak enfolding them.

"You are wet and cold," he said gruffly, refusing to loosen

his hold. For even though it was torture to have her softness pressed against him, he discovered that it was a sweet torture in the other imaginings it conjured up.

"I have been wet and cold before," she persisted, so close that her cheek was warm beneath his chin. "I do not mind it."

"*I* mind it."

His breath tingled at her ear and down the side of her neck, causing her to shiver anew with a far different sensation that spiraled through her to settle beneath the weight of his arm at her breast.

"And if you persist, demoiselle," he warned, his voice still harsh with that gruffness she didn't understand, "then I shall have you bound and trussed before me," he assured her. "And you *will* be wrapped in this mantle. The choice is yours."

She didn't struggle again, but there was no surrender in her tense body.

As the hours passed, he felt her sway as fatigue overcame her. She stiffened and stubbornly held herself rigid in the saddle before him. Eventually exhaustion won out. Her slender chin drooped. She eased against him and did not pull away.

Night began to fall and even their slow pace became impossible in the darkness that closed around them. At the edge of a wood, Rorke ordered his men to make camp for the night.

His Saxon captive jerked awake with that sudden alarm that is a mixture of bone-aching weariness and uncertainty of one's surroundings. Rorke had experienced it many times in the aftermath of battle in countless foreign lands.

Her slender hands clutched at his arm, her body retreating further into his. His arms closed protectively about her. He allowed himself the luxury of the feel of her hair, like warm satin, at his lips as he whispered to her.

"*Sa se bien, demoiselle.*" His warm breath stirred gently against her cheek. Exhaustion slowly cleared from her senses.

He felt the rigid tension return to her body. She pushed away from him, her eyes wary and bright in the fading light.

"What is this place?"

"We'll make camp here for the night and continue in the morning."

Rorke removed the mantle from about them and dismounted. Relieved of his weight the large warhorse stood trembling, its glossy black coat caked with mud, sweat, and lather. Steam rose from the animal's back, misting the night air. Long powerful legs that had borne two riders over many miles quivered, the large head sagging with exhaustion.

Vivian shivered at the sudden loss of Rorke FitzWarren's heat. Her back ached and her legs cramped from sitting at the saddle for so many hours. She slipped to the ground and would have sprawled in the mud had he not caught her.

He pulled her against him, supporting her weight on his arm as the feeling slowly returned to her legs and feet. At first there was only a faint tingling sensation, then heat burned down through her legs and spread to her toes. She pushed away from him.

No squire appeared to relieve him of his armor or tend his horse. Instead, he unsaddled the stallion himself.

He glanced toward the forest. "If we are to eat, and keep from freezing tonight, we will need wood for a fire."

She looked at him with more than a little surprise. She had fully expected to be bound. It intrigued her that he did not intend it.

"Aren't you afraid that I might escape?" she asked in amazement.

"You're afoot and it is a very long walk back to the abbey," he pointed out. "You are not foolish."

"I might choose to hide out in the woods," she suggested tartly. "You would not know, then, which way I had gone."

"Aye, but eventually you would be found. However, I could not guarantee that it would be my men who would find you first."

That intriguing combination of vulnerability and strength, which he'd seen at the abbey, flashed in her eyes. Her chin came up.

"I am not afraid of Vachel."

"No, but the villagers of Amesbury have reason to fear him, and it is the first place Vachel will send his men if you should disappear." He assured her, "If you are found, he will burn the village. If you are *not* found, he will still burn the village.

"Vachel is like an animal," he warned. "And like an animal he is best at hunting. When not hunting he should be chained, but his master rarely keeps him chained."

More death and destruction. She shivered again. This time it wasn't from the cold, but from the memory of her vision in the heart of the stone. Of a creature born in fire and blood that would sweep across the land, and a growing sense that she was being drawn toward something she could not yet understand, nor prevent.

"I will not try to escape," she said softly as she turned toward the trees. "You have my promise."

"Do not go far," Rorke warned.

She found no answers in the solitude of the forest, only a vague awareness that slipped across her senses, like the warning whisper of the wind as it moved through the trees.

When she returned, she discovered that Rorke had made their camp near the horses. His mantle was laid across the trunk of a massive fallen oak. An area had been cleared away in front of the tree trunk. Rolls of thick furs lay at the edge of the clearing.

The campfires of his men rimmed the clearing. Vachel's men made their camp under the canopy of trees. They laid fires, striking metal against stone while others went into the woods to hunt.

She layered dry leaves and pieces of bark with small twigs that she found in the shelter of the fallen oak. Heat spiraled smokily on the chill night air. Then a small flame burst to life.

It fed hungrily at the pieces of bark and twigs, quickly consuming them. She added more pieces, building the fire until it flared and danced about thick logs that would burn long into the night.

Seized by a sudden chill, she extended her hands toward the fire. But not even the heat could drive away the cold ache that settled low inside her as she sensed danger.

Vivian stood abruptly and whirled around, knowing who she would find. So quietly had Vachel come upon her and she hadn't heard him, but instead sensed his presence.

Surprise leapt into Vachel's dark eyes, no doubt at losing the advantage of surprise. Firelight played across his broad, flat features and the ribbon of dried blood at the wound that seamed his face.

Vachel had removed the cumbersome battle armor, his compact, barreled body moving easily as he crossed the clearing to the fire as though to warm himself. He had thought to take her by surprise, but that hope was now gone.

"You are indeed skilled, mistress. You have a warm fire while others still struggle to strike the first spark."

Watchful eyes gleamed in the flat planes of his face, reminding her of a weasel. She remembered Rorke's warning.

"It requires no great skill," she answered carefully. "I was fortunate to find dry wood." She put more wood on the fire.

He crouched before the fire with an agile movement that contradicted the thickness of his body. A blade gleamed at his hand—one that had not been there before. He probed the tip of it into the embers that had begun to form at the fire.

Vachel turned to look up at her, his lips pulling back over stained, uneven teeth. He passed a hand over the slash at his cheek. But her gaze was fixed on the blade at his hand. He was playing with her, much the way an animal plays with its prey before striking.

She sensed his dangerous mood and thoughts, as clearly as if he had told her of them, and sensed, too, the humiliation that seethed within him like a festering wound. She had disgraced him before his men and then slashed him. It mattered little that she was protecting those she loved. He had come for revenge.

"He leaves you unbound and unguarded. Rorke FitzWarren is a fool."

He sprang at her like an animal, a blunt hand seizing the thickness of her hair as the blade came up in the other.

"The blade is hot. It will burn as well as cut." His hand twisted in her hair, pulling her closer until it was wound about his fist.

"Before I am through, demoiselle, you will cry mercy." His stale breath made her skin crawl as if she'd been touched by something foul. Bile rose in her throat. Pain throbbed where his hand knotted in her hair, but she refused to cry out. Like an animal, she knew the fear would only make him bolder.

"I will tame you, demoiselle," he vowed as he brought the blade up beside her face. "And then I will force that stubborn Saxon pride from you as you lie beneath me."

"Never."

Rorke heard the painful yelp, like that of a wounded animal, and swore an oath as he crossed the camp. He shouldn't have left her alone.

In the light of the campfire, he saw Vachel at the clearing, standing a few feet away from the healer, who lay sprawled on the ground. Firelight gleamed from the blade of a knife that lay on the ground between them.

Rorke's hand closed over the handle of the short blade at his belt as he reached the clearing. Several of his men and Vachel's followed close behind, their hands at their weapons. His hand went still at his own blade as he realized it was not the healer who had cried out.

Vachel screamed an agony of pain as he clutched one hand in the other. The flesh of one hand was reddened with raised welts as if he had laid it to the fire.

"The Saxon whore attacked me!" He swung around for all to see. "Look what she's done." And then on a snarl, "She burned me! I will have the bitch's head on a pike!"

"Cease, Vachel!" Rorke ordered.

"I *will* have justice for this," Vachel sputtered. "Either that or she will be subject to William's justice for attacking one of his knights!"

"I see two people before me," Rorke said, his gaze traveling from Vachel to where Vivian knelt in the dirt before the fire.

"You doubt what I say?" Vachel demanded.

"I do not doubt that you have suffered some injury," Rorke told him, "but I will also hear the cause of it from the girl."

Vivian slowly lifted her head and gazed at the circle of Norman knights that had gathered. On the faces of Vachel's men she saw an animal lust for blood. Rorke's men seemed less certain. The strangely dressed, blue-eyed warrior watched her with an unsettling intensity.

Norman justice, she thought. The same justice with which William had seized the crown of England?

"He burned himself with a blade at the fire," she answered, telling a simple truth.

"She speaks lies!" Vachel accused. "She burned me, with a stick! She has it in her hand."

Rorke extended his hand to her. She placed her empty hand in his.

"Your other hand as well, demoiselle."

She looked up at him with a gaze as brilliant as blue flame. If he thought to discover either malice or deception there, he saw neither.

"You do not believe me."

"I do not disbelieve you."

An angry fire leapt into her eyes. She extended her other hand and opened it.

A vibrant strength coursed beneath the warm satiny skin, pulsing strong and sure at the slender curve of wrist where tendons joined bone. That same hand had calmed his warhorse and brought ease of suffering to the sick and wounded of Amesbury. He could almost feel an energy, like that of the sun, in the flesh, muscle, and bone cradled in his hand. With something very near reluctance he released her hand.

He turned to Vachel. "There is no weapon."

Fury twisted the flat features as Vachel stalked past him to his own men.

"She attacked me," he insisted, knowing they would believe whatever he told them. "She has hidden the weapon to keep blame from herself. The Saxon is dangerous and should be punished." His men muttered agreement; they seemed to be of a similar mind.

"Perhaps this is the weapon you speak of," Tarek al Sharif suggested as he rose from where he had crouched before the fire. He held a knife in his hand. He gave it to Rorke FitzWarren.

Rorke turned it over in his hands, a distinctive blade with a boar's head handle. "I believe this belongs to you, Vachel," he suggested, holding the weapon out to him.

Vachel's gaze narrowed as he stared at the blade. "It must have fallen when she attacked me."

As he reached for the knife to take it back, Rorke seized him by the arm. With a powerful grip, he dug his fingers in between tendon and muscle at Vachel's wrist forcing his hand open.

"You claim she burned you with a stick from the fire."

"I have said it is so! It is there for anyone to see." Vachel flung back at him. He swore an oath and struggled, but could not free himself.

What was there for all to see in the light from the campfire was the long, slender, burn mark like a brand across Vachel's palm, much as he would hold a blade, and identical in shape to the blade he claimed to have lost.

"Anyone can see," Rorke growled, shoving Vachel away from him. To Vachel's men, he suggested, "Return to your campfires. The night will be long and cold."

They slowly turned and retreated, until only Vachel remained. With a barely controlled violence, he resheathed the knife at his belt, then turned and stalked away, slipping into the darkness beyond the ring of the campfire. He reappeared briefly near the campfire of one of his men. Something was said, the blade flashed in the firelight. Vachel was like a wounded hound that turned on the pack. Then the blade was resheathed and he disappeared from camp.

As she watched him, Vivian was seized again by the foreboding of something that lay in the future, something that seemed to have followed them from Amesbury, but which she could not see, because it lay shrouded in darkness like a pervasive, malevolent force. She shivered as if taken with a sudden chill in spite of the warmth of the fire. It was Tarek al Sharif who spoke her thoughts aloud as if he had read them.

"It will end in blood."

"If he so chooses," Rorke answered as he, too, watched Vachel.

They saw no more of Vachel that night, but it made Vivian feel no easier. She knew he was out there, like the darkness, waiting just beyond the edge of the campfire.

Tarek had hunted and brought back from the forest two partridges, which were roasting over the fire. Across the clearing other cook fires burned, the aroma of cooking meat mingling with thick woodsmoke. At others, men murmured amongst themselves as they sat bundled in thick furs against the freezing cold that hovered at the edges of the campfires and already frosted the ground in between.

Vivian hadn't realized how hungry she was, her stomach grumbling noisily as the blue-eyed warrior nimbly carved a wing and leg portion from the roast partridge and handed it to her. She shivered again at the precise, slicing strokes as she imagined that other curved blade in his hands.

Each movement was perfectly executed with no waste, accomplishing precisely what he chose, which was to sever limbs from carcass. She imagined that skillful blade in battle and wondered with a shudder how many Saxons this exotic, intriguing warrior might have killed.

Still, she felt no fear of him. Quite the contrary. She sensed that here was someone she could trust—someone very like herself. Although he was not a captive as she was, he was not

Norman. Rorke's men accepted him with the deference accorded a respected warrior. Vachel's men did not.

After they had eaten, Rorke laid several more pieces of wood on the fire, then retrieved several rolled furs from the edge of the clearing.

"It is late and we leave at first light." He untied a thick roll of fur, spreading it on the ground before the fire.

"You will sleep here," he told her.

Tarek sheathed his blade and sprang nimbly to his feet. He laid out his fur at the other side of the fire, between them and the rest of the encampment. His curved sword gleamed deadly as he laid it beside him. He drew a thick mantle over him, his hand resting on the handle of the blade.

Across the camp, conversations died as the other knights made their pallets before their fires.

Vivian huddled before the fire. "I cannot take your blanket," she told Rorke, her chin lifting slightly as she gathered her shawl more tightly about her.

He looked up from the broadsword that he carefully drew from its leather sheath. Like the others, he had removed the cumbersome chain mail tunic and chausses, leaving the supple leather undertunic and breeches. He laid the broadsword on the fur as Tarek al Sharif had, and beside it the smaller blade as well.

"It was not my intention that you should, demoiselle," he said matter-of-factly. "We will share it."

Her startled gaze met his across the clearing that suddenly seemed to narrow to the width of the heavy fur that lay between them.

"We cannot," she protested with sudden alarm. "There is barely enough for one." Then, edging closer to the fire, she hastily added, "I am quite used to the cold."

"I am not used to the cold, demoiselle," he said bluntly, giving the distinct impression that the matter was ended before they'd even discussed it. He had retrieved his mantle from the fallen oak and approached the fire.

His voice gentled. "The night is long and will grow much colder. If my men have no objection to sharing their warmth with one another, surely you cannot."

She glanced across the fire to where Tarek al Sharif lay rolled alone in his fur and mantle, seemingly already asleep.

"He is a very restless sleeper," Rorke commented. "It can be dangerous to sleep too close."

She then glanced to his sword.

"I am not a restless sleeper," he assured her, then added as if to convince her, "You are fully clothed, demoiselle, and I am not given to ravishing young maidens as they sleep."

With the bitter cold already seeping around the edges of her shawl, Vivian reluctantly accepted the fact that if they were to survive the night, it must be together. She slowly approached the fur pallet, taking only a narrow space at the edge for herself and leaving the larger portion for him.

He did not immediately join her, but instead spread the mantle over her. Then, she heard the rhythmic sound of a stone being drawn repeatedly across metal as he sharpened the blade of the broadsword.

He seemed to be giving her time to adjust to their unusual sleeping arrangements, or perhaps lingering as if he, too, was waiting for something. But what?

Was it possible that he expected Vachel to return during the night? By the blade beneath the blue-eyed warrior's hand, it seemed more than one anticipated it.

She felt no alarm at the possibility, only an acceptance of what she knew to be true. It would come. Vachel would strike again, for such was the nature of animals. But it would not be tonight.

The fire warmed across her face, the heavy mantle and thick fur warmed the rest of her. Her eyes grew heavy.

Exhaustion ached through her, creeping into her bones with a sort of liquid feeling as if she were sinking into herself. Then there was only the darkness of sleep.

Much later, Rorke joined her at the fur pallet, drawing the

mantle over them both. She lay on her side, knees drawn up, feet tucked beneath the hem of her gown. She shivered slightly at the sudden intrusion of cold air but did not waken. Instead, she curled more tightly within herself.

The fur was meant only for one person and Rorke had no intention of waking in the morning with frostbitten hands, feet, or backside. And he was certain the closeness of her body on the pallet couldn't be any more disconcerting than sitting with her before him in the saddle.

Exhaustion and sleep had eased the rigid tension from her slender body. She lay pliant and completely relaxed in the deep fur, one slender hand pillowing her cheek, the other falling over the edge of the fur.

He reached to tuck her hand beneath the thick mantle. Her fingers were icy cold as they closed over his, drawing his hand beneath the fur to lie nestled against her breast.

He discovered precisely what was worse than sitting astride a saddle with her slender body nestled against his mail-clad flesh—her slender body nestled against his unrestrained flesh with his hand pressed between her soft breasts.

"Sweet Jesu!" he swore softly. It was going to be a very long night.

Four

The slopes of the hills surrounding the valley were covered by dense forest. They rode through stands of alder and red oak, leaves stained brilliant red in the setting sun and drifting to the ground.

As the slope flattened and fanned out into the valley, they passed a mournful caravan of creaking carts. A lifeless arm had fallen through the slats of one. The sleeve wrapped about that outthrust arm was that of a plain, coarse woolen tunic of a style commonly worn by Saxon thanes.

Vivian shuddered as an icy hand moved deep inside her. All the horrors she had foreseen and dreaded had come to pass, for the carts carried the bodies of Harold's dead soldiers. Mounted behind her in the saddle, Rorke was stoically silent.

A distance apart, hunched figures lined the ridge of a low ravine. They were darkly ominous shapes in the fading light, in appearance greatly resembling those harbingers of death—black crows.

As they rode closer, Vivian saw them bend and straighten, bend and straighten in a kind of macabre dance as they threw spadefuls of earth into the ravine.

At the bottom were grotesquely twisted shapes—the bodies of mounted soldiers and their horses—some still astride, bodies trapped beneath the crushing weight of their fallen mounts.

They were piled on top of one another as if some giant hand had swept them into the ravine. Horrified, Vivian realized they had fallen to their deaths in a downhill charge toward Harold's army.

"They are Norman," Rorke said, his voice low and seemingly devoid of any emotion.

Her foreknowledge of Harold's defeat at Hastings had brought with it an overwhelming sense of loss for the countless Saxons who had died there. But those grotesquely twisted bodies reminded her that Norman soldiers—a great many of them— had died here as well.

As a healer she'd seen death among the families at Amesbury. From disease or an accident. An old woman whose time was at an end, or an infant whose time had come too soon and could not live. But nothing in her life or her gift of foreknowledge had prepared her for what she saw now.

Instinctively, she wanted to hide from the death and destruction she saw. But she knew she could not. Her gift of inner sight would not allow it as her senses filled with an awareness of the battle now past.

Though she tried to block them out, they still came, that prescience of vision of things past and future, that was both gift and curse.

What old Meg had told her since childhood was never more true. The power of sight that she'd been born with, and her mother before her.

"Your special gift can bring great joy as well as great sorrow," she had explained. *"You must be strong enough to accept both, or it will destroy you."*

"If I see sad things, then I do not want it." Vivian remembered telling her. Meg had smiled at her tenderly, laying a hand that was old even then tenderly against her cheek. Her voice was filled with her own sadness.

"The choice is not yours to make, little one. It was made long ago, by one far older and wiser than you or me. He knew you would be strong enough. You will find the strength within yourself to bear it."

As Meg had said would happen, in time she had found the strength to bear the sadness along with the joy that her visions brought. But bearing it had not made the gift easier to accept.

Now, even though she tried to push away the ghastly images, she saw again the terrible battle that had taken place here.

A cold knot formed low inside her and expanded until she shivered violently at the horror that unfolded before her—of two armies plunging headlong toward each other; the cold clash of steel blade against war ax and the painful screams and agonized cries of the dying; the dust that rose to engulf them; the overwhelming emotions of confusion, fear, hopelessness; and, in the aftermath, the bodies of both Saxon and Norman dead lying on the cold hard ground.

Hot tears slipped down her frozen cheeks as she stared out across the valley and saw the distant fires glowing eerily through the gloom of mist and smoke.

Larger bonfires were scattered some distance apart. As the carts rumbled along toward them, she realized they were not bonfires but funeral pyres for the dead.

A creature born in fire and blood . . .

The crest Rorke FitzWarren carried on his shield was the image she had seen in her vision. She had no understanding of it then. But now she understood.

They rode on in painful silence. But she was aware that the gazes of the soldiers and knights who rode with them were also fixed on those distant fires.

They finally stopped before one of several large tents in the heart of the Norman encampment.

Rorke dismounted, pulling her to the ground beside him. Several armed soldiers immediately appeared, making her aware this was an armed encampment.

"Bring your medicines," Rorke said.

He strode ahead to draw aside the tent flap. Another armed soldier just inside the tent immediately appeared. A guard? He glanced at Rorke, recognized him, and stepped aside.

Tarek al Sharif had dismounted his horse and walked beside her. Vachel had not followed them into the camp, but had departed with his men as soon as they entered the valley. He was nowhere to be seen.

Stephen of Valois and several of Rorke's knights walked behind them, like an armed escort. A frisson of uneasiness slipped down her spine.

Beware, my child.

The warning slipped across her senses as Vivian untied the leather bundle from the saddle.

The bitter cold wind gusted inside the open flap as they entered the tent, stirring a fire in a brazier and guttering flames at several lamps. As the flap fell once more back into place, cutting off the intrusion of wind, the flames settled and glowed steadily once more.

There were several mail-clad, well-armed knights inside the tent. They ringed a raised cot, partially blocked from view by the phalanx of sword and armor.

"Milord." One of the young knights stepped forward and greeted Stephen of Valois. Vivian saw the nod of acknowledgment that passed between the two young men and immediately sensed a bond of deep friendship.

They were of a near age, as were several others of the knights in the tent, except for one who was somewhat older than Rorke. In this man, she sensed the wisdom and counsel of many years, many battles fought, and deep, abiding loyalty. She sensed other things, but they were fleeting images.

Most of what she sensed was a great urgency—that same urgency had grown in her throughout the day as they rode closer to Hastings. And she knew it was for William of Normandy.

"Are we in time, Gavin?" Rorke asked the nearest knight.

The one called Gavin nodded, his face taut. "He is alive," he said with solemn voice.

But hardly more, Vivian sensed, in the knight's unspoken thoughts.

Rorke glanced about at the heavily armed knights. His eyes narrowed as his gaze fastened on someone who stood behind one of the knights at the head of the cot.

"What is she doing here?" His voice was as cold as the steel of a blade. The knight moved aside, revealing a woman in the light of the oil lamps.

"Milord FitzWarren," she greeted Rorke with silky voice. The pale blond beauty stepped forward, her manner aloof. She spoke in French and her kirtle was of the finest heavy satin.

Vivian had seen little of the encampment, but she had seen no other women. It seemed odd now to find a woman, and one so finely dressed, in the middle of a military camp. Perhaps she was the wife of the man who lay on that cot.

"I gave orders that no one other than my men was allowed in here," Rorke snapped.

"I am not one of your knights," the woman reminded him as she stepped closer to the cot. "You have no authority over me." Then she added, "He asked for me. My place is with him."

Vivian sensed the spasm of tension that moved through the tent. From the woman she sensed many things—the coldness of ambition, the heat of anger and passion, and traces of a sensual, almost erotic, memory that reached out to Rorke FitzWarren. Vivian knew that in spite of the anger that seemed to leap between them, they had once been lovers. Perhaps they still were.

"It seems odd, milady, that one so grievously wounded and unconscious would have the strength to summon you," Rorke responded coldly. He glanced to Gavin, and Vivian saw the man's subtle shake of head, silently disavowing what the woman claimed.

"Remove her," Rorke ordered.

"You may not have me removed," she cried out. "My place is at his side!"

Rorke turned with a deliberate slowness, and again Vivian was reminded of that earlier impression of a dangerous creature. His features were hard, forbidding; she was certain that icy gaze was capable of freezing one where they stood. For all her boldness the Norman lady indeed seemed wisely frozen where she stood.

"The only woman who may claim that privilege is his *wife*," he said in quiet voice completely at odds with the scathing look he gave her. Then with a jerk of his head he signaled Gavin to have her removed.

"Take your hands off of me," she cried as Gavin turned to escort her from the tent. She wrenched her arm free of his grasp, wrapping her cloak about her as if it were the finest battle armor. She turned on Rorke, her voice dripping with haughty disdain, "I will leave, milord FitzWarren. But I shall return when *he* asks it."

"He will not ask it," Rorke assured her.

When she had gone, he turned to Gavin. "Tell me everything that has happened."

"Naught is amiss," the young knight assured him. "Now that you have returned."

Vivian heard the qualification of his reply, but more, she sensed the knight's unspoken thoughts of some trouble that he chose for the time being to keep to himself. Rorke sensed it as well. He nodded.

"We will speak of it later. There are more crucial matters here." He stripped away mail-covered gloves and shoved back the mail hood from that mane of silken, tangled dark hair. The circle of knights parted as he stepped to the cot.

"Christ's blood!" he swore softly, but with a ferocity that turned Vivian cold with apprehension, as he gazed down at the man who lay on the cot. She heard the undercurrent of emotion at his voice—anger laced with incredulity

"How is it possible that he is even still alive?"

The man she glimpsed briefly as Rorke knelt beside the cot lay wasted and emaciated, his skin a gray, bloodless color above bloodstained leather garments. Over the mournful howl of the wind that sent the loose edges of the tent flapping she heard the ragged breathing that was too rapid and too shallow. By Rorke FitzWarren's urgency, this wasted man could be no other than Duke William of Normandy.

"Not Christ's blood," Gavin informed him, his lips thinned with contempt, "but more of his own." He gestured to the stained blanket that lay beneath the injured man.

"Yester eve," he explained, "I found the bishop and that butcher of a healer's apprentice bleeding him."

"Sweet Jesu!" Rorke swore. "He has already lost enough blood for two men." He stood abruptly and called an order back through his men.

"Bring the girl."

Almost as one, the knights and soldiers filling the tent turned and stood apart. They were dressed in their bloodied and mud-caked battle armor, swords unsheathed and held at rest in their gloved hands. To a man they towered over her, their gazes by turn speculative, doubtful, and fierce.

This was what her people had confronted. No matter how bravely they fought with their clubs, axes, and sticks, they were no match for these well-armed, professional soldiers whose sole purpose was war and death. With an ache of sad-

ness so intense that it stilled her breath in her lungs, she knew
the fates of the men of Amesbury—indeed all of Saxon England—had been sealed before they ever met the Norman army
on the battlefield.

Her vision had seen all, and she had been powerless to stop
it.

Vivian realized Rorke had again summoned her. She glanced
up at the collective countenance of those fierce warriors turned
toward her and experienced something of the emotion that
Harold's beleaguered Saxons had felt—raw, naked fear.

As she slowly walked toward the cot, she had a prescience
of time moving out of itself, of events unfolding that she was
being drawn into but could not yet see, much less prevent.

"I have a name, milord," she said softly. Gray eyes glittered
dangerously as he stared back at her; yet his voice was carefully
restrained.

"Vivian of Amesbury," he acknowledged. "Your skills are
greatly needed by the one who lies here gravely wounded."

She approached the cot, through that gauntlet of fierce, heavily armed knights. "I will do what I can, milord. The rest is up
to God."

"God has already done his part." His tone was filled with
unmistakable contempt, with no attempt to disguise what would
seem to be blasphemy. And she wondered what might account
for such coldness of heart in a man who had shown such compassion at the abbey.

"The rest is up to you, and you will not fail."

Vivian knelt by the cot and looked with pity upon the man
who lay there, shrunken by fever and loss of blood. He seemed
a skeleton already except for the pale skin that clung to his
bones.

"Hold the lamp close," she told Rorke. "I must see what
must be done."

There was another who stepped to the opposite side of the
cot, the young knight Stephen of Valois. As she reached to draw

back the side front of leather tunic that covered the injured man's chest, Stephen's hand closed over her wrist.

"If he dies," he warned, "I will personally see that your life is forfeit for his."

Through the contact of his hand clamped painfully about her wrist, she sensed his own much deeper pain, and the fierce, warring emotions that reflected in the taut, rigid expression at his face. She sensed a deep, silent anger, an aching need for some long-denied love, and the conflicting emotion of intense hatred, as if they fought each other within him.

She felt his inner pain with such an intensity and fierceness that her heart ached. And she sensed something more, glimpsed in the shadow of his thoughts that he attempted to keep hidden from everyone, including himself. The man who lay on the cot was his father!

"Let her help him, my young friend," Rorke FitzWarren said beside her, his own hand lying gently, but with firm restraint, on the younger man's shoulder. Still, Stephen of Valois did not release her. Instead his fingers tightened about her wrist, with a brutal strength that threatened to snap slender bones.

Vivian silently communicated to him with her thoughts, allowing him to feel her compassion and concern. She felt his resistance, fighting her, pushing her thoughts back from his own. He was a fierce warrior, but in his heart she sensed the greater fierceness of his love for the man who lay between them.

Trust me, she spoke silently to Stephen of Valois, willing him to feel the truth of her thoughts. *I will not let him die.* She sensed his emotional struggle as he tried to understand the thoughts that moved through his, as if someone had spoken. Eventually, she felt those fingers loosen about her wrist, and, though they left red marks at her skin, she felt no physical pain, only his deeper emotional pain. Finally, he nodded and stepped back from the cot, but remained close enough, his hand at his broadsword as a silent warning.

She slowly rounded the cot, in turn lifting crudely made bandages that had been pressed against the wounds to stanch the flow of blood.

In most places the bleeding had stopped, leaving the bandages glued to the wound with the dried blood. At others, the wounds still seeped. She wet them with water from a basin, gently easing them away from the torn flesh, examining wounds that were obvious to the eye. Though there were several, including a deep one at his side, none by itself threatened his life.

When she moved down the length of cot at the opposite side, Stephen of Valois impatiently blocked her, his expression challenging.

"Enough of this!" he growled. "He lies here dying while you take your time as if you were at market. Get on with it!"

"It is not yet enough," Vivian told him gently but with an authority of voice few would have dared. "I must know exactly how badly he is wounded if I am to help him." Behind her, she sensed a movement.

"Her skills are great," Rorke FitzWarren told the young man. "Allow her to do what must be done."

Vivian looked over at him in surprise that he should speak so highly of her. What did he know of her except from rumors among Saxon peasants?

There was a moment of silent challenge between the two men. Then Stephen stepped once more out of her way though he remained close.

She moved past him, concentrating on the wounded man who lay before her, fingers moving along muscle, sinew, and bone, seeing with that inner eye the wounds that were not obvious— two broken ribs and several bruises.

In good health William was no doubt a powerfully built man. The bones were heavy and solid. Though sunken from fever and loss of blood, his features were ruddy beyond the pallor of illness, his hair a russet color. His eyes, she knew, would be brown like his son's. Then she lifted the blanket that covered the lower half of his body and discovered the wound at his leg.

Though the leg was laid out straight, the long lower leg bone was shattered, fragments piercing through the flesh. Like the others, a crude bandage had been placed over the wound. But little else had been done and maggots now crawled inside the torn flesh.

She shuddered, her stomach turning over as nausea backed into her throat. Her hand trembled at the bandage with a mixture of horror and anger that he had been cared for so badly.

Rorke FitzWarren's hand closed over hers with surprising gentleness. The warm strength in those scarred fingers flowed through the contact of skin on skin, stunning her.

"Do what must be done."

"He is dangerously close to death," she said softly. "The loss of so much blood . . ." She did not say the rest, for it was dangerous to speak out against others.

Those fingers tightened over her wrist. "What may I do to help you?"

"I must have more light and it must be warmer in here. He has a fever that may just as easily take him as the wounds. All drafts must be sealed. Then I will need more blankets, hot water, fresh bandages, and a very sharp knife."

He hesitated at the last request, then nodded as he turned and gave orders for the bottom edges of the tent sides to be buried and the opening sealed off.

More braziers and fuel were summoned, along with another basin of hot water set to simmering, heavy furs, and clean bandages. Rorke handed her his own blade, which she laid across the coals that glowed at the bottom of a nearby brazier.

The Conqueror's tunic, breeches, and boots were removed, the furs laid over the upper part of his body and his uninjured leg.

She sprinkled crushed leaves over the simmering basin. A bittersweet fragrance spiraled steamily in the air. Three more braziers appeared, their fires stoked high to give more light and more warmth.

Outside the tent she heard the sound of blades striking the

earth as trenches were dug and the edges of the tent buried all around to seal out drafts of air and seal in the heat. A thick carpet on the earthen floor was rolled and carried outside where it was hung over the entrance.

She set two more small bowls on the braziers. Water was added to one and soon simmered. A white powder was added to the other and the mixture turned golden brown on the heat. She removed Rorke's blade from the coals.

"The flesh decays," she explained. "In order for these wounds to heal, the dead flesh must be removed. He sleeps now because of the fever, but may still feel the pain. There is a potion I can give for the pain, but it wears off very quickly. It must be saved for his leg."

Rorke nodded as he moved to stand at William's head, prepared to hold him down if necessary. One of his knights moved to stand at each side. This was something all warriors understood.

At Rorke's nod she worked quickly, deftly removing the putrefied flesh from wounds that had festered, all the while silently cursing the fool who had ordered that William be bled as a means of saving his life.

Bloody barbarians! she thought. *Have they no common sense about the way of wounds?*

It was an agonizingly slow and painful process. Each wound needed to be cleaned of debris and filth, the decayed flesh removed. Then she spread each with a salve mixed from one of the bowls and bandaged them with clean linen. He was bound about the waist with lengths of linen to aid the broken ribs in healing.

Excruciating pain roused him from the stupor of fever. Weak as he was, he would have been too strong for her and it would have been impossible to continue had Rorke and his men not held him down.

Cold sweat sheened across his body and poured off him. His skin took on an even deadlier pallor, his eyes glazed with pain, fever, and delirium.

Vivian worked quickly. Three times she called for more water to clean the wounds. Her back and arms ached. The heat in the tent added to her tension. Perspiration beaded across her forehead, dampening tendrils of hair that she wiped back with a bloodied hand. When she sagged with exhaustion, she felt Rorke FitzWarren's unspoken support in the touch of a hand or a gently spoken word of encouragement.

"Sa se bien, demoiselle. Sa se bien."

Finally, she straightened, pressing a hand into the small of her back where a dull ache had set in from bending over the cot. The smaller wounds had all been cleaned and bandaged. The worst she had saved for last—the badly maimed and shattered leg. Into a tankard she poured a portion of the sweet-smelling brew that had been simmering over a brazier.

"He is very weak, but the leg must be mended. He must drink as much of this as possible or he will never survive the pain."

She saw the uneasiness that passed from one man to the other. They understood the need for bandaging wounds. But drinking unknown potions was another matter. All too well, she understood their concern. The war to conquer England—everything depended on the man who lay on the cot. He must live. And she was a Saxon healer who had every reason to hate him and wish him dead.

"If I wanted to do him harm," she asked logically, "would I have gone to so much trouble first?"

Stephen of Valois reached out and seized the tankard. "I will drink from it first," he declared.

She saw the look that passed between him and Rorke FitzWarren. If the potion were poisoned, Stephen would fall from it and she would be put to death. All waited for her to stop him.

She did not, but nodded, "You will experience a very pleasant feeling of warmth. Eventually you will not be able to move your arms or legs. The potion blocks out feeling; therefore, it also blocks out the pain."

He nodded and took several swallows of the faintly sweet liquid.

After a moment, he leaned unsteadily against the cot, but his expression was no less fierce than before, his grasp of words or thought no less clear.

"Do what must be done, healer."

It was a slow, painstaking process, but finally, with Rorke's help, she poured the contents past William's pale, slack lips and persuaded him to swallow.

From their previous reaction to the pain potion, she sensed the answer for what she must now ask, but it was necessary. She set the tankard aside and turned to Rorke FitzWarren.

"For what must be done next, you must trust me. I must be alone with him."

Stephen's reaction was immediate as his hand clenched over the handle of his broadsword.

"What treachery is this?" he demanded. "Do you think you have gained our trust by the test of your potion?"

Already, the effects of his drink had begun to wear off and he stood, drawing his sword.

"No matter her skills, she is still Saxon," he argued. "The bodies of the Norman dead lie in yonder graves. You cannot allow what she asks. I do not trust her. What is it that must be done that we cannot see?"

She saw the contemplation that settled in Rorke FitzWarren's cool gray gaze and heard the sounds of other weapons being drawn from their sheaths.

Imploringly, Vivian cast her thoughts out to him as she had with Stephen of Valois, desperate to make him understand, to bend his will to her own. But she discovered she could not. He was not like the others who might be persuaded by her thoughts.

"Please, milord," she begged. "He is dying. 'Tis a small thing I ask." Somehow she had to make him understand, for no one, not even Meg, had seen what she must do. She appealed to his honor as a knight sworn by an oath to the very man who lay so gravely injured.

"The healing ways are ancient and known to only a few," she went on to explain. "They have been entrusted to me with a sacred vow. Surely, you understand that I cannot break a covenant of trust." She laid her hand on his imploringly. "You must not ask it of me."

As a healer, Vivian had touched people hundreds of times. Physical contact soothed and gentled. But she gasped at the intensity of touching Rorke FitzWarren. His muscles tensed as his fist clenched, and she experienced a raw, sensual power that was stunning in the contrast of the heat of his scarred hand beneath her cool one. His fingers closed over hers. As if with a will of its own, her hand opened to the sensual heat of his touch, unleashing sensations that were stunning and terrifying.

Five

"Can't you see her treachery?" Stephen of Valois demanded as he shouldered his way around the cot to stand before her, his youthful features twisted with anger, pain, and fear.

"I will not allow her to be alone with him!" Stephen turned to her. "You will do what must be done, healer. And *none* will leave."

She could not reach Rorke FitzWarren, she thought in despair, but she might be able to reach this young, reckless, impassioned knight whose father—whom she sensed he both loved and hated—lay dying.

With lowered voice that only Stephen of Valois and those standing immediately about him might hear, she told him with the certainty of all her powers, "If you wish your *father* to live, you must do as I ask. If you do not, then his death will be on your hands."

Stunned surprise leapt into his eyes that she knew William

was his father, then his questioning gaze turned to Rorke FitzWarren.

"I told her nothing," Rorke assured him. When he looked at her, Stephen's expression was tormented and suspicious.

"What treachery is this, Saxon?" he demanded. "I could strike you down where you stand!" he whispered fiercely.

"Aye," she calmly agreed, "and then he will surely die. The choice is yours." She saw that her words were not lost on Rorke FitzWarren, for he had given her much the same sort of choice about the people of Amesbury.

Finally, Stephen, spat out, "So be it! But if he dies, you will quickly follow."

As a warrior Rorke had experienced many wounds and relied on the dubious talents of healers, many of them butchers who learned their trade flaying fowl or butchering pigs.

A few among them, in the Eastern empire, were healers of rare skill, whose knowledge and ability was very near miraculous. This young woman's skills were not merely that of mixing powders and potions. She understood the body's healing ways and skillful surgical techniques that rivaled those of the ancient Egyptians.

"I brought the healer," Rorke said for all to hear, his decision made. "The responsibility for what passes here rests with me."

His decision made, he announced, "Two of us will remain. The rest will leave." He nodded to Tarek al Sharif.

"Surely, demoiselle," he said to her, "you understand a vow of honor cannot be broken."

Vivian felt helplessness wash over her. She could not persuade this fierce Norman warrior to leave. There was no choice and there was no more time, for even now she felt William's life ebb.

"Aye," she reluctantly agreed. She could not prevent his staying, but perhaps she could prevent his remembering.

The expression on Stephen of Valois' face was filled with a turbulence of emotions. He did not want to leave, but he had given his word. He sheathed his blade.

"I will wait outside with the rest of your men, milord," he told Rorke. His gaze rested briefly on Vivian, then he and the others turned and left the tent. The heavy tapestry whispered into place after them.

Vivian moved back to the cot, trying to sort through her own emotions. Tarek al Sharif stood at the other side, his hand resting lightly on the handle of his blade. Rorke FitzWarren stood beside her.

She shivered, for the cold that seemed to find its way into the tent in spite of the fires that burned in the braziers and the drafts that had been sealed.

She laid a hand lightly on William's chest, feeling the thready life force within.

Glancing over at Rorke, she asked, "What do you believe in, milord? Are you a man of faith?"

"I have seen the corruption of faith," he said bluntly, wondering if she was about to ask him to pray, which he would not. "I have no patience for it."

"Do you believe in miracles?"

"I believe them to be the illusions of questionable minds."

"The ravings of lunatics?" she asked with a faint, sad smile. With an ache of compassion she wondered what it was in his life that had caused such coldness of cynicism. Was it possible he was of so little faith? She needed him to believe in miracles, for there was no logical explanation that most people might believe in what she must do. If he did not believe, what then might he think of what he was about to see? That she was a witch, a conjurer, and then have her put to death?

"Call it what you like, demoiselle. I believe in what is real. The earth beneath my feet, the strength that flows through my hand."

"The sword in your hand?" she suggested, trying to find some way to reach beyond the barrier of that wintry gray gaze, for if he doubted too strongly, he would stop her.

His gaze narrowed as he tried to guess her purpose. "Aye, for it is a knight's true strength."

"And what of the wind, milord? You cannot see it or hold it in your hand."

He thought on it at great length. "I can see it moving in the trees and feel the force of it at my back."

She glanced down at William. "Then so, too, you must accept what you will see, milord, and not interfere. For his life depends upon it."

He nodded gravely. "You have my word that I will not interfere, as long as you do not endanger his life."

She glanced across to Tarek al Sharif. He nodded his agreement.

With a sense of something irrevocable unfolding, Vivian looked down at the man whose life slowly ebbed.

No visions came to her. No voices whispered to guide her. There was only the certainty that this man must not die or England would lie in chaos as it had once before hundreds of years ago, prey to whatever invader chose to lay waste to it. England would not endure that, and she was the only one who could save him.

She took the blue crystal from about her neck and laid the stone over William's heart. Slowly she pressed her palms together and closed her eyes. Then she breathed in deeply, closing out everything about her—the glow of the candles and the fires in the braziers, the smell of burning tallow, leather, sweat, the warmth from those fires, the coldness of uncertainty. Turning inward to that place where time and place no longer existed, where there was only the life force of the power that burned within.

She let go of her awareness of everything else about her as the power grew, like the small spark that becomes a flame, and then becomes the inferno, until everything within her was focused on the power of the inner flame. Ancient words taught long ago whispered through her senses and she repeated them in the old language of the ancient ones.

Her head was bent over her hands, her flame-colored hair falling forward in a thick satin curtain, making it impossible to see her features as she whispered the strange-sounding words over and over.

She spoke softly, ancient words whispering through the tent, surrounding the flames that burned in the braziers so that they seemed to quiver with each word.

Rorke knew little of faith and trusted it even less. But these were not words of any faith that he understood. They were like a song, or incantation, whispered over and over again.

He knew of spell casters. An old gypsy woman lived on his father's estate, her hovel of a cottage reeking of foul-smelling concoctions that supposedly would rid a person of infirmities.

Pathetic, forlorn creatures sought her out when all else failed. A crippled child who longed to walk, barren women who longed to bear children, and impotent old men. Her remedies more often than not were the powdered eggshells of some lizard, eye of newt, or dragonfly wings to be ingested. All failed miserably.

Occasionally a woman got herself with child after consulting with the old crone, but there was never cause to believe it would not have happened anyway. As for the old men who went to see her, only one could claim a cure. And that administered by a fourteen-year-old girl on the estate!

Rorke had no belief or patience for such things. But now, when he moved to put an end to it, Tarek al Sharif stopped him with a powerful hand clamped over his arm.

"Do not!" he whispered a vehement warning, staring past Rorke to the Saxon girl.

Her unbound hair cascaded a fiery torrent about her shoulders and down her back as her head lifted. Her skin glowed pale and luminous as though from some inner light. With slender arms thrown wide she repeated the ancient words.

"Element of fire, spirit of light, essence of life, awaken the night."

"Fire of the soul, flame of life as light reveals truth, burn golden bright!"

The walls of the tent billowed as though caressed by the wind. Candle flames fluttered wildly. Coals in the braziers, which had burned low, suddenly burst into flame, filling the tent with blazing heat.

But it was not the flames suddenly flaring to life from coals that were almost dead, nor even his friend's hand that stopped him. It was her eyes, as they slowly opened.

They were an unnatural, compelling blue, rimmed by brilliant golden light like the heart of a flame as if she was not a creature of this world, the same color as the crystal that glowed where it lay over William's heart, as if the same fire burned through both.

She seemed completely oblivious to everything about her. There was no recognition or even the least acknowledgment of his presence. As if she were in some deep sleep at the same time she was awake. Or, as if she was not truly there.

She looked up, her blue gaze meeting his and at the same time seeing through him. He touched her hand and felt a fierce, wild energy in the skin beneath his fingers. The contact was intense, the unusual light in her eyes reaching out and enfolding him, suffusing him with heat. But once again there was no reaction, as if she had not felt his hand on hers.

She did not reach for the knife, nor did she apply any of the healing balm she had prepared for the other wounds. Instead she laid one hand at William's chest over his heart. The other she laid over the angry, festering wound at the mangled leg.

Vivian reached out, letting her consciousness flow through her fingertips into the injured warrior, reaching deep into his consciousness.

The contact was frenzied and chaotic, like stepping into a storm of past experiences, memory, and dreams, as she bonded with the life force within him. And it was intense.

Childhood experiences overlay those of the grown man, then flashed with glimpses of his young manhood. A fall from a childhood pony, the wrenching separation from his mother while still so young, painful rejections that spawned a fierce pride and stubborn willfulness, the physical contests of his warrior's training, the test of countless battles, a pretty young

woman's face, a child's, then that of the woman she'd seen in
the tent.

She saw and felt everything about William of Normandy. His
ambitions, fears, strengths, weaknesses, hopes, deepest desires.
All of it in a whirlwind of intense emotions, light, and color so
vivid that she felt those emotions, saw the blood and death of
those countless battles, including the battle at Hastings. Then
she felt the pain and fever that wasted him.

As if it was a tangible thing that she could hold in her hands,
Vivian reached deep within him, surrounding his pain with her
energy until she felt it begin to flow through her, the connection
between them like a silken thread that must not be broken.

Rorke had no understanding of this ancient ritual. Yet, as he
watched, William's body visibly relaxed from the tortured, painful spasms that had seized him. His skin lost its deadly pallor
as color returned and the death rattle eased from his lungs.

The heavy tapestry at the opening of the tent was torn aside.
Dust, smoke, and bitter cold wind swept inside.

"In the name of God! What is the meaning of this?"

Several candles guttered out. The fires that had burned bright
in the braziers suddenly smoldered and threatened to extinguish.
What light remained gleamed almost obscenely on the silver
crucifix that hung from the neck of the man who stood silhou-
etted in the opening of the tent, the grayish pallor of smoke
from the encampment swirling about him.

"God in Heaven!" he said with horrified voice as he strode
into the tent, surrounded by a half-dozen men. His gaze swept
the tent and then came to rest on Rorke FitzWarren.

"Is there no limit to your blasphemy?"

As the flames died, Vivian cried out. Pain tore through her
as the fragile bond with the dying man was suddenly threatened.
Searing fire and bitter cold seized her. Her lungs felt frozen,
each breath an agony as an overpowering weakness robbed her
of strength.

Swept back into the world of her own consciousness, her

gaze was drawn to the man who had caused the intrusion that now threatened the life of the man who lay before her.

Their gazes met briefly. She glimpsed powerful emotions—contempt, barely restrained anger, and other dark emotions she would not have imagined in a man of the Church.

Tarek stepped to block him from advancing any further. The bishop's men immediately drew swords, including the one who stood at the right hand of the bishop—Vachel.

"By all that is Holy, FitzWarren," the bishop vowed, "you dare too much. My men were sent to bring the healer. Who is this creature? What is this unholy act you dare to bring here?"

Then, turning to Vachel, he commanded, "Get her out of here!"

"Nay!" Vivian cried out as a new and different pain moved through her cold as death—William's death. The fragile connection to her was all that sustained him and must not be broken.

"Please, milord," she beseeched Rorke, "I must be allowed to finish, or he will die."

Rorke's glance went to William, who lay silent as death on the cot. So much hung in the balance, so much that had been wagered and might now be lost if he died. He saw the shallow rise and fall of that broad chest, saw too the slender hands that possessed some strange healing power he could not understand. The light in the blue crystal wavered and grew dim.

Though he had no explanation for it, he believed what he had seen with his own eyes, and knew in his heart that William would die without her.

Even now the Conqueror weakened once more. His skin had once more taken on a deathly pallor, painful spasms wracked his injured body, and his breathing was labored, as if each breath might be his last.

"Get them all out of here!" he commanded his men. "Including the bishop!" As Vachel stepped toward him threateningly, Rorke's blade sighed from its sheath.

"By all means," Rorke told him, "draw your blade. It would

give me enormous pleasure to separate your head from your shoulders."

Vachel hesitated, his gaze fastened on the bishop.

"You overstep yourself," the bishop warned Rorke with icy authority. "You intercede in matters of the king. How dare you interfere!"

"Be warned, milord Bishop," Rorke told him, angling the blade on a level with his throat. "Or you, too, may find yourself carrying your head. Bishop or no, makes no difference, for I have no fear for my soul."

The bishop hesitated. His gaze swept the tent, and Rorke FitzWarren's men. The anger faltered, tempered by cunning.

"You *will* fear for your soul," the bishop vowed. Then, with a harsh order, he swept from the tent, his men following behind him.

Rorke's men followed, forming an impenetrable phalanx against any further intrusions around the entire perimeter of the tent.

Rorke turned back to Vivian. His hand closed gently over her wrist.

"Do what must be done, mistress."

Beneath his fingers he felt the wild energy that poured through her. As before, he stared in amazement at the visible changes as she bent to her strange healing way.

Her slender hands spasmed and grew taut. She gasped as though suddenly in great pain while, beneath her hands, the painful spasms eased from William's tortured body. The blue crystal once more glowed bright.

Her skin became fevered to the touch, as William's cooled and no longer glistened with sweat. William's heartbeat slowed and strengthened. She turned deathly pale. It was as if she had given William her strength.

Finally, she lifted her head, her face drawn and pale, her breathing shallow. Rorke caught her as she collapsed and swung her up into his arms.

* * *

He held the goblet to her mouth, trickling the wine past colorless, cold lips. Eventually, she roused, dark auburn lashes lifting over eyes that were now the color of pale morning sky.

Slowly the color returned to her cheeks. As he looked down at her, he saw recognition and then memory return in the space of a heartbeat. Her gaze immediately went to the cot. The tension eased at her slender shoulders as if she was pleased with what she saw there.

She drank several more sips of wine. Beneath his hand at her wrist, her pulse once more beat strong and steady.

"I have no understanding of what I have just seen." Rorke spoke, awed in spite of himself. That vivid blue gaze came back to his, then angled away.

She offered no explanation as she attempted to stand. He refused to release her.

"He was near death."

When she still would not speak of it or look at him, he forced her head up with his fingers beneath the curve of her chin.

"Do you deny it?"

He had no idea how near death, Vivian thought, nor could she explain it to him so she sought refuge in safe answers. "Only God has the power of life and death, milord. Surely you believe that."

"God was not in this tent."

There was warmth and strength in that battle-scarred hand—a strength found in wild creatures that may be held but never tamed, and the warmth of some equally untamed emotion that both terrified and fascinated her.

The healing had left her senses and emotions naked, exposed, and vulnerable. The simplest contact of his fingers against her skin caused a heat she'd never experienced before.

A memory flashed through her thoughts, of a warm summer day when she was twelve and had gone into the forest near the abbey to gather herbs and roots, and come upon two young lovers.

She knew them from the village. The girl Bronwyn was not much older than Vivian. The boy, Ham, was the goatherd.

They lay together in the meadow, the warm summer air filled with their whispers, laughter, and other sounds. A moan low in Ham's throat as he touched her, followed by Bronwyn's startled gasp and then her sighs of pleasure.

Words drifted back with that memory. Lovers' words as clothes were discarded. Words of pleasure as naked flesh met naked flesh, then words of urgency that matched the urgency of their joining.

She had been terrified to leave lest she be discovered, and too fascinated to look away.

As she watched, a tightness grew low inside her like a longing of anticipation but for what she did not know.

Afterward, wanting some explanation for the strange feelings, she had told old Meg of what she had seen.

"Such things are not for you," Meg had warned. "Bronwyn is a simple, foolish girl, while you are learned in very special ways.

"Does she have the gift of sight or the power to heal? Can she call the birds from the sky?"

"Nay, child! You have very special powers and a unique destiny. Such things are not for you as they are for other mortals," she repeated. "For you would lose your powers. It would destroy you."

So long ago had it been that she had almost forgotten it. Until Rorke FitzWarren touched her. And she remembered now the inexplicable sadness Meg's words had brought.

"Please, milord," she begged, restless with a new urgency to be as far away as possible from the disconcerting gentleness of his touch. Then, with the excuse she was certain he would not refuse, "The bone must be properly set and bound."

Sensing her uneasiness, Rorke released her. "We will speak of this again." As she turned to William where he lay on the cot, Rorke moved toward the entrance of the tent.

"I will have food and blankets sent," he told her.

The bright satin of her hair shifted in the light from the braziers as her head came around.

"I would like to leave as soon as I have bound the leg."

"That is out of the question," he said, his voice cold and once more remote.

"There is no reason for me to remain," she protested. "I have told you that he will live."

Though she sensed that Meg and Poladouras were both safe, she wanted to return to Amesbury. Surely this was the meaning of her vision—the creature rising from the flames—the knight who sought her out to save William's life. It was done now. There was no reason for her to stay. In the weeks that lay ahead, the people of Amesbury would need her.

"There is more than enough reason," he informed her coldly. "I will not allow it."

Her uncertain emotions pushed her to anger. "I have done your bidding," she glared at him. "You have no more need of me."

"Aye, you have done my bidding," he acknowledged. "And far more than I had hoped. But I cannot allow you to leave." There was no threat in his voice, but the finality of his answer made her anger reckless.

"I will not stay," she told him adamantly.

Rorke's gaze narrowed thoughtfully. She cared not for herself. He had seen it at Amesbury. But there were others she did care for.

"Would you so heedlessly jeopardize the lives of the people of Amesbury?" he asked with a reasonableness of logic that stopped her. Once again there was no threat by tone or action, but merely in the simple asking of the question.

At that moment she hated him even more than she first had at Amesbury. Then, she understood his urgency, but she understood nothing of it now. Incredulous, she asked, "You would use their lives to bind me to you?"

"I would," he said with that same promise of voice.

"To what purpose?" she demanded, anger rising.

"To the purpose of guaranteeing William's safe recovery. I have seen healthy flesh turn and sicken when a wound is all but healed. By what I have seen this night, mistress, you have the skill of extraordinary healing. I will not jeopardize his life by allowing you to return to your villagers."

Her cheeks blazed with color. The flames of the candles reflected in her eyes. "Is that your final word?"

"It is."

"How can you then be certain that I will not be neglectful in his care?" she challenged.

He smiled so certain of himself. "Because the villagers of Amesbury mean far too much to you."

She shuddered at the depth of his coldness. Inwardly, she wept silent tears at his cruelty. Her voice was filled with loathing. "You are no different than Vachel."

"I am far different, demoiselle. He would have destroyed the village for the simple pleasure of it. I spared it for a purpose."

She was caught by her love and loyalty to the villagers of Amesbury. And he knew it.

"And will your men remain outside?" she asked, her voice dripping with contempt.

"They will."

"To guard me?"

"To protect you."

"I do not want your protection."

"Nevertheless, demoiselle, the guards remain."

To report back to him, if she should attempt to leave, so that he might then carry out his promise. She whirled back angrily to the cot. At the table the flame of the candles quivered and flared brightly.

Tarek met him at the opening of the tent as he was leaving.

"Guard the duke of Normandy and the healer," Rorke told him. "I trust no one else."

After he had gone, Vivian said angrily, "He has left you to

stand guard over me." Vivian speculated after Rorke FitzWarren
had gone, the tent flap closing behind him.

"I am to guard the duke of Normandy," Tarek responded
quietly.

"To prevent me from leaving?" she demanded, facing him.

His bright blue gaze met hers, the color of his eyes startling
in that darkly handsome face. She could sense his thoughts and
emotions, yet he was equally as dangerous as Rorke FitzWarren,
whose thoughts she could not sense.

"To keep others from entering," he replied stiffly.

She frowned as she sensed he was telling the truth. She had
expected him to deny it and she would have known that it was
a lie.

When he moved to the side of the cot as though to give
assistance, she stopped him.

"I can do what must be done," she assured him. "But we
will need more wood for the braziers."

That strange blue gaze met hers and for a moment she wondered if he sensed her deception. Then he bowed his head
slightly and went to the opening of the tent to tell Rorke's men
that more wood was needed.

The moment his attention was turned elsewhere, she removed
the fur that lay over the duke of Normandy's injured leg. She
worked quickly, covering the open wound with a poultice
soaked in a simmering concoction of horsetail and comfrey. The
horsetail would prevent the wound turning bad, while the comfrey would hasten the healing.

She was grateful that he spoke at some length with one of
Rorke's men. No doubt seeing to the details of her imprison-
ment. When he returned, he carried several pieces of firewood
and two pieces of straight wood of an even length.

The firewood he divided among the braziers set about the
tent to provide warmth through the cold night. He handed her
the straight pieces of wood, which looked like slats from one
of the carts. His gaze narrowed as he looked at her.

"You are indeed a skilled healer," he commended her. "I have never known a bone to be so quickly set, and especially one shattered to pieces. Your ancient ways must be rare indeed."

" 'Tis no great accomplishment," she assured him, and then added, with a small shrug, "The bone was not as severely broken as it first seemed."

Although she sensed his doubt, he seemed to accept her explanation. He sat at a small stool before one of the braziers, while she finished splinting and wrapping the broken leg.

He removed the curved sword from his belt and began sharpening it, making her wonder precisely whom he guarded against.

William's squire, escorted by one of Rorke's men, brought wine, food, and several furs. The meal was laid out, the furs spread before the braziers.

"You must eat," Tarek told her, when she had assured herself that William rested comfortably. He passed her a trencher of cold meat and bread. Exhausted from the healing ritual and the wine that made her senses feel as if they were wrapped in fleece, Vivian merely nibbled at a crust of bread.

Tarek al Sharif had returned to sharpening that oddly curved steel blade. It caught the light of the brazier and winked golden death.

"Who was the man who tried to stop me?" Vivian asked.

There was no attempt to disguise the contempt in his voice. "He is the count de Bayeau, bishop of the Church of Rome, and Duke William's brother."

"His brother?"

Nothing she had sensed about the man had revealed it. In fact, she was able to sense little other than what she had seen of his appearance and that gleaming silver cross.

"And Vachel serves him?"

Tarek nodded, the whetstone gliding along the curve of blade with a deadly hiss. "Like the jackal serves the night."

His comparison startled her, for she, too, had sensed a darkness about the man. Puzzled, she stared at him.

"He sent Vachel to find me, yet he would have prevented me helping his brother. I find no reason in it."

He gave her a telling glance. "He has his own ambitions, and they are not entirely bound to the Church."

He refused to say more, and Vivian was too exhausted to understand any of it, though something that had been said kept prodding at her thoughts—Rorke FitzWarren's accusation that Vachel had gone to Amesbury to kill her. She had no idea what any of it might mean.

Tarek al Sharif had laid out his own pallet some distance apart, guarding the entrance. He did not immediately seek his own bed, but continued polishing his blade.

Vivian gazed into the flames of the brazier as she curled deep into the furs and lay beside the fire. The flames curled lazily over the wood, slowly consuming it, shifting and separating into spiral strands of brilliant blue, soft gold, bright yellow, and red like silken stands that threaded the darkness in the tent. As she watched, an image slowly took form in the shifting colors—that of a woman sitting before a large open frame.

The flames shifted again and she saw that the woman sat before a tapestry loom, bending over her work. She was dressed in blue, the loom was a dark void framed in gold. But she could not see who the weaver might be, for the young woman was turned away from her.

The darkness of the tapestry seemed to spread, bleeding beyond the boundaries of the loom until it all but consumed the weaver. The woman slowly turned toward Vivian, but before she could see her face, the vision was gone, as illusive as smoke.

She tried to find some meaning in the vision but could not. Exhausted, she drifted into restless sleep filled with troubled dreams of war, death, and a fierce creature born in blood and fire—a creature with the features of a man. He reached out to her, rousing sensual dreams of two people in a forest glade, their bodies entwined in passion.

Rorke FitzWarren was the phoenix and she was the flame, and he arose reborn from the inferno of their fierce joining.

Six

The tent flap was thrown back, framing Tarek al Sharif in a swirl of early morning mist.

Rorke looked up as he finished strapping on padded leather chausses. His features were drawn with fatigue from having been up half the night listening to reports from his knights about events in William's camp during his absence.

The Persian's expression was taut, filled with fury. Immediately wary, Rorke demanded, "Is it William? Has he worsened?"

"He rests well for a man who was near death but a few hours past," Tarek assured him as he came into the tent. "The fever is gone and the wound no longer seeps."

Rorke's relief was visible in the lines easing about his mouth. He smiled at his friend, who was always so serious and intense, like that curved blade that he carried—always sharp and eager to draw blood.

"What is it then?" he asked. "Has some new Saxon army shown itself on the ridge above and now swarms down the hillsides to overrun us?"

Tarek glanced to Rorke's squire. With a nod from Rorke the young man was gone, removing chain mail battle armor badly in need of repair. When he was satisfied that none would overhear them, Tarek told him. "The *Saxon* has not overrun us, but retreated."

"Aye," Rorke agreed, mistaking his meaning, "vanquished by William's army not more than six days ago on this very battlefield."

Tarek shook his head. "Hardly more than six hours ago."

Humor slowly faded. Rorke became wary. "What are you saying?"

The Persian's expression was grim. "The Saxon I speak of is not an army of men, but one Saxon girl, fled in the night."

Gray eyes narrowed. "Fled?"

"Aye, the one with hair like a flame and the powers of a Jehara. She is gone."

Rorke didn't bother to summon his squire. Instead he hastily finished pulling on leather boots. Anger replaced the fatigue, emphasizing each movement—the slap of leather, the snap of the belt, the thud of a booted foot stomped into the earthen floor.

"How is it possible," Rorke demanded, his voice taut, "that a simple maid has the ability to accomplish what the finest trained mercenaries in all the Byzantine Empire could not, in slipping past you?"

Tarek answered matter-of-factly, "I would like to know that as well. If the girl is found, I have several questions I would like to ask her. It is very puzzling how she managed it."

"When she is found," Rorke emphasized, "you will have your answers. As will I."

Unshaven, his features were gaunt and filled with shadows. The expression in his eyes was cold as the wind that sliced through the opening of the tent.

"Have you spoken to anyone else of this?" he demanded harshly.

Tarek shook his head. "Only your men who guarded the tent. It was necessary to question if they had seen her."

Rorke nodded as he seized a short-bladed knife and slipped it down the inside leg of his boot, then seized his leather gauntlets.

"No one else is to know she is gone." He snapped out his orders. "I want no interference from Vachel. See that William's tent is well guarded."

Tarek assured him, "It is already done."

"The horses?"

"Saddled and waiting outside. I have put out the word that we ride in search of Saxon rebels."

Rorke's lips thinned. "That is not far from the truth."

Outside the tent, a chill wind stung exposed skin, whipping smoke from cook fires to sting at the eyes.

The horses sensed their mood and moved restlessly, heads tossing as they strained their tethers. Rorke seized the reins and vaulted into the saddle.

"Did anyone see her leave?" he asked, as he controlled the restless stallion.

"No one saw anything," Tarek replied as he mounted his Arabian mare. "But I found a set of lightly made footprints that could not be made by a soldier's boot, several hundred yards beyond William's tent."

"How is it," Rorke asked through his teeth, "that no one saw her leave and that these prints suddenly appear some distance from the tent? "Would you have me believe that she sprouted wings and flew from the tent?"

"I do not know," Tarek admitted.

Rorke swore heavily, for it was not like his friend to be uncertain in anything. Never in all the time he had known him, since they met at Antioch—two warriors willing to sell their services in a personal quest, thrown together by fate and the threat of the Turkish sultan—had he ever known the warrior to falter.

Tarek was the half-caste son of a woman of noble Persian birth and a foreign raider, a Viking whose fleet of ships had laid siege to Antioch and held the city for a fortnight before being driven back. But in that fortnight the Norsemen had laid claim to more than riches of gold and silver. They had laid claim to the daughters of several noble families, who in the ensuing months gave birth to the Viking blue-eyed babies.

Tarek was the result of such a union, taken from his mother at birth to hide her shame and raised by a merchant and his childless wife. But always he carried the shame of his birth and the hatred for his father, who had left Tarek's mother with a child in her belly and a gold Norse medallion that Tarek wore about his neck.

Out of shame and a broken heart at being parted from her baby, his mother had taken her own life, and Tarek had vowed revenge for her death and his own shameful birthright. Shunning the life of a merchant, he became a warrior, selling his prowess with a blade to the highest bidder. For only with gold and in the service of foreign kings might he find the father who wore the emblem of the dragon head and had abandoned him and his mother.

In all of Byzantium Tarek al Sharif's skill with a blade was well-known. He was a warrior without peer, until the day by a strange twist of fate, which he believed to be the workings of the Divine One, he found himself under a Norman blade. Spared from death by Rorke FitzWarren, he was in the dubious position of owing a debt of honor to an infidel. But fighting with Rorke FitzWarren rather than against him offered another advantage besides the gift of his life.

It offered him the opportunity to travel west, closer to the lands of the Norsemen. Then he received word that a man who carried the badge of a dragon was rumored to be in the far north of Britain and he had thrown in his lot with Rorke FitzWarren and the knights who pledged themselves to William of Normandy's cause to take the English throne.

Knowing his friend as he did, and with a profound respect for his skills as a warrior, Rorke frowned. It was for those reasons he had left Tarek to guard William and the maid. For he was certain no one would get past Tarek al Sharif. He had not considered that the maid would get past him. Nor could he fathom how she might have done what no other warrior had ever done. But he knew beyond doubt that he must find the maid and bring her back lest William suffer a relapse and worsen without her care.

He had no clear explanation for the healing technique she had used the night before. Whatever its origin, it had been effective. The future of England was at stake, and along with it his own future. William of Normandy must live to claim his throne.

"Did you see which direction she fled?" he asked.

"East toward the sun," Tarek informed him.

Rorke frowned. "Then she has not returned to Amesbury," he said with more than a little surprise, for he was certain that was the direction she would take.

His eyes scanning eastward, Rorke realized why she had taken that direction. He had only forbidden her to return to Amesbury or forfeit the lives of the villagers.

"Jesu!" he swore. "She has set out across the battlefield. Does she not know the danger of wandering alone through a field camp filled with soldiers?"

Rorke's gaze narrowed as he scanned the edge of forest that rimmed the battlefield. She could easily conceal herself among the trees. She had spoken of it on the journey from Amesbury.

"What was it you called her?" he asked Tarek as they set off following those tracks in the muddied earth, with his men fanning out about them for some other signs of those same tracks that might indicate she had taken a new direction. "Jehara? I do not know the word."

"They are the enchanted ones who live between the worlds of what we can and cannot see," Tarek explained. "It is said they have great powers, among them the ability to move between the real and spiritual world."

Rorke glanced over at his friend, who was a great warrior and believed as he did in the power of the sword that a man held in his hand.

"Do you believe in such things?"

"I believe there are a great many things that we know little about. I know that she was in the tent one moment, and then gone. I left only once and your guards were at their positions at all times."

"What are you suggesting?"

"It is said the Jehara may take many forms."

"Into what, pray tell?" Rorke snapped. There were times his friend's odd beliefs were amazing. "A gnome or elf? Perhaps a troll small enough so that you could not see her? That would account for the small tracks you found!"

"There are many such legends among the Saxons," Tarek speculated. "As there are in my own culture. The most widely held belief in such creatures is the one called Merlin."

Rorke frowned. "The sorcerer who made Arthur king of all Britain." He shrugged, dismissing it. "I have heard of the legend. There are many such legends among all cultures. Among the ancient Greeks, there are similar legends of gods and goddesses and mythical creatures with extraordinary powers. Legends and myths."

"And yet," Tarek pointed out, "there are those who believe in them. Among my mother's people it is believed that such creatures also possess great healing powers. Can you otherwise explain what we saw in William's tent last night?"

"I cannot explain it," Rorke admitted, his voice low and thoughtful. "An ancient Saxon remedy perhaps. The girl is gifted in the healing arts and I have need of those skills. I care not the source." He whipped his horse forward. His voice rose in anger. "She will be found."

Mist blanketed the ground, swirling on currents of air one moment, then shrouding everything in shades of gray. Silent as a wraith, Vivian slipped past the Norman guards into the Saxon encampment at the edge of the battlefield.

She had been roused by dreadful dreams that were like images of the day before and the horrible death scene they'd come upon as they entered the valley. The faces of the dying Saxons haunted her, their voices whispering to her through the dark veil of sleep, and she knew she must go to them.

They were there, they must be—the injured Saxons who had somehow lived through the dreadful battle of Hastings and even now lay wounded and in need. She had seen the Norman guards as they rode into camp and wondered whom they guarded across the wide-open field. Then she realized that not all those fires were funeral pyres. There were shapes huddled before them, in groups of two, three, or more. And so, at dawn, as William rested peacefully from the tisane she had given him, she knew she must go to the battlefield and do what she could to ease the suffering of the Saxon prisoners.

She rose from her bed of furs, taking the pouch of medicines with her. Then she opened her thoughts, reaching out to Tarek al Sharif where he slept at the entrance of the tent. Her thoughts closed around his like a shroud drawn over the senses so that he would not awaken. That left the guards that she knew surrounded the tent. Vivian stepped to the east wall of the tent.

The blue crystal once more hung about her neck. It glowed brightly as she closed her eyes and once more turned her thoughts inward. Concentrating on the power of the old ones that lived within her, she imagined herself walking through the tent wall, continued to imagine herself moving unseen to a place apart from the camp.

She felt the heavy fabric of the tent wall wrap about her, then the sudden sharp bite of the bitter cold wind. When she opened her eyes, she stood several paces away from the tent. There was no shout of alarm from inside the tent, nor did the guards appear to be aware that anything was amiss. Clutching the pouch of healing herbs and powders tightly under her arm, Vivian turned and fled the Norman encampment for the battlefield where Saxon survivors lay scattered, huddled in the cold morning air, too badly injured to move.

She followed the cart path and quickly found them, avoiding the guards in the same way she had eluded Tarek al Sharif, by merely controlling their thoughts so that they were not even aware of her presence.

A few of the Saxon injured had been able to forage wood and built meager fires that smoldered, adding to the pervasive pall that hung over the encampment. Others lay with blank, pain-filled eyes, waiting for death.

There were women, too, wives and lovers who had followed them to Hastings and risked much to now care for their sons and husbands.

"Water," a feeble voice called out. "Do you have water?"

Vivian quickly knelt by the man and let him drink from the skin she had brought with her. She bandaged his wound and then quickly moved on, for there were so many. And always there were the cries for water and food. Some, giving her a description, asked if she had seen a companion, brother, or son.

She moved among them, drawing only an occasional glance from the Norman guards, for she no longer bothered to control their thoughts. They had no reason to think she was other than what she seemed, a Saxon woman who tended the dying. Moving from one meager fire to the next, she handed out powders and herbal remedies for pain, bleeding, and fevers. Whispers of gratitude followed her. And then she moved on, her heart aching at what she saw.

Images hovered at the edges of her vision. When she looked to see them more clearly they disappeared. They were the images she'd experienced the day before, arriving in the valley where the battle had been fought. The memories of pain, misery, and dying became her memories.

Like a dream that was very real, she clearly saw the battle unfold.

Hopelessly outnumbered and armed with crudely made clubs, wood axes, and the simplest peasant tools, they had fought afoot in defensive lines so tightly packed together that as the dead fell among them under volleys of Norman arrows, they were pinioned shoulder to shoulder beside the living.

They had been relentlessly hacked to pieces. Those who survived had been positioned at the ends of the line. As the line fragmented, they had fled and regrouped. But the outcome was inevitable.

With an army made up of untrained peasants, thanes, and house carls, Harold had been doomed before he ever set foot on the battlefield at Hastings.

She saw it all clearly, the threads of gray smoke, bleak defeat, and crimson blood, emerging in a pattern beneath the weaver's hand at the loom just as she had seen it in her vision.

A tapestry not yet woven, a distant voice whispered through her senses.

But she knew the first threads had been set on this battlefield. The threads of an unknown future lay in the basket of thread at the weaver's feet.

She moved on, offering what comfort she could. And with each group she encountered, she searched for a familiar face from the village of Amesbury. But she saw none.

One of the guards turned to stare at her curiously. She darted out of sight around the end of a cart with a broken wheel, a cart like the ones she had seen the previous afternoon piled with bodies.

A man lay on his side beneath the cart. By his tunic and breeches, Vivian realized he was a Norman soldier.

Tentatively, she laid a hand at his shoulder, then swallowed her cry of alarm as he suddenly rolled toward her.

Flies, disturbed by the intrusion, buzzed noisily as they swarmed the front of his bloodied tunic and dead, sightless eyes.

She had sensed his death the moment she touched him and should have been prepared for it. But neither was she prepared for the way this Norman soldier's death affected her, as deeply as that of the Saxons she had seen.

He was young, with his hair worn in the tonsured style, and clean-shaven. He looked no different than the Saxon soldiers, except that his clothes were leather, padded for protection, and a battle sword and shield lay beside him.

Like the dead Saxon soldiers, there was nothing she could do for this enemy, but she thought of those who would mourn him. He was some woman's son, lover, or husband who would not be returning to his home, just as many Saxons would not return to theirs.

She knew she must return to William's tent. The sky had lightened considerably. It was only a matter of time until it was discovered that she was gone. Already she imagined Rorke's anger at finding her gone. She could not control his thoughts as she could others, and she would not be able to *persuade* the anger from him. Nor could she control her own thoughts when she was around him.

A sudden, brilliance of heat shimmered through her at his remembered touch. Yet she shivered, drawing her shawl more tightly about her and feeling the unwanted sensations that poured through her at just the memory of his hand on hers, and the thought sprang unbidden of what it might feel like to have his hand touch her in other places. She cast it away, the forbidden thought, as she rose to leave, reaching to the side of the cart to steady herself.

Suddenly, a hand clamped over her wrist. Before she could protest, another hand smothered over her mouth.

Vivian struggled to free herself, but she was no match for her assailant. Her feet went out from under her and she was dragged to the ground. Vivian kicked and fought, but that hand made it impossible to breathe. She clawed at those fingers at the same time she struggled to control her emotions and thoughts. For it was her only chance as she was dragged behind the cart.

Seven

"Do not cry out!"

Slowly the hand dropped away from her mouth. An arm loosened about her waist and she was released. Vivian twisted around.

"Conal!" Now, she understood why she hadn't sensed any danger.

The shepherd from Amesbury looked quickly around. Then,

satisfied that the Norman guards hadn't seen them, he dropped back to the ground behind the cart.

Vivian was stunned. She couldn't imagine how Conal had come to be here. Fear tightened around her heart at what would happen if he were found.

"Why are you here?" she asked anxiously.

"I set out as soon as the storm cleared," Conal explained in a low voice. "Poladouras gave me his palfrey." His lean features softened, making the bruise on the side of his head seem less severe. With old Meg's care he seemed to have recovered from the beating at Amesbury.

Touched by his loyalty, Vivian knew the danger he risked and she protested, "You should not have come. It is too dangerous."

"Aye," he answered, "and dangerous for you as well. You're not harmed?"

"Nay," she assured him. "I am well. But how did you find this place?"

Conal's expression contorted. "It was not difficult. I followed the trail of dead and wounded." His voice was filled with a contempt of bitterness.

"Aye," her heart constricted as she thought of the dead she'd seen. "Many died here."

Then Conal's expression lightened. "I watched the Norman encampment all night and saw you leave this morn. Now we can leave together." He had taken her hand between his, the palms hard and callused from working with the sheep, but as gentle as if he cradled a newborn lamb. He rose, pulling her to her feet.

"We must leave now," he said urgently, his gaze scanning the open field beyond the cart with a keen shepherd's eye, as the mist cleared and sun broke through.

"I left the palfrey in the forest not far from here."

He pointed to the edge of the forest; Vivian pulled her hand from his grasp.

"I cannot," she said sadly. "You must go back without me."

Conal looked at her as if she had taken leave of her senses.

"I will not go back without you," he protested. "You are the reason I came here. It is dangerous for you here. You saw how they treated the people of Amesbury." He glanced cautiously around. "We must leave together, now, before we are discovered."

Everything within her longed to return to the remote safety of Amesbury and those she loved. But sadly, Amesbury was not safe. Rorke FitzWarren had vowed what would happen if she was to leave. He was a dangerous man—a man who would keep such a vow.

"No, Conal," she said, desperate to make him understand. "I will not go with you. You must go back alone."

In all the time they had been friends Conal had never shown anger toward her. His gentle eyes took on a hard, determined look.

"I will not leave without you, Vivian." His face was grim. "We will hide in the forest until nightfall and travel by night. Come morning we will be halfway to Amesbury." His hand shot out and once more clamped painfully about her wrist.

"You're hurting me," she cried as he began to pull her toward the edge of the forest.

Behind them, she heard distant shouts from the Norman guards and terror seized her.

"You must go!" she told him. He had turned and stared past her as another shout went up. His fingers bit into her tender flesh. Then he looked down at her, his gaze filled with a dark pain.

"I came here for you!"

More shouts joined the first ones, closer now. Through the shifting, swirling veil of mist, Vivian saw the outlines of several mounted horsemen.

Poladouras had read to her from the Bible of the four horsemen of the Apocalypse—war, famine, death, and pestilence. These dark shapes, shrouded in mist and smoke, seemed like those four horsemen come to life, and a portent of the death they would bring if he did not go now.

"Please go, Conal," she begged frantically. "I could not bear your death."

His gaze too was fastened on the approaching horsemen. As he hesitated, his hold on her arm loosened, and Vivian twisted free of his grasp.

She backed away from him, back toward the cart, even as she wished in her heart that she could run into the forest with him, and leave this place of death.

The expression on his bruised face was contorted with anger and helplessness. "I love you, Vivian. I have always loved you. I will find a way." Then, as the horsemen broke through the mist, their weapons catching the dull gleam of the sun, he turned and ran into the heavy undergrowth at the edge of the forest.

Through the shifting clouds of mist that swirled along the ground, Rorke's gaze scanned the edge of the Saxon encampment.

They had lost Vivian's tracks when the guards stationed about the encampment informed them that a woman had been seen in the encampment, moving among the injured Saxons.

As the mist shifted and separated he glimpsed a cart at the edge of the field and a woman. Beneath the edge of her shawl he also glimpsed fiery red hair. He cursed as the mist swirled before them and he lost sight of her.

The sun broke through as they rode in the direction of the cart and he caught sight of her again. This time on the other side of the cart and running back toward the field. Then he glanced past and saw a man running into the forest, by his simple clothes a Saxon!

"There, at the edge of the forest." Tarek al Sharif had seen him as well. "I will take some of the men and see what we may find."

"Aye," Rorke acknowledged, with narrowed gaze fixed on the edge of the forest. "Take care you do not find too many Saxons hiding out in the forest."

Tarek and Gavin de Marte rode toward the forest, battle swords drawn and resting across the front of their saddles.

Vivian saw several knights angle off toward the forest and she prayed Conal was safely hidden. If he was found, she feared what Rorke's men might do to him.

She drew in a fearful breath, seeing Rorke riding steadily toward her, leaving no doubt that she had been seen. Neither he nor his men wore their battle armor, but instead the leather breeches and tunics usually worn under their mail. Perhaps, she thought with a small, faint hope, more bloodshed was not their intention, and his only purpose was to find her.

In her concern for the injured Saxons, she had stayed longer in the prisoners' encampment than she had intended. If she had returned earlier, her absence might never have been discovered, and Conal would be safe. But there were so many wounded who needed her help.

She stood, head lifted slightly, meeting Rorke's gaze, which was cold as the morning mist, as the powerful warhorse and rider approached.

"Good morn, mistress," he said, as he pulled the stallion to a stop. Beneath the simple greeting she heard the ribbon of anger.

"Milord," she greeted, and then, stepping aside of the cart, she indicated the man who lay underneath.

"I fear he was already dead when I found him." She shivered at the memory of his young dead face, and added softly, "There was naught I could do."

Rorke's glance angled to the Norman soldier who had died so pitifully beneath the cart before his men could reach him.

He nodded, his expression grim, but whether it was for the Norman soldier's death, or with anger at her, she could not tell.

"I will have someone tend to him," he said not unkindly. " 'Tis a hard thing to die alone so far from home."

His words startled her, for she had not expected any tenderness of feeling, much less compassion.

She grew uneasy under that silent scrutiny and, fearing he

might be distracted toward Conal and the forest, tucked her pouch of herbs under her arm and walked past him as if it was most natural for her to be in that field, in the early hours of the morn.

"I feared some harm might have befallen you," Rorke commented as he swung the warhorse about to follow. She heard his undertone of anger.

"As you can see, milord," she said with even voice as she continued walking. "I am quite safe. There was no need for your concern."

He guided the warhorse slowly forward until he was beside her. "Tarek al Sharif was most concerned since I had entrusted your safety to his care. He takes his responsibilities most seriously. He was very perplexed that you were able to leave without his seeing it."

He saw the sudden rise and fall of her shoulders as she took a breath that betrayed her uneasiness. But her gaze was direct and unafraid as she turned and looked at him.

"Then I shall have to give him my apologies," she said, making no excuses, nor offering any explanation of precisely how it had been done. Instead she was exchanging polite pleasantries as if she was unaware of the cold fury that glittered in his eyes, the powerful hand that flexed over the handle of his battle sword, and his men who rode along the edge of the forest with their own battle swords drawn.

She was the most magnificent creature he had ever encountered. As bold and proud as any knight, like a beautiful, defiant flame threading the mist. Causing him to strongly consider having her bound and flogged as he would any other escaped prisoner. At the same time he wanted to make love to her.

He had never before found himself so truly vexed by a maid, or at the same time undone by one.

It took no power of second sight to know that he was very angry with her. She had prepared herself for it, and even now braced for the outcome of that anger. Recalling the brutality that had been handed out at Amesbury without cause, she could only guess the punishment he intended for her. And if Conal was found, he would doubtless be put to death.

Gathering her skirt in hand to keep from tripping over the uneven ground, Vivian continued walking. Her slippers were poor protection against the hard-packed, frozen earth, but she dare not stop, for every step drew him further away from the forest and Conal.

"You deliberately disobeyed me." His voice was as cold as the wind that whipped at her.

She continued to gaze straight ahead, concentrating on her footing to keep from stumbling, her slender chin angled slightly.

"I did not, milord," she calmly informed him.

"I forbade you to leave the encampment." His voice rose as he reminded her, his hand taut at the reins as the stallion tossed its head uneasily at the huddled shapes gathered about the Saxon campfires they passed.

"You did not," she said matter-of-factly. "You said only that I might not return to Amesbury. And as you can see"— she gestured across the encampment—"I have not returned to Amesbury but remain within your encampment. Therefore, I have not disobeyed you."

She continued across the field, taking a direction she had not walked when she left the Norman encampment.

Lips thinned, he fought to keep control of his temper as he rode along side.

"You twist my words against me, Vivian. My meaning was clear and you understood it well. You were not to leave William's tent. I had my reasons for giving such orders."

"And I had my reasons, milord."

A woman struggled to her feet as they approached. She was thin and poorly dressed, her features haggard with a mixture of fear and starvation. Beside her a Saxon soldier lay curled toward the feeble fire, his body wracked by violent shivering. Vivian sensed only fear and desperation could have made the woman approach them.

"Please, mistress, have you water?" she begged. "Or a crust

of bread? My husband is too weak to walk, and without water he will die."

Wary and mistrustful, she reached an imploring hand, keeping well out of the way of the striking distance of that broadsword.

"I have medicines and food," Vivian told her, speaking in Saxon English that caused the woman's sagging face to brighten with feeble hope.

"You are Saxon."

"Aye," Vivian said, going to her. "I am Saxon." The woman's gaze darted past her to the warrior astride his warhorse.

"Come, you must help me," Vivian told her, drawing the woman back to the fire with her. She immediately saw the source of her husband's fever. A sword wound that had festered. Knowing that she risked much in stopping to help them, Vivian pressed her last crust of bread into the woman's thin hand. It was all that remained of what she had brought with her from William's tent.

"It is all I have," she apologized. Then she took the woman's other hand and poured a handful of crushed leaves into her palm.

"Sprinkle this into the wound and then bind it. It will draw the infection. I wish that I had water to give you, for it would be best if you could brew a tisane from the leaves as well." Her heart ached into her throat. "But I have none."

Tears glistened at the woman's eyes. She clasped Vivian's hand between her thin ones and pressed it to her sunken cheek.

"Bless you, mistress!" She shivered pathetically as the mist blocked the sun. Her shawl had been wrapped about her trembling husband. Vivian quickly removed her own shawl and wrapped it about the woman's thin shoulders.

"You must not," the woman protested. "How will you keep warm?"

"I shall manage," Vivian assured her, wondering how they would possibly survive another night without water and shelter. There was a shift of movement behind them. The woman cringed as she turned and saw Rorke's giant warhorse looming over them. Her arm came up across her face in anticipation of a blow. But there was none.

Instead, Rorke lowered the skin of water that hung from his saddle and extended it toward the woman. Mistaking his intention, she flung her arms up to protect herself.

"Nay, milord!" she screeched, crawling to protect her husband. "Have mercy I beg of you."

An odd expression contorted his features as Vivian reached to comfort the woman. A mixture of anger, pity, and what might even have been regret.

"I have no intention of taking your life, woman!" The words started in anger, but ended gently. "Take the skin of water. Perhaps it will ease your husband's fever."

Vivian's surprise was as great as the woman's as she stared up at the fierce Norman warrior, and tried to understand what could only be seen as kindness.

"You have done all that you can," Rorke said, not ungently.

" 'Tis not enough!" she answered fiercely.

His expression hardened as before with taut features, making him seem more than ever the fierce creature of her vision. But just as she had not been prepared for his kindness, she was not prepared when he extended his hand to her.

Rorke saw her hesitation, the shift of uncertain emotion in those flame blue eyes. Then, she laid her hand in his.

He lifted her to the saddle before him. He was a formidable presence in full battle armor astride the tall warhorse with war lance and broadsword.

But with battle armor removed, powerful arms and legs wrapped about her, each shift of heavy muscle felt through every part of her, Rorke FitzWarren was far more formidable in ways that pierced through the protective barriers of her own emotional armor.

His hand closed over her hip as he settled her more securely before him, recalling the hours they'd ridden that same way from Amesbury.

The warmth of his hand, felt through her thin kirtle and shift, was disconcerting, slightly possessive in the lingering weight when he did not immediately remove it. She shivered suddenly as strange feelings spiraled through her.

Thinking her cold, Rorke said, "You should not have parted with your shawl."

Vivian shook her head as she tried to control her uncertain emotions. " 'Tis a small thing. She will have better use of it, and I could not wear it knowing of their suffering."

"Yet you are cold." His hand shifted, moving across her waist to pull her back against his warmth. Did he know how she burned at his touch?

"I will survive it, milord," she assured him, and prayed that she would survive that sensual awareness which spiraled through her as he held her against him.

She silently prayed to all the powers of the Light, trying to find some understanding of the wild, chaotic feelings he roused in her. What was it in this dangerous enemy's touch that affected her as no other ever had?

He did not ride back to the main part of the Norman encampment but instead turned the warhorse on a line parallel with the edge of the forest. Cold fear gripped Vivian—fear that he had seen Conal after all and was determined to make her part of the hunt.

A shout went out, and the fear congealed in a knot at her stomach.

It wasn't possible! She had not foreseen Conal's death. Please let him be safe! And yet in other matters her sense of things had abandoned her. Since Rorke FitzWarren had come into her life with such a violence and destruction. Her heart leapt into her throat as Rorke whirled the warhorse about. Gavin de Marte pointed not to the forest, but to the sky overhead.

His men had been taking aim with their bows at the noisome swarms of pesky crows that swept in small dark clouds over the encampment, occasionally alighting to pick at some bit of refuse.

Several of his knights had loosed their arrows, bringing the crows to earth with deadly accuracy.

She felt no sympathy for the wretched birds, whose raucous sound was like rude laughter as they dived at carts laden with the bodies of the dead. The archers pointed not at the crows, but at another, larger bird that glided above them.

The bird was sleek and dark, riding the currents of the wind far above, occasionally swooping low with head angling back and forth as though it, too, hunted.

It disappeared into the forest, then emerged to swoop so close that the bronze and gold among sable feathers was visible on outstretched wings. Rorke's men took new arrows from quivers and set them to their bows.

"No!" Vivian cried out. "Please, do not let them kill her." She tried to loosen his arm about her at the same time she struggled to push away.

"Please," she begged again, as several arrows were released. Her cries and efforts to free herself startled the warhorse, and it was all Rorke could do to keep both of them from being unseated.

"Cease at once!" Rorke snarled, jerking her against him. But she seemed not to hear.

"Please, you don't understand!" Frantically, Vivian tried to make him understand. "She is tame. Do not kill her!"

She had drawn the attention of his men, and, as they hesitated with drawn bows, she sent her thoughts and her fears skyward to the small falcon.

Fly far! There is danger. Do not come near!

But if the falcon sensed her thoughts, she gave no indication, for she swept lower still.

Tears streamed Vivian's cheeks, like cold rain in the bitter wind. With every power that she possessed, she tried desperately to make Rorke understand.

"Please, stop them!"

Rorke finally brought the stallion under control. Vivian leaned forward in the saddle. Her face was turned skyward, that compelling blue gaze fastened on the falcon, her cheeks wet with painful tears.

When he set out from William's encampment he had prepared himself for anything if he found her—anger, defiance, lies. But after everything she had been through and seen, he was not prepared for tears shed over a small peregrine.

Gavin de Marte looked at him questioningly.

Rorke had no explanation for her reaction to their hunting a small, insignificant falcon. But it had affected her deeply. How was it possible for someone who would face down the Norman army to be undone by the loss of a single falcon? The more he knew of her, the less he discovered he knew.

Other women had cried their tears for him—lovers and courtesans he left when he tired of the charms that masked their own ambitions for his wealth. But he found he could not bear her tears.

"Leave off and return to camp," he told Gavin. "There will be other days for hunting. This small falcon is not worth the loss of your arrows. You might well have need of them elsewhere."

Gavin nodded and called out to the others. Tarek al Sharif rode up to Rorke. "Where do you go?" he asked. "It is not wise to ride out alone."

Rorke shrugged dismissively. "William's guards are nearby, we will be safe enough. And I have my battle sword."

Still Tarek hesitated. "Those same guards allowed a simple Saxon maid to pass by."

"As did you," Rorke reminded him, with a faint, sardonic smile. "Our enemies will not be so bold as to strike this close to the main camp. Return to William's tent, my friend. I would rather have you there."

Tarek nodded reluctantly and turned his mare about to join Gavin and the others, who grumbled among themselves at the loss of the falcon.

She was taut as a bowstring, her body arched away from him,

tears staining her cheeks, her breathing rapid and faint. Slowly, he loosened his arms about her.

"Vivian . . ." He felt the emotion that quivered through her.

He was a warrior, well trained to the subtleties of challenge, battle, an enemy met and conquered. But none of his training prepared him for dealing with the subtleties of emotion. And yet, as instinctively as he knew when to draw his blade, he sensed her need to be comforted.

He touched her cheek, brushing back the flame colored hair. She turned at his touch. The look in her vivid blue eyes was shaded with those myriad emotions. He could not imagine that such a simple thing had undone her so.

"I give you the life of the falcon. None of my men shall harm her."

Her watery gaze met his. "Thank you, milord."

He grunted a response, " 'Tis a small thing."

"Not to me, for I value the falcon highly. She is a true friend."

"Then you are acquainted with this creature?"

She nodded. "Aye, she is trained to my hand."

"You brought her with you?" he asked with more than a little surprise, for he had seen no such creature on the journey from the abbey.

Vivian frowned as she shook her head. "She was hunting the morn Vachel and his men . . ." It was on the tip of her tongue to say the morning that Vachel and his men raided the abbey, but she thought better of it. For though there seemed to be no love lost between the two men, they were still both Norman and she was Saxon.

"The morning they came to the abbey," she said softly, unable to forget Vachel's brutality. "She must have followed from Amesbury."

Rorke looked at her speculatively. He had never seen her quite this way, vulnerable yet fierce over something she so obviously loved, and he felt an unexpected twinge of envy that the falcon was so loved.

"Call her down," he told her. "I would like very much to see this creature that has come so far to find you."

He offered her his heavy leather gauntlet.

"There is no need," she assured him. "She is very gentle."

Then spotting the falcon, she whistled the familiar three-note signal. The sleek bird's meandering glide immediately altered as she began a swift downward plunge.

At a height that barely skimmed the treetops of the nearby forest, she broke her descent with a graceful glide and several backward strokes of powerful majestic wings, slowing her descent.

Vivian held out her arm, but instead of settling there, the falcon skimmed past her toward Rorke. Experienced with falcons, he had watched the sleek huntress, and, as she refused one perch, he instinctively offered her another on his gauntlet-covered arm.

With a graceful billow of outspread wings she settled on his arm. Her touch was light, merely enough to balance and settle her wings. Remarkably, not a single talon pierced the leather.

"She has never done that before," Vivian remarked with surprise.

"My apologies. Perhaps she was distracted. But I see there was nothing to be concerned of, for she has a rare, gentle touch."

"Aquila is never distracted," she said, auburn brows drawing slightly together at the falcon's odd behavior. Until today, she had never taken another's hand.

The falcon was small and graceful, golden eyes studying them both thoroughly as she cocked her head first in one direction then the other. That lethal beak that so easily snapped the necks of prey was slightly open as she made soft whistling sounds.

"Aquila," Rorke repeated the bird's name. Her sleek head angled toward him. "You have named her for the constellation of stars near Lyra and Cygnus."

With some surprise, Vivian remarked, "You know of it?"

"Aye, but I would not have thought an abbey-raised girl would also know of it."

"Poladouras is a student of astrology. He taught me all of the constellations," Vivian explained in a quiet voice, so as not to frighten the falcon.

Unafraid of those lethal talons, she held her arm lengthwise along his, gently rubbing the falcon's belly. The sleek bird moved from one human perch to the other, her grasp gentle.

"Did he also teach you how to handle and gentle a falcon to your hand?" he asked, for she seemed to have a rare calming effect on the bird who turned her sleek head toward Vivian's voice.

"She taught *me*." Vivian smiled, as though at some jest at herself. "One learns quickly when dealing with a wild creature what to do and not to do, though in truth she has never harmed me."

Rorke watched, fascinated, as the falcon cocked her lovely head this way and that to catch the soft nuances of Vivian's words and realized that he, too, listened for the different shadings of her voice. Especially as now, when she seemed less wary and guarded, and a soft smile hinted at one corner of her mouth.

He discovered he longed to know all of that smile as he reached an ungloved hand and stroked the falcon's downy breast; it recalled the satin texture of Vivian's skin.

"Did you also teach her to trust the touch of a stranger?" he asked, watching for her reaction rather than watching the bird. A faint frown wrinkled her forehead, knitting slender auburn brows together.

"She has never taken a stranger's hand before today, nor tolerated another's touch."

"And what of her mistress?" he asked, reaching with that ungloved hand to stroke the back of a finger along the curve of her lower lip.

His voice had gone low in his throat, as though he sought to gentle her with both touch and words. Her startled gaze met his, her breath quivered out between softly parted lips. With his arm at her back, there was no retreat or escape.

She felt the rough scrape of that hard, callused hand, inexplicably gentle, as if she were the falcon that sat perched awaiting his touch and the sound of his voice.

Strange feelings, remembered vaguely from a summer day long ago, spiraled through her, from the pit of her stomach upward, and settled just under her breast, as if his arm still bound her, making it impossible to breathe.

How was it possible that such a hard, brutal hand could be so gentle?

Senses strained for some understanding, some essence about this man. But there was nothing, except the touch of his hand beckoning to her other senses—and wildly, improbably, without her inner sight to reveal him to her—she wondered at the taste of a man. Was it very much the same as the feel of him? The roughness disguising the tenderness beneath it.

He felt the tension that quivered through her. Her skin was incredibly warm to the touch in spite of the coldness of the day and her meager garments. The heat of innocent sensuality glistened at her parted lips.

A raw desire, naked and powerful, clenched inside him like a taut fist low at his belly. His sex strained against layers of leather chausses as he imagined her slender hand stroking him as she stroked the falcon.

Confused even frightened by what she should not—must not—feel, Vivian jerked away from him.

"You frighten the falcon, milord," she said softly, concentrating all her senses on the sleek bird.

"The bird, or the one who holds her?" he asked, his voice deeper still with the effort of drawing breath through clenched teeth. She looked at him then, eyes as brilliant as flame.

"You do not frighten me, milord."

He sensed that it was true. She had no fear that he would harm her. It was something else that she feared. He reined in the desire that burned through him like a white-hot flame.

"Tarek al Sharif is most confused about how you left the tent without anyone knowing of it." Rorke watched her carefully for her reaction, forcing himself under control.

"He is convinced that you have the powers of a Jehara and became like the falcon, and flew from the tent."

Her eyes widened slightly as she listened, but whether with surprise at the unusual thing he told her or some other reason he could not guess.

"What are these Jehara?"

"Creatures endowed with very special powers, including the power of healing."

She frowned and said dismissively, "Was no great feat, milord. I but waited until he had left the tent. Your guards were changed at the same time." She shrugged a slender shoulder. "In the confusion it was a simple matter to slip past them."

Rorke knew his men well, having trained them himself. It was not a simple matter, but he sensed that if he questioned her further, the answer would still be the same.

"Is the falcon a pet, then?" he asked, deciding for the time being to pursue the matter no further. He couldn't be certain, but he thought she seemed relieved that he did not ask of it again.

"Pets are tame creatures. She is my companion, but she is completely free. She is also my teacher. I have learned much from her. It might be more truthful to say that she owns me."

It was an odd comparison that he had never before considered. Such a thing as ownership suggested ties that bound as surely as a falcon's jesses.

"She is free, yet she wears leather thongs," he pointed out.

" 'Tis only to secure the bells so that I may know her from others. She is never bound. I could not bear to see her bound or imprisoned."

Her meaning was not lost on him. "You are as free as the falcon, Vivian. There are no jesses binding you."

Her eyes saddened. "The promise you made me forswear

binds me as surely as any lash. I cannot risk the lives of others and well you know it."

"It was a bargain well made, each receiving something in the making of it," he reminded her.

"A bargain suggests something freely exchanged," she retorted.

Rorke sought to assuage the anger that flashed in those brilliant blue eyes. He much preferred her gentleness and humor. And her cooperation. However reluctant, it better served his purposes. And he found he far preferred the healing balm of her gentle smile, rather than the fire of her anger. As if sensing their uneasy mood, the falcon flared her wings.

"I once had a teacher such as your falcon," he said with lowered voice so as not to excite her further.

"A hound pup brought back to my father's estate from the Pyrenees Mountains. It was a fierce-looking creature, all teeth, muscle, and legs. My father loathed the animal, but I gentled it."

He grew thoughtful, recalling the silver-blue-coated hound that was like a shadow to a lonely, young boy.

"What you said was true. I was more owned than owner. We hunted the hills together. He taught me much about myself." His voice had lost its edge and softened at the childhood memory.

"He was my only companion," he went on to explain as he carefully stroked Aquila's head, "other than my brother, whom I was allowed to visit only when my father was away." His voice changed, and it required no gift of inner sight to sense the pain that threaded the words.

"Was your brother also fond of the hound?"

He nodded, his gaze suddenly very far away, as if he saw beyond the encampment to another time and place, before all the death, before the battle, before the events that had transformed a boy into a cold, hardened warrior who refused to allow himself to feel anything at all, and vowed revenge against his own father. Before he discovered that he felt nothing at all except the need for that revenge.

"Aye, Philip was fond of the animal," he said with the beginning of a smile as he remembered. "I took the rangy beast to see him. That last time was a very good day, for our father was away."

"A good day because he was away?" she was confused. "I should like very much to be able to spend time with my father."

"I suppose that would be true if your father was kind of spirit. My father was not. He was a cold, forbidding man. I was ten and two at the time, my brother but six." His expression hardened.

"Our father returned unexpectedly and discovered the beast. As my punishment for disobeying him, he took the hound away from me."

"But surely he returned it to you afterward."

"Aye, he returned it." His voice had gone as wintry cold as the gray of his eyes, staring into that faraway memory as if he could see it all again.

"After he had it killed to teach me a lesson."

She was horrified at the thought. Her voice broke softly at the pain she knew he must have felt.

"What lesson could something as dreadful as that possibly teach a young boy?"

He looked at her then, and she shivered at the look in his eyes.

"It taught me to love nothing in this world, for it may be easily taken away. It is a lesson that I learned very well." His expression softened at her distress.

"But you need have no fear," he told her as he stroked Aquila's silken breast with a gentleness that belied the young boy's rage and pain that still burned in his heart.

"I have said you may keep the falcon. And once made, I never break a promise."

"Will you promise to let me leave once William has returned to good health?" she asked.

It was on his lips to do so, for in truth that had been his purpose in seeking the healer in the first place. But something stopped him, for in promising, he would be forced to let her go.

"Do not ask too much of me, Vivian," he replied, his voice suddenly gruff. "There is only so much I will grant you."

Eight

They returned to the Norman encampment in uneasy silence, Aquila perched on Rorke's arm.

Vivian wanted to hate Rorke FitzWarren for what he was and the dreadful destruction he had helped bring upon the Saxons and all of England. But for every reason she found to hate him, she discovered two why she could not.

His men had returned to camp ahead of them. As they rode in, she felt the stares of the other Norman soldiers, curiosity mixed with surprise. Tarek al Sharif was waiting outside Rorke FitzWarren's tent.

Vivian sensed Tarek's gaze. Her first thoughts were of William of Normandy, but her senses also told her that his condition was unchanged and that he slept peacefully from the healing draught she had given him.

"You have had word of some kind?" Rorke inquired of Tarek.

"A great number of Saxons have been seen by our soldiers," Tarek informed him. "No doubt survivors from the battle. They gather but a half day's ride from here and are heavily armed."

Rorke nodded grimly as he lowered Vivian from the saddle, then swung down beside her.

"Has Robert of Mortain been told of this?" he asked.

Tarek nodded. "He has ordered your men to make ready to ride immediately."

Uncertain whether she should remain, Vivian had turned to leave. Rorke stopped her with a hand closing around hers with gentle but firm restraint as he listened to Tarek's information.

"Order my battle armor," Rorke commanded. "Tell Mortain to be ready to ride in an hour's time."

Vivian felt frozen at the news, a new fear closing around her heart. More Saxons would die. She pulled away from Rorke's hand, unable to bear being near him.

"Vivian," he said, his voice as gentle as the restraint of his hand. He sensed her torment and saw it in the expression at her lovely face, her gaze fastened on the ground at his feet.

"I am sorry, Vivian."

She heard the apology in his voice, but there was no room for it in her heart.

"And yet, you will still order your men to go after them."

"Because I must," he said, his voice still gentle.

"Must what?" she asked, not understanding at all. "Kill more Saxons? Are not the ones you've already killed enough?"

She watched the color of his eyes go from soft gray to cool ice. "It is what I must do, because to wait for their attack here would be the worst foolishness. If they can be found before they are ready to strike, mayhap it will be possible to spare them."

She knew he would not be persuaded by anything she said, and even realized that what he said was true in the context of the battle that had already been fought and the lives already lost.

William the Conqueror had come to lay siege to Britain, not for one afternoon's sojourn onto a grassy field. Those Saxons and Normans alike who had already died were testament to that. Neither William, nor Rorke FitzWarren, who led his great army, would now yield or turn and run. Not until all England was theirs.

Her chin quivered with the enormity of the emotions she

fought to control. For reasons Rorke couldn't begin to understand, this one maid's valiant effort to keep from crying went
further toward undoing him than all the dead at Antioch or
Hastings.

"You may keep the falcon in my tent," he told her, trying to
find some means of assuaging her pain. "She will be safe there,
and my squire is adept at handling falcons. She will not want
in his care." She said nothing, her gaze still fastened at the
ground.

"Gavin will remain in my stead," he then told her. "If anything should happen—" It was then her gaze came up, watery
blue, filled with countless emotions, and fastened on his, causing him to wonder if the thought of his death distressed her.

"He will see to your protection and safety until William is
recovered." He added fervently, "I would trust him with my
own life."

"How long will you be gone?" Her voice was as watery as
that dark blue gaze that he had always thought so like a flame,
but now looked more like flame seen through a glass sheened
by rain. He cast an eye toward the sky.

"A half day's ride will find us at their encampment. If, pray,
we are successful in finding them before they attack, then mayhap we will be able to return by midday on the morrow."

His squire appeared, informing him that his battle armor was
in readiness. Rorke handed the falcon over to him with instructions to her care and feeding. Vivian bade the small peregrine
good-bye with soft words and a gentle touch.

With a look at Vivian, Rorke told his squire, "The falcon is
not to be bound."

The young man looked at him quizzically, then nodded and
strode toward the tent with Aquila perched lightly on his gloved
hand. As Rorke turned to follow, Vivian laid a hand on his
sleeve.

"I would ask a favor, milord."

He turned, those gray eyes contemplative. "I displease you
so, and you ask a favor?"

At the sudden change in his voice, Vivian looked up to find him actually smiling at her. The effect was intoxicating and at the same time unnerving. Rorke FitzWarren, stern of face with hard-set features was formidable, powerful, and dangerous. Rorke FitzWarren smiling, those hard features softened to mere masculine handsomeness with gray eyes looking at her with cool speculation, was far more dangerous.

"I would like to be allowed to return to the Saxon encampment to treat the injured. Their need is great and it seems that William would be more in need of healthy Saxons than more Saxon graves."

He contemplated both the request and the one who had made it, her uneasiness all too apparent and more than surprising for one who seemed to have no fear of Norman knights or Norman punishment. He smothered the smile, attempting a stern expression that he suspected fell somewhere in between. God help him, but he found her to be the most fascinating creature.

He was inclined to grant her request. However, she still had not explained to his satisfaction how she had escaped Tarek and his men. Yet, if he refused her, might not she be inclined to do just as she pleased in the first place.

"I will suggest a compromise," he told her, watching with delight the wary expression in eyes that were once more like blue flame.

"Our need is just as great." He went on to explain precisely what the acceptable compromise would be. "There are many injured Norman soldiers in the encampment," he began. When she would have objected—no doubt to inform him that she did not care if his men rotted where they lay—he held up a hand that he was not yet finished.

"If you will lend your capable skills in aid of injured Norman soldiers, then I will allow you to send medicines and curatives into the Saxon encampment with one of my men and instructions as to how they may be administered."

"But it is not that simple," she protested. "A mistake might easily be made."

"With your exemplary skills I am certain you will see that does not happen." When she would have protested further, he cut her off gently but firmly.

"It is the only compromise I will consider, Vivian. The choice is yours."

"Very well," she replied reluctantly. "I accept."

She watched an hour later as they rode from camp, and though she told herself she was glad to see them go, she couldn't help feeling a greater loss than their mere departure, as though something had been set in motion which she could not sense.

The day grew cold, the sun like a bright red-orange ball through the gray pallor of a wintry sky.

She went first to William's tent to check the poultice she had wrapped about his leg the night before. She drew up short, uneasiness slipping across her senses, at sight of his brother, the bishop, standing beside the cot. Then she saw Vachel, standing in the shadows behind him. Both men looked up at her and her uneasiness turned to fear. Why were they here when Rorke had given orders that they were not to be allowed in William's tent? Why had Rorke given those orders against William's brother?

The bishop had been less than pleased at finding her there the previous day, calling her healing ways blasphemous. Such uncompromising hostility was not unknown to her. Poladouras had lived with it for many years, ostracized by his fellow monks at nearby St. Anne's because of his study of sciences which were also considered to be *blasphemous*.

She wished Gavin had come with her, for she had no desire to be alone with the bishop and Vachel. She might even have turned back if not for a compelling sense that she must not— that something was very wrong here.

At a movement on the other side of the tent, she was relieved to see William's squire stirring a simmer pot at one of the braziers. The air inside the tent smelled faintly of lavender from the sleep tonic Vivian had instructed him to make the night before.

"I did not mean to disturb you, milord," she said uneasily, aware of the conflict of powerful emotions within the bishop.

He was dressed in finely made black velvet raiment, tunic, breeches, hose, and mantle. The simple luxurious fabric was enhanced by the winking of several jewels sewn on the fabric, and the prominent silver cross that hung from an elaborate silver chain about his neck.

The bishop was as tall as William, but not as stocky, and several years younger. His fair hair and features made him resemble one of the golden saints portrayed in the intricate stained glass window at St. Anne's Abbey. Unlike the saints' eyes, his were not celestial blue, but black as night.

Though his coloring was not the same as William's, the features were similar and there was no mistaking the common parentage. Both, she knew, had been sired by the old duke of Normandy, but of different mothers. Poladouras had told her the story when William first laid claim to the English throne.

William's mother was the old duke's mistress. His wife had borne him three sons, half brothers to William the Bastard. Yet the old duke favored his firstborn son and made William his heir over his legitimate sons, who were left either to seek their fortunes through knighthood or pledge themselves to the Church. It was said William had been generous with all three of his brothers, bestowing land and titles on them.

"Ah, the healer," the bishop murmured, in a careful voice. "You have not disturbed me. I but sought to assure myself that my brother truly lives."

She approached hesitantly. It might have been her imagination but the candles and oil lamps seemed to stop their quivering and glow more steadily as she drew nearer the cot.

"He lives," she assured him. "God willing, he will grow strong and recover."

"I assure you, mistress, God is very willing. But it is not lost on me that you have conjured a minor miracle in the matter of my brother's recovery. For it was known to all among his most trusted knights that he was near death." The ornate silver cross gleamed coldly at his chest against the black velvet of his tunic.

Conjured? She thought it an odd choice of words. She laid a hand on William's arm above the edge of the fur, uncertain why she felt the need to reassure herself that he but slept peacefully.

Through the simple contact, she felt the steady, slow beat of his heart. His thoughts were peaceful as well. Covertly she studied this bishop of God who also carried a sword. She thought it odd that a man sworn to peace and spiritual fulfillment felt no conflict in the taking of lives.

"You objected strongly to my skills yestereve," she commented, careful with her words. "Yet you sent Vachel to find the healer."

The bishop inclined his head and angled her a sideways glance, as though studying her.

"I am a man of devout faith," he explained. "Certainly you can understand, demoiselle"—he made a dismissive gesture with his hand as if it were a trivial matter now—"that I expected to find the healer brewing a curative for a poultice. Such methods as I witnessed are not usually considered acceptable by the Church."

Across the tent, William's squire finished his task and silently left the tent. Vachel followed like a silent, stalking shadow. And again Vivian experienced an uneasiness of some pervasive evil.

With new uneasiness, she asked, "Such methods, milord? What is your meaning?"

She sensed the need to carefully conceal all emotion and thought, though she could not have named the reason for such feelings. She sensed other things about the bishop as well. He was not a fool. Beneath the mask of saintly benevolence was a shrewd intelligence and an even shrewder ambition. He was not a man to be taken lightly.

He smiled then, and she wondered if this was the expression he used with the devoted at Sunday worship, for it was a cold expression, shaded with something very near cruelty.

"My concern," he explained with that careful expression, "was for my brother's well-being. Certainly you can understand that. It is second only to my devotion to God and the Church of Rome. William has many enemies. It is my duty to protect him against those enemies.

"For many years I have been the sword at his side, albeit I also wear the cross. I fight his mortal enemies with the one and his spiritual enemies with the other." He gave her a sharp look. "When I saw you standing there in that strange trance I could only assume that you meant him some harm."

Again it seemed that he was trying to attach some particular meaning to her healing ways, and she sensed that it might be dangerous.

"Aye," she agreed, choosing her words carefully, "the ritual is quite ancient, known for at least a thousand years."

There was no outward change of expression, only the subtle shift of light reflected back from those dark eyes that hinted his satisfaction, as if he'd caught her at something.

"I often find it comforting to pray," she went on to explain, pleased at the expression of surprise that now crossed his face. "I believe, milord, you are also familiar with the power of prayer. Surely you did not think your brother in danger because I prayed over him. I would have thought you, most especially, would understand the necessity of it."

That dark gaze hardened, and, for a moment, she glimpsed something frightening, a pervasive darkness so evil that no other emotion existed at all, and then it was gone.

"Ah yes, prayer." His voice was like silk. "Most assuredly it is a very powerful influence. However, I would not have thought it common to a healer."

"I was raised in an abbey, milord. My guardian since childhood is a most-learned monk of enormous faith."

His surprise was immediate. He smiled to cover it, that false smile she knew did not reach his heart but carefully concealed some other emotion.

"You have reminded me, demoiselle, of something that I have

experienced oft enough in the past but had forgotten in the midst of war. God works in mysterious ways and He often places such matters in man's skilled hands. Or in this particular instance, in a woman's skilled hands."

He was standing so close that had she closed her eyes she could have felt his presence. That awareness confused her and he caught her unprepared when he took her hand between both of his.

Then, amidst the muttering of the flames in the braziers and the sighing movement of the walls of the tent that shifted with every breath of wind, she heard the Voice—a softly whispered warning.

There is great danger . . . Though she listened for more, there was nothing. Only that brief, urgent awareness of warning.

"Your skills as a healer and your power of prayer are a gift for which I am deeply grateful," the bishop continued smoothly. "Am I forgiven for the circumstances of our first encounter?"

She tried to pull her hand from his but found she could not. "Forgiveness is God's gift to bestow," she said, frowning. "Mine is to heal."

At last he released her hand, turning his cold gaze on his brother as he lay sleeping. "He will recover from his wounds?"

"Aye, milord," she assured him, clasping her hands together to warm them as she felt a sudden chill. "In time, and with rest and care. The leg must be given a chance to heal properly."

"Most remarkable," he said, "when it was certain he would lose the leg, if not his life." He nodded farewell. "When he awakens, tell my brother that I shall visit again when he is awake and stronger." As he left the tent, she heard him greet Vachel, who had waited outside the tent. Their voices were carried away on the wind, making it impossible to know what passed between them.

The flames of the candles and the braziers smoldered low as he left the tent. Then they steadied and once more grew bright. Vivian shivered, as if some evil presence had left the tent with him.

When William's squire did not immediately return, she busied herself with preparing a stout curative broth for when William awakened. He had lain wasting for several days with fever, but it had lessened with the strong tea of white willow bark. If he was to recover, he must have nourishment.

She worked quietly, unaware that she hummed the ancient Celtic folksong to herself until William stirred at the pallet.

"Are you an angel then?" he murmured painfully in Norman French through dried and cracked lips.

"Or have I perhaps ventured in the other direction? Although you are far too lovely to be the devil unless he has taken on the guise of a woman."

"I am neither, milord," she answered tentatively in English as she slowly approached the cot.

His mind was surprisingly clear in spite of his exhaustion from fever and the wasting infection of his wounds.

"You are the Saxon healer," he said gruffly and with much effort, narrowed eyes studying her. "My squire spoke of you this morn, or perhaps during the night." His eyes closed as he gathered his strength. "I find I cannot remember."

"I am Vivian of Amesbury," she replied, laying her hand on his shoulder. The pain eased from deep lines at his face.

The dark amber eyes opened once more and slowly focused on her. "My squire also said that I owe my life to you."

She felt the life force strong and sure within him, along with a sense of his frustration at his infirmity.

"You owe your life to God." Then she smiled, for she did not find William of Normandy quite as fierce as she had been led to believe. Instead, he rather reminded her of Poladouras when he occasionally became ill—one of her most quarrelsome and uncooperative patients.

"You do, however, owe your leg to me."

His surprise was immediate. "You were not forced to remove it?"

"I thought you would be better served if the leg was saved."

To reassure him, she lifted the edge of the fur blanket, to

reveal the proof of her claim. His relief was a visible thing as his head fell back to the pallet. After a moment he turned toward the bubbling sound that came from the brazier.

"What is that vile-smelling brew?" he demanded.

She sensed his next thoughts as easily as if he had spoken them aloud as he glared at the simmer pot as though its contents had come alive and grown teeth. She smiled faintly. It seemed Normans and Saxons were alike when it came to curative potions.

"It is not poison," she assured him, "although some have said it tastes far more vile than death. Such is often the way with the most effective curatives," she assured him, as she slipped her arm beneath his head and spooned two mouthfuls into his mouth. "And I would not destroy some of my finest handiwork. Had I intended that, it would have been much easier done while you were delirious with fever."

He shuddered as the medicine went down, taking a deep breath to recover. "Yet you are Saxon and no doubt consider me the cause of some grief to you. It would not be untoward for you to hold deep grievance against me."

"Aye, I do," she admitted without hesitation, then added, "but equal blame must lie with Harold, I think. For he lost his army, many innocent Saxon lives, and his throne."

Thinking of the visions she had seen of the coming conflict, she added sadly, "It could not have been otherwise." She poured a cup of lavender tea.

"Drink this, milord. It will banish the taste of the other."

When he lay once more back upon the pallet, he implored her, "Sit a while, demoiselle, for I grow weary from so much sleep." His breathing remained even and no more pain filled his face. He regarded her with calm strategy, as though studying an upcoming battle.

"You see things far differently than most Saxons," he commented. "Others would not be so kind or generous of thought."

"It is neither kind nor generous, milord," she told him with a blunt honesty. "I but see the truth of things that others are not willing to see."

He smiled weakly and nodded, thinking of other things. " 'Tis said you worked a miracle in saving my life. Is there truth in that?"

"I leave the matter of miracles to Poladouras, the monk at Amesbury abbey."

"Does this monk have a particular skill in such matters?"

"He does," she said, brightening with thoughts of the jovial monk whom she loved like a father.

"He is honest, humble, and a shrewd bargain maker. He would have made a good merchant if he had not been determined to be a monk."

"Ah, a merchant of miracles. And does God barter? I have been told that He makes bargains with no one."

"It is not necessary that he bargain with God, for they fight the same cause."

"Ah, yes"—William sighed—"the forces of darkness. You say he is a shrewd merchant?"

"Oh, aye," Vivian assured him. "He is rich in saved souls."

"I should like to meet such a man," he said with what she sensed to be sincerity. "I will have great need of all the shrewd bargain makers I can find."

"Your men had him beaten nearly to death," she said evenly. "He would have paid with his life had he refused to hand over what they demanded."

Heavy lines formed once more at his face. "What did they demand that the monk was reluctant to surrender? Most are not men of property."

"He would not surrender me to them."

"Ah, then he bargained with them, for you are here now."

"He did not," she assured him. "I handed myself over to your men."

His gaze narrowed. "And the bargain you made, demoiselle?"

"I bargained for the lives of the villagers of Amesbury."

"I thank you for the bargain made, demoiselle. I owe my life to that bargain. And the monk?"

"I pray he has recovered, but I cannot know, for I was taken from Amesbury immediately thereafter and not allowed to tend him."

He nodded. "I shall inquire about him for you. I will not have my men abusing monks." His eyes closed then, and she thought surely he dozed once more, but he only rested with eyes closed.

"If it was no miracle that saved my life, that but leaves magic. Are you witch or sorceress, Vivian of Amesbury?"

She was stunned and grateful that his eyes were closed. With much surprise, she said, "I would not think that William of Normandy would give credence to such things."

And added to reassure him, "I am not a witch. I am a healer."

"And I suppose you will demand payment in exchange for your skills? What is your price, save that of your freedom, which I cannot grant to you as I most obviously have further need of your skills."

Again he surprised her. By his own word, she was prisoner in his camp and yet he spoke of a boon he would grant.

She wisely said, "We will speak of it later, milord. I must give the matter much thought so that I take full advantage of your generosity."

He laughed at that, a faint chuckling sound that brought on a spasm of pain. "If not a witch, are you then a sorceress?" he asked. "As king of England I would have a sorceress by my side . . . like Arthur and the fabled Merlin." His head turned at the pallet, those amber eyes gazing at her thoughtfully.

"Do you believe in the legend, Vivian of Amesbury?"

"Many believe 'tis true," she conceded, drawing the thick furs about him once more. His eyes closed as though thoughtfully considering her answer.

"But after all," she said softly, "Merlin was a Saxon."

He did not stir at her answer and she realized that he slept deeply. She checked the bandages on his wounds. Satisfied then that he would probably sleep through the rest of the afternoon and evening, she sought out Gavin to assist her in organizing the medicines she wanted sent into the Saxon encampment.

She found chests of curatives, vials of medicines, and packets

of crushed condiments that had belonged to William's personal
healer. The man had perished during the channel crossing Tarek
had told her—his death had set off the Norman's hunt for the
fabled healer of Amesbury.

Most she was able to identify and added to her own precious
hoard of medicines. Those she could not were destroyed, for his
journals were poorly kept and gave no indication as to the various curative remedies.

William's squire agreed to take the medicines into the Saxon
encampment accompanied by one of Gavin's men. Midaf-
ternoon they set off in a cart filled with herbal curatives and
powdered medicine with specific instructions for the most common wounds.

Also included were scrounged blankets. She assured Gavin
that Rorke had approved she send them along with skins of water,
various pilfered cups and simmer pots, and loaves of bread.

As she watched the cart rumbling down the crude road that
had been formed by the trampling of hundreds of Norman
warhorses, she prayed lives might be saved by her meager efforts.

Then she turned her attention to the injured among Rorke's
men, going from campfire to campfire, tent to tent, with Gavin
ever present at her side.

She dispensed extract of shepherd's purse to stop bleeding,
tea made from star thistle to ease fevers, crushed horsetail to
make countless poultices, and crushed comfrey to aid the healing
of assorted surface wounds, blisters, and minor broken bones.

She worked until the afternoon set with a bitter chill and mist
lay just beyond the perimeter of campfires. She ached all over
from bending long hours over campfires and mixing medicines,
preparing bandages and poultices. There were so many injuries
that Gavin had enlisted the aid of his own squire and two other
men to care for the most common ailments.

"It is late, mistress, and the light fades," Gavin said with
unexpected concern. "It would do William no good if you were
to become ill with fatigue. There is the morrow."

"Aye," she agreed, but insisted, "just this last tent."

She recognized some of the men gathered before the tent as Vachel's men from that day at Amesbury.

When she had bandaged the last one she stood to leave, then paused, sensing a presence inside the tent. Thinking that there might be an injured man inside the tent too weak to move, she made to enter. One of the other men seized her arm to stop her.

"There's no need," he told her gruffly.

Vivian felt a sudden surge of anger. "I will determine if there is a need," she replied and started to push past him. When he stepped to block her, Gavin grabbed him roughly by the tunic.

"Do not interfere, Soren." The challenge quickly ended as the one called Soren reluctantly retreated. As soon as she stepped into the tent, Vivian knew what it was that she had sensed.

"Mally!" She rushed to the girl's side.

"Mistress Vivian?" the girl whimpered weakly.

"Aye, I'm here. Oh, Mally. What has happened?" But even as she asked it, she knew the answer. Against Rorke FitzWarren's orders, Mally had been abducted by Vachel's men and hidden for their own pleasures once they returned to camp.

Vivian's heart ached for she sensed that the girl had suffered far more than the bruises she'd received at Amesbury. She'd been used repeatedly and no doubt by more than one man. The stains of it covered her torn clothes. And along with heartache Vivian felt rage.

"You're coming with me," she told Mally.

"No! You mustn't. It isn't safe for you. They'll hurt you, mistress."

"It's perfectly safe!" she assured the girl, thinking of the boon William had promised. Surely the gift of a Saxon girl would not trouble him.

"Come along," she gently urged the girl.

"Where are you taking me?" Mally asked, trembling.

"A place where you'll be safe." Vivian helped the girl to stand, taking most of her weight as they walked together from the tent. Soren immediately leapt to his feet.

"You can't take the girl!" he protested. "Vachel's orders." Gavin's sword met his next protest.

"We're taking her," he said harshly. "Should Vachel care to protest the matter he may take it up with me, or with milord FitzWarren."

Soren immediately fell silent. They all knew the repercussions that were likely once Rorke learned they had deliberately disobeyed his orders.

Gavin's squire came forward to help Vivian. He was an older man who had been injured young and could not hope to attain his own knighthood, but with a deep loyalty to Gavin's family. He slipped an arm gently about Mally's waist and lifted her.

"Milord?" he asked of Gavin.

"Take her to my tent and notify my men that she is to have my protection."

Inside Gavin's tent, Vivian gently cradled Mally's head in the curve of her arm and spooned sweet lavender tisane between the girl's swollen and bruised lips. Mally moaned a protest and tried to turn away as the warm liquid stung slightly.

"You must drink it all," Vivian coaxed her. "Then you will sleep for a very long time. When you awaken the pain will be gone." The girl nodded bravely, taking the last of the tisane with a shuddering breath.

"I wish to die," she cried softly. "Why did they not kill me and be done with it?"

"It was not their intent." Vivian acknowledged the harsh reality of what had been the girl's intended fate, that of camp whore.

"You should have left me," the girl wailed. "What good am I now? I can never return to my family."

"The good of it," Vivian told her firmly as she eased her back down onto the thick pallet Gavin's squire had provided, "is that you are alive. That is important above all else."

"But look at me, mistress. I am ruined." Mally wept. "I am not fit for any man now. What is my life to be?"

"I am looking at you and I see bruises and wounds that will heal. In time your heart will also heal."

"But it will only happen again. Vachel's men will come for me." She trembled violently in fear.

"It will never happen again," Vivian said with a fierceness that brought a look of stunned surprise to the girl's eyes. She gentled her voice as she promised, "I will see to it."

"With a spell?" Mally asked, her eyes filled with fervent hope. "You could turn them all into mice or toads."

Vivian smiled that the girl really believed in such things.

"I do not think a toad is a vile enough punishment," she said, as she stroked the girl's cheek. "You must sleep now, Mally. I promise you are safe."

Mally curled onto her side, burrowing deep into the warm furs like a child seeking comfort, reminding Vivian of how very young she was. But no longer innocent.

"Will she be all right, mistress?" Gavin's squire asked. His name was Justin and he had hovered near since they brought Mally to the tent, providing bowlfuls of warm water, discreetly looking away as Vivian bathed her, then providing one of his own tunics, large enough for a gown, that she might wear.

"The bruises will heal," Vivian said, adding with a deep frown, "There are other wounds that will take longer to heal. But in time, they too will be gone," she vowed, lightly stroking her fingers across the sleeping girl's forehead.

Except for one, for with her gift of inner sight, Vivian already sensed the greater damage that had been done that Mally could not know of. A child, conceived from one of the joinings that had been forced upon her in the days since they'd left Amesbury. And she felt sick at heart, knowing the difficult times that lay ahead for the girl.

The wind had come up, billowing the sides of the tent, and Vivian shivered. She took her pouch of herbal medicines with her, for she must check again on William of Normandy. But she hesitated, reluctant to leave the girl.

"She will be safe," Justin assured her, his hand resting on the blade at his belt. "I'll look after her, mistress. No harm will come to her while she is in my care."

She sensed the older man's gentleness of spirit and genuine compassion for Mally.

"Aye, Justin. Thank you."

Outside and gathered about a roaring fire, Gavin and his brother had been joined by several of their men for the evening meal. The weapons close by their sides belied their casual conversation. No one would be allowed to enter Gavin's tent without first passing through that armed guard.

William had not roused since the last time she saw him and she found no reason to wake him when he slept soundly. She'd given him enough of the healing tisane to carry him through the night, and so to let him rest. She was a firm believer that rest had an amazing curative ability. For while one slept, the body healed itself.

Guards lined the outside of the tent and William's squire had already made his bed beside his master's cot.

She made her own pallet of the furs where she had slept the night before, but sleep was not soon in coming. She was troubled by thoughts of Mally and her own encounter with the bishop.

She could do nothing more about Mally tonight, but when William awakened she intended to ask his protection for the girl. As for the bishop, she had no answers for the uneasiness she sensed—an uneasiness that followed her into troubled dreams.

The tent was dark when she awakened, an urgency of warning moving across her skin like a cold hand. At first she thought all the braziers had smoldered out, but then she saw that several burned brightly. It was only here, immediately about her, that the light did not reach.

Darkness surrounded her and she sensed a vile, evil threat exactly like the danger she had first glimpsed in her vision within the blue crystal. Something was wrong. There was great danger!

Rising quickly from her pallet, Vivian went to the brazier. The flames burned brightly once more with a welcoming warmth, but still the danger was there. She could feel it, hovering just beyond the light. Slowly, she extended her hand toward the flame.

Its warmth reached out, banishing the cold, radiating toward her. Then, as she slowly extended her hand into the flame, it surrounded her as she whispered the ancient words.

"Fire of the soul, flame of life, as light reveals truth, burn golden bright."

The flame built higher and higher, gold threads blending with bright orange and deep crimson.

She was not burned. There was no pain at all. Only the light of the flame reaching inside to the light within, illuminating with its brilliance.

At first she saw only a void. Then as that day at Amesbury just before Norman soldiers appeared, she saw it clearly—the flame in the world of darkness. Like a fiery flower that slowly opened and revealed a creature at the heart of the flame. The creature raised its fierce head—a magnificent bird bathed in shades of fiery orange, yellow, and red. *A creature born in fire and blood.*

As in her first vision, the creature spread its magnificent, powerful wings. Unlike her first vision, it did not rise from the heart of the flame.

The colors of the vision shifted and changed. Brilliant yellow-and-orange flame was bathed in crimson that spread, drowning the other colors until everything was washed in blood. She saw the portent of death—Rorke FitzWarren's death.

Nine

As Vivian pulled her hand from the flames, she cried out, as though she had experienced that death herself.

Rushing from William's tent, she was stopped by one of Rorke's guards.

"You must take me to milord FitzWarren's tent," she demanded and saw the alarm that leapt into his face.

"The falcon is there. I must see to her." He finally nodded and turned to hurry beside her to Rorke's tent.

Before they reached it, Vivian heard the falcon's wild, frenzied calls. As she entered the tent, the falcon's sleek head angled toward her, with eyes that were brilliant golden pools of light.

"She has been like this for some time," Rorke's squire told her, obviously upset.

"Aye," Vivian said, approaching the perch with no fear of those powerful wings and deadly talons. She crooned softly to the falcon.

"You sense it too, my sweet," she murmured, stroking the falcon's glossy chest as it calmed. "Aye, it is there. I feel it though I cannot see it." Then taking the falcon onto her arm, she stepped outside.

The first light of dawn streaked the sky with fingers of gold. Rorke's squire and his guard watched, perplexed, as she continued speaking softly.

"Stretch your wings, *mo chroi,*" she whispered, letting her thoughts join with the falcon's. "See what I cannot see, be where I cannot be." She spoke in the ancient Celtic language. Then, extending her arm high, she sent the falcon aloft. When Rorke's guard would have stopped her it was too late, the falcon was already seeking the dawn-lit sky.

"Now, you must take me to Sir Gavin," she commanded. The guard hesitated. "Take me to him, you fool," she snapped. "Or Lord FitzWarren's blood will be on your hands."

Gavin immediately roused from his pallet, his brother Guy stepping to the entrance of the tent with him. Both carried battle swords.

"What is it?" he asked, frowning. "What has happened?"

"There is great danger," Vivian hurriedly explained, fear tight around her heart. "You must take your men and ride after him."

"What foolishness is this?" he asked.

"Or a trick, perhaps?" Sir Guy suggested.

Desperate now, Vivian knew there was no time to waste on lengthy explanations.

"It is no trick. What would be the purpose? My escape?" she asked him, demanding that he think logically. "Think!" she implored. "I am surrounded by the entire Norman army. How could I possibly escape?"

And yet she knew he recalled the day before, when she had easily left William's tent with Rorke's men guarding it.

"You must go now!" she demanded. "You may well save milord FitzWarren's life!"

She knew that he was unconvinced. There was only one other means by which she might persuade him.

"Please, Gavin," she begged. Calling on her power, she reached out to lay a hand at his arm, her fingers gently closing over the hard muscles beneath, even as she felt the darkness grow ever more dangerous.

"You must not fail him," she implored, giving him her thoughts now, conveying to him through the physical connection of her hand at his arm the same images she had so clearly seen in the flames. Her growing sense of danger told her she must bend his will to her own.

Gavin's expression was at first bewildered. Then, gradually, she sensed his acceptance as the sense of danger became his own.

"Aye," he finally said, an urgency in his voice. "I will go."

"The falcon will guide you," Vivian said with a rush of relief so intense that it was almost painful.

Dawn was full upon them by the time they were ready to leave the encampment. Vivian stood at the opening of William's tent, the darkness invading her thoughts, filling her soul with a cold ache and the certainty that the entire future lay in the balance.

Hurry! she sent her urgent thoughts with Gavin. Do not delay. And then her thoughts lifted, climbing the skies on outstretched wings as she prayed they were not too late.

At midday Rorke and his men stopped at the edge of a stream to water the horses. The respite was brief, his men taking their

own food and drink quickly as they continued their search for
Saxon rebels who still filled the forest.

The twoscore of handpicked men rode in groups of four,
fanning out from each other in the shape of an arrow tip piercing
the dense forest. One was always within sight of the next group
lest they come upon a group of Saxons who'd fled the carnage
at Hastings and then regrouped to take up the fight in smaller
roving bands.

The Saxon King Harold's army might be broken, but it was
not yet defeated. It was a lesson Rorke had learned well at a very
young age on his first battlefield. An army that defended its
homeland was like the mythical creature Medusa. You might
sever one serpent's head, but there were a dozen others still capable of striking with deadly poison. And with William gravely
injured, there was always the chance of another strike. It could
come in any one of a dozen different places and times. It was a
tactic that had ultimately defeated more than one invading army.

It was for that reason that he had taken unofficial command,
sending soldiers far afield to track down Saxon leaders who
might each have it within himself to band another small army
together to spring a surprise rebellion. The Saxon dukes and
earls must also be dealt with, but that was for William to determine when he was stronger.

They had eaten cheese and bread for the midday meal, part
of the stores William had ordered brought across the sea. A
prolonged occupation would quickly deplete those stores, creating a new concern—the feeding of a massive invasion army.
Rorke glanced over at Tarek as they angled through the forest,
following the directions of the mapmaker William had brought
from Normandy.

A learned young man who had traveled extensively with his
Saxon merchant grandfather about the whole of Britain, he had
acquired invaluable knowledge. It was young Merrick's map
they followed.

Rorke glanced across at Tarek, whose scowl had been a per-
manent fixture since leaving the Norman encampment. Sky blue

eyes constantly scanned every stand of trees, thickets, and out-croppings of moss-covered rocks. He caught a lethal glare from the friend who had made it his mission in life to defend his as repayment for a debt of honor.

He had specifically given Tarek orders to lead one of the other groups, as he had Stephen of Valois. He trusted the skills and prowess of both men completely. Stephen had taken command of the guard to his right, Tarek had politely refused.

"I fight by your side," he said simply, which was exactly what he always said whenever the matter arose even though Rorke was in command. He was again reminded that only Tarek al Sharif made decisions or gave orders to Tarek al Sharif.

"You do not like the forest," Rorke commented as their horses picked their way through the tree and brush cover. "You much prefer to be out in the open."

"This cursed forest hides a thousand enemies," Tarek spat out irritably. "I can feel their eyes watching." And to make certain there was no doubt how he felt, "It is dangerous! Unwise! We should leave this place."

"And leave our quarry to hide out, group together, and possibly become a strong force to be dealt with later?" Rorke offered logically in what was a frequent argument. "I would much rather fight one wolf than a pack of wolves."

"There are other ways to fight," Tarek commented, and at Rorke's look, said, "Burn the forest, and all within will perish."

"Including the forest itself and all the wildlife within," Rorke pointed out. "What will the people use for fuel at their fires in the winter? What will they eat? No, my friend. That is not William's purpose." He found himself repeating what Vivian had argued very recently.

"William is not interested in ruling over a land of graves and funeral pyres. There is no wealth in graves." His comment was greeted with a snort of disdain.

"More than one lion has been felled by a pack of wolves," Tarek pointed out.

"That is why the lion must seek out the wolves before they attack," Rorke replied reasonably.

The mist had burned off over the tops of the trees, exposing a brilliant blue sky that appeared in patches amid burnished gold and evergreen foliage. Beyond the sounds of their own presence were the sounds of the forest. The chittering of birds gathering seed from the forest floor in places where snow had melted. The scolding of a squirrel, the curious stare of a muskrat at the opening of its burrow as they rode past.

The trees thinned and opened onto a clearing where late afternoon sun warmed through cold armor. Two more groups, the phalanx of the arrow's tip, emerged a short distance away flanking both sides. A sleek, graceful shadow swept across the sunlit clearing, drawing Rorke's gaze skyward. He immediately recognized the falcon for the trailing leather jesses woven through with a blue ribbon.

"Aquila!" he said in surprise.

Tarek's gaze followed his, a deep frown, etching his features. "How is it the falcon has followed us? I thought you left her with the maid for safekeeping."

"She would not follow us of her own accord," Rorke answered with grave certainty. His gray gaze was fixed on the sleek bird as she swooped low along the rim of the clearing, plunged into the forest as if suddenly spotting prey, and then immediately reappeared her talons empty.

She swept toward Rorke, veering so close that his warhorse snorted nervously, so close that Rorke saw the glossy gold and sable feathers of her wings, and so close that he could have sworn her brilliant yellow eyes glowed deep, fiery blue. She did not seek the perch of his arm as he offered it, but angled past toward the trees. He stared after her, trying to discern the falcon's odd manner.

"She was sent to find us," he said of a certainty.

As he spoke dozens of birds suddenly plunged skyward, startled from their perches in the surrounding trees by some unseen creature. Or creatures.

"Battle swords!" He shouted the alarm to his men, his war cry shattering the peace of the forest.

Steel sang as it was drawn from sheath and scabbard, gleaming deadly in the bright afternoon sun from a dozen locations about the clearing. No sooner were they drawn than the attack was upon them.

Saxon rebels came from the trees and the cover of rocks, swarming into the clearing, a full score outnumbering the Norman knights. At Rorke's signal, they formed a defensive circle at the heart of the clearing, turned their warhorses into the onslaught, and prepared to meet the attack head-on.

There was no time for more. As it was, the precious few seconds' warning they had been given by the startled birds meant the critical difference between immediate slaughter and a fighting chance to defend themselves.

The attack had been well calculated and the Saxons were well armed, many carrying Norman battle-axes, mace, and swords no doubt stripped from the dead at Hastings. They outnumbered Rorke and his men three to one and were not encumbered by heavy mail armor or the unwieldy horses forced into close proximity with one another.

The Saxons fought like seasoned warriors, surprising Rorke with their prowess and cunning. If Harold had possessed a full army of such men, he might easily have won the day at Hastings and the outcome would have been far different. One of Rorke's men was struck a fierce blow from a battle-ax, sagged, and fell from his mount. Beside him, Stephen of Valois' vulnerable right side was exposed to attack.

"Protect him!" Rorke shouted at Tarek as he wheeled his warhorse about to block a blow with the hilt of his sword. He saw the moment's hesitation that crossed Tarek's fierce expression, then Tarek swung his own mare about to join Stephen.

All about them were the familiar and terrible sounds of a fiercely fought battle—the feral shouts of the Saxons who had already been defeated at Hastings and no doubt felt they had precious little more to lose; an agonized scream as a Saxon met death beneath the slashing hooves of a Norman warhorse; the painful cries of wounded men as they fell on both sides; the animal sound of a dying warhorse as it toppled to the ground, taking its rider with it.

Rorke met blow after blow with his sword, guiding the stallion about with the hard pressure of one knee and then the other, as if the animal were a weapon. Striking down one Saxon with his sword, another was staggered off-balance by the lunge of the horse's massive shoulder, long enough for Rorke to recover and thrust his sword deep into the attacker.

He felt sudden resistance as the tip of the sword met bone beneath the Saxon tunic, then the soft-as-butter yielding of muscle and sinew. The man cried in agony as he took the sword deep. Then he was forgotten and Rorke was swinging to meet the next blow.

His arm grew weary. He felt the stallion stagger and grow tired beneath him. Still the stallion responded gallantly, shifting and dodging at his command.

Within his field of vision he saw the falcon suddenly burst skyward, and then the sound of battle seemed to increase tenfold as mounted soldiers poured from the forest into the clearing. The Saxons found themselves trapped between Rorke's men in the middle of the clearing and Gavin's men, who surrounded them from every direction.

Heartened by the sight of their fellow soldiers and knights, Rorke's men rallied. The two lines of Norman soldiers converged, crushing the Saxon attackers between. The battle, which had seemed all but lost only moments before, was turned and brought to a quick, decisive conclusion.

"Hold your weapons!" Rorke shouted the command, echoed all along the Norman line until one by one his men ceased fighting. The Saxon dead littered the clearing. Few remained standing. Of those who did, most had been severely wounded. One man broke from the others and ran for the trees. Sir Galant quickly rode him down.

With a booted foot thrust into his back, the man stumbled

and fell to the ground. He rolled and quickly came to his feet a long-bladed Norman knife in his hand.

"Yield!" Sir Galant ordered him, sword drawn. "The day is lost. Drop the weapon and live." The Saxon glanced wildly back to the clearing, at his fellow Saxons fallen in the bloodstained clearing.

He nodded, and for a moment it seemed he would do as Galant ordered. Then, without warning, the Saxon turned the knife on himself and, with both hands, plunged it deep, taking his own life.

"You fool!" Sir Galant shouted, horrified by what the man had done, and at the same time powerless to stop it from atop his warhorse. He quickly dismounted and went to the fallen Saxon.

"I would have spared your life!" he told the dying man as he bent over him. "Why did you seek your own death?"

There was no answer, only the rattling sound of the breath that died in the man's lungs and the strange smile at his lips. Galant cursed the dead Saxon.

"There was naught you could have done," Rorke assured as he reined in the warhorse beside him.

"If he had not taken his own life, he would have taken yours. And without the remorse you have shown at his death. I consider this the better bargain, for you, my friend, are alive."

"But why?" Galant demanded. "Why would he chose death?"

Rorke said with sudden, dragging weariness. "I have seen it on the battlefield before. Those for whom defeat is so repugnant that they would rather forfeit their lives than be part of an uncertain future."

"But that was in the Byzantine Empire," Guy argued. "These were Christian men. To take one's own life is a sin in God's eyes."

Rorke remembered the macabre sight of the enemy taking their own lives, impaling themselves on their blades rather than be taken prisoner by those they considered to be infidels. His brother Philip had died in just the same way and even now he could feel the cold knot of anguish that he could not reach him in time to save him. Even now, he rubbed his hand against his tunic as if though trying to wipe off Philip's blood.

"Whatever his reason," Rorke said, those old memories cling-ing to him like heavy chains, "he has taken it with him. Come, my friend, let us find your brother Gavin and thank him for his prompt arrival. Or we might well have been the ones lying on this bloodied field."

"You've bloodied your tunic," Tarek commented as Rorke and Galant returned. "Some Saxon got too close and now regrets it."

Rorke brushed a gloved hand across it with a grumbled com-ment. He listened thoughtfully as two men were reported dead. Several others had been wounded, but would survive. Three horses were lost. His scowl deepened at hearing that a full score Saxon had died. Others at the perimeter of the fighting had fled.

"Stephen!" he called out among his men, not having seen the young man after the battle.

"The young pup is here," Tarek grinned. "He fought well. He would make a father proud."

"Are you unharmed?" Rorke demanded of the young knight. Stephen grinned as he swept back his mail coif, revealing a Saxon blade had struck frighteningly close, laying open a slender ribbon of flesh above his left eye.

Angrily, he asked, "Where is your helm?"

"He removed it because he could not see?" Tarek explained with tongue in cheek.

"And almost lost your eye in the bargain!" Rorke growled.

"It was cumbersome," Stephen defended. "I would rather have the ability to see my foe than find him at my back." His grin deepened. "A scar or two, a little blood impresses the maids." He gestured to Rorke's hauberk.

"Perhaps you will have a certain Norman lady begging at your feet with admiration for the bloody banner you now wear. There is nothing like a *grave* wound to ease a woman's heart or the entrance to her charms."

A round of good-humored laughter met his ribald comment, a healthy release for pent-up tension and fear after the battle well fought.

Rorke wiped again at the blood that seeped down the hauberk

"It seems this banner is flowing," he commented, as pain began to burn through the fatigue and settle at a familiar place low at his side where the hauberk had been hacked through in the battle days earlier.

"You are injured!" Tarek frowned at the blood.

"It seems that I might be," Rorke responded with a grave smile. "This brute of a stallion was a bit slow on one turn." His friend was immediately beside him, gently probing between broken links of chain mail.

"The brute you curse most probably saved your life," Tarek informed him. "The blow was struck from behind. Had it struck true, half of you would be astride the brute and the other half lying in this clearing."

Rorke winced and cut him a threatening look for his painful inspection. "It was the falcon's warning no doubt saved all of our lives."

"Bring the healer!" the cry went out as Rorke and his men returned to the Norman encampment just before sundown.

Vivian had been restlessly pacing William's tent. As the first call that riders had been seen went out across the encampment, she rushed to the opening of the tent. Her heart felt frozen as her fingers clasped about the blue crystal, for she had seen nothing of Rorke's fate when she tried to call a vision from it. Even now, she could not sense the seriousness of his injury, and relied on the fact that they summoned her that he still lived.

Unbidden, a prayer sprang to her lips that he was not dead.

Gavin's brother, Sir Galant, hurried her to Rorke's tent. Sir Gavin and Tarek al Sharif were there, along with Stephen of Valois. Torches blazed outside the tent. Rorke's men were gathered there, weary, battered, and bruised, reluctant to seek out their own tents until they knew Rorke's condition. The tent flap was pulled back and Vivian stepped inside.

It was warm, for Rorke's squire had kept the braziers lit in anticipation of his master's return. There were no shadows of darkness here. Large candles set into iron bowls blazed brightly, flooding every corner of the pavilion nearly as large as Duke William's.

"You have brought your healing potions?" Tarek asked, his darkly handsome features lined with worry and fatigue. Vivian nodded, her gaze seeking out Rorke even as she dreaded what she might find. Tarek's hand closed about her arm, guiding her through the men who stood clustered at the far side of the tent.

They made way as she drew near, the leather roll of her precious hoarded herbs and powders clutched under her arm. She halted mid-stride, momentarily taken aback. Rorke FitzWarren sat on a bench among them and she saw for the first time what her vision had not revealed to her. He was alive! She almost cried out her relief.

He had removed his steel helm, the mail coif pushed back to his shoulders much as that day she had first seen him, reminding her all over again of the raw power of his presence that moved through her in strange and unexpected ways. Leather gauntlets had been thrown down onto the table beside the bench. His right hand was wrapped around a goblet of wine. His squire hastened to refill the goblet as it was quickly emptied.

Rorke's face was drawn, features haggard. His usually healthy color had gone to shades of gray beneath the shadow of dark beard. There was a small cut above his right brow, most likely made from the steel helm rather than any blow. The blood had dried and crusted. He leaned against the table far more than mere fatigue warranted, supporting his weight with his right arm, the goblet in his left hand. His mouth was tightly set, eyes closed as he swallowed another ample draught of wine as he steeled himself against the pain of his wound.

The mail hauberk showed the evidence of a fierce battle, iron links were bent from blows. There was a crease in the mail armor low at his left side, the place where iron links had been cut through, revealing the protective leather tunic underneath also severed through, and the fresh blood that seeped through both.

"The armor will have to be removed," she said, almost fearfully, for she knew it would cause him more pain. His squire and Sir Gavin carefully removed the mail hauberk and coif. Rorke said nothing, but the way he held himself rigid as the weighty armor was hauled from his shoulders, she knew the pain must be intense.

Motioning for a candle to be brought closer, she knelt beside him. With a fresh linen his squire provided she stanched the flow of blood in order to determine the extent of his injury. With the light pressure of her touch, his eyes slowly opened. Cold as winter's morn, gray as a northern storm, those eyes were now bleak with pain.

" 'Tis hardly more than a scratch," he assured her with an effort.

" 'Tis a great deal more than just a scratch," she informed him shortly, and then bit at her lip. She should not care that this Norman knight was injured. She should rejoice in it. Why then did she feel like weeping?

His voice took on a steeliness that brooked no refusal. "There are others whose need is greater. I would have you see to them first. An army is of little use without its soldiers."

"Soldiers are of little use without someone to lead them," she pointed out. His eyes narrowed, mouth thinned in disapproval.

"I am not accustomed to having my orders disobeyed."

"I am not accustomed to having *my* orders disobeyed," she informed him, finding some solace in his anger, for if he could rouse enough strength to be angry with her, he might just live. She began giving orders like a field general for the items she would need to clean the wound.

"Two basins of hot water, one placed over a brazier to steam," she instructed Rorke's squire, and then set about issuing similar orders to Tarek and Stephen of Valois, as if they were there but to do her bidding. And as if they were there for just that purpose, they brought fresh linens, more candles, cleared the tent of everyone else, and secured the flap against cold drafts.

Moving the bowls of water closer, she cut away the thick woolen undershirting, much like the Saxons wore.

"It would seem there are some things Saxon that you approve of, milord," she commented as she wet a strip of linen in one of the bowls of warm water the squire had quickly provided.

She pressed it gently against the wound at his side where the wool had also been cut, the frayed edges sticking to the edges of the wound. Those bleak gray eyes glittered through narrowed slits. His voice had gone thick and low at his throat, with pain and some other emotion.

"I find there are many things Saxon that I approve of."

A shiver passed through her at the underlying meaning in his intense tone. Her fingers trembled at their task. She focused her attention and carefully soaked the frayed threads of the torn garment loose from the wound. When it was done, his squire removed the wool tunic. She knelt between his spread legs, encased in heavy leather breeches and boots.

The wound was worse than she had hoped. He had taken a glancing blow, evidenced by the indentation in the chain mail, the tip of a sword finding the vulnerable place where the links had given way from a previous blow, possibly in the battle of Hastings.

"It would have been far more serious had we not been warned beforehand. The falcon warned us of it in the wood."

She looked up, her gaze meeting his, a thousand questions weighting the air between them. The flames of a dozen candles placed nearby quivered as though stroked by some unseen whisper of wind. He waited for her explanation.

Vivian had known her decision to send the falcon would open a door that might never be closed again. What lay beyond that door, she could not be certain, for the vision in the crystal had not revealed the future, nor her part in it. The only thing she had been certain about was, even though Rorke FitzWarren was her enemy and had no doubt taken countless Saxon lives, she must not let him die. She bent to her task of cleaning the wound.

"Then you are most fortunate, milord."

His eyes held hers. "Aye, or perhaps it had nothing to do with good fortune at all." He stilled her hand with his larger one, her slender fingers trapped by those long, callused ones.

"We searched for the falcon afterward." There was a new hesitance in his voice that brought her head up. "But could not find her. I fear she might have become lost."

"There is nothing to fear. Aquila has an uncanny sense. She shall return."

He did not release her hand but held it captive in his. "It was surprising how she found us," he speculated, watching for her reaction.

"It is not so surprising, milord, when she already knows your hand."

Rorke wasn't fooled by her explanation. His features were predatory, watchful, as he studied her, as if he stalked a particular quarry. In a way, he did. He sought the truth of this beautiful, ethereal creature whom he had seen work true magic with her healing touch.

"I think not," he murmured. "I have seen her loyalty to you. She would not leave your side, unless commanded."

"There is always a first time. She has been restless, unsettled by these new surroundings. Perhaps she sought to hunt."

"Aye," he told her in significant tones, "she hunted, and hunted well." With a gesture at Tarek and Gavin, he dismissed the men. They were alone.

"We were outnumbered four to one," he explained, watching as she bent to concentrate on cleaning his wound. Ignoring the pain, his gaze fastened on the warm gleam of her hair, like fire spilling over her shoulder. When she refused to comment, he continued to describe the attack in detail.

"They were seasoned warriors. We would have been hard-pressed to defend ourselves had we not known of their presence before they were upon us." She said nothing but reached for a clean square of linen. He slipped his fingers beneath her chin, forcing her head up and her gaze to meet his once more.

"You knew we would be attacked. You sent the falcon to warn us and Gavin followed the falcon, although he could not explain the reason to me." He studied her through narrowed eyes.

"When I then asked him why he was convinced there was such great danger, he could not say."

With head bent, her expression concealed in shadows, Vivian felt an enormous relief. Gavin had not remembered their strange encounter when she had merged her thoughts with his and allowed him to see the vision of impending death. She shrugged a shoulder.

"Gavin is your friend and a stalwart warrior. No doubt, he sensed the danger as you would have, milord. Surely it was nothing more than a warrior's instinct of things."

He watched the way the firelight from the nearby brazier seemed to catch in her hair and then move with languid grace at the lift of her shoulder as if it truly was a flame.

"It is a much different thing. He could not have known precisely where and when the attack would come. You sent the falcon, you saved my life. Why would you do such a thing?"

"I . . ." She faltered under the demanding scrutiny of those gray eyes.

What could she possibly tell him?

That it was for the same reason she knew she must accompany him to the Norman encampment that day at Amesbury? That she had seen a powerful vision of a magnificent creature born in fire and blood—the very same creature that he carried upon his shield? And knew that her fate was inexplicably linked with his?

How could she possibly explain the gift she possessed to see deep inside others, to sense their emotions, their true hearts, their very thoughts? But that she could not sense those things about him?

And, finally, how could she possibly make this fierce warrior enemy understand the forces that even now gathered around them and forming the design of that unwoven tapestry of what had been, what was, and what was yet to be when she herself did not understand? Instead, she went back to the task of bandaging his wound.

At her movement, brilliant blue light glinted and winked behind the fiery veil of her hair. She was startled as he brushed back the silken fall, the glow from the brazier reflecting off the magnificent blue crystal that hung from her neck. Long fingers wrapped about the shimmering clear blue crystal as though he would seize it from her.

She held her breath, waiting for his cry of pain at touching the crystal. None had ever touched it without being burned. It was for that reason that she kept it hidden.

Only once had someone other than herself ever touched the crystal and not been horribly burned by it—old Meg, when she carried it on her pilgrim's journey, charged with the care of a small babe, the crystal wrapped in a chrysalis of spun silver.

Meg had woven a silver chain from the threads of the chrysalis and when Vivian was but two years old, had placed the chain with the blue crystal about her neck without a single mark upon the old woman's hand. Once it had been given to her, Meg refused to touch the crystal again.

"I must not," she had explained when Vivian asked her the reason. "Only once was it possible for me to touch the crystal, and that in the giving of it to you. If I were to touch it now, I would be horribly burned, as would anyone else who attempted to remove it. That is the protection of the crystal. Only she, to whom the crystal belongs, may touch it and remain unharmed."

But now there was another who had touched the crystal, and remained unscathed as he cradled the crystal in the palm of a scarred hand.

Rorke had seen such rare blue stones of a like quality when in Persia. But never of the size or unusual cut of this one. It was magnificent, a deep blue oval sapphire polished perfectly smooth on the outside, with the illusion that one could see through it.

But as he turned the sapphire it caught the light from the brazier as it had when hanging about her neck and he realized that it was not perfectly clear. There were myriad patterns in the heart of the crystal. The patterns were no haphazard formations of nature as the sapphire was formed, but spirals of precise design, as if some highly skilled craftsman had cut the stone.

"It is a fine rare crystal," he said, his voice low, as he speculated how a simple Saxon maid who wore a peasant's kirtle might come by such a gem. "And it is of the same blue as your eyes, and seems to hold the fire within, the way your eyes seem possessed of fire."

It took no gift of inner sight to know the question that turned in those cunning, quicksilver thoughts. She saw it in his eyes.

"It was a gift," she said hastily, her fingers closing over his in an effort to retrieve the crystal. But his fingers were not easily pried from about the gleaming blue orb.

"A fine gift of costly value. You must have held a special place in the heart of the one who gave it."

Knowing he would not be satisfied until he had an answer, she hastily explained, "It was a gift from my father. It was all that he could give me before . . ."

"Before . . . ?"

"Before he was forced to send me away. It is all that I have of him. It is called the Eye of the Dragon." Her fingers slipped between his, trying to loosen them. Instead, as their fingers entwined about the sapphire, she felt the sudden glow of warmth from the heart of the crystal. Not fiery hot to burn, but a languid heat that seemed to meld their hands together, a mesmerizing, sensual warmth as if it bound their hands together around the crystal.

Ten

Rorke reluctantly relinquished the crystal, and Vivian tucked it into the bodice of her kirtle.

"The Eye of the Dragon," Rorke mused. "Do you believe in dragons, Vivian?"

She shrugged her shoulders in a dismissive gesture as she bent to her task of bandaging the wound at his side.

"Some people believe in them. It is said that a dragon guards the Holy Grail in a deep cavern far to the north."

"Ah, legends," he commented dryly. As many countries as he'd traveled at William's side, there were a like number of legends about the cup of Christ. "No doubt, then, you also know the legend of Excalibur."

"The sword of King Arthur," she commented without looking up. "I know of it. According to legend it possessed extraordinary powers."

"Aye," he replied thoughtfully. "The Sorceror's sword set in stone and the only one capable of removing it was the boy king. 'Tis also said that the handle was set with a magnificent blue stone."

"Legends oft take on magical qualities in the telling," she commented.

He grunted a painful response as she pressed a cloth against the wound. She knew he still watched her; she could feel the scrutiny of those wintry gray eyes. From the corner of her eye she saw him reach once more for the goblet and raise it to his lips. "What do you believe?" she asked softly.

"I believe in what I can see and hold with my own hand. A warrior's sword is his own true strength, not some mythical sword sprouted from legend."

Still he watched her. Untying the leather bundle, she spread it upon the table and searched among the powders and herbs until she found the ones she wanted.

White willow leaves and shavings of bark were tossed into the second basin of steaming water to bathe the wound against infection, horsetail and ground yarrow for a poultice.

"No magical healer's touch to close the wound?" he asked, watching every move she made.

"It will heal well enough with sufficient care and proper healing powders, and there will be no fever. I have taken precautions against infection."

"I am indebted to your unique skills," he said, the words

fraught with myriad meaning. "You must explain it to me, for I have a curiosity of such things."

"White willow protects against festering," she explained while she worked. "Crushed horsetail will stop the bleeding."

He winced. "Hopefully you didn't pluck it from the tail of my warhorse. He might heartily object."

Her mouth quivered at the corners. She couldn't resist smiling, "Not your horse, milord. I took it from Vachel's."

Those cool gray eyes glinted with amusement, stunning her in the way it transformed his entire face as she applied a portion of the salve to the poultice, another portion directly onto the wound.

She applied the poultice, holding it in place with a length of linen that she wrapped about his waist.

His skin leapt at her touch. The muscles at his belly, above the leather breeches, flattened and went hard as stone with his sucked-in breath. As she bent to pass the linen from one hand to the other at his back, her hair brushed his shoulder and he ceased to breathe at all.

"Why did you send the falcon?" he asked, when he could reclaim his breath. Her hands went suddenly still at the task of tying off the bandage.

Fear—vicious weapon of the unknown—knifed through her. She had never felt it before. Before, all things were known to her. She saw them in her visions and dreams, sensed them with a single touch that stripped away all pretense and disguise, and exposed a person to her completely. But this man was unknown to her. She could sense nothing about his inner being.

She feared him—feared what she could not see, feared the other senses that she was forced to rely on—feared her own reaction to him.

She refused to look at him, even though the question demanded it. Instead, she hurriedly tied off the bandage so that she could be gone. But her fingers, skilled and certain, fumbled over themselves as if they mocked her.

The flaming cascade of her hair swept forward at her shoulder, but failed to completely conceal her features—that small, stubborn chin, the full curve of her mouth, the small indentation centered above the bow of her upper lip, the slender arch of her nose, the high angle of cheekbones lightly sprinkled with freckles invisible now in the shadow of her long hair, and those magnificent blue eyes that were like the heart of a flame.

His fingers flexed and then fisted with the desire to run his hands through that torrent of fiery hair. He wanted to see again the look of stunned surprise in those flame blue eyes as he had that morning on the heath when he found her among the Saxon dead, her expression wild, tumultuous, uncertain, rather than this carefully controlled coolness she cloaked herself in.

He longed to feel again the warm satin of her skin. Not with the touch of a healer but the touch of the woman that hid inside. And with a raw, rare hunger he ached to taste the fullness of her mouth.

She felt his warrior's hand in her hair and the gentle but insistent forcefulness that drew her head back and compelled her gaze to meet his.

His features were hard, forbidding, all the more so for the scar that etched his cheek from the corner of his eye to the angle of that bearded jaw, and by myriad other scars wrought by time in the lines at the corners of his mouth and between those dark drawn brows.

Then the taut lines eased about his mouth, the wintry coldness shifted in those gray eyes, and they took on a much darker shade of some new storm that gathered, stunning her with the transformation from cold and forbidding, to something she sensed was far more dangerous.

His scarred warrior's hand closed over the thickness of hair that hung loose at the nape of her neck. He twisted it into a silken rope, binding her to him.

"Jehara."

The ancient word was low and fierce in his throat. At the same time it whispered on the wind that sighed against the walls of the tent, and caressed the trembling flames at the candles with unseen hands. His mouth hovered close to hers. His breath, wild and sweet, bathed her.

"Sorceress, Tarek has called you."

Trapped between his legs, imprisoned by that strong hand in her hair and unable to escape, a fear greater than any she had ever known tore through Vivian. The inner sight that always guided her had now abandoned her, leaving her naked, exposed, completely vulnerable for the first time in her life.

"Touching you is like touching the sun."

Her skin trembled as his other hand came up to cup her face, callused fingers fanning across her cheek, lightly grazing her skin with a rough tenderness that made her long for more.

"The taste of you . . ." The tip of his tongue flicked at the curve of her lip, as light as the stroke of a butterfly wing.

". . . is like tasting fire." He groaned, and the words became a shuddered whisper as the fiery heat of his mouth took fierce possession of hers, stunning her.

Vivian was caught, trapped by the strength of that powerful hand clasped in her hair. There was no opportunity for escape, nor any hope of it. There was only the warrior strength of his kiss scattering the precious herbs from her stunned fingertips, as he scattered the thoughts from her head and then invaded her senses. Terrified, she tried to push him away.

He tasted of wind, steel, and sweat, overlaid with the dusky sweetness of warm wine laced with exotic spices hinted at in the contact of his lips, discovered in an explosion of intoxicating heat as his mouth opened to hers.

She tasted of wild heat, lost, ancient dreams, and an unexpected innocence that knifed through his baser desires to open a breach in the wall of ice around his heart.

He felt the heat of her hands at his bare shoulders, the insistent pressure as she attempted to end the kiss, the bite of her fingertips like the frantic grasp of a young falcon's talons uncertain whether to fly or hold on.

From beyond the tent he heard an insistent voice. Then the tent flap was suddenly thrown back.

"Forgive me, milord." His squire hastily mumbled an embarrassed apology. "I tried to stop her."

Abruptly the kiss ended and Vivian was scrambling frantically as a startled falcon to pull away. Rorke experienced an intense ache of loss equaled only by the cold fury of the words that immediately leapt to his tongue at the intrusion.

He snarled an oath. "I gave orders I was not to be disturbed!"

"I'd heard you'd returned, milord." Judith de Marque's silken voice permeated the tent as she stepped forcefully past his squire, then halted at the sight of the flame-haired girl who knelt between Rorke FitzWarren's legs.

Stunned, bewildered, humiliated, and terrified at what she should not, must not, feel, Vivian struggled to free herself. But that powerful hand, twisted with gentle restraint in her hair, held her as surely as a falcon tethered by leather jesses to its master's wrist.

Her eyes were almost iridescent as they reflected the flames from a nearby brazier. There was such agony of pleading in those eyes that Rorke let his fingers loosen, the silken ribbons of her hair slipping from his hand like liquid fire.

"Stay!" he commanded, at that moment loathing Judith de Marque with an intensity he would not have believed possible. But like the falcon that sought the sky, Vivian rose and hastily gathered her herbs and powders.

"Nay, milord," she whispered, "I cannot." And she fled the tent. Suddenly, it seemed colder, the shadows deeper, as if she had taken the light with her.

"You are amused by the Saxon slave," Judith commented as she poured warm wine from the pan over a brazier into a flagon. She brought it to the table where he sat flexing his left arm against the stiffness that had set in from blows he'd taken. Standing between his spread legs, she refilled his goblet.

"Spoils of war," she commented, pouring slowly, so that the wine sighed into the goblet with a faint murmuring sound, until the deep burgundy color edged the rim, its pungent, faintly spicy fragrance drifting upward between them. She handed him the goblet.

"And yet, you hesitate to take what you could easily take by right of conquest."

He grimaced, both at her remark and the pain that radiated from the wound at his side with every movement. "She is not spoils of war to be abused and poorly treated," he grunted his comment. "Her skills are needed."

"Aye," Judith remarked, a tawny brow lifting over pale blue eyes far different from those fiery blue eyes he saw in the heart of every flame he looked into. "I suspect her skills were much needed, yet the little bird has flown."

She knelt between his legs as Vivian had. Unlike Vivian, there was nothing that could be mistaken as innocent about Judith de Marque as she retrieved the cloth from the bowl at the table and wrung it out. Leaning forward between his thighs, she stroked the cloth up the length of his left arm.

"She is too young and far too simple to comprehend the needs of a warrior," she purred as she drew the cloth down over the curve of his chest.

"And you understand those needs perfectly," he said, without the least effort to disguise his cynicism. She dipped the cloth again in the warm water, continuing to bathe him where he sat before her.

"I know them well, milord. Mayhap you have forgotten." She leaned closer then, the front of her mantle falling open to reveal that she wore nothing underneath. As she leaned to stroke the cloth across his belly, she gave a faint shrug of her shoulder and the mantle fell to the dirt floor.

Her breasts were large and pendulous, brushing his arm as she leaned forward. The flat moons of her dusky nipples puckered and hardened at the contact.

"But I have not forgotten," she said huskily, the bathing forgotten as her fingers stroked across his belly then downward over the hardened ridge of engorged flesh that pressed thickly up against his belly beneath the leather breeches. He watched her through narrowed eyes as she laughed, a deep, throaty, satisfied sound, again reminding him of a cat licking her lips over a bowl of cream.

"Aye, milord, you have indeed remembered," she said, satisfaction gleaming in her eyes.

"What of your loyalty to William?" he asked, the coldness of his voice matching the wintry chill of his narrowed gray eyes.

"I am as loyal to him as he is to me," she said with silken voice, which both knew meant not at all. "He brought me to England to ease the cold nights because his duchess is large with child. He will send for her to join him in London, and when she has brought forth the child, he will again be loyal to her."

She slid her hand down the length of his erection to the bulge at the base and her voice lowered to a hungry growl. Then she smiled, and her voice had gone lower still and thickened with desire.

"I can feel how well you remember," she whispered smokily as she squeezed with one hand while the other stroked the fullness of her own breast, squeezing and pinching at the nipple as she watched for his reaction, then stroking down over her flat belly through the thatch of pale hair, to the cleft of her body.

Laughter was thick at her throat, her fingers glistening, as she brought them to her lips and licked each one like that hungry cat he had imagined. Judith de Marque had never lacked for imagination or enthusiasm. Then the laughter died and she smiled triumphantly with the last stroke of her tongue.

She slipped her other hand behind his neck and murmured huskily as she pulled his head down for her kiss. "Taste how well I remember."

The kiss was deep, thorough, as intimate as the physical joining her body craved.

Abruptly, Rorke thrust her away from him, the taste of her thick and redolent with the muskiness of desire at his lips.

"I am tired unto death, Judith, and the wound is like a poker thrust into my side." His expression was void of any emotion except that cold, empty stare. "Perhaps one of the count de Bayeau's men would appreciate your loyalty this night." The words cut like shards of ice thrust deep.

Stunned by his rejection, Judith moved stiffly away. She reached for her mantle, the expression behind her eyes cold as stone. Her features hardened, no longer sultry with invitation but a mask of undisguised hatred. Angrily, she wrapped the mantle about her, then fled the tent as Tarek al Sharif stepped past her.

"That is an expression I have never seen before on the leman's face," he commented. "Have you lost your taste for a woman's charms?" he asked with some bemusement, for it was no secret that Judith de Marque still longed to share the bed of the count d'Anjou, even though she had willingly shared William's bed. She was a woman of ambition and rare appetite. For a while Duke William had fulfilled her ambition, while the count d'Anjou had fulfilled that rare physical appetite.

Rorke refilled his own goblet, downed the ruby red contents, and refilled it again, trying to drown the whore's taste from his mouth.

"I find I have lost my taste for a certain woman," he said with disgust, at the same time longing to recapture the sweet-burning essence of another.

"What will you do?" Tarek asked, both amused and curious at his friend's unusual dilemma.

Evading an answer, Rorke reached for a large parchment scroll carefully wrapped in leather. He untied the leather bindings and opened the scroll, spreading it across the surface of the table. The parchment was a map of Britain.

"It is imperative that William take London. Only then can the throne be assured. We shall wait until he is strong enough to travel, fortify ourselves, and strike before the Saxons strike at us."

Fire hissed in a nearby brazier as the coals feebly struggled to warm the cold air inside the tent. His squire moved about, preparing a late supper, setting out garments for the morrow, including a second mail hauberk. Few were as rich as his lord and therefore capable of affording two such garments, nor were others as needy of two from constant warring.

Tarek al Sharif, on the other hand, eschewed such weighty trappings, preferring instead to strike first with that deadly curved blade and lightning swiftness his mailed opponents were soon given cause to envy.

"How is an enemy best taken?" Rorke asked thoughtfully, as though considering strategies of war.

Tarek shrugged with an air of faint boredom, for they had discussed such matters at great length. "Strike hard, strike fast, and then strike again where it may least be expected."

"Aye," Rorke acknowledged, studying the map. "With decisiveness, strength, and cunning."

"Do we speak of England or a single Saxon maid?" Tarek asked, failing to hide his amusement. It was long known that his friend's only ambition was the bounty offered by William for aligning his army with that of the Conqueror. That bounty would assure him the duchy of Anjou. Was it possible that something was causing his friend's ambition to waver.

Rorke's level gaze met his across the table, then returned to the map. "We will make our plans to take Canterbury next."

Tarek knew of this place called Canterbury, spiritual heart of Saxon England, and saw the cunning of Rorke's plan.

"Claim the heart of the creature and then capture the soul, and do it when and where none will expect it." He nodded his appreciation of the plan. "There will be opposition," he warned. "There are those who will say you overreach yourself, my friend."

"What do you say?" Rorke asked him.

Tarek grinned with approval as he lifted his goblet. "To London."

Eleven

Vivian sat up suddenly at the insistent shaking of her shoulder. The mist of the dream slowly disappeared, sleep clearing from her thoughts as she became aware of the cold that seeped through the thin blanket and her much-mended kirtle. The hand at her shoulder belonged to Sir Gavin's squire, Justin.

"What is it?" she asked, since she'd had no foreboding of it. "Has the duke of Normandy worsened?"

" 'Tis not His Grace, but Mally," he said with a worried frown that betrayed his feelings for the girl. "She's fearsome sick even this many days after . . ." He hesitated to speak aloud of the abuse she'd suffered at the hands of Vachel and his men.

"Aye," Vivian acknowledged, for the first time realizing that the girl was gone from their meager shelter under the cart where they had sought warmth at night since the journey from Hastings had begun days earlier.

Though Duke William was far from strong enough for the journey, he was determined to press on to London, insisting that it was imperative that the city be taken as soon as possible in able to ensure his claim to the throne. He and Rorke met daily, discussing battle plans, numbers of soldiers lost at Hastings, and the strategy for taking control of London.

William's wounds were healing well, the bone and tissue in his leg knitted and mended. She always rose early before sunrise, attended the duke in the small tent that was erected each eventide for him, and then left before Rorke arrived with Gavin and the knights.

During the day Rorke and his men rode far afield, fanning a protective line out through the forest well ahead of the main column of soldiers, to protect against Saxon attack as they drew closer to London.

The illness that plagued Mally, however, had nothing to do with bruises or broken bones, nor threat of starvation and deprivation. She had already suffered the worst that could be suffered at the hands of Vachel and his men. She had found at least temporary safety in Sir Gavin's care. Vivian had made certain of it, telling the kindhearted knight that the girl was much too ill to be moved elsewhere. He had agreed to allow the girl to remain with his entourage, and Vivian had remained with her to see to her care.

"Where is she?"

"Down by the water," Justin worriedly informed her.

Vivian gathered the thin shawl about her shoulders. It had been given to her by one of the camp followers out of gratitude for healing the man she traveled with, a soldier in Sir Gavin's retinue. Justin accompanied her, indicating the place where he'd last seen Mally.

The girl was on her knees by the water's edge, bent over at the waist, and retching violently into the rocks on the shore. When the spasms seemed momentarily to subside, Vivian gently laid a hand on her shoulder.

"Mally?"

The girl turned her head to look at Vivian. There was such misery in her expression. Her skin was deathly pale, and, in spite of the coldness of the morning, a fine sheen of perspiration beaded her skin and plastered her lank hair damp against forehead.

"Mistress Vivian?" she said miserably. It was all she could manage before she was immediately seized with another wave of nausea. Vivian gently bent Mally over her arm, holding her, while she held the girl's hair back with the other.

"Set a small pot to boil over the campfire," she instructed Justin.

He hesitated, fear warring with indecision in the expression at his face.

"She will be all right," she assured him. "But I need your help. A fine tea brewed from some of my seedlings will relieve the sickness. Now, please go." He did, but reluctantly, pausing to take Mally's hand between his own and squeeze it with undisguised affection. The girl didn't shrink from his touch as she did others, but instead smiled feebly. He turned and scrambled up the embankment toward camp.

Vivian had seen it coming from the moment she had Mally taken to Sir Gavin's tent. Justin was in love with the girl. If he knew the true nature of her illness, Vivian held no doubt he would have taken up a sword and gone after Vachel and his men single-handedly for what they'd done, for she had come to realize there was a deep contempt and loathing between Rorke's and Vachel's men.

"Oh, mistress Vivian," she moaned. "You must give me a healing potion. I don't know what's the matter with me, but I don't seem to be gettin' no better. And if milord FitzWarren finds out, he'll have me put out for certain so no one else gets sick."

Vivian tore a strip from the hem of her linen chemise under her kirtle, wet it in the clear, cold water of the stream, then wrung it out and folded it into a square. Holding Mally's hair out of the way, she laid the cold cloth across the back of the girl's neck.

"They will not put you out," she said vehemently. "Not when your illness is of their own making!"

"Their making?" Mally groaned, her voice small and childlike as she leaned weakly against Vivian. "I don't understand mistress."

Vivian hugged the girl against her. "Your sickness is not from disease or fever," she told the girl gently. "It is from joining with a man."

Mally was only ten and four, but she was bright and quick. There were seven children in her family. She had assisted the births of the two youngest. She had been raised in a single-room cottage with all the members of her family crowded around the fire at night. With that many children, four of them younger than Mally, it was impossible for her to be ignorant in the ways that men and women came together.

"You haven't had your monthly flux since we left Amesbury," she went on to explain.

The girl turned away from her, arms wrapped about herself, as if holding on, or holding herself together. Eventually, she nodded.

"I told myself it couldn't be true. I didn't want it to be true. Oh, mistress Vivian. What am I going to do? What will become of me?"

She hugged Mally tightly, anger burning through her like a live flame for what the girl had been forced to endure and must now endure further.

"The child is innocent," Vivian said gently through her own tears. "No matter how it was created. Don't worry," she assured the girl. "I'll take care of you and the baby." But in her thoughts, silent, where the girl could not hear, she cursed all Norman soldiers.

"You must tell Justin," Vivian went on as gently as possible. "You can't let his feelings for you continue and not tell him. It wouldn't be fair."

Mally jerked away from her, her eyes wide with misery. "But I can't tell him. He mustn't know. He'll hate me."

"He won't hate you," Vivian said with a certainty, knowing exactly where Justin's hatred would be directed. "You and the babe are innocent in all of this. But you must not delay, for he would be deeply hurt if you deceived him." Mally nodded miserably against Vivian's shoulder.

When the girl was better they returned to camp. It was late, the sun was already climbing the sky. Preparations were being made to get under way. She had just finished instructing Justin in the brewing of tea made from anise for Mally that would ease her nausea and make travel bearable, when Sir Gavin arrived to escort her to Duke William's tent.

The only thing that set the small, inconspicuous tent apart from any of the others was the heavy guard of soldiers that surrounded it.

Saxon rebels might be anywhere, and with the attack days earlier, no chances were being taken. The tent flap was drawn back and she went inside. She had been overly delayed in arriving. Rorke had already arrived, rolls of maps bound in leather spread across William's cot before him. She felt the weight of his gaze as she crossed the tent.

As they had at her last encounter with him days earlier, all her senses seemed overly aware of him. The simple cut of padded leather tunic, leggings, and boots that enhanced the lean, hard muscles beneath rather than disguising them. His face was cleanly shaven. Gone was the shadow of beard that had given him a rough animal wariness, replaced by an even more fearsome countenance in the sharply carved angles of cold, hard features. But beneath the coldness, beyond the wintry gray at his eyes, she saw the flare of predatory light that gleamed there. Like the fiery stare of the hunter, making her aware, as he had with his kiss, that there was fire beneath the ice.

The duke's brother, the bishop, was also there, as were several squires to see to the duke's needs. The bishop nodded to her, those dark eyes silently measuring, contemplating, assessing behind the benevolent facade of the gleaming silver cross he wore. She reminded herself that though he might be a bishop with vows sworn to God, he was also a warrior with fealty sworn to William. The warrior-bishop. An odd juxtaposition, and she silently wondered at the conflict such devotions might arouse.

"Good morrow, mistress," William greeted her. In spite of the rigors of travel with the wounds still so fresh, he looked none the worse for it. He was freshly shaven and sitting upright, wearing a clean tunic and breeches. His sword, cleaned of the blood of battle, lay gleaming at his side.

"Have you broken the fast?" he asked, spreading a hand to the ample fare that filled a tray at his bedside. She nodded, even though her stomach rumbled with hunger. Her thoughts were full of anguish for Mally and how she had suffered at Norman hands. She quickly went about her work, anxious to leave the tent and the presence of Rorke FitzWarren.

"I owe you my life," William stated matter-of-factly. "It has been much on my mind these past days. I owe you a boon. You have but to name it."

He watched her with keen interest. She could feel Rorke watching her as well. Days ago the answer would have required little thought. She would have asked to return to Amesbury, and not even Rorke FitzWarren would have gainsaid his liege lord. At a glance she saw that he expected it even now.

But there were other concerns that weighed much more heavily now and she doubted that William, with all of his apparent benevolence, would be inclined to grant more than one boon to her this day.

"You are very generous, milord. There is a boon I would ask." She took a breath, wondering if his generosity would stand up to his brother's objections. For Vachel was the bishop's man, and he had left no doubt of his intention to see Mally returned to his tent. Only Sir Gavin's intervention and her slow recovery—which Vivian had prolonged longer than was possible or wise—had prevented the girl's being returned already.

Over the days since discovering Mally in Vachel's tent, she had become aware there were other women in the Norman encampment. They were an odd mixture of Norman, French, and foreign women, some who had married soldiers, but most were the camp followers—the whores who plied their trade on the fringes of the moving army.

With them were children, bastards who might have claimed any one of a dozen different fathers. She'd even noticed a few Saxon women who'd chosen to throw in their lot with the conquering army. Vivian was determined that would not be Mally's fate.

"I do not ask it for myself, but for another."

William's russet brows lifted, with no attempt to conceal his surprise.

"You might ask for clothes." He gestured to her own clean, but much-mended gown and the meager slippers that covered her feet. "You might ask for gold, for I value your skills highly."

"What good is gold when some Norman soldier would only take it from me?" she asked with undisguised candor. "What good are clothes when they will suffer the fate of those that I wear? To be torn and shredded when blows are struck? These things hold little value for me, milord. The boon I ask is a girl."

"A girl?"

She was immediately aware that the bishop's gaze narrowed as he watched her. Rorke FitzWarren leaned against the edge of the nearby table, arms folded across his chest.

"Aye, milord. A Saxon girl taken from Amesbury the same day I was taken under threat of death to those I love and hold dear. She is here in this camp even now and has been badly abused by some of your men."

"Is this true?" William looked to Rorke.

"The girl was taken against my orders. She was poorly used and has been recovering in the care of Gavin de Marte."

"I protest such a request," the bishop intervened. "The granting of favors to a Saxon slave?" he indicated Vivian.

William held up a hand for silence, as he asked Vivian, "Will the girl recover?"

She was aware of the dark, angry look that crossed the bishop's face. "She will recover," she assured the duke of Normandy.

"Aye," he acknowledged, "in your care there can be little doubt of it. And yet, you ask not for yourself but for her. Why is this, Vivian of Amesbury?"

"The reasons are threefold, milord. I have need of the girl. She has assisted me before and is learned in many healing ways."

He nodded as he considered her request. "The second reason?"

"The girl, Mally, was poorly used, worse than the lowest animal that crawls the earth." She felt the bishop's hard stare, but refused to acknowledge that she was aware of it.

"I would not see her so abused again for she might easily perish from it and would be of little use to milord."

"I see the wisdom of your request," he answered. "And yet if I grant this boon for the reasons thus given, I would grant it for the girl herself, for it seems she has suffered greatly and with no just cause."

He was equally blunt as he added, "I will have England at the end of my sword, but I will not have it under my boot. A kingdom such as that is not a kingdom at all but the worst sort of prison and worth nothing to me."

He was equally blunt, and she realized William, duke of Normandy, was not a man to play with words.

"Ah, but there still remains the boon you have earned for yourself. You did say, mistress, the reasons were threefold."

"The third reason is that if I ask anything for myself, your generosity to me will be fulfilled."

He nodded his agreement as his own eyes narrowed with keen speculation. "Pray, continue."

She smiled faintly. "Therefore, I will not ask the boon for myself now," she went on to explain. "But there will come a day when I will ask it and you must grant it for you have so sworn before witnesses, including your own brother, the bishop."

A shrewd strategist, he admired the same quality in others and grinned appreciatively.

"By God, mistress Vivian, you remind me of me. Had I such a shrewd bargain-maker on my campaigns into the Byzantine Empire, the kingdom would have been mine. You are a healer of both the flesh and the spirit.

"I accept your decision. I will grant the boon for the girl. She will remain with you, under my personal protection."

"Thank you, milord," she murmured, as she set about changing his bandages. It was quickly done and she asked that she be allowed to take her leave. At the entrance to the tent, she paused.

"I would ask your permission to gather herbs and roots from the forest, for my medicines have been greatly depleted and not all of what I need can be found in your physician's stores."

"Is that the boon you ask then, mistress?" William inquired with a speculative look.

"Nay, milord," she assured him. "I ask it on your behalf. 'Tis your health that will benefit from the granting of it."

He chuckled, his face lined with fatigue from the morning activities that required his attention. "Then so be it." He added, "One of my men will accompany you."

"You are most generous, milord."

Within hours they were under way toward London, William's decision made that he would delay no further. Tents were collapsed and packed in great lumbering carts to follow the main army.

Aquila had returned unharmed to the Norman encampment the day after the Saxon attack, as if she had but hunted in the forest, returning with a fine fat hare which ended up in the evening's stew pot. But late that night, after the rabbit had been consumed, Vivian took a thick morsel to the falcon, crooning soft words to her, communicating with that special bond they shared.

By day, as the Norman army traveled, Vivian gathered what herbs, roots, and late, shriveled berries could be found along the old Roman road they traveled. The remainder she sought from the hedgerows and forest edge after they had made camp.

Their travel was slow, limited each day to William's endurance. When he tired and could travel no further, the journey was halted. Sir Galant accompanied her into the forest to gather what grasses, shoots, and tender roots could be found this late in the season beneath the late afternoon frost.

With winter hard upon them, the remedies she preferred were difficult to find. Many would not reappear until the following spring and summer. As they returned to camp, her basket filled with chiseled pieces of bark and root dug from beneath the frosty ground, she began making mental substitutions of ingredients that might be used from the supply found in the healer's chest.

Along with her meager daily gatherings most of the soldiers' needs could be seen too if there wasn't an outbreak of fevers or serious infestation.

Gavin's squire and retainers had set up camp. A fire burned a welcoming warmth. The falcon, Aquila, had hunted in the forest and swooped low to reclaim the perch that had been provided for her. With so many soldiers and guards about, Sir Galant bade Vivian farewell to return to his own camp nearby.

Mally worked over the cook fire, helping prepare the evening meal. The longer periods of enforced encampment allowed for the preparation of hot meals of fresh roast fowl in place of the hard, stale bread and cheese that had sustained the army for weeks since crossing the English Channel.

Vivian laid out the leather roll, carefully spreading the twigs, bark, and roots that she'd gathered. She worked quickly in the fading light, separating and sorting each, for none could be wasted. Even though the fire was warm, she still shivered as though a sudden coldness swept over her. She sensed his presence.

But even with the forewarning, she looked up with sudden uneasiness. At first she didn't see him in the shadows at the edge of the campfire, as though he belonged to the darkness. Then, as he realized that she was fully aware of his presence, he stepped from the shadows into the light that rimmed the campfire. Golden flames reflected at the silver cross he wore.

"I see you've been gathering your precious herbs and strange medicants," the bishop observed, coming to stand closer, hands extended before him toward the warmth of the fire.

"Not so very strange to those in need," Vivian answered evenly.

"Spores, molds, and fungus?" he inquired with a bemused expression that made her realize he considered such things to be the foolishness of peasants even though many of the healing cures could also be found among the Norman healer's potions.

She gave him a measuring look, trying to discern what it was about him that eluded her. "They're all beneficial in healing"— and then with a faint smile of her own—"as is the spider's web and the application of leeches. There are many things of benefit to be found in nature.

"But I think, milord," she added, "that you did not come to discuss healing potions."

"Ah, ever the quick mind. You surprise me much, mistress Vivian."

"For a Saxon?" she speculated.

He chuckled softly. "I am oft surprised by God's strange workings in finding one so gifted in a heathen realm. But I have noticed that you do not wear the sign of the cross," he speculated. "You wear instead the symbol of the earth in a blue stone. Is that not the way of the heathen Celts?"

"If I do not wear the cross about my neck, it does not mean that I do not wear it in my heart," she informed him. "God is everywhere and in every thing."

"Was that taught you by the monk at Amesbury."

She sensed his disdain. "Poladouras is exceptionally well learned. He has taught me many things."

"Including the ways of mixing potions of molds, frog eyes, and spider's webs?"

"I learned the healing ways from the old ones."

"Ah, the Celts." With a stick seized from the edge of the fire, he stirred the newly formed bed of coals. "Do you also believe in faeries, trolls, and mystical spirits who inhabit the trees and rocks?" he asked.

"I believe, milord Bishop," she said with a certainty, "that you did not come to discuss healing potions or matters of faith."

"You are right, mistress. In truth, I came to inquire about the girl you bargained for with my brother."

Behind her, in the shadows of the cart, Vivian was aware of a movement and knew that Mally hovered close by.

"Is she recovering from her injuries?" he asked in a way that made Vivian aware he chose his words very carefully.

"She is," she said with quiet introspection, trying to discern what the bishop's true purpose was, for she could not believe that he concerned himself with a simple Saxon peasant girl. He looked past her as though he could see into those shadows where Mally hid.

"You need not fear me, my child. I am a man of God. I would but offer absolution for your sins and protection from your enemies."

Sins? Vivian felt a ripple of irritation. What about Vachel's sins and the sins of the other Norman soldiers committed upon innocent Saxon women and children?

Mally had stepped from the shadows, not toward him, but toward Vivian. Vivian moved beside her.

"She will be safe enough here," Vivian said evenly.

"But there are dangers everywhere," he protested with such concern of voice. "She would be safer in my protection."

"Safer than under the protection of Duke William himself?" she inquired. "Would you hold yourself above your liege lord?" She was reminded that Vachel was the bishop's man. A curious alignment for a man of God, but perhaps not so curious for a warrior. Why would the bishop want the girl? Had he perhaps promised her to Vachel?

The smile was still in place, but there was a sudden sharpness at those dark eyes that warned she had perhaps been too outspoken. She bantered not with a fool, but with a very clever man who wielded much power.

"No man is above God," he countered. "Not even a man who would be king of England."

At the cart she was aware that the falcon had become agitated on her perch. It was not the restless movement of the need to be at the hunt, but the uneasiness of alarm.

"Especially a man who would be king of England," she responded. Anger flashed in his dark eyes and she realized she had perhaps struck too close to the truth. The falcon seemed to sense his anger as well, for her wings flared as though she was ready to spring into flight.

The bishop reached out, touching the edge of her sleeve. "These are precarious times, mistress. Be careful that you do not overstep yourself."

It was a simple enough gesture, yet inexplicably a great coldness swept over her. The falcon screeched in alarm at her perch. When Vivian tried to calm her, she immediately leapt into the air, powerful wings sweeping low, talons outstretched as she swept past Vivian. She flew so close that a talon grazed Vivian's arm.

A look of genuine alarm appeared on the bishop's face and his hand went to the sword at his scabbard as the falcon winged so close with those deadly talons that he could feel the brush of feathers at his cheek.

The falcon swept low under the canopy of the trees and sought a distant perch. She sat on an outstretched limb, wings unfurled, that lethal beak open, golden eyes reflecting the gleam of flame from the campfire. From across the encampment dozens of voices called out, swords were drawn, and soldiers gathered.

"Stand away!" The order was barked amid the gathered soldiers and they stepped aside. Rorke FitzWarren quickly strode through the circle that had gathered.

"What is amiss?"

"That creature tried to attack me!" the bishop accused, gesturing to the falcon that now sat calm and watchful on a low-hanging limb nearby. Golden eyes seemed to reflect the flame of the fire.

"If she had wanted to attack you, milord Bishop," Vivian

assured him, "she would have done so and there would be no doubt of it. But as you can see your tunic is intact and you are unharmed. You frightened her is all."

The bishop's taut expression eased. "I have been too long at war," he said by way of explanation. "I have forgotten the finer points of falconry. I assure you I will not forget them again. I would not care to lose an eye or find myself flayed open for my carelessness." He then turned to Vivian with a wary eye toward the falcon to make certain he didn't frighten her again.

"You have reminded me, mistress, of a valuable lesson about wild creatures. They can never be completely brought to hand and must be guarded against constantly." Then he smiled, as if to make a jest of the entire matter.

"I will take my leave, before she decides to go hunting again. And I suggest that you keep her to tether about camp," he added. "My brother, the duke, has brought his own hunting birds. They are fierce creatures. Your small falcon would be no match for them. You would not wish to find her maimed or killed."

"Thank you, milord," she murmured. "I will remember."

The soldiers sheathed their weapons and left to return to their own campfires when they realized the cry of alarm was not over Saxon rebels attacking the encampment.

As Rorke also turned to leave he saw the blood that dripped through fingers clasped tightly over her arm.

"You've been injured," he said with more than a little alarm.

" 'Tis nothing," she responded and tried to turn away, but he prevented it, hands closing about her upper arms.

" 'Tis more than nothing," he remarked tight-lipped as he stared down at her bloodied hand. "Did the falcon strike you?"

"No harm was done," she insisted, trying to pull away.

"You said the falcon has never wounded you," he reminded her, prying her fingers apart.

Just the simple contact of his fingers against hers recalled the possessive touch of his hand in her hair and the feel of his mouth against hers.

"It has never happened before," she explained. "It was not intentional. She was startled was all." She found herself repeating what she had explained to the bishop. " 'Tis only a scratch."

" 'Tis more than a scratch, Vivian," he insisted. "I've seen my share of wounds and any that bleed like this are indeed serious."

"Mally is quite skilled," she hastily assured him. "She will see that it is properly bound."

But he was not to be persuaded otherwise and succeeded in prying loose her fingers. He stared at the sleeve of her kirtle, shredded by the falcon's lethal talons as she had swept too close, and the pale, unmarred flesh at Vivian's arm.

"There is no wound!" he said with stunned disbelief. "Not even a mark." He gently turned her arm this way and that, still unable to find any wound or even a scratch.

"I saw the blood! How is it possible that there is no wound?"

She refused to meet his gaze as she finally pulled her arm free and stepped past him. "You were mistaken is all." She washed the blood from her fingers.

"The falcon hunted in the forest while I gathered herbs," she explained. "No doubt the blood was from some prey that was captured."

Gray eyes narrowed as he studied her, making her wonder who was now the predator and who was the hunted.

Twelve

"It seems," Rorke said reluctantly, "that I must accept that you have told the truth. By your own words, you are incapable of a lie."

"What other truth could there possibly be?" Vivian asked in a low voice.

"What other truth indeed!" he countered.

Tarek appeared on the other side of the campfire, and Vivian let out a sigh of relief for the end of the uncomfortable silence that had closed around them and the disconcerting scrutiny of those gray eyes that saw far more than she had told him.

"William has asked to see you," Tarek informed Rorke. "Plans must be made for the march on London."

"Aye," Rorke nodded, his gaze never leaving hers as if he still sought some other truth there. His handsome mouth curved into a frown of displeasure as he wrestled with new, far weightier matters.

"This might well end in a bloody siege because of foolish decisions. And this army cannot survive another siege, fragmented as it is across the whole of England because of ill-advised decisions." Both he and Tarek knew the bishop had advised just such a decision—split the army into a dozen smaller forces and spread like pearls along a golden chain—a very thin chain capable of being broken. Vivian heard the undercurrent of disdain that flowed through the words and sensed Rorke had not welcomed the decision.

"Perhaps," Tarek suggested, his tone filled with unspoken meaning, "it was an exceptionally ingenious decision."

Rorke's gray eyes sharpened as he considered that precise possibility. Vivian's senses sharpened. What she could not discern about Rorke FitzWarren, she succeeded in sensing from Tarek. They suspected some sort of danger from within.

"Perhaps," Rorke speculated as some undercurrent of understanding seemed to pass between him and Tarek. He turned to leave, but not without another long, speculative look at her apparently uninjured arm.

"Be careful in handling the falcon," he cautioned. "It would be best if she was tethered until we reach London." As he turned to follow Tarek to the duke of Normandy's tent, he assured her, "We will speak of this again."

* * *

Too weak to lead his army, Duke William reluctantly relinquished command to his generals. Vivian discovered, that like King Arthur's five hundred years earlier, William's army was made up of generals, trusted knights, and fellow noblemen who had proved themselves in battle at his side over the years.

She learned that he entrusted his brother, the bishop count de Bayeau, with matters of faith. But in matters of conquest, he entrusted his army to Rorke FitzWarren. That dangerous dichotomy was not lost on Vivian, who attended William and daily became more aware of the undercurrent of resentment and enmity between the two men.

It was also rumored the bishop considered command of the army his by right of blood. But over the days and weeks, as she learned more about Rorke FitzWarren, she realized that he had more than earned that right, by a much different rite of blood.

He had been apprenticed as a squire at the age of fourteen and earned his knighthood by the age of sixteen. When his father, the Count d'Anjou, had refused to support his knighthood, he had blackmailed the old man into sponsoring him by threatening to pledge his sword to the king of France, a longtime enemy of Anjou.

Though his father eventually sponsored his knighthood, Rorke refused to take the crest of Anjou for his shield. Instead, he took the mythical phoenix rising from the flames—a creature born in fire and blood, destroyed and then reborn in the flames.

Gavin revealed little about Rorke's relationship with his father. Only that the old man was a cruel, forbidding man who had sacrificed one son for another and lost both in the bargain. More than that he would not say. But with what little Rorke had shared with her that day in the Saxon prison encampment, she knew the hatred was deep and painful and whatever had separated father and son had never been forgiven.

It was on the battlefield at San Cristabol in the Mediterranean provinces when he was but eighteen, that Rorke met William of Normandy. Their friendship was forged in blood and common ambition, and Rorke had pledged his loyalty to William.

Now, fourteen years later, London was surrounded with legions of William's army, like the links of a massive chain. Canterbury had fallen to the Norman army two weeks earlier. Just two days before, with the whole of the Norman army encircled about London, the sheriff of London had finally capitulated and negotiated for peace.

The carts, wagons, litters with the wounded, camp followers, squires, and retainers, had moved to the back of the Norman line. There was no place for them among a fast-moving invading army.

Because there had no doubt been rumors of William's injury at Hastings, and any weakness would be seen as vulnerability and perchance an opportunity for the Saxon barons to refuse him as king, it was of critical importance that William be seen in full battle armor among his men.

Though none of the other women were allowed to accompany this vast, moving army, but ordered to follow with the supply columns, Vivian accompanied him to see to his care. Afraid to leave Mally behind, she insisted that the girl be allowed to accompany her.

The girl had not wanted to leave Justin's care, for they had become very fond of one another. But Vivian insisted. Mally had been given William's protection. She knew not what might happen to the girl beyond the reach of that protection.

It was a cold night. The Norman campfires rimming all of London no doubt were clearly seen by the inhabitants of the city. Deep in her heart, Vivian wept for the inevitable outcome that she had foreseen and could not stop. Yet, Rorke FitzWarren still did not order the Norman soldiers into the city.

A bitter wind swirled across the landscape, making Tarek al Sharif wish for the warmer climes of Antioch, that distant home he had not seen since boyhood, when he had set out to find his father, but which he remembered in his blood. A sharp gust guttered at a nearby campfire, sending clouds of smoke into the bleak night sky. It whipped at the flaming ribbons of Vivian's hair as she stood staring into the night. She wore only the threadbare shawl gathered around her shoulders over the thin woolen gown.

Tarek found her at the edge of the encampment, one of Rorke's personal guards hovering nearby. Her slender figure was outlined by the glow of the campfire. Haunted shadows played over delicate features. She was like fire—fascinating, tempting, wildly dangerous, unafraid, untamed, and unconquerable.

She stood with arms folded about her as if she were trying to hold something in rather than hold the cold out. He made no sound as he approached, yet somehow she sensed his presence, her head turning slightly in acknowledgment. It was not the first time he had noticed that uncanny ability, almost as if she had a sense of foreknowledge about such things.

"What do you see in the darkness?" Tarek asked, coming to stand beside her.

"I see death, great sadness and loss, and change that no one can stop."

Tarek smiled. "William would be pleased that you see the success of his ambition."

"Success bought at the cost of human suffering?" she asked sadly, still without looking at him.

"William merely claims what was his by right."

"By what right?" she asked wearily.

"By right of a deathbed promise from the old king, so I am told," Tarek explained. "That promise then broken by the king's counselors when they held the witan and elected Harold king of England."

Poladouras had spoken of the promise and the inevitability of war that might come when the old king died and Harold was made king. "And if the promise had not been made"—she turned to look at him—"would William have been satisfied with Normandy?"

Tarek shrugged. "It is said that England was his by right of blood, through his grandmother. There was none other who had equal or greater claim."

"Aye, by right of blood," she murmured, closing her eyes as she did so and still seeing the eerie, bloody images behind closed lids as the portent of things to come.

Lust. Greed. Betrayal. But whose? And against whom?

"Come back to the camp," he said, shivering in spite of the heavy robes he wore. "It is cold here. And there are no answers to be found in the dark. I know, for I have searched for them." He gently touched her arm to draw her back to the camp. Her skin was warm to the touch, vibrantly so, as if some wild, untamed fire burned through her and he again thought of the legendary Jehara, who inhabited the world between the worlds.

Beware the faith that has no heart, the sword that has no soul.

The words she had first heard that long ago day at Amesbury whispered back to her on the wind. But she could not discern who spoke them, any more than she could see beyond the growing darkness that closed around them.

"The answers are there," she said softly, as if she hadn't heard him but spoke to someone else. Then she seemed to return to the earthbound world, turning to look at him.

"Will it be tomorrow?" she asked.

"I do not know. He tells no one of his plans. When the time is at hand it will be done."

"Will Rorke FitzWarren be merciful?"

"He will be just."

She prayed she could believe that, for he had shown himself to be a just man in other things. Which was more than she could say for the bishop.

It didn't happen the following day, or the next. Nerves were drawn taut, as the waiting continued. Vivian knew it must be that much more difficult for the inhabitants of London.

Another emissary arrived from the sheriff of London, in whose care the defense of the city had been left upon the death of Harold. No answer was given and still the waiting continued.

Finally, the morning of the third day past the agreed-upon date for the surrender of London, with nerves drawn to the breaking point, Rorke FitzWarren gave the order for the march on London. Soldiers, both mounted and afoot, and all heavily armed, were to enter the city from a dozen defensive locations around the city. The duke of Normandy would not be among the first to enter the city, a decision that did not sit well with the battle-hardened soldier.

"I will lead my army into London!" he roared his disagreement with Rorke's decision as they all met in William's tent, including his brother, the bishop.

"And possibly ride into an armed ambush? We know not the temper of the people of London," Rorke argued. "We must assume they will defend the city to the last man. If it were Anjou, I would defend it until my blood ran into the soil beneath my feet."

"These are not soldiers!" William pointed out. Cold sweat from the exertion of argument beaded his forehead. "They are merchants, tailors, and innkeepers. Think you they will defend the city with writing quills, sewing needles, and tankards?"

"Only a fool rides into a fortress not knowing the strength that lies within," Rorke pointed out. "By your own words, the fiercest enemy is one that defends his hearth and home."

"You use my words against me!" William roared. The bishop had moved to stand beside him, by his silent presence indicating whose side he took in the argument.

"I use your words to keep you alive!" Rorke told him without hesitation. "What good is an army if the commander is slain? What good is a throne if there is no one to wear the crown? You might ask good king Harold those questions."

"By God! I would have any other man struck down for what you've said!" William shouted.

"Aye," Rorke agreed, unaffected by the threat, "the truth is often a bitter medicine to swallow." And on that thought, he turned to Vivian.

"What say you, mistress? Is he strong enough to mount a pitched battle within the city walls? Is his sword arm strong enough to wield a blade? Is he recovered enough to sit a warhorse, or shall we fasten him to the top of a cart?"

At that moment, Vivian glimpsed the cold ruthlessness she had sensed him capable of. The questions were rhetorical. He didn't really expect an answer. Or in the very least not one that would disagree with his plans. But William wanted an answer— a very different one. And the expression on the duke of Normandy's face suggested it might be unwise to give any answer other than what he wanted.

"Be advised," Rorke told his liege lord, "the maid has informed me that she is incapable of lying." He turned to her then.

"Well, what say you? Are his wounds sufficiently healed to allow him to participate in full combat?"

"By all means," William slyly encouraged her. "Be completely honest. After all"—he leaned forward from his cot— "you have nothing to fear of FitzWarren for telling the truth, my dear. I shall abide by your decision."

He was so confident of his recovery that he encouraged her to tell the truth. She sensed it, and had to fight to suppress a smile. He wasn't going to be at all pleased with the truth.

"I will tell you, milord, what I would tell any other man with your injuries," she answered, diplomatically as possible.

"You are alive only by the grace of God. The wounds linger and must be given more time to heal—"

"Nevertheless," he said, cutting her off.

Undaunted, she continued. "The leg is not yet mended. If you attempt to sit a horse, you will fall flat on your face. You cannot hold a quill in your hand to write the simplest missive, let alone a sword. You have four broken ribs that pain you to draw the smallest breath, let alone sit upright in full battle armor—"

"Silence!" he roared. "By God, you are a mettlesome wench!"

"You did insist that I tell you the truth, milord," she pointed out. He glared at her from beneath that wild, russet brow.

"What then is your plan for my campaign?" he demanded of Rorke, while massaging his weak right hand with frustration.

"We will secure the city against any skirmishes and uprisings. As far as anyone in London is concerned, it will be the duke of Normandy leading his army."

William's head came up, eyes narrowing.

"Explain yourself."

"With your permission, I will wear your battle armor and carry your standards. We are of the same size. With the helm in place, none will be the wiser. And your *presence* at the head of the army will be a strong deterrent to attacks . . . and rumors of any injury that may have traveled ahead of us."

"It could also make you a target for an assassin," William pointed out as he nodded his assessment of the plan. "I have always accepted the full responsibility of my actions. I would not have another man die in my place."

"With the duke of Normandy seen to lead his army into London, there should be no need for any man's death."

William nodded. "And once you have established control of the city?"

"I will send Tarek to escort you into London. To all outward appearances, the *duke of Normandy* shall meet with the Saxon earls and barons and make his rightful claim to the throne. None will be the wiser."

"I must protest!" the bishop objected, his dark eyes narrowed. "William must be seen leading his army into London. Do you believe the Saxons will be fooled? Such trickery establishes a dangerous precedent." Then he turned his argument on William.

"FitzWarren is your most powerful commander. He already commands more than half of your army. He is ambitious. Do not allow this, my brother. It is too dangerous."

"As dangerous as leaving William's side during the thick of battle?" Rorke flung at the bishop angrily, the words filled with accusation.

"What are you suggesting, FitzWarren?" the bishop's voice suddenly low and dangerous.

"I *suggest* nothing, milord Bishop," Rorke answered, his eyes a deadly shade of gray. "I will say plainly what all know to be true. You were not there to defend William's side when he was injured."

"Cease!" William ordered. "I will not have this enmity between men that I have a need of." He nodded to Rorke. "You have my trust. I agree to your plan. I shall await the escort you send." He turned to his brother. "You will accompany FitzWarren. It would seem *unusual* if you were not at the side of the duke of Normandy."

The subtle, silken message of what hadn't been said was equally clear. His brother's sudden disappearance at the battle of Hastings had been noted and was not forgotten. The bishop bowed his head in reluctant obedience to William's decision.

"Godspeed," William told Rorke. "And safe journey, my friend." Rorke nodded and quickly left the tent.

Vivian sensed the bishop's anger over the confrontation and knew he would give full vent to it with William. The bishop tolerated her presence at best, in the very least considered her skills crude and unnecessary in spite of the fact that she'd saved his brother's life. She had no desire to be caught in the middle of their argument and immediately followed Rorke.

The duke of Normandy was the only one allowed a tent in the fast-moving column that had surrounded London. The cold blast of frigid morning air beyond the tent stunned her. She shivered, pulling her shawl tighter about her shoulders as she hastened across the camp after Rorke.

Her slippered feet made light crunching sounds in the frosty mantle that covered the ground. She caught up with him at his own encampment, where even now Gavin assisted him with William's cumbersome chain mail armor.

It had been carefully cleaned and mended, but still bore the marks of the blows William had taken at the battle of Hastings.

All about the camp mounted soldiers and those afoot made preparations for battle.

Iron swords, finely polished, gleamed dangerously in the gray sunless morning light. Heavy chain mail chausses and hauberks were buckled into place. Steel helms with nose plates were donned as were heavy mail gloves. Painfully, Vivian recalled that morning at Amesbury, when it seemed the whole of the Norman army had descended on the abbey, bringing with it death and destruction. The only difference was the standard that fluttered overhead on the icy wind and the kite-shaped shield that lay across the saddle.

Instead of the phoenix rising from the flames, both carried William's emblem of an eagle rampant on a field of purple, the standard with a fringe of black, gold, and purple threads—like the threads of an unwoven tapestry that tossed on an uncertain wind.

Rorke turned at the touch of her hand. He had not yet donned the mail coif or steel helm. His dark hair lay in thick layers to his shoulders for want of skilled shears. He was clean-shaven, the strong features of his face etched like stone in the cold morning air that held the hint of a pending storm. Eyes that she had once thought as cold as winter ice softened at the sight of her.

"Do you come to wish me farewell, demoiselle?"

"Yes," she answered truthfully. At the same time she tried to quell the fear in her heart at what might happen, for they were prepared to battle for London if necessary. She should not feel this way—this ache of fear and uncertainty that he might be killed. "And to wish you safe journey," she added.

He stopped jerking leather straps snug at the mail armor and looked at her speculatively.

"Could it be that you might feel some small measure of regret at my death were I to perish on the streets of London?" he asked, the deep timbre of his voice moving across her skin like a warm hand.

"Yes, of course, I would," she blurted out, and then, realizing how easily what she'd said might be misunderstood, she hastened to correct herself. "No! . . . What I mean is . . . If anything were to happen . . ."

Rorke smiled. "In the short time I have known you, Vivian of Amesbury, you have never lacked for words. Say what you will and be quick about it, before you freeze to death."

"Very well," she answered, her breath pluming on the chill morning air. "My concern is for Mally."

"Mally?" he responded with more than a little irritation. He leaned over and jerked a leather strap into place, snugging the mail chausses over a long, muscular thigh.

"What has the girl to do with the taking of London?"

"She is protected from Vachel and the others by William's order and given into your care. If anything were to happen to you in London . . ."

" . . . You fear that the girl might come to some harm," he finished what she seemed to be having some difficulty saying as her teeth chattered from some malady other than the cold.

Vivian nodded, holding the shawl more tightly about her, certain that it must be the cold that made her shiver. "She's done nothing, but still suffered the worst abuse. What will become of her?"

"Cease," he ordered, but not ungently, as he suddenly stood upright once more beside the tall warhorse. "Do you always go abegging for others?"

"I am not begging! I am merely asking for what is just," she argued.

"The girl has William's protection if anything should happen to me. She will be safe. But what would you ask for yourself?"

"Myself? Why would I ask anything?" she responded in surprise. "I have all that I need. And you have clearly stated that you will not grant that which I would ask—the safety of the people of Amesbury."

"But what of your freedom?" he spoke softly, his voice deep.

"If something was to happen to me, what of you then, Vivian of Amesbury?"

At his words, she felt a sudden coldness sweep over and through her. "I would return to the abbey."

"And if William or the bishop would not allow it?"

She answered with complete honesty. "They could not stop me if I chose to leave."

His eyes narrowed. "Yet you now remain within William's encampment when you have no desire to be here. Wherein lies the difference?"

She glanced away, seized by a sudden violent shivering. "I cannot say." His touch was as warm as summer sun against her skin as he forced her gaze back to his with fingers gently clasped over the curve of her chin.

"Or will not say?" he speculated.

"Will you give your word for Mally's safety?" She avoided a direct answer, quite simply because both were only half-truths.

"Aye, I will give my word for her safety. And yours," he surprised her by adding. He reached for the heavy mantle that lay across the saddle.

It was midnight black wool, finely woven, and lined with soft white fur. He draped it around her shoulders, snugging the heavy fur collar about her neck. The mantle, large enough to accommodate his large frame donned with battle armor, framed her slender shoulders with a comforting heaviness like being wrapped in a warm cocoon.

"I cannot wear this," she protested, feeling the warm caress about her arms and legs, the scent of him—faintly spicy and of the wind—permeating the rich fabric and thick fur.

His hands lingered at her shoulders, fingers brushing her neck, causing a thrill of excitement at her skin.

"Nor can I." He pointed out the brilliant purple mantle brought from William's tent, replacing the black mantle at the front of the saddle.

"Wear it for me," he told her, his voice suddenly low at his throat as if something unspoken lay behind the words. "You may return it when we have secured the city."

With an ease that belied the weight of the heavy mail armor, he vaulted into the saddle, adjusting William's mantle with the easily recognizable gold lion emblazed at the hem for all to see so that they would know that William the Conqueror had conquered London.

He pulled on heavy gauntlets and gathered his reins. He glanced briefly at Vivian, with an expression that was almost tender. Then he looked to Gavin and said with unspoken meaning, "You have your orders, my friend. Do not fail me."

"I have always fought at your other side," Gavin said, his voice heavy with protest.

"You will fight at my side again, my friend. For now I must entrust both sides to another."

Beside him Tarek nodded. "I will be like the eagle he wears on his mantle. None will be able to touch him while I fly at his side."

The command was given and echoed along the entire column of soldiers, formed six abreast with lances and maces held at the ready, broadswords unsheathed and laid across saddle pommels, and stretched beyond the encampment into the rolling mist like some phantom army appearing then disappearing on the currents and eddies of the mist so that they might have numbered five hundred or ten times that number.

Vivian stood back, clutching the folds of the mantle about her to hold out the unbearable cold that ached through her. That small legion of soldiers that day at Amesbury was only a mere whisper of the size and force of the number that now marched to lay siege to London. And, mournfully, there was nothing she could do to stop it. Indeed, she was part of it—part of that unwoven tapestry that was the future, the threads of which tossed and waved on a cold, bitter wind.

* * *

It was the middle of the next night when she was awakened
from troubled dreams by an insistent shaking of her shoulder.
It was Gavin.

He was dressed in full battle armor rather than the leather-
padded pants and tunic she'd last seen him in. His expression
was resolute, yet there was a boyish eagerness that softened the
hard line of his mouth and glinted at his eyes.

"It is time, mistress. The signal flares have been seen at the
heart of the city and a messenger arrived but an hour ago. We
ride into London."

For two days they had waited with no word, only the flare of
fires that appeared throughout the city, glowing from rooftops,
and then eventually smoldering to a lambent glow. Vivian had
stood on the small knoll of the encampment, forcing herself to
watch as flaming threads of the tapestry wove the night sky and
she thought of a mythical bird that rose reborn from the flames.

Unbidden, as if with a will of their own, her thoughts reached
out to Rorke, to feel some essence of him, to know that he was
safe, to somehow quell the ache inside just to see him again,
to hear the gentle roughness of his voice, to feel those cool eyes
watching her from a distance, and his hand lightly brushing her
shoulder or her cheek. She did not understand how she could
long for a simple touch, she only knew that she had as she
longed for sunlight, air, and the warmth of fire.

Now, they mounted horses, surrounded by a heavily armed
guard. It was necessary that Vivian accompany the duke of Normandy. Mally rode beside her.

Her experience with horses was limited to Poladouras' aged
palfrey, a docile creature that the good monk claimed was given
to dozing between strides. She and Mally were given cart ponies
to ride, rather than the larger, more high-spirited warhorses.
They sat astride, surrounded by Gavin's guard.

Refusing the aid of any man, the duke of Normandy appeared
at the opening of his tent. He wore chain mail battle armor. It
concealed the gauntness from the fever and infection that had
laid waste to his body, making him appear formidable in height

and size. He waved Gavin aside when he would have assisted him astride his warhorse.

"By God! This at least I will do for myself!" Then he motioned for his squire and gave instructions.

"Send a messenger to the ships that await on the coast. The time is at hand and I would have Matilda brought to London so that she may be crowned queen as I am crowned king of England." Then he turned to Gavin.

"You have the route by which we are to enter the city?"

"Aye, milord." Gavin nodded. "By the north bridge. An escort will be awaiting us."

The Norman encampment was less than a league from the city. Any infirmity of pain William suffered was disguised by his determination to ride into the city, claiming it for his own.

The north bridge quickly came into view, outlined by torches set along the length connecting one side of the river to the other. An armed escort rode across to meet them.

Instinctively, Vivian found her eyes searching among the mail-clad knights for one who was taller, leaner of frame, with wide-set shoulders, protective mail coif impatiently cast back about his shoulders. But Rorke FitzWarren was not among them.

She did recognize de Lacey, Montfort, and Sir Guy. Greetings were exchanged. Their expressions were resolute, grim with their purpose of escorting Duke William of Normandy into London. Word passed through the Norman guard.

There had been continual skirmishes and armed encounters with Saxon rebels and those who refused to surrender the city. Many had been wounded as they fought from street to street in spite of the official surrender the sheriff of London had so passionately negotiated. But for those isolated pockets of resistance, London had fallen to the Conqueror and William of Normandy would officially lay claim to it that night.

They rode a circuitous route through the city, through back streets, cobbled alleys, and places where cobbles gave way to dirt, across another bridge, and past a central square with the spires of Westminster Abbey looming ever closer.

Vivian felt the stares and stolen glances from behind shuttered second story windows, above shops, inns, cottages, and stables as the inhabitants of London looked out on the heavily armed escort that wound through the streets. She could feel their fear and apprehension at these strange invaders, their entire lives turned upside down with the death of Harold and the defection of the archbishop of Canterbury and enough Saxon earls to guarantee William the throne of England.

Occasionally they passed blackened and burned-out rubble, all that remained of a cottage or shop where there had been skirmishes and fires. But for the most part the buildings were intact.

Poladouras had been to London and spoke often of it. He had told her of the grand Winchester cathedral, the royal houses built within a square park beside a wood, and the ancient Roman ruins where other invaders had once held court.

Vivian discovered it was also a rabbit's warren of stone, thatch, and wood buildings, crammed all side by side like squat nesting hens, water spilling from rooftop cisterns and freezing to ice almost before it reached cobbled streets where rats darted and floated among the flotsam of refuse and garbage, the stench congealing with the acrid smoke from their torches that cast eerie, shifting shadows along walls and fronts of buildings as they passed by.

Their destination was the royal tower where Harold had held court and where the council of Saxon barons and earls had held the ancient witan proclaiming the boy Edgar king of England, in futile defiance of William's claim. It was here that William was to officially lay claim to the throne.

Then a new urgency ran cold through her blood, sharpened her senses, and had her pulling back sharply on the pony's reins and motioning for Mally to do the same.

"What is it?" the girl asked anxiously.

"Something is wrong," Vivian said as the urgency moved through her. "There is danger very near."

Without clearly seeing it she sensed a deadly danger that closed around them. She called a warning to Gavin. Riding just ahead, he reined in and turned at the sound of her voice. The warning came just as the flash of axes and swords exploded from the shadows at either side of the narrow street.

Orders were quickly shouted. Horses jostled against one another, trapped within the narrow confines of the buildings that lined both sides of the street. Steel blade rang out against steel blade. Beside her, Mally screamed. Vivian grabbed the reins of her pony to keep them from being separated in the confusion.

A mounted soldier riding on the other side of the girl reeled from a blow, feebly tried to bring up his maimed sword arm, and was dragged from his saddle by an attacker. The riderless horse reared, hooves slashing the air. Vivian turned both the ponies and tried to reach Duke William.

He motioned her to safety behind him at the same time he tried to wield the heavy broadsword with his weakened left hand. It was a gallant but hopeless gesture as the shadows closed in on them from all sides.

They were caught, trapped by the buildings butted together by common walls, and with no hope of escape. Montfort's warhorse screamed in pain as it took a sword in the neck and fell to the street amid jostling horses and slashing hooves. Sir Galant defended against one attacker while another moved at his back. The Norman soldiers were better trained but horribly outnumbered. Without help, death was certain.

Again, Vivian was seized by the horrible anguish of divided loyalties. She was Saxon. The Norman soldiers and Duke William were her enemies. They'd already killed countless numbers of innocent Saxon men, women, and children, and yet there was a certainty that went beyond the circumstance of her birth.

She had seen it in her vision—a creature born in fire and blood spreading its wings across the land.

The end of all Saxon England had already been written. There was nothing she or anyone could do to prevent it. Now, the Saxons had no leader. Poladouras had long spoken with dread of the consequences if young Edgar should eventually be named regent, for he was but a child and sickly, incapable of protecting England against the invading hordes that would no doubt come as they had for centuries before the Saxons.

She knew William to be a good and just man, and a strong, decisive leader. He must not die.

Amidst the sound of battle, Vivian heard a heavily accented Saxon war cry, "Kill the Norman bastard! Kill them all!" and she knew that she must protect William.

"Heed me, powerful one," she whispered, and with bowed head turned her thoughts inward to that place of visions and ancient dreams, and summoned the power of the Light.

Within her thoughts she imagined the buildings, the street, the soldiers and their attackers, the images forming strong and clear as if they existed there within her mind. She saw them fighting, struggling, falling, and dying as the Saxons closed in on them.

Spreading her hands before her, she spoke the ancient words.

"Element of fire, spirit of light"—she threw back her head, eyes tightly closed as she flung her arms wide—*"Essence of life, set ablaze the night!"*

Thirteen

The explosion filled the night sky with fiery light. Rorke shuddered. He had seen such intense light many times over the past two days when buildings were set afire, some by accident, others in foolish protest by the owners over the presence of Norman invaders in London.

It seemed as if the inhabitants of London were intent on burning the city to the ground if need be to deny it to the Norman captors.

Most of the fires had been put out, or left to burn themselves out in buildings set apart from others and posing no further threat. But this fire was a fireball that exploded. It cast city rooftops into sharp relief against the night sky, and from a part of the city that made his blood run cold in his veins. For it was the route William was to enter the city.

For several days, since entering the city, the deception had worked. Duke William was *seen* all about London, hale and hearty, leading his troops in full battle regalia, his standards flying high for all of London to see and know that they had been conquered.

It was a psychological strategy in a deadly game they couldn't afford to lose. For if any guessed that only weeks before William had lain near death and was still too weak to lead his army, the Saxons would no doubt have struck with renewed fervor.

The timing was now perfect for William to enter the city in secrecy and take his rightful place. He was due to take up residence in the tower fort, official residence of the king, and meet with the council of Saxon barons in two days. Everything hung in the balance. If William were injured or perhaps killed, all would be lost.

Rorke shouted orders to his men, commandeering them from their different posts. The Bishop rode with them, his expression betraying nothing of his inner thoughts. Their number grew as they rode hard through the littered and abandoned streets toward the North bridge. All rode with battle swords and lances drawn, archers with arrows ready at their bows, for Rorke expected the worst.

They drew up at the end of the street at the carnage that met their eyes.

The attack had been at the center of the street where there was no hope for escape. Saxon insurgents had come from both ends of the street, effectively cutting off any retreat or advance. The battle had been grim, like too many he had seen before on

countless fields across the whole of Normandy, France, and the
rest of Europe and the Byzantine Empire.

He had long held the belief that what a poorly armed soldier
lacked in weaponry he more than made up with in fervor of
defending his hearth and home. There was a sort of frenzied
passion in fighting for one's entire existence that went beyond
the prowess of a trained soldier, making such a man a fierce
adversary. The Saxons had been such fierce adversaries, giving
no quarter, showing no mercy.

He counted at least a dozen dead Norman soldiers and knew
there would be more as they took assessment. Among them was
an equal number of fallen Saxons, forming a ring of bodies
around the core of William's escort. There the Norman soldiers
and Rorke's own knights had made a last, defiant stand, forming
a wall, four men deep all around, to protect Duke William. In
a precise circle between the fallen Saxons and the inner circle
of defending Norman soldiers who still stood or were astride,
was a ring of small, dying fires like flaming jewels strung on
a necklace.

Most of the insurgents had fled, abandoning their attack,
weapons thrown down as though fleeing some terrifying, un-
godly force. A few remained, refusing to yield. Rorke's men
charged into the battle, their warhorses flinging aside Saxon
attackers as he drove to the heart of the tightly fortified core of
William's soldiers.

He told himself it was William that he sought among the
sword-wielding soldiers, that if William fell, all of England
would be lost. But in truth, his thoughts were filled with visions
of that fiery explosion and another sweet fire that he sought—
the fiery satin of long, brilliant hair, a slender form, and eyes
as blue as the heart of a flame. For he knew Vivian would be
with William.

An unexpected fear locked around his heart and clenched at
his vitals as he searched for sight of her, determined to find her
as the same time dreading what he might find. When had she
become so important to him? From the beginning, the answer

came effortlessly, sliding along his senses, reminding him in flashes of memory of all the ways—the curve of her smile, the fire that leapt so easily into her eyes when defending someone she was loyal to, or the sweet torment of her taste.

It wasn't enough! he thought with a fierce rage of anger. For the first time in his life someone else mattered, and the short time they'd shared, was not enough.

He frantically urged his warhorse forward, the animal hastily stepping over a Saxon who lay facedown, sword in hand. He'd died from sword wounds, but his face and hands were oddly blackened with soot, as though he'd ventured too near a fire.

Norman lances were quickly lowered, swords returned to their sheaths, arrows unnotched from bows. Gavin charged forward from amidst the tightly defended coterie of soldiers that surrounded William, greeting Rorke with a grim nod.

"We were attacked. They came from all sides"—Gavin gestured to the doors and windows—"and from the buildings and rooftops."

Rorke quickly gave orders and soldiers swarmed from their mounts and into the buildings. There were loud screams and shouts of protest as they began a systematic search for Saxon attackers.

"The duke of Normandy?" he anxiously inquired. Again there was a grim nod, this time edged with satisfaction.

"I am well enough!" William shouted as the soldiers parted around him. "But we were sorely pressed to defend ourselves and might have perished if not for that ring of fire you set upon them."

"Vivian?" All his desperate rage formed in the sound of her name as he looked past William to the shadow that moved at his side—a much smaller pony dwarfed by the massive warhorses, and the slender figure that sat astride.

She was wrapped in his heavy black mantle, the soft white fur framing the brilliant flame of her hair. Her eyes were wide and luminous, as if they possessed a fire of their own, and set in the pale heart shape of her face.

As instinctive as breathing, Rorke reached for Vivian, pulling her from atop the pony into the saddle before him. Her slender hands closed over his forearm as though she were holding on for her life.

The chain mail that bound his forearm scraped Vivian's fingertips raw as she clung to him as though he were the calm center in the middle of a storm, a safe haven when all about her was chaos. She leaned heavily against him as though seized by a sudden weakness. Nearby, Mally slumped wearily astride her pony, her eyes wide with fear at what had just passed.

In a gesture that was both rough and tender, and filled with urgency, Rorke shoved the fur-lined hood back from Vivian's head, his large hand going back possessively through her hair.

"You are unharmed?" he asked gruffly and with a harshness she'd heard dozens of times before when giving orders to his men. Now he spoke with a dangerous intensity that reached deep into her soul with a new depth of awareness, as though something predestined had passed between them. Her gaze locked with his.

"Aye, milord," she whispered, for she could not trust her voice, when strange, inexplicable feelings burned through her at the simple touch of his hand in her hair.

"Those who can ride have been given horses," Tarek informed Rorke as he rode up. "The more severely injured will be carried on litters. It is best we leave this place as soon as possible."

"Aye," Rorke acknowledged, with a grim look over the top of her head. "An open field rather than a forest, my friend? This time I am inclined to agree with you." He turned and gave orders to his knights.

"Bring whatever prisoners have been taken." His cold gray eyes narrowed. "I would ask them questions about the attack, since William's route of entry was known only to a handful."

Tarek nodded grimly. "We must consider that we have a traitor in our midst."

Rorke agreed and said with low voice, "But for now, it is important that William reaches the fortress safely. Then we will see about ferreting out this traitor. For now, nothing to anyone." He turned to William.

"Can you ride, milord?"

"Well enough to show these Saxons that I am not easily slain."

"The fortress has been made ready, milord."

What had once been King Harold's royal residence—a series of sprawling stone and wood residences linked by corridors and a small central court—had been turned into an armed fortress surrounded by a stout wall of heavy timber. The timber was fresh-cut and smelled strongly of forest pine, runnels of sap glistening in the light of torches as the riders passed through a massive lowered gate across a causeway.

Vivian shivered as they passed through the first set of gates and then a second set of iron gates, her senses assaulted by myriad images and impressions. The attack in the streets had been a portent of the danger that surrounded them—a danger she felt even more intensely inside those stout walls that had been erected in preparation for William's arrival in the city.

Though apparently uninjured, the attack had nevertheless taken its toll on William's meager strength. His shoulders sagged beneath the weight of the cumbersome chain mail. Yet, as they rode through the gates, he sat taller in the saddle, straightened his wide shoulders, and looked very much the conqueror come to claim his throne for all to see.

As they rode into the dirt courtyard a group of a half dozen men stood on the steps awaiting their arrival. By their manner of dress—richer by far than any she had before seen, yet distinctly different in style from the Norman battle armor—Vivian realized they were Saxon nobility. A small contingent of the Saxon council that had negotiated for peace days earlier had no doubt come to greet Duke William of Normandy, albeit reluctantly.

One, dressed in the elaborate headpiece and robes of the Church, with an ornate gold cross worn on a massive gold chain about his shoulders and with gold scepter, came down the steps of the royal residence toward them.

Rorke swung down from the tall warhorse and reached up for Vivian. "Say nothing," he warned in a tense low voice.

She felt his tension in the crushing strength of his fingers clamped around her upper arm.

The entire royal guard, all Rorke's knights and soldiers, had dismounted, but still William sat astride. Even with the enormous will of self-control that he possessed, Rorke's fingers gently bruised as they waited.

Neither he nor any of his men made any attempt to assist William, as they had when he had mounted the warhorse for the ride into London. Vivian realized it was of utmost importance that he do this alone as the deception concerning his complete return to good health was carried out.

It was possible that Saxon soldiers had seen him struck down at the Battle of Hastings. They would most naturally have carried that story far and wide, including to London, in the vain hope that the Norman invaders might yet be put down with either the loss or grievous injury of their commander.

It was now of paramount importance, Vivian realized, that the Saxon earls, any Saxon loyalists who remained within the royal enclosure, indeed all of London bear witness to William's physical prowess as a soldier and his ability to rule without question as to his health. Even she felt herself holding her breath in anticipation. She should not have doubted the outcome.

More than once, in their countless conversations, she had glimpsed that indomitable strength of will, the sheer forcefulness of William's personality and his determination to claim the English throne. He had come this far. The few steps necessary to claim officially what he had staked his life and fortunes to claim would not deter him now.

With that powerful, enigmatic presence that she had seen on so many occasions the past few weeks, William pushed back the nose plate of his steel helm with an impatient gesture. She sensed the enormous strength of will it required just for him to remain upright, yet his expression betrayed nothing of that battle or his pain.

His features were grimly set, amber eyes narrowed with what appeared to be critical assessment though she knew, in truth, it was pain. His mouth was taut, also with pain, yet the sum of his expression conveyed not pain but a resolute strength and ferocity that roused even her grudging respect. And the time that he lingered in the saddle only heightened the anticipation rather than raising any doubts of his physical prowess.

He seemed to take inventory of all that surrounded him, including the Saxon earls and the man with the golden scepter who had begun to fidget noticeably beneath his heavy robes.

"Milord," the berobed man greeted him, with a faint bow of his head. "May I present the royal council."

This was spoken clearly for all to hear, in English, and Vivian was aware of the faint mockery that underlay the man's tone. The choice of English for their solicitude was also a mockery. They assumed, she realized, that William was ignorant of their language and sought to publicly humiliate him—the Norman Conqueror who could not even speak the language of the people he had conquered.

"In due time, Archbishop," William responded in clear, precise English that immediately caused a shuffling of surprise and discomfort among the council members. They realized not only had they been misinformed by the archbishop of Canterbury, who had yielded the city of Canterbury but also campaigned for surrender, as to the health of Duke William. They'd been made fools in their attempt to humiliate a man they considered to be low and common.

He was neither low nor common, nor ignorant of their language or strategies. The archbishop of Canterbury could only smile weakly, his expression a mask of anxious uncertainty and chagrin that he had perhaps made more than one grievous error.

Eventually, William pulled off his gauntlets, drawing out the tension as he kept everyone waiting, while silently gathering what little strength he had left.

"I would reward you most heartily for the greeting I received upon entering London," he commented sharply and with obvious meaning. Vivian heard a hastily stifled cough from one of the barons, as though he were seized by a sudden malady, and wondered what the man might know of the attack.

William handed the reins and gauntlets to a squire who had magically appeared at his side. Even more magically, he had taken on the oversize, stalwart proportions of one of Rorke's knights rather than one of William's personal attendants, who were of somewhat smaller stature.

No doubt the *squire's* assistance was meant to disguise any infirmity on William's part when he dismounted—a helping hand lest William should fall from weakness. But he waved all such assistance aside, his gaze hard and purposeful, the sharp look of one who knows all too well what is expected of him, as he swung a leg over the warhorse and dismounted.

Vivian held her breath as he lowered his substantial weight— even after the wasting fevers that had racked his body—down onto the barely mended leg that she had carefully set and repaired.

There was only a faint betrayal of the enormous pain she knew he must feel in the sudden flinch in his eyes that no doubt seemed a grimace of barely suppressed disapproval of the Saxon nobles, who also waited with held breath in anticipation of William the Conqueror, whose cunning, forthright manner, and rumored brutality had preceded him.

"There will be time for meetings later," he informed them in a strong voice, clearly establishing his authority.

"Tonight there are other strategies to be planned, and inspection of the royal apartments. I would have everything in readiness for the queen's arrival. I will meet with you accordingly."

Then, gathering what little strength remained, he mounted the steps, with Rorke and his guard surrounding him, and swept past the astonished Saxon barons and the archbishop.

Inside the royal residence with the archbishop and barons left to trail behind like farmyard chickens pecking about for pieces of grain, William strode to the center of court with all the authority of a king.

"Your private apartments are in readiness." Rorke strode quickly forward. "Perhaps you would care for some food and drink?"

"Aye, that I would," William replied with all the gusto of a man who possessed an ample appetite, rather than one who had subsisted on meager broth the past several weeks. His large hand was pressed against the front of his mail hauberk as if hunger gnawed from the inside out.

"You will accompany me," he told Rorke, in what must seem a customary order of a king to his knight.

With a curt nod, Rorke led the way across the small inner court with its raised dais newly relieved of Harold's royal pendants. William's own standard, that Rorke had carried into the city, had been set beside the throne, symbolic of the warrior king who now claimed the throne.

Gavin and Sir Galant accompanied William, one on either side, their voluminous, heavy mantles concealing the supporting arms they placed about their king as he turned his back on the Saxon barons and the archbishop and sought the private royal chambers. Vivian felt Tarek's hand tug gently at her arm.

"You will be needed," he said with lowered voice, and escorted her with the others. Mally followed closely behind her, carrying her pouch of medicinal herbs.

Inside the private royal chamber, all was in readiness for William's arrival. In lieu of William's guard, which had not yet arrived from the Norman encampment, Rorke's personal guards stood heavily armed on both sides of the entrance.

Once the door was closed behind them and barred against

any unexpected intrusions, the extraordinary performance she'd watched with growing admiration abruptly ended.

His strength gone, driven by sheer force of will, William sagged with exhaustion and would have fallen to the floor if Rorke's men hadn't supported him.

"Bring him to the bed," Rorke ordered. "And then remove his battle armor." He turned to look for Vivian, but she was already beside the bed, efficient fingers quickly unbuckling the cumbersome hauberk.

William cursed. "I am well enough!"

"You are not well enough," Vivian informed him. "You are bleeding and quite heavily. The wound in your shoulder has reopened."

"Do you mean to heal me or slay me?" William grumbled as she roughly jerked open the front of his padded undershirt even before the mail hauberk was lifted clear of his shoulders, to reveal for all to see that indeed the wound had reopened, undoubtedly during the attack in the street.

" 'Tis a question that would require some consideration before answering," she answered without the least trepidation.

"Healed you have a penchant for doing yourself more harm. Were I to choose the other, I would be relieved of constantly mending your rents and tears." There was a grunt of disapproval at her bold comment from the bishop who had accompanied them into the chamber. But William merely laughed.

"Thank God, you are at least honest in your dislike of me. I cannot abide simpering, weak-blooded maids. You will like my Matilda. You are much alike in many ways." He winced as she deliberately applied a square of bandage too firmly.

"I do not dislike you, milord," she replied with complete honesty. "I merely dislike what you have done to England, and it would be far safer for my neck, milord, if I am able to greet your wife with her husband's improved progress and return to good health, rather than bearing news of his stubbornness and illness."

"She is well acquainted with my stubbornness."

"Aye," Vivian commented. "I can well imagine." She quickly gave orders to everyone, including Rorke, for the preparation of a steaming pot, fire at the hearth, clean linens, and some of the French wine William was so fond of.

"You would make a formidable general," William commented with a weak smile.

"I have no ambition to lead an army, milord," she responded, aware of the oddly amused look Rorke flashed her. "I have no use for battles or wars."

"And yet you waged a fierce battle to save my life these past weeks," William commented. "Why is that?"

"Because I was taken prisoner and forced under threat of death to those I love," she answered, offering him the wine.

"I think there is none who might force you, no matter the sword they held against you." He drank the wine but refused the soothing powder she offered to aid his sleeping.

"I must remain alert," he explained. He grunted from pain as she applied the poultice with healing salve and snugged it tightly into place to stop the seepage of the wound. "The pain will assure that I remain alert."

"You should rest," Vivian said with a firmness of authority.

"There are matters which must be discussed," the bishop insisted, moving near the bed.

"They will be of little importance if he succumbs from his wounds," Vivian pointed out. The bishop glared at her. But she refused to cower or leave.

"Several of your men were injured in the attack," she explained to William, "including Sir Guy. With your permission, I would see to their wounds."

"By all means, mistress," William nodded. "I would not deny my soldiers and knights what has so magically aided in my recovery. In the meantime I shall rest. I find that I am quite weary from the day's events."

When the bishop obviously would have pressed for an audience, Rorke interceded.

"There is nothing that cannot wait until the morrow," he told the angry bishop. "The hour is late. To all outward appearances William but retires to eat and sleep. Surely you would not deny him much-needed rest."

"You overstep yourself, FitzWarren," the bishop spat angrily. "One might think that you aspire to be king of England."

"And you, sir Bishop," Rorke countered, his eyes as cold as winter ice. "To what heights do you aspire?"

Fourteen

There was only silence in the chamber at the bold and reckless accusations that had been made.

Vivian shivered at the animosity that leapt between the two men in Rorke's suddenly tense stance and the bishop's furious gaze. Rorke's hand had gone to the handle of his broadsword and with a sudden terror she realized that if provoked, he would not hesitate to draw it.

"There are none who doubt the effectiveness of her skills," Rorke said with dangerous warning.

"Would you offer yourself so eagerly to her care, milord?" the count snarled.

"I have," Rorke informed him coldly. "And I found nothing lacking in her care."

"Nor her bed?" the bishop added in a vicious tone, the expression on his face sharpening.

With sudden, brutal clarity, Vivian realized the bishop assumed Rorke had claimed her for his bed.

"Be careful what you say," Rorke warned. "I have no fear of striking down a bishop."

"Enough!" William ordered sharply. "I will hear no more of it!"

To Vivian, he said with a gruff gentleness, "I value your

skills and your kindness, mistress. Please see to the others who have need of your care." She nodded, grateful for the opportunity to leave.

To the others, William ordered, "Get out!" All but the bishop turned to leave. William reached a hand and touched Rorke's arm in the gesture of ease between friends.

"I would speak with you, alone" he said, dismissing his brother along with the others. The bishop nodded stiffly and flashed a furious look at Rorke.

"You have but to call, brother," he said with barely concealed anger, "and I will do your bidding."

"My bidding is that you leave," William said firmly but not unkindly.

When they had gone, he dropped any effort to disguise the pain that suffused every muscle and joint. His face was heavily lined with fatigue, his skin pale with the weakness that seemed to drag the flesh from his bones.

"You knew there would be an attack?" he questioned Rorke.

"I feared there might be," Rorke replied. "There is danger all about. There have been pockets of resistance continuously since we took the city."

"Can we hold the city?"

"London is yours," Rorke assured him. "We will hold it, no matter what the Saxon resistance."

"Who knew the route by which I entered the city?"

"Only a handful. Myself, Tarek al Sharif, Gavin, Montfort, and your brother."

"It is difficult to keep secrets when the walls have eyes and ears," William commented thoughtfully. "What Saxons remain within the royal fortress?"

"The Saxon council, several of the barons, the archbishop, all of whom seek an audience with you, and several royal retainers that I thought necessary to keep near for all to see as you take control. Also for their skill and knowledge in matters of Saxon rule."

William nodded his agreement. "Most necessary if we are

to wield control effectively over this foreign land. It is good that you had the foresight to ride out with your guard to the meeting point. We were outnumbered by our attackers and in such close confines would have been hard-pressed to fight them off. They might have accomplished what all of Harold's army could not." He sighed heavily as he drained his wine.

"The ring of fire was an effective weapon," William acknowledged. "I commend you on the tactic, for it proved effective."

"I would claim credit if it was my doing," Rorke admitted and then confessed, "but it was not. In all truthfulness, I cannot say how it occurred."

William's gaze narrowed thoughtfully. "Perhaps it was the doing of one of your men," he suggested. "They fought well. I owe my life to them."

"Aye," Rorke speculated, "perhaps." But he was of a different thought, for he had already questioned his men about it. They knew nothing of the cause, and he had no other answers.

Vivian finally finished binding the last of the wounds that had been suffered in the attack. Mally had accompanied her, fetching basins of fresh water and linen for bandages.

A half dozen soldiers had been killed in the attack, one had died after reaching the royal residence. The others would survive, including Sir Montfort, whose horse had been cut from under him.

Sir Guy had a deep gash on his head and several bruises to show for the encounter, which his brother, Gavin, jovially declared hardly more than what they'd suffered at each other's hands as children.

"He's got a very hard head." Gavin slapped his brother on the back. Sir Guy glared at him as he tenderly pressed fingers against his bandaged head as though to keep anything from seeping out.

"Our brother once was forced to get his attention with a tree stump. As you can see, he recovered very well from the encounter."

"Stay away from tree stumps and maces for the next few days," Vivian advised, and with a hidden smile, thought it might do him equally well to stay away from his brothers, for they were a rough and boisterous threesome given to challenging each other to wrestling and armed combat when boredom set in, as it had many times during their enforced encampment while waiting to enter London.

She looked up as two of Rorke's squires appeared. They were dressed not in the usual costume of leather breeches and tunic but in a simple fine costume bearing Rorke's red-and-gold colors.

She had become so accustomed to seeing soldiers about in full battle dress, with swords and lances at their sides, that their lack of either startled her. But they were not entirely defenseless, for she saw the slender blade in the leather scabbard that hung from their belts.

"I have been instructed to escort you to your sleeping quarters, mistress," one informed her. "Arrangements have been made for the girl to take a room off the kitchen pantry." When Vivian started to protest, he assured them both. "Milord FitzWarren has posted guards. Upon their arrival in the morn, she may transfer to Sir Gavin's household."

Vivian assured Mally. "You will be safe. I have his promise on it."

Mally nodded reluctantly. They bid each other good eve and Mally accompanied the young squire to her quarters near the pantry. Vivian sagged with fatigue as she followed Rorke's other squire.

Candles that had been lit had guttered low. The hall, earlier filled with throngs of soldiers and armed knights, was now all but empty except for guards positioned at each doorway and entrance.

She was so weary even the straw that covered the floor of the main hall seemed inviting, even though she suspected that

Harold's household staff was not in the habit of changing it often, nor obviously had Rorke's men thought to change it.

She recognized the corridor where he led her. It was the same corridor that led to the royal chamber where Duke William now slept, evidenced by the guards positioned outside his door. The squire opened the door onto a room immediately to the right of the royal chamber.

A heavy tapestry hung just inside the doorway across the coved entry that led into the chamber. Rorke's squire held it aside for her to enter.

The chamber was not overly large, but adequately furnished. A large raised bed stood against the far wall. Thick furs and fleece had been thrown across for warmth. More furs covered the stone floor, smothering the cold draft that swept about her ankles.

Logs had been added to the fire. A trestle table and two chairs sat before the hearth for the ease of warmth the fire offered. Heavy tapestries of various elaborate designs covered the walls to subdue the bone-chilling drafts inherent in all stone buildings. It made her think of the achingly cold mornings at the abbey when it seemed there were more holes than stones in the walls.

No matter how much she had stuffed and chinked the crevices, there were always new ones. And always drafts that made Poladouras' bones ache and caused Meg's joints to stiffen so that she could hardly move. But here every simple comfort had been seen to.

A chain mail hauberk lay across a large trunk that had been set against the sidewall. The contents of a decanter shimmered deep ruby red at the table, where a platter of fresh fruit, cheese, bread, and several portions of cold, sliced fowl had been laid out. Her stomach grumbled loudly.

The last three days all seemed to blend together in a blur and she couldn't recall when she had last eaten or slept. She was exhausted, cold, and hungry. Both the food and the bed beckoned with equal appeal.

She frowned as she stood back and looked at the bold pattern woven into one of the tapestries—a figure of a golden bird set in stark relief against a blood red background, rising from a fiery bed of flames. The red and gold threads of the fringe played through her fingers, wrapping around them with satin warmth, as though warm fingers entwined with hers, gently holding on, caressing, stroking each finger, recalling with startling clarity the touch of Rorke's hand.

She jerked her hand back at the forbidden feelings that remembered touch roused deep inside her, a different sort of hunger growing low in her belly.

Stepping back from the tapestry and that fierce, predatory, almost sensual creature, Vivian demanded of Rorke's squire, "Whose chamber is this?"

"It is mine."

Vivian whirled around at the sound of the voice that echoed the dangerous power of that fierce creature wrapped in the sensual heat of warm satin. Not his squire, but Rorke FitzWarren himself.

"Yours?" she asked incredulously. "But surely there must be some mistake. I cannot stay here." She looked about for his squire to tell him that some other arrangement must be made.

"There is no mistake," Rorke assured her as he crossed to the table, seized the carafe, and poured wine into both goblets.

"I took this chamber for my own when we first arrived in London." He pushed one of the goblets across the table toward her.

She shook her head, pressing fingers against the dull ache at her forehead that had set in from too little food and no sleep. "Your squire indicated that I was to sleep here." She stared at him puzzled.

"Aye, he was following my orders."

She winced as the pain intensified and she realized it was

neither lack of food or sleep that was the cause, but a vague warning that drifted across her senses.

"That is impossible. I cannot," Vivian protested. "I will not stay here. Surely there is another place. The scullery, the armory, or the mews." Gavin had told her that was where Aquila would be taken. Yes, of course. That was it. A simple solution. She would sleep in the mews.

But Rorke FitzWarren shook his head adamantly. "It is out of the question. William still has need of your skills. He is much weaker and his condition less improved than he would have anyone believe."

Vivian had worried that his exertions might reopen the wounds that had very nearly taken his life only a few weeks earlier. She more than anyone knew he still had not returned to the robust strength that was so inherently a part of his character.

"And no one must know of his weakened condition," Rorke continued with a grim-set expression that emphasized his haggard features. She knew that he must be as exhausted as she.

"The barons remain inside these walls. In due course, William will be meeting with them to carry out the transfer of power. No one," and he repeated emphatically, *"No one,* must suspect he is anything less than in perfect health and fully capable of carrying out his duties as king."

"If the barons or the archbishop of Canterbury were to guess that he lay near death but a handful of weeks ago and that his health is still precarious, it would guarantee renewed insurrection among the Saxons, and . . . more bloodshed."

There it was again, that subtle but unmistakable threat of more Saxon deaths.

"If you were to make daily visits to his private chamber," he continued, "they might become suspicious." He gestured to one of the tapestry panels that covered the eastern wall.

"There is a doorway beneath that tapestry that leads directly to William's chamber. I can enter to discuss matters of import whenever it might be necessary without requiring his presence at court in full battle armor. You may enter whenever there is a need to administer your potions or change the bandages. And none will be the wiser for it."

"But it will seem to them as though . . ." her voice trailed off with the sudden tightness at her throat.

"As though we are lovers?" he asked coolly. "It has also been said that you are Saxon and cannot be trusted, that you would bring harm to the duke, and yet you give no import to these things."

"There is a difference," she argued helplessly, knowing the argument was already lost as in everything that had been lost to her the past weeks.

"I think the difference lies only in the truth or falsehood of such matters," he suggested.

"Are you not concerned what Judith de Marque will think?" she inquired.

"Judith de Marque knows her place, and the consequences if she goes beyond herself," he replied. "The matter is settled, Vivian."

"Very well," she said, too tired to argue the matter further with him. She crossed toward the hearth, gathering thick furs and fleece-lined rugs. She laid them before the warmth of the fire.

"You may take the bed," he told her when he saw her intent. "Any sleep I get this night I will take with my men."

"The floor shall suffice," she informed him, determined to set physical boundaries between them.

Though they had slept close before, on the journey from Amesbury, even using the same pallet and wrapped in thick furs, the very notion of walls closing them in together rather than the forest or an open field created an intimacy that was far too disconcerting.

"It is not so hard or cold as the ground." Turning her back on that equally disconcerting gray gaze, she laid the furs across the stone floor before the hearth, making a thick pallet for a bed.

"There is another matter I would discuss with you."

"Can it not wait until the morrow?" she sighed wearily.

"Nay, it cannot."

He crossed to the hearth, his tall presence making her feel small and vulnerable. He handed her a goblet of wine.

"Drink it. It will help you to sleep."

"I need no elixir to aid my sleep. I assure you I shall be oblivious to anything within moments of retiring." She couldn't have been more obvious in wanting him to leave than if she had asked him outright.

"Drink it," he commanded.

She took the goblet and sipped carefully. She'd tasted the ale that Poladouras was so fond of, but this was her first taste of wine. With only her previous experience of the bitter ale, she was pleasantly surprised by the warm, lusty sweetness of the dark red wine that hinted of some other tangy taste and an exotic hint of spice.

"It is mulled wine," he explained, "particularly soothing when one is very tired."

She took another sip and found the pleasure increased as the warmed wine with mysterious flavors both bold and subtle spread to her arms and legs, and fingers and toes, filling her with a wonderful lethargy. It didn't dull her senses as she knew it did with some, but instead heightened them.

The chamber took on a rich, golden glow. The colors in the tapestries at the walls seemed much darker and vibrant, as if they had come to life. Beneath her fingertips, which rested on the edge of the table, she could feel each grain of wood, the diagonal of a scar etched in the surface, and the soft satin of edges worn smooth.

"William and I spoke of the attack in the street," he said over the rim of his own goblet and it seemed that his voice was like warm satin, soothing as it wrapped about her senses.

"We spoke of the Saxons, the suddenness of the attack, the

location within those narrow streets that made any hope of escape impossible . . ."

She looked up at him, her gaze drawn by eyes as cold and gray as stone—like a wall she realized with sudden clarity—a stone wall that carefully protected his emotions, letting no one inside. And yet, she knew, there had been moments between them . . .

"You rode beside William," he continued. "And in the midst of battle when all seemed lost and you would all surely die, he distinctly recalls that you spoke strange Celtic words. Then there was suddenly a ring of fire all about."

She set the goblet down abruptly. It wobbled beneath her hand—a hand that was always so steady and sure when holding a surgical knife, cauterizing blade, or needle for closing wounds.

His hand closed over hers, steadying the goblet. He didn't immediately release her hand but instead turned her hand in his and studied it as though he possessed the powers of a conjurer and could divine some great truth from the patterns of delicately carved lines across smooth, supple skin.

"Where did the fire come from, Vivian?" he asked without looking up.

"There were fires all about," she stammered. "It was a sudden explosion is all. Perhaps one of Gavin's men . . ." she said, grasping for any possibility that might satisfy that sharp curiosity of his.

"Perhaps he made the fire appear out of his pocket?" he suggested as his fingers tightened about hers, and in a tone that suggested he did not believe it. "I inquired. All were as mystified as William at the appearance of that ring of fire, although extremely grateful. It turned the tide of the battle." He studied her carefully. "All would have been lost if not for the fire."

"Perhaps it was contrived among the Saxons as part of their trap," she suggested, trying to free her hand. She felt naked, exposed, trapped like a falcon tethered by golden jesses that can only fly the length of those rich chains.

"According to Tarek, the Jehara possess great powers," he continued, "the powers of light and darkness, earth, wind, and fire . . . the power to transform themselves into anything they desire . . ."

"I thought you did not believe in such things." Her voice was hushed with fear that he knew.

"I believe there are many things between Heaven and earth that cannot be explained." As he spoke, those strong fingers dug gently into her wrist, leaving pale white indentations. She laughed softly in spite of the fear that twisted deep inside her— fear of the cold, warrior's brutality that she knew him more than capable of, fear that it was not really the brutality but some other equally terrifying passion, and, finally, fear of her own vulnerability to that passion.

"If I possessed such powers, would it not be a simple thing to transform myself and escape the danger, and then escape from your men and return to Amesbury at my choosing?" she asked, forcing herself to calmness.

"Aye," he replied thoughtfully, the expression behind that implacable gray gaze shifting, growing darker with some new thought. "So it would seem."

"As I am still your prisoner, it would seem, then, that Tarek is mistaken." She kept her voice even, uncertainty disguised by a logic that could not be denied at the same time her heart pounded fiercely.

"I cannot tell you where the fire came from," she added truthfully. "Perhaps," she suggested, becoming desperate, "what Sir William heard were my simple prayers."

He sighed almost as in defeat. His fingers finally loosened about her wrist.

"I am very weary," she said, without looking up. She dare not, terrified he would see that she had not told him the complete truth, more terrified that he would see another truth—the truth of her wild, chaotic feelings at his simplest touch.

"I would like to sleep now," she whispered. "There are few enough hours left in the night, and William will have need of me when he awakens."

"You need not sleep on the floor," he said with that roughness of voice that she felt along every nerve ending like a fire of passion. "You will take the bed. It will be very late when I retire for the night, if at all. I will have no use for the bed."

"You are most generous, milord, but I cannot," she protested.

"What are you afraid of?" he asked, coming to stand before her, so close that she could smell his special scent as though she had known it all her life—the richness of leather, laced with the essence of night mist, earth, and wind, with the tang of strong male sweat. It moved across her senses with an intoxicating and terrifying power.

"I am afraid of nothing," she answered defiantly. Her gaze fastened on a place below his chin instead of meeting that penetrating gray gaze. She quickly discovered the inherent danger in her choice as she stared at the strong pulse that beat low at his throat. In a panic, she lowered her gaze farther still and concentrated on the stitchwork of his leather tunic.

Though she could not see it, she could feel the strong pulse that beat like a fire in the blood that moved through his veins, felt it as surely as if it flowed through her own.

"You are like the untrained falcon," he said, the sudden gentleness of his voice surprising her so that she suddenly did look up and made the mistake of meeting that compelling gaze.

His fingers gently held her chin. She could have pulled away, but she did not. Something much stronger than fear immobilized her—like the falcon fascinated at the sensations that poured through her.

"Intelligent, beautiful, wise in so many ways," he said softly, "yet wild and untamed." His hand lowered then, his fingers touching her at precisely the same place on her throat where she had stared at the pulse in his. As though he knew her every thought.

"Ready to fly the unknown hand." His fingers stroked the

small hollow at the base of her throat and then across the ridge of bone, her skin shivering at his touch.

"Yet always lured by the treasure that may be found there."

Fifteen

Vivian took William his late afternoon herbal tisane. It helped ease the discomfort he still suffered from his wounds.

In the weeks that followed their arrival in London, she rose long before anyone else each morning to prepare the herbal medicines for Duke William of Normandy.

William had brought his own cook from Normandy and quickly installed her in the kitchen previously occupied by Harold's cooks and servants. The woman was amiable and made a place for Vivian to prepare her medicines. Mally often joined her there, and the cook quickly took the girl under her care, putting her to work with the other serving girls.

This afternoon she had happily been making tarts, setting aside one for Justin. Vivian had quickly made the steaming tisane and returned to William's chamber through the door that adjoined it to Rorke's.

Now, William sat wearily in a large chair, his squire massaging his sword arm. Deep circles lined his eyes above gaunt cheeks, making him look haggard.

Within days of their arrival in London William began holding daily court to dispel any possible rumors about his health. He met each day with the Saxon earls and barons, the English archbishops, and his own leaders as he took steps to establish the framework for the transition toward Norman rule over Saxon England. He discussed important matters now with his brother, Rorke, Tarek, and his other knights.

She listened tentatively as they spoke, pouring the tisane into his wine, then busily preparing the poultices for the wounds that still slowly healed.

"What say you, mistress?" William startled her by asking. "Should a London merchant be levied by the crown on goods in his shop, or only upon a sale to a customer?"

Vivian looked around uncertainly and saw that all gazes had turned to her. All that is, except one. The bishop seemingly frowned over his goblet of wine, but she sensed the true cause—his growing resentment of her.

"I know little of these matters, milord," she said by way of an excuse.

"But surely you have an opinion about such things." William snorted. "Everyone else has one."

She glanced at Rorke, and he nodded his encouragement for her to speak.

"It would seem, milord," she suggested hesitantly, giving great consideration to the weighty matter, for it effected her people, "that if you levy the merchant before sales are made, he might soon be out of business. If he is out of business how then are you to collect the levy? Methinks, 'tis better to nibble at the turnip than try to squeeze blood from it."

William studied her intently. "I see the logic in what you say. I will consider it. And what of the lands held by Saxon earls and barons?" His gaze sharpened, for all knew where her loyalties lay. "I have promised certain rewards to my own knights and barons. Promises must be kept, mistress, or I may not hold England at all."

She wished that he had not asked it, for if she spoke in favor of his plan it would be seen that she betrayed her own people. If she spoke out against it, William might take offense, for he could not go back on his word.

"Nor can you long hold it if there is constant rebellion," she pointed out and nearby heard an exclamation of anger at her honesty. William raised his hand for silence.

"Continue. I would hear what you have to say."

Again she looked at Rorke. His expression was bemused, his

mouth curving into a smile at one corner which he hid behind his goblet as he drank from it. But his gaze found hers over the rim and in it she saw a fierce strength of pride.

"A great many men died at Hastings," she began, choosing her words carefully. "Their widows and children cry for them. But rather than throwing them off the land of their ancestors, it might be more logical to bind them to you at the same time you allow them to stay on their land."

"Go on," he said carefully, sipping the tisane of medicine.

She had given the matter some thought, for she had heard the saxons and earls grumbling about the hall, and knew they feared all might be lost. Their mood was dangerous and fearful. Such led to war. What, then, might avert war? she had wondered silently as she had heard Rorke speak of the dilemma.

"Have you given thought, milord, to marrying those of your men who are acceptable with these widowed Saxon baronesses? You would thereby guarantee the Saxon tie to the land at the same time creating a bond to the Norman nobility that may not be broken."

William's gaze narrowed thoughtfully as he stared at her. "Aye," he considered. "Conquer by marriage and birth what might otherwise be conquered only by death."

"It would seem a way to appease both."

William's hand slammed down on the arm of his chair. He roared with laughter.

"By God, I should like very much to meet this monk who taught you so well. You have a logic that sees to the heart of difficult matters and offers a solution to all arguments." He smiled at her graciously. "Thank you, Vivian."

"Aye, milord." She quickly gathered her herbal potions and left, for she sensed the bishop's animosity while the others had listened attentively. She returned to the adjacent chamber and was startled when Rorke followed her. He caught her at the doorway behind the tapestry that covered the entrance. His warm hand closed gently over hers, preventing her escape.

"Was there something you wanted, milord?" she asked hesitantly, far more unnerved by the touch of his hand—gentle yet possessive—than she had by anything William asked, or the bishop's steely scrutiny.

"Aye," he said, his voice low almost to a whisper and as dangerous to her senses as his touch. "There is much that I want."

Vivian shivered as fire spiraled inside her. Those few words seemed to hold a portent of so much more. She gasped softly at the sudden contact of his hand at her cheek, his rough, callused fingers inexplicably tender, recalling memories of other ways he'd touched her at the same time it created wild imaginings of other places that longed for his touch.

"I want," he began gruffly, and then continued, "to thank you for your honesty. There are many things you might have said. Many foolish things that others would have said. For that I thank you."

Shaken by his touch, unable to say anything more, much less think it, she said, as she stepped away from him, "You are welcome, milord."

With so many armed Norman guards about, Vivian was given a great deal more freedom in London. She was aware of the speculative glances that fell her way and the rumors that were whispered in the main hall, for it was soon known that she had the ear of William.

For that reason she avoided the central hall where William held court, so that she might avoid those speculative glances and sly whispers. But on this particular morning she had the misfortune to encounter Lady Hertford in the passage outside the central hall. It almost seemed as if the woman was waiting for her.

Lady Hertford was a dour, pinch-faced woman whose family had once possessed vast estates. Now she had been reduced to penury, her estates confiscated by the man she secretly called the Norman bastard.

She had been widowed in the Battle of Hastings. Now her only hope of salvaging her family estates was for her to make an opportunistic marriage among the Norman nobles whom she disdained as nothing better than drunken peasants.

"I would have a word with you," Lady Hertford announced in a tone that suggested it was of necessity rather than personal choice, since it was assumed the *mistress* of Rorke FitzWarren might enjoy a certain influence at the Norman court.

"You seem to have a certain . . . *favor* with the Normans," the haughty woman began, choosing her words carefully. "I have waited three days for an audience and can wait no more. You will arrange for me to meet with him."

Vivian was taken aback by the woman's boldness. "I am sorry, madam," she politely refused, trying to hide her aggravation. "But I cannot." Then she excused herself and made to step past Lady Hertford. Vivian was grabbed by the arm and pulled around.

"Perhaps you did not understand," Lady Hertford said in a barely civilized tone Vivian was certain she reserved for her servants.

"You *will* arrange a meeting for me with the duke of Normandy immediately. My late husband was Lord Hertford, a man of considerable influence and wealth. I demand an audience to discuss matters of import." Her voice quivered with anger. "I will not be pawned off on some Norman barbarian as I have heard of others."

"It is you who do not understand," Vivian attempted to explain with civility, struggling with her own anger and humiliation at being treated so cruelly. "I cannot arrange it. I have no authority at William's court." Then, she coolly demanded, "Let go of my arm."

Lady Hertford's fingers tightened. "I am not used to being dismissed, and certainly not by a Saxon peasant who whores herself to that Norman bastard, FitzWarren!" She finally let go of Vivian with a vicious pinch.

"You will do as I say," she informed Vivian. "And you will learn proper obedience." Then her eyes gleamed as she looked down at a slop basin that had not yet been removed from the night before and sat against the wall. She kicked it over, the contents sloshing across the floor. If Vivian had not quickly stepped back, it would no doubt have splashed her slippers and the hem of her gown. Lady Hertford was undaunted.

"You will clean all of this, Saxon bitch," Lady Hertford snapped. "And when you are finished, then you will do as I say."

"Good morn, demoiselle. Is something amiss?"

The sound of Rorke's voice brought Vivian's head around with a snap. Humiliation burned across her cheeks.

"Naught is amiss," she said, hoping to convince him of it before he saw just what damage had been done. Pain tightened at her chest at the woman's cruelty, for they were both Saxon. Yet, as Vivian sadly realized, she was not looked upon as such. She was considered the enemy in her own homeland. Then she saw the dangerous expression on Rorke's face that belied his casual greeting.

In the past weeks he had grown impatient with the Saxons' whining and wheedling about the fortunes lost in Harold's futile campaign against William, as if they expected William to give restitution for their losses.

Though Vivian had no fondness for Lady Hertford, she still felt sympathy for her. Her entire way of life had ended with the death of her husband and Harold's defeat, her life reduced to begging for favors.

"A spilt pail, nothing more," Vivian hastily explained, hoping to convince him of it. "I will clean it immediately." She bent to the task only to be stopped by the firm strength of his hand beneath her elbow, and she knew he was not convinced of it.

"You will not," Rorke stated decisively.

For a moment their gazes met in the flickering light of the torches that lined the walls of the passage. She saw neither pity nor ridicule, but a glimmer of anger that quickly shifted to an icy resolve as he turned to Lady Hertford.

"*You* will clean it, milady" Rorke informed her, and then explained precisely how it was to be done. "On your hands and knees with pail and brush. And when it is finished, then you will clean the entire hall."

He paused briefly to see if she would offer any objection. She might have if she had not been robbed of all breath, her face pale and pinched as though someone's hands were clamped about her throat.

"If you refuse," he continued in that silken voice that carried far more dangerous promise than any shouted threat, "I will have you stripped naked and chained to the wall of the main hall with the hunting dogs. Then we will see who is the Saxon bitch."

"You cannot order me to do this!" Lady Hertford gasped. "My husband was Lord Hertford."

"Your husband is dead," Rorke pointed out coldly, and then assured her, "and I shall order you about as I please."

With the toe of his boot, he kicked the basin toward Lady Hertford. It wobbled and then righted itself, precariously sloshing the remaining contents across the satin hem of her gown.

"Every stone of the floor in this hall is to be scrubbed," Rorke reminded her so that there would be no possibility of misunderstanding. "And when you are finished, I shall inspect every stone. If they are not clean as I have ordered, then you will begin again, and tonight you will sleep among the hounds."

With stories of Norman atrocities running rampant in the royal household—whether true or not, Lady Hertford trembled. Memory of stories of this particular Norman knight's cold brutality on the battlefield, reflected in her fearful eyes. She hastily nodded and bent to pick up the pail.

Rorke took Vivian gently by the arm and escorted her to the central hall.

"Are you all right, demoiselle?"

"Aye," she assured him. " 'Twas a minor thing and did not require punishment."

He assured her, "Lady Hertford's punishment was not what I could have given her, nor what I preferred." With his fingers beneath the curve of her chin he lifted her gaze to his.

"I will not have you treated so, nor would William take such a matter lightly. He would have dealt far more harshly with her, for he has come to value you highly."

"It is a small thing, and finished. Please, do not speak of it to the duke of Normandy," she implored him, lest more severe punishment fall upon Lady Hertford. "He has matters enough to concern him."

"You plead mercy for them even when they would demean you," he said, thoughtfully studying her face. "I fear we have brought you to this. It was not my intention that day at Amesbury."

"They cannot harm me, milord," she protested in defense. "They lash out in pain and fear of an uncertain future they cannot see."

"And yet you do not," he observed, his mouth curving in a speculative smile that had the unexpected effect of transforming cold, forbidding features almost to a handsomeness. He still held her prisoner by the simple contact of those strong fingers at her chin, yet held her with only the gentlest restraint. She could have resisted and turned away had she wanted. She did not. His touch mesmerized her as the unexpected warmth of that simple contact spread across her skin and cascaded through her body. An expectant heat that made her lean into his touch.

"Do you perhaps see what they cannot?" he asked.

"I see the hopelessness of more deaths," she whispered, the memory of her vision sharp as her breath fragmented at the tip of his thumb stroking along the curve of her lower lip.

Rorke watched as blue fire leapt into her eyes, enveloping the midnight dark iris, banishing it until it seemed her eyes were shimmering blue flame. The heat of her startled breath caressed his skin.

Desire, sharp and long denied raged through Rorke. He silently cursed that he should feel such a rage of need midmorning with two hundred soldiers, knights, and assorted Saxons crowding every square inch of the hall.

He wanted to take her then and there. To push her skirts up and discover all her woman's secrets. Against the wall, or on the stones of the floor would not have mattered as he felt his flesh press hard against his belly.

He wanted to feel her beneath him and all about him, to hear her soft cries, to burn with her heat, to watch those magnificent eyes as he joined his flesh with hers, to discover the passion that defended a tumbledown abbey and a broken-down monk, defied a conqueror and reduced both a bishop and his men to her bidding.

He wanted to lose himself in her and in the loss perhaps find something more that he couldn't even name.

A voice sliced through the desire, cooling the heat with tones of urgency.

"Mistress Vivian!"

It was the girl, Mally, as she suddenly came from the great hall. At seeing Rorke, she faltered and stammered, "Forgive me, I didn't see you there, milord." An apprehensive expression crossed her face as she chewed at her lower lip, hands twisting before her.

"What is it, Mally?" Vivian asked, telling herself she was grateful the girl had appeared when she had, even though she knew it was a lie. She ached for his touch with a longing of something more. Much more. Her thoughts slowly cleared.

It was odd for Mally to be in the great hall. Since there were frequently many soldiers about, she stayed away from the hall, confining herself to the kitchen, where she helped the cook, or, like a silent shadow, followed Vivian as she went about her chores.

"Is something amiss? Has someone taken ill?"

"Speak up, girl," Rorke ordered.

Still Mally fidgeted, casting worried glances from Vivian to Rorke and back again.

"It is a private matter, mistress."

Mally had gradually improved since their arrival in London. But now, Vivian sensed something fearful in the girl's chaotic thoughts and wondered if something had happened she might not have been able to sense.

"Whatever it is, you may tell me and have no fear, Mally," she gently encouraged the girl, stroking her arm soothingly. It was then the girl's thoughts joined with her own in the sound of two names as if she had heard them.

Poladouras and Meg! And they were there that very moment, in the great hall of William's London fortress.

Vivian turned abruptly to Rorke. "Please, milord," she begged. "It is a personal matter." And then, with a sudden thought, " 'Tis of a womanly nature." The deception was not entirely untrue.

Rorke saw the change in her manner. The faint furrow of auburn brows and then the startled look that flashed in her eyes as if some silent communication passed between her and the girl. Something was amiss, but he instinctively knew that if he pressed the matter, she would not speak of it.

"I must find Gavin de Marte," he said, excusing himself and crossing the great hall in the direction opposite to that from which Mally had come.

It was crowded and noisy, filled with the usual petitioners who waited for William to arrive at court. When he was blocked from their view by several of his men who were also always in attendance, with their swords at their sides, Rorke turned and watched as the girl led Vivian across the far side of the hall, where several Saxon merchants, peasants, and monks had gathered to speak their cause.

Vivian glanced anxiously about as Mally led her across the crowded hall. Norman guards were everywhere.

Dozens of questions filled her thoughts. How had Meg and Poladouras gotten there all the way from Amesbury? Why had they come, and at such great risk? Then she feared they might be seen, and apprehension tightened at her throat.

She, too, saw the crowd of peasants and pilgrims that crowded the far wall, their numbers increasing each day as more filled London in the wake of William's defeat of King Harold. Then, as if a hand had reached out and touched her arm, Vivian sensed a presence deep in her heart. That presence of love and caring that had borne an infant girl child from the far west country to a tumbledown stone abbey so many years before, guided by a magical falcon because her eyes could not see the way.

"Meg," she whispered softly, tears filling her eyes as she turned to the small form beside her, features shrouded in a monk's robes and hood.

"Mo chroi."

The rim of the hood lifted just enough to reveal that dear, lined face that was ageless to her. Meg's thin hand reached out from the voluminous sleeve and closed over Vivian's wrist in the ancient bonding way. Immediately a connection of love and fear passed between them, followed by the assurance that each was well and for the moment safe.

Holding on to the old woman's hand, Vivian glanced about for Poladouras, but failed to find his face or corpulent form shrouded by any of the monk's robes that surrounded Meg.

"Do your senses fail you, child?" a voice asked behind her. "Appearances can be deceiving."

She whirled around to find a merchant in much-mended clothes, with a cask of mead clutched under his arm. His face was shrouded by heavy growth of gray beard that blended with the wild mane of his hair, barely restrained by a woolen cap.

He wore breeches with leather leggings that barely wrapped to his knees, and a coarse woolen tunic belted by a length of rope for lack of a suitable belt, and smelled of the brew he carried.

If she had not sensed who it was beneath the ridiculous disguise, she would have known it in the warm brown eyes that glinted back at her.

"Meg dresses as a monk and you disguise yourself as a village merchant?" she asked incredulously, her eyes brimming tears with a mixture of joy and disbelief at the danger they risked.

Poladouras' eyes crinkled, his smile lost somewhere in the mat of beard. "It seemed logical. Who would bother a simple merchant bearing a gift of mead to Duke William?" he reasoned, then winked at her. "And it provided sustenance for the journey."

"Does any of the ale remain?" Vivian asked, smiling through her tears, knowing well his appreciation of fine brew.

His eyes widened that she should ask such a question, then crinkled again with laughter.

"It would be a shame to waste all of it on the Normans, who have a taste for wine instead. It might be a bit watered down." He shrugged. "They will never know the difference." His large gentle hand clasped hers.

"Dear child! You are well."

"Aye, well and safe," she assured them both, then, with a worried glance about the hall, "But why have you come here? It is dangerous."

Poladouras leaned close and winked again at her. With a nod toward Meg, he said, "This old woman would not let me rest until I agreed to come to London. Threatened to turn me into all sorts of vile creatures unless I brought her. Determined, she was," he muttered. "And unable to find her own way without the falcon."

Vivian clasped both their hands in hers. "I've seen Conal. He followed me to Hastings."

"Aye," Meg whispered, "the lad was near crazed after you were taken. Is he about?"

Vivian shook her head. "He spoke of dangerous things that I feared might get him killed. I had hoped he might have returned to Amesbury and given up his foolish plans. I pray he is safe, but it is not safe for you to be here," she protested, even as she felt joy in seeing them again and grateful they had suffered no lingering infirmity from the horrible beatings of that day at Amesbury.

"You cannot stay. You must leave now before you are seen!" she went on with growing urgency. She sensed Mally's sudden apprehension and, turning to the girl beside her, saw it in the fearful expression on her face.

It was already too late, as a familiar voice behind her commented, "Surely your friends are not leaving so soon, demoiselle." Fear clenched around her heart as Vivian recognized that voice. She slowly turned to confront the wintry gray gaze of Rorke FitzWarren.

"Milord," she said slowly, the breath trapped in her lungs. She tried to gauge his mood as she realized he had recognized Meg and Poladouras.

"William will be most interested to meet both of you," he told them, but his gaze was fixed on Vivian.

When informed of the latest arrivals at his court, William immediately summoned them to his chamber.

"So, you are the monk, Poladouras," he exclaimed as they stood before him. "I have heard much about you. Please, come closer so that we may talk."

"Brother," the bishop warned, "I strongly advise against this. We cannot know what treachery the monk plans. My men have told me how they were attacked at the abbey. The old woman went at one of my men with a meat ax."

Vivian watched him carefully, for he was most certainly aware who Meg and Poladouras were. She felt a new fear of the lies Vachel might have told him about that day. For certainly, the bishop carried great influence with William. She wished desperately Meg and Poladouras had not come to London.

"Aye," William acknowledged in grave tones. "I've been told of it. Forty-odd, heavily armed men held at bay by a monk, a blind woman, and a young girl. Formidable odds indeed. Be at ease, brother," he admonished the bishop. "Unless you believe them to be armed and scheming to strike against me in my own chamber with over two hundred of my men just beyond that door."

"I would have them searched," the bishop demanded.

"By all means." William nodded to Rorke FitzWarren. "Make it so." And when the search failed to produce anything more than Poladouras' cask of ale, William again nodded.

"A formidable weapon indeed," he told the bishop with a sarcastic tone. Then he asked Poladouras, "Is it a decent brew?"

"Aye." Poladouras nodded. "The finest made by old Anselm of Amesbury."

"Then stay, monk," William commanded, despite his brother's further protests. "We shall share the cask, for I have been told you are learned in many things and a shrewd bargain-maker. I would ask your counsel on certain matters. So you see there is more than one reason for you to remain in London as my guests."

With an awe of new respect, Vivian realized William's shrewd purpose. For in binding the monk to his court, so too he bound her.

"What of the old woman?" the bishop asked. "It is said among my men that she has the way of an enchantress about her."

William roared with laughter, causing Meg to look at him askance—all the more disconcerting with that pale, colorless, blind gaze.

"What say you, old woman?" William demanded. "Are you an enchantress?"

Meg smiled, the transformation in her features hinting of the comely young woman she had once been. Vivian held her breath, for the old woman had no fear of William of Normandy or any man, and there was no telling what she might say.

"You flatter an old woman," Meg said with a sly smile. "It has been many years since I was called *enchanting.*"

"Somehow I disbelieve that," William said with far more wisdom that any who did not know him might have given him credit. As Vivian had learned, he was a shrewd judge of character.

"She has knowledge of healing," Rorke told him, drawing a curious stare from Meg, who quickly remembered his voice and picked it out from the others. "Her skills would be valuable to us."

"Aye," William nodded. "Then the matter is settled."

Vivian was greatly relieved that William had not ordered Meg and Poladouras beaten for what had happened at Amesbury, for it would have been within his right to do so.

She grew anxious, however; for his brother, the bishop, was not pleased with William's decision to allow them to stay in the royal hall and had argued long against it. She feared he might have them chained and imprisoned, or worse. In the end William grew weary of his arguing.

"The matter is settled and I will hear no more of it. If either the monk or old woman show themselves to be traitors, then they shall be dealt with accordingly. But in truth, I deal with nobel Saxon barons and earls who would far more willingly slit my throat had they the chance. And," he added, with a shrewd look, "I rely upon you to protect me from my enemies no matter the guise they wear."

William then rose, for there were matters he must attend to at court. "Return this eventide and join me for supper," he told Poladouras. "I understand you are a man of shrewd intellect and I confess that so far I have found shrewdness lacking among the Saxon barons." Then he turned to Meg.

"The girl Mally may find a place for you with her near the kitchen."

"I would stay with my mistress," Meg protested.

"For that you must ask permission of milord FitzWarren," William informed her, "for she occupies the chamber adjacent so that she may see to my wounds obtained at Hastings, and the chamber is his."

Meg turned toward Vivian, who sensed the burning question in the old woman's thoughts.

Rorke's response was adamant. "Near the kitchens will suffice. I am certain the girl may make her comfortable."

Vivian accompanied Meg to the kitchens, where she made the acquaintance of the cook and was made comfortable in the small chamber off the pantry that Mally occupied.

"I hear whisperings," Meg said, laying a hand gently on Vivian's arm, when Mally had gone to find something with which to make the old woman a pallet. "The walls say that you are mistress to milord FitzWarren." Her face was lined with worry.

"The walls are wrong," Vivian adamantly denied. "They whisper about what they see but know nothing of. I was given the chamber adjacent so that I might attend William without others knowing the extent of his injury, for he nearly died at Hastings."

"And what of your vision at Amesbury?" Meg asked, her voice trembling.

"I know no more of it now than I did then. I know only that my destiny lies with Rorke's. Please, ask me no more. You are here now. Perhaps together we may find it."

"Nay," Meg said sadly, laying a hand unerringly against Vivian's cheek. "I fear only you may find your destiny. I can but wait, and perhaps protect you as best I can. As I always have since you were born. That is why I came to London. I was with you the first moment you drew breath. I was the first to hold you when you slipped from your mother's womb. And I have been entrusted with you since. I will not abandon you now, my child, whatever path your destiny takes you. Only I pray, beware of everyone, for I sense danger in this place."

It was eventide and just before supper in the great hall when she returned to Rorke's chamber and found him returned from the practice yard.

A fire burned at the hearth, taking the chill from damp stone walls. Candles had been lit, casting pools of golden light across the floor.

He stood before a basin of steaming water, his tunic removed, wearing only breeches and soft leather boots. Pools of light gleamed across the muscles of his shoulders and chest; patterns of old scars stood out in sharp relief against bronzed skin. She should have looked away but found she could not.

As a healer she knew and felt so much through touching. She wanted to touch him, to learn the contours of hardened muscle and bone, to feel that golden skin and all the ridges of scars that defined his life so that in some way she might know more of him. Her fingers burned with the longing of it and she curled them into tight fists, trying to deny the sensations just the sight of him roused. But she could not, for her hands grew restless, fingers flexing and curling with the effort of not touching him.

Droplets of water sprinkled his hair, glistening in the shaggy lengths of the rich dark mane, and at the hard planes and angles of sharp features at his face. A flagon of wine also sat at the table and two goblets, as if someone were expected.

"Forgive me, milord," she said on a startled note and turned to leave.

"Stay, Vivian," he said, his voice gentle but nevertheless a command. He toweled the water from his hair and face with a square of linen. He missed the sprinkling of droplets that glittered in the dark hair of his chest like a handful of precious crystals on dark velvet. Beneath the downy midnight darkness was the fine, pale satin patchwork of scars both old and new. She stared with fascination at the dark whorls of hair, his skin shades darker than her own. Male nipples were flat and pebbled in the chill air, and she felt a tingling at her own breasts at the imagined contrast of her nakedness against his. She wondered, was every part of him dark, powerful, and hard, like the muscles of his arms and chest?

"Is there a matter you wish to discuss?"

"It will wait, milord," she replied breathlessly, desperate to pull her gaze away from his half-naked body, but even more desperate to see more of him.

"I would have you tell me now, Vivian. What matter brought you here? Is William unwell?"

Her gaze came up. "Nay, he is in remarkably good health for a man near death but a few weeks past, but he pushes himself far too hard."

"If not William's health, then what matter of import could make you seek me out when I am aware you make every effort to avoid me." He smiled, further disarming her.

" 'Tis not true," she protested, finding it necessary to take an extra breath at the devastating power of his smile that transformed the glowering phoenix into another far more formidable predator—a predator of the senses.

He laid the linen down on the table. Making no attempt to retrieve his tunic, he poured wine into the two goblets.

"Then stay a while and prove it a lie," he told her, with cool self-assurance.

She began hesitantly. "I came to thank you for your kindness today. It was not necessary."

"Ah, but it was most necessary." He handed her one of the goblets, gray eyes watching her thoughtfully with an expression she had glimpsed before when he contemplated some matter of strategy.

"Had I ordered them beaten and thrown from the fortress, you would have been angry, perhaps even demanded to leave as well, though I could not allow it."

She looked at him incredulously. She knew him to be cunning, but he was as shrewd as William. "So you therefore sought to bind me to you with your generosity to Meg and Poladouras." She saw the wisdom.

"William sought to bind you to him," he told her, "as you once explained might be wiser in dealing with Saxon barons." He reached out, taking a strand of her hair between his fingers and gently stroking it.

"They are not Saxon barons and have nothing of value," she reminded him between carefully drawn breaths as she watched her hair trapped possessively between those long, callused fingers, like leather jesses that bound her to his hand.

Still, she had only to pull away. She did not, but remained where she was. At the same time, terrified and fascinated by feelings she'd never experienced before.

Like the falcon that he'd compared her to, she imagined him carefully holding a powerful, majestic hunting bird. Imagined, too, the sweet warmth of his breath gently acquainting the creature with his essence, the caress of words spoken low that taught his sound, the stroke of his hand at the creature's rounded breast that learned his touch.

He gave her a knowing look. "Their value lies in your devotion to them."

She watched with stilled breath, unable to respond, as he

slowly wound the tendril of her hair possessively about his finger, drawing her closer to him with gentle, demanding tugs.

"Is the old woman completely blind?" he asked, confusing her with the sudden change in direction of their conversation.

"She has been blind since birth," she explained. "But I have always felt that she sees far more than others." The air quivered out from between her parted lips. Her breathing was rapid, jerky, panic-filled, and at the same time filled with some other response that she didn't understand.

"What do you see, Vivian of Amesbury?" His voice was low and warm.

"Milord?" the question startled her.

"Look at me." Not a request, but a command, given and expected to be obeyed, but with such gentle persuasion.

No falconer's gloved hand, protected with heavy padding, chain mail, and metal spikes, pulled at leather jesses, but instead his vulnerable bare hand, exposed, naked, giving at the same time he took possession of her. A bond that could easily be broken if she chose it. Yet both were aware she did not.

She looked up and, in doing so, sensed that something irretrievable had slipped from her grasp, and in its place, something new, undiscovered, and yet as inevitable as the sun passing across the sky into night.

She saw it in his eyes as gray as winter sky with the portent of a powerful gathering storm. Unlike winter's icy blast, she discovered the hidden fires that lay beneath winter's icy mantle in the myriad golden lights that flecked the gray.

"What do you see?" he repeated, the words lower still in his throat and sending terrifying pleasure across her skin.

A month, a week, or even the day before, she would have answered truthfully that she saw nothing. For it was as if her ability to see and sense things about him as she sensed them about others had been blinded. From that first day at Amesbury he, above all others, remained closed to her in ways that she had never experienced before. It had terrified her.

But now, as though some force inexplicably moved between them and at the same time connected her to him, she was seized by flashes of powerful emotions. They were not the visions of clear understanding that she perceived in other people, but instead bursts of pure emotion like flashes of color in a void of darkness, and light so intense that she felt it along every nerve ending.

She sensed rage, as old as memory and long denied, some enormous wounded pain carried deep in his soul, the darker gray shadows of other things that haunted him and were a part of his past, some startling new emotion that she'd never experienced before. Yet she felt it with such intensity that the only possible comparison was with fire that burned out of control and threatened to destroy everything in its path. Finally, there was a void of darkness of longing so deep that it was like a pain unto itself and made her cry out.

Vivian pulled away, breaking the tender connection of his hand in her hair, and at the same time, severing the sensual connection. She made a hasty excuse, stumbling over her words.

"I see that it is very late," she said, covering the more truthful answer he sought as she glanced out the high, narrow slotted window. "I must prepare a tisane for his lordship."

"Why do you run away from me, Vivian? What is it that you fear? Do you fear what I make you feel?"

She avoided his gaze. "I do not understand."

"You understand very well, for you have felt it just as I have felt it." He seized her hand in his. With his thumb he stroked her fingers apart then brought her hand to his chest and flattened it over the curve of hard muscle.

"Please! Do not!" she implored him.

"What do you feel?"

"I feel nothing!"

"You feel what I feel. Heat, fire burning through me at your simplest touch. I know you feel it."

"I feel nothing!" Still, she denied it, but her desperate struggle to free her trapped hand made her a liar.

"Please!" she implored. "I cannot bear it."

She looked at him with an expression that warred between terror and longing, between a forbidden prophecy and the destiny of a vision in flame.

"I have already told you," she repeated, her voice barely more than a whisper. "I do not feel what others feel. It is impossible."

She jerked her hand from his, aware on some level that it was only possible because he allowed it. The connection was broken. Cold chilled her skin as though something had blocked out all light. The ache of loss for something she couldn't even name was like a wound deep inside that opened up and seemed to swallow her heart.

She gasped at the intense emotions of longing, need, and then despair that she had never before experienced. Human, mortal emotions that she had always been protected against by the certainty of her destiny. She felt as if she were dying and was certain she would if she did not leave him.

Vivian hastily searched for the leather pouch that contained what was left of her herbs and powders. It lay beside the hearth, ties dangling loosely. She frowned slightly, her thoughts, usually so clear, muddled by the unfamiliar emotions and sensations that poured through her. She quickly gathered it up, taking no time to roll or retie it.

She hurried to leave when he stopped her, strong fingers digging powerfully into the soft flesh of her arm.

"Vivian." His voice was both harsh and gentle, filled with a conflict of emotions as overwhelming as her own. But it wasn't the sound of her name that stopped her. It was his touch, felt without even making contact.

She sensed those conflicted emotions, sensed the anguish that ran through them, sensed, too, his touch, with a longing so deep that it was painful.

With one painful glance at the anguish that etched his face, the powerful, scarred hand that so easily wielded a deadly sword on a battlefield and now trembled with longing, she implored, "Please, do not!"

Then, hastily stepping beyond his reach, she pulled open the heavy chamber door.

Judith de Marque's surprise was as great as her own, but her recovery at finding Vivian in Rorke's chamber was far quicker. A cunning expression sharpened in the Norman woman's eyes as she stood at the threshold to the chamber, then became dismissive as she swept past Vivian.

"I came as soon as I received your message, milord," she told Rorke. "I see you've poured wine for us." Her voice was like warm honey as she closed the stout door firmly behind her.

Vivian leaned against the stone wall outside Rorke's chamber, eyes closed as she tried to bring her dangerously chaotic emotions back under control by sheer force of will. Jealousy and longing spiraled through her. Jealousy of the woman she was certain must still be Rorke's mistress, and a longing that it was she who longed to share the wine with him and so much more. She stifled back a painful sob.

The vision that she'd experienced so long ago came back vividly to her. A creature born in fire and blood that spread its wings across the face of England. Rorke FitzWarren. Her fate was inextricably linked with his. It was no accident or random twist of fate that had brought him to Amesbury Abbey. It was destiny, seen in a vision.

Clutching the brilliant blue stone that hung about her neck, she cast her thoughts far, beyond the stone walls, beyond London, beyond time and place into the swirling mists where present and past merged in a time of hopes and dreams, in a faraway place that existed only in ancient hollow hills. The words whispered through her tormented thoughts.

Please, father. Help me!

A loud crash shattered the peaceful morning air in the gently swirling mist of the world between the worlds. The sound of metal being hurled against stones followed by an agony of furious curses in a half dozen ancient, half-forgotten languages.

Ninian hesitated at the bottom of the narrow stone steps and wondered if she dare climb them to the top. Another burst of curses, followed by an agony of pain, settled the matter as she gathered her shimmering silver skirts in hand and hastily ran up the steps.

The chamber was in complete disarray, utensils and their contents scattered about the floor. A dozen ancient books littered the table, stacked one upon the other as if some hand had hurriedly searched the pages. The flames of a dozen candles burned a lambent glow, but the scattered droplets of rapidly drying wax revealed the chaos that had gripped the chamber but a few moments before.

The metal brazier had been hurled against the stones. It lay on its side, its smoldering contents glowing on the stone floor. Her husband stood before the raised stone hearth—of a height the same as a table—where the brazier had sat only moments before.

His weight was braced by his hands on the stones, head hanging forward between slumped shoulders; the folds of the midnight blue robe he wore draped his tall frame, concealing the gauntness that had set in. For the first time, he seemed completely unaware of her presence and a new fear knifed through her. She went to him, laying a slender hand on the wide shoulder.

"Dearest, love," she whispered. "What is it? What has happened?" He stood there for the longest time, and then slowly turned to look at her.

The handsome features had become more so with time, the lines about his eyes and mouth adding strength and character to his face. They were strong, aquiline features that suggested an ancient royal lineage, and clearly Celtic forbears. Long ago he'd chosen to grow a full beard.

As a very young man it had been russet in color, then silver, now white, and kept closely clipped about that stubborn, set chin. His hair had also turned white and was kept closely cropped about his head. But his brows were still that fiery, russet color above the set of brilliant blue eyes that held a far different fire of their own.

Time had not diminished her love for him. Indeed, it had deepened it, giving it distinctive, new qualities like fine wine never tasting the same twice, the myriad colors discovered and then rediscovered all over again in a rainbow, the constantly changing rhythms of the earth, wind, and sea. But never before had she known such anger.

Ninian sensed his anger and saw it in fists clenched with impotent rage until his knuckles showed white through the skin of his hands, heard it in the litany of curses that still charged the air of the chamber with a wild, chaotic energy, and felt it in the trembling beneath her hand.

"Dearest, please," she said gently. "You need to rest."

"I do not need rest! I must reach her. I must find a way," he said with growing helplessness, hands thrust out before him. It was then she saw the painful, ugly red slash of raised flesh across his hand where he'd burned it at the brazier.

"Come," she said insistently, pulling him with her to the bench that sat before the table, mindful not to touch his burned hand. She gently pushed him down onto the bench. Taking several medicinal herbs from the shelf on the wall above the table, she laid them out precisely, along with a fresh strip of linen cloth. She sat down before him and took his hand between both of hers.

"What did you see in the flames?" she asked, tenderly stroking his hand between hers, across long, strong fingers, then back across those whitened knuckles, and all around the slash of burned flesh across his palm where he had taken hold of the brazier and hurled it across the chamber. He refused to answer at first and eventually she looked up at him.

His expression was tortured with such a sadness of helplessness. Tears glistened in those fiery blue eyes.

"Dearest Ninian," he whispered, his voice breaking softly over her name. "I was unable to see anything. Not even the barest glimpse. Nothing, but a growing darkness."

"It has been like that before, my love," she consoled as she continued to stroke his hand, eventually gliding her fingers across the burned flesh, taking away the pain, healing the damaged flesh with the power that burned within her.

"No! Not like this," he said with helpless frustration. "Always before there was a connection. I could reach her, but lately it is gone. I thought that perhaps through the light of the fire . . . But there was only darkness!"

"There has been darkness before," she reminded him. "Darkness always follows day." Her voice was as soothing as her touch, lyrical, faintly musical, usually as calming as her magical healer's touch. He stared down at his hand, where only moments before the flesh had raised an angry red welt, the blister already forming underneath.

She had bandaged it carefully with a special poultice that would make the skin strong again and protect against new injury. He stroked the linen bandage thoughtfully.

"You always take care of me, sweet wife. You bandage the wounds of the flesh and ease the wounds of the spirit. That which would not even be bearable, you make more than tolerable. You have brought me hope, faith, and love, and made this prison that is my existence a treasure beyond compare. What have I given you that I deserve such as this?"

"You have given me truth, honor, and a passion rare. You have given me your heart and soul. And you have given me fine, beautiful children when I despaired that I might ever enjoy those mortal pleasures. I am by far richer for the bargain, my love."

"But I have not kept the bargain," he lamented, taking hold of her hand with his without any lingering trace of pain. "I had thought that I could keep her safe, but I cannot. I fear this darkness, Ninian. It is not like the darkness that follows light of day."

He stood and walked toward the chamber window. "It is a darkness that consumes the light, destroying it, obliterating all that was before and may ever hope to be."

He buried his head in his hands. "And now I cannot reach

her. I cannot warn her of it!" She went to him, wrapping her
arms about him, feeling the ache of despair that spread through
him, hiding her heart from him so that he would not see the
fear there.

"We will find a way, dearest husband. She is part of us both.
She is strong and fine and true. We will find a way to reach her."

As she spoke she turned her face into his shoulder, terrified
that he would see the doubt in her face or the tears of helplessness at her cheeks, for her children so long gone from her for
their own sakes to places where they might be safe, and for this
immortal she loved and had given up her own mortal life to
share his. Her husband, lover, and mate through all eternity.
Merlin, whose pain she could not assuage.

He bent his head to hers, cupping her head with its rich fall
of thick golden hair, like the sun burning through the mist even
after all these years.

Ninian. Lady of the lake, who had stolen his heart, healed
his soul, and given him the sweet, precious gift of life. He held
on to her, drawing strength from her.

"I will find a way to reach her," he vowed.

Sixteen

The narrow passage that led to the kitchen was cold and damp
as Vivian's feet skimmed over the stones. She hugged the folds
of Rorke's woolen mantle more tightly about her, the fabric
redolent with his masculine scent. The flames of the torches
quivered at her hasty flight.

The sudden warm blast of heat from the oven and cook fire
was heady with the aroma of fresh-baked bread and meat already turning at the spit for the evening meal.

The cook cursed in French at one of several young girls who

helped her. From the coarse exchange, it seemed the girl had returned late from the soldiers' barracks. She was hollow-eyed and sluggish in her chores, causing the cook to wave a stout knife at her menacingly.

Vivian had left Mally and another girl busily preparing William's chamber for the arrival of his wife Matilda in time for the coronation. Now, she looked for Meg and found her stirring herbal leaves into a small simmer pot over a brazier in the adjacent pantry.

The potion was for the painful stiffness that plagued the woman in the damp coldness of the royal fortress. Although the noise from the kitchen would have made it impossible to hear, still she sensed Vivian's presence and smiled as Vivian reached around her to steady her hand at her stirring.

"Dear child, I despaired that I would ever have a chance to speak with you." Meg said as she turned and put her arms about Vivian. "You are kept so busy and well guarded there is never a moment when we might be alone."

Taking the old woman's hand and pressing it against her cheek, Vivian said, "I sensed your thoughts and came as soon as I could. It is difficult," she admitted, and, glancing over her shoulder at the cook who was busy with her own chores, said, "It seems the most private moment might be here."

Meg nodded. "You are well?"

"Yes, very well. You must not worry so."

"How could I not worry?" Meg sighed. "You are as much my child as if I had borne you. I am old and my powers are not as yours, but whatever the meaning of this vision, I could not let you face it alone." She pulled Vivian aside to the sacks of flour that lined the wall. They sat upon them and spoke of things there had been no time to speak of that last day at Amesbury.

"Has the vision revealed anything more to you?" Meg asked with concern in her voice.

Vivian shook her head gravely. "I have seen nothing more in the stone. But I have sensed a presence."

Meg heard the hesitation in her voice. "What do you mean?" she asked, sensing something more.

Vivian hesitated. "It is difficult to explain, for I have never sensed anything like this." She glanced back over her shoulder to be certain no one listened, for what they spoke of might easily be misunderstood by those who were superstitious about such things.

But even though no one glanced their way, indeed, could not have heard over the crash and clatter of cook pots and kettles, she sensed a listening presence. And so she sought to communicate with Meg in the old way, by giving her her thoughts. She held the old woman's hand against her cheek and opened her thoughts to her as if she spoke the words aloud.

"In the vision I saw a cold, evil darkness unlike anything I have ever known, but I had no meaning for it. The vision did not reveal it to me. Since then I have not seen it again in my visions, but I feel its presence. It is here, in the shadows just beyond my ability to see it. As if it were waiting for something, or someone. Tell me what you know of it."

Beneath her hand she felt Meg's quiver against her cheek. Before any thought was shared with her, Vivian sensed the old woman's anguish of fear.

"Not for five hundred years has anyone spoken of the Darkness. When I was a child it was whispered about, a tale to frighten children, I thought. Nothing more. It is said to have come over the land in the time of ancient kings."

"It is said," Meg continued, her wizened old features pale and drawn, *"that the Darkness destroyed the ancient kingdom."*

"Did no one try to stop it?"

"Aye." Meg answered, now with a clarity of understanding of Vivian's vision that she had not possessed before. *"Someone did try to stop it."*

Vivian knew her next thought. *"And he was destroyed because of it?"* she asked fearfully.

"Aye, banished from the kingdom forever."

Tears filled Meg's blind old eyes, as she once more communicated with spoken words, "I fear for you my child. Leave this place. Come away to Amesbury. We can leave now. Poladouras will take us."

Vivian sadly shook her head. "You know that I cannot. I have seen the darkness in my vision. I am part of it. If I were to leave, it would only find me again. You know the truth of the visions—once seen they cannot be altered. It is what has not yet revealed itself that may yet be altered."

"The future," Meg said with tremulous voice.

"Like a tapestry," Vivian answered. "The threads are not yet woven." She felt a small flame of hope. "The future is not yet certain and it lies in the hands of a creature born in fire and blood, and . . ."

"And all is in your hands," Meg said with much sadness of voice. "Your fates are intertwined. I see now that you are right, though I had prayed it was not so. He is Norman. He brings blood and death to the Saxons."

All the emotions she'd felt over the past weeks swept through her. Her fear of Rorke, her fear of her own feelings, and the prophecy that bound them together.

"That fate was already certain before he and his knights came to Amesbury," Vivian acknowledged sadly, "for I saw it clearly in the stone, just as I knew that I must go with him."

One of the cook's girls came into the pantry, glancing at them with wide-eyed curiosity as she seized a bag of flour. Vivian rose to leave, for she had been on another errand when she stopped to see Meg. Sir Gavin had promised to escort her to the London market so that she might replenish some of her herbal medicines.

"William has given his permission for me to go to the market," she explained to Meg. "I will bring leaves to fix an elixir for the pain in your hands."

Meg waved her gnarled old hand as if it was of little importance. "I am an old woman and my needs are few. My greatest concern is for you my child." Her hand was surprisingly strong and warm with the life force that still moved through her in spite of the fragile, gnarled old bones.

"Though your fate is linked with his, beware," Meg warned in a low voice. "For I have sensed his feelings for you. They are dangerous. You are a child of the Light," she reminded Vivian. "You must not forget the warning of the prophecy, for if your powers are lost, then all is lost."

And what of my feelings for him? Vivian wondered, even as she reassured Meg that she must not worry. Why did these mortal emotions and needs stir within her as they never had before, at his simplest touch?

"I will take care," she promised, but her thoughts were filled with doubt and uncertainty as she left the kitchens and continued down the passage that led to the sally port at the east wall of the fortress, where she was to meet Sir Gavin, for she had spoken to him earlier and he had said he would accompany her to the market. A dozen mail-clad soldiers sat astride their warhorses, waiting for her.

In the days since she'd arrived in London, William's soldiers had removed their mail armor. There was little need of it inside the walled fortress. The sight of it now reminded her that while they but ventured to market, there was still danger of armed attacks.

The soldiers stood beside their mounts, mantles carefully draped over their armor, broadswords concealed from sight. Mist swirled about the mounts and their riders. She approached the one she was certain must be Gavin, her breath pluming on the frosty morning air with a greeting.

"Good morn, Sir Gavin. I apologize for keeping you waiting."

"Good morn, mistress," the knight commented as he turned around to reveal that it was not Sir Gavin who waited for her, but Rorke FitzWarren.

"Where is Sir Gavin?" she blurted out, startled by the unexpected appearance of the very man she had been avoiding for the past several days, since the unhappy encounter in his chamber with Judith de Marque.

"Called away on another matter."

"But he assured me that he had nothing of import to attend to this morn," Vivian responded, shock giving way to uneasiness.

"He was mistaken," Rorke informed her sharply. "Therefore, I shall ride in his place. Surely you have no objection."

"Nay," Vivian assured him—not any that she could explain. " 'Tis only that I would not take you away from important matters. It is a matter that can wait until Sir Gavin is able to accompany me."

"It might not be for some time," he informed her. "I would not have William's return to good health endangered by your lack of medicines. Surely my men are capable of escorting you about London."

"Of course," she protested weakly. " 'Tis only that I would not bother you with such a trivial matter."

He assured her, "Matters of William's health are not trivial. You spoke of a need to go to market. Therefore, you shall go to market, accompanied by my men. And for your safety, you will ride with me."

A tentative calm had settled over the city while negotiations for peace took place between Duke William of Normandy, the archbishop of Canterbury, and the Saxon barons.

Merchants opened their shops. Markets bustled with activity. Inns and taverns, which had been boarded up only days earlier, overflowed and did a bustling trade providing food and lodging for the very same invaders they had fought.

The people of London bitterly resented the presence of the Norman invaders, and the duke of Normandy even more, but there was a harsh reality to be confronted. Commerce meant profit, and profit meant survival.

"How is it the cook or one of her women could not acquire the necessary ingredients for you?" Rorke inquired as they rode through the bustling streets toward the marketplace.

People grudgingly made way for them, stepping aside from the large warhorses so as not to be trampled by the great beasts, casting resentful looks in their direction, hissing curses when they assumed they could not be heard. But Vivian heard the words and, with Rorke's understanding of the English language, she knew that he heard and understood them as well.

He gave no indication of it, but kept his gaze fixed straight ahead. Or at least she thought he did, until she cast a quick glance over her shoulder and saw that she was mistaken. He only gave the appearance of looking straight ahead when in truth his gaze constantly scanned the street, buildings, and rooftops ahead of them.

"There are many different varieties of the same plants," she explained in answer to his question. "So, too, are the potions made from them different. I must see them myself to choose the correct ones. If the merchant does not have what I need, then I must choose something else that will work as well."

His mood seemed to have eased and he accepted the logic of this. "I suppose it would not do to use the wrong medicine. It might prove lethal."

"Only with much stronger medicines," she responded. "However," she added, "an incorrect medicine can cause strange results." When he made no attempt to change the conversation but instead listened with interest, she went on to explain.

"The leaves used in a salve to treat boils are very similar to another that causes an unusual amount of hair growth." From the corner of her eye she caught sight of the thoughtful expression that appeared on his strong features.

"Hmmmm," he commented. "Considering the area usually afflicted, that might prove to be most disconcerting."

She was held firmly in place before him by a strong arm wrapped about her. The humorous timbre of his voice rumbled warmly through her. It was not an unpleasant sensation and she relaxed against the curve of his mail-clad chest, her mood lifting by degrees.

"Oh, I fear it was most disconcerting," she continued with mock seriousness. "In the village, old Anselm took it upon himself to treat a fierce case of boils. He knew the name of the plant I used for making the salve but he thought to make it himself, with disastrous results."

"He still has the boils," Rorke speculated.

"Aye, and more," she replied, her expression solemn. "According to his wife, his arse is covered with more hair than his head. She says he can't figure out which end is up."

From the corner of her eye she caught sight of the smile that began at one corner of his mouth and heard his low chuckle. "Are there other such treatments which might be confused?" he asked with a grin.

"Oh, many others," she said. "There is a plant which provides a medicine for treating coughs."

"And there is one similar that causes far different results?"

She nodded. "It looks exactly the same except for the number of leaves in a cluster on the branch of the bush. It does nothing to relieve coughing, but causes a dreadful amount of wind."

Pressed firmly against him, Vivian felt the laughter that he tried to suppress. With great effort he remarked, "Considering there are three hundred or more soldiers within the fortress it could indeed be a very explosive situation if they were to get hold of the wrong medicine."

"Very *explosive* indeed," she agreed, forcing a serious tone. "But there is another that is far worse. There are roots of certain plants which provide a salve for treating toothaches. But there is one similar which produces a salve that causes a certain . . . *flaccidity* of the limbs."

"Flaccid limbs?" Rorke looked at her askance, more than a little amusement pulling at his mouth as he imagined such catastrophic results.

"Aye," she said. "It can make it very difficult to walk, or remain upright." She felt the laughter that rocked through him.

"I can imagine that it would."

The largest market was located near the river, where barges and flatboats brought cargoes from ships that filled the harbor.

Carts drawn by oxen added to the congestion of people in the streets crowding the stalls stocked with fresh fish, squawking chickens, squealing pigs, kegs of ale and mead, a limited supply of winter vegetables, sacks of apples, pears, and various nuts. Cook fires provided an array of meats and fish. There were also sticky, honey pastries.

One merchant sold bundles of uncarded wool, while another sold iron cook pots, platters, and utensils. Still others sold sacks of grain, flour, and pots of honey.

Then there were merchants who sold household goods, including brooms and brushes, tools, leather hides piled high and still reeking from the tanner's table, while others sold lengths of fine woven wool, muslin, and satins, ribbons and lengths of satin cording with an eye toward selling to the Norman noblemen and their knights, who frequented the market with—it was rumored—gold pieces in their pockets.

If they had been forced to surrender their kingdom, they might at least be compensated by the inflated prices they asked for their goods.

The Norman knights on their warhorses stood out in spite of the simple gray woolen mantles that concealed the battle armor. They received a variety of stares, glares, and open taunts as they passed the market stalls. Vivian held her breath in anticipation of trouble, but, remarkably, there was none.

Rorke's knights rode three on each side with stoic expressions, eyes looking straight ahead while still watching for any warning of violence.

She felt his arm tighten about her, but it was the only outward sign of his own wariness. On any other occasion it might have been no more than a gesture to steady her in the saddle before him. Only she was aware of the deeply corded muscles that did not completely relax, and the tension she felt through layers of cloth and mail armor.

"I had not realized it would be so dangerous." She felt the lift of Rorke's shoulder against hers in a shrug.

"It is always equally difficult for the invaders as it is for the vanquished."

Accustomed to being able to sense inner thoughts and emotions of others, she found it disconcerting that she could not sense his. She turned her head slightly to ask, "Have you a great deal of experience in such matters?"

"Aye, some."

He did not easily reveal details of his life. In that same congenial mood she asked, "Which is it? Invader? Or vanquished?"

"Both."

She turned with more than a little surprise. "I would not have thought the Count d'Anjou would have allowed himself to be vanquished."

He continued to stare over her head, his gaze scanning the street before them with the practiced ease of a warrior experienced with such matters.

"No one allows it, or plans it, but when you are sixteen and inexperienced in such matters much can go awry."

She was startled. "Sixteen? So young."

His lips thinned. "Aye, and a soldier for sixteen more. Half my life has been spent on the battlefield." He made no attempt to disguise the weary disillusionment in the words.

She heard the loneliness, like a heavy mantle that he wore. "When did you last see your family and home?"

"I was but ten years of age when last I saw Anjou." There was a poignancy of longing in his voice that flattened and became as hard as stone as he said, "I have no family."

The ease they'd found with each other earlier had disappeared like the sun behind a cloud, taking with it the warmth of laughter. Whatever it was that had taken a ten-year-old boy from his home and family had left deep wounds that had never healed. He spoke no more of it and Vivian concentrated on the purpose that had brought them there.

She finally found the market stall she was looking for. "I must get down," she insisted.

"It is too dangerous," Rorke warned. "Make your selections and I will have one of my men pay for it."

"It cannot be done that way. I must do it to be certain of what I am buying."

He reluctantly agreed. "Very well." At a nodded signal, his men dismounted. Rorke dismounted as well, lifting her from the saddle and gently lowering her to the street. The pressure of his gloved hands lingered at the curve of her waist.

"You will stay close at all times," he spoke low. "Make the necessary purchases and I will pay for them. It is dangerous for you here."

"Yes, it is," she agreed with a certain sadness that somehow reached beneath his hard, warrior's facade and touched a place somewhere beneath the chain mail armor, the thick underpadding and beneath the sheaf of hard muscle and the shield of his ribs.

"I wish that it could be otherwise," he said with sudden gentleness. His expression shifted with some emotion that she'd glimpsed before. First on the plain at Hastings when bandaging the wound at his side and again when she'd gone out among the wounded and he'd gone after her. He lifted a gloved hand and touched her cheek; she felt his warmth through thick layers of leather.

"I wish I could regret that you were the healer I found that day at Amesbury, instead of the old woman," he confessed and then with equal honesty, told her, "but I cannot."

Unable to sense any of his inner thoughts, she heard the intensity of the words that came low at his throat. With her newly discovered woman's sense she knew the words were neither easily said or lightly given.

So disconcerting were these new feelings that she tried to step away from him, putting distance between them, but found she could not. The warhorse blocked any retreat.

"Please, milord," she beseeched, struggling to understand what she had never felt before. "I would not unnecessarily delay your men from returning to their duties." She fixed her gaze at the intricately designed twin medallions that secured his mantle about his shoulders—the images of two lions in hammered gold.

"They are my men. I say what their duties shall be. Even if it is escorting beautiful maids about the marketplace."

Her startled gaze lifted and met his. No one had ever said that about her . . . called her beautiful.

For the first time in her life, Vivian experienced uncertainty—in the meaning of the words, the peculiar way he said them, as though it was an endearment spoken between lovers. A sudden intense longing welled within her, bringing a flood of unwanted emotions.

All at once she wanted to scream, cry, and laugh, with absolutely no idea as to the cause of such a malady, except that it both excited and terrified her.

His smile eased the uncertainty, beginning at one corner of his mouth and lifting to those gray eyes. Sensing her discomfiture, he stepped back, allowing her escape.

Like a startled falcon, uncertain of the hand that flies it, she flew from his side to the first market stall to inspect the merchant's wares. In that moment, it was as if he'd lost the sun from the heavens in the loss of her radiant beauty by his side.

"Follow close at hand," he instructed his men. "I want no surprises." Handing the stallion's reins over to the nearest knight, he walked with her.

When it came to marketing, he discovered she had a quick eye, an extraordinary grasp of numbers, and, as she had once pointed out, she was a shrewd bargain-maker. She showed enough interest in everything she considered to whet the merchants' appetites for a sale and make them overly confident of the coin that would soon line their pockets.

They resented her. She was finely dressed with Rorke's mantle concealing the much-mended gown beneath, and she spoke their own language with a fluency that revealed she was indeed Saxon.

There was only one conclusion to be drawn from her presence among the Norman knights and escorted by a Norman nobleman without restraint of chains. If she was not his prisoner, then she was his whore.

Rorke saw it in their degrading glances and heard it in their rude responses to her questions about this herb or that one, or some powder substance, or liquid in a vial. Yet, she treated each person she encountered with kindness, seeming not to notice.

She purchased leaves, picking through them carefully for just the right ones. She also purchased sprigs of other varieties. When the woman offered the contents of a particular basket for her inspection, Vivian waved it aside and pronounced it inferior for her use. She then selected an appropriate substitute.

The purchases were weighed, separately wrapped, and handed over to one of Rorke's men. The woman announced the sum for the purchases. Before the good knight could hand over the appropriate coins, Vivian plucked three from the handful and gave them to the woman, who immediately set up a protest. Vivian leaned close so that only the woman could hear.

"I have given you a fair price," she informed the woman. "If you protest, I shall make it known to everyone in this market that you weight your measuring baskets with stones, thereby driving up the cost of each purchase and cheating your customers."

So as to leave no doubt that she would do exactly as she promised, Vivian seized the woman's thin, grubby hand, forced it open, and dropped several stones that she had picked from among the herbs and plants into the cupped palm. With an icy glare, the woman's hand snapped closed over the stones.

"Is there some difficulty?" Rorke inquired.

"No longer, milord," Vivian said with a small smile.

As they walked to the next stall, Rorke recalled what she had told him the day before. "Always give more than you intended, but less than is demanded?" he quipped, gray eyes warm with tiny flecks of golden light.

"Since I could easily find most of those herbs and plants in the forest, you paid far more than I intended," she pointed out. "And the old crone will not find herself flogged or in chains, which she would have if I'd paid what she demanded. So the bargain is well made."

"I will be most careful not to enter into any bargains with you," he responded, smiling down at her. "I might find myself without my warhorse, sword, or any of my men."

Heads turned as she walked past each stall. Fierce expressions softened when she stopped to make an inquiry about this item or that.

She never failed to draw a merchant into conversation, their crude comments forgotten as they stared into that luminous blue gaze; the musical softness of her voice had a strangely soothing effect, as did the gentle touch of her hand on the head or face of a grubby, wide-eyed street urchin.

I feel like those children, Rorke thought, fascinated by those unusual blue eyes, drawn by the sound of her voice, longing for the touch of her hand. His own hand played over a length of particularly fine woven wool in a shade of pale mauve and he imagined how it would look next to her skin.

She moved ahead, surrounded by her well-armed guard. Rorke paid the merchant for the length of wool and tucked the wrapped bundle inside his mail hauberk. He caught up with her at a stall where the merchant was selling tallow candles, soaps, and fragrant herbs. She cupped a handful of herbs, eyes closed with pleasure as she inhaled the fragrance.

"Another curative?" he inquired.

"Hmmmm, a curative against the stench of lye and tallow."

Previous experience with some of her concoctions, not to mention the tales she'd told him, made him cautious. Gently seizing a slender wrist, he cradled her hand in his, the sweet fragrance almost as pleasing to his senses as the touch of her skin. He smiled pleasurably at the scent of lavender.

"This surely cannot cure much," he teased. "It does not smell of rotten eggs, sting the eyes, or choke at the throat."

She laughed, a warm, magical sound filled with golden light and its own healing balm, making him long to hear it again and again, when evening shadows grew long and there were only the sounds of soldiers' voices raised in lewd, drunken revelry.

Or in the darker hours of night, when the only sound was the anger that haunted his dreams.

Or at first light, when ghosts haunted the dawn.

She poured the contents from her palm back into the vendor's basket. "No, but it soothes the spirit and makes one remember spring in the midst of winter." To the vendor she said, "I will take a large basket of the tansy instead. For all the finery of the Saxon barons, there are enough bugs crawling about the royal household to move the stones in the walls. I will not abide fleas and mites."

"Best make it two large baskets," Rorke commented. "Half the garrison is acrawl." Vivian moved on ahead while he paid for the purchases.

The men had grown hungry and thirsty, and looked longingly at some of the food and drink that was offered. At the next vendor's stall, they purchased mugs full of Hogsbreath Ale.

Accustomed to French wine, they stared dubiously at the dark, frothy liquid. With a muttered toast, or what might have been a curse or prayer, they downed the ale.

They looked at each other with expressions that varied from amazement to horror to satisfaction.

"It tastes like a hog's breath, all right," one of the men commented, and they all burst out laughing.

From the next vendor several meat pastries were purchased and passed round. Rorke balanced one on his gloved fingers.

"It's called shepherd's pie," Vivian announced, eyes filled with laughter at the expressions that crossed the knights' faces. One by one the meat pies were popped into hungry mouths and consumed.

"Aye," commented one, with a twinkling eye, "Tastes like a shepherd."

Vivian laughed as she walked ahead. She had not thought to enjoy the morning when she first discovered Rorke waiting for her. But the first wariness had passed. There seemed to be no threat of danger in the marketplace, and Rorke had not questioned her about the attack against William in the streets of London, nor the unusual ring of fire, as he had promised he would.

She inspected thick rolls of linen cloth and thought of all the bandages she'd made from bits and pieces of old cloth and shirts. She made her purchase and was about to turn and look for Rorke. His back was turned as he inspected some woolen cloth. Suddenly she sensed a familiar presence beside her that she had last sensed at the battlefield at Hastings. An arm closed around her waist and a hand clamped over her mouth. She was pulled behind a curtain hung between two of the vendors' stalls. She finally pried that hand away from her mouth and stared in surprise at the familiar face.

"Conal," she whispered, "You shouldn't be here. It's much too dangerous." He pulled her to the other side of a cart that stood behind the vendor's stall.

"I followed you. I've joined with others here in London."

Fear clenched about her heart. "No, you mustn't!"

"We have weapons," he assured her, lifting his tunic to reveal the short-bladed knife that hung at his waist. The knife was woefully inadequate compared to Norman bows, broadswords, and war lances. She glanced over her shoulder. Any moment her disappearance would be noticed.

"I came for you," he repeated. "I'll get you out of London before we strike at these Norman bastards!"

"No!" Vivian cried vehemently. "You must not!" She tried desperately to make him understand. "I cannot go back to Amesbury. Not now." Her voice softened as she struggled with the uncertainty of her own visions. "Perhaps never."

"What are you saying? I will take you there. You'll be safe."

"Conal, please! You must understand. I cannot leave."

"You are not their prisoner," he argued. "You are not chained or bound. You must leave with me now."

"It is not that simple." She tried desperately to find a way to make him understand. She could not tell him of her vision or the terrible, spreading darkness. He would only say that it was Duke William's Norman army. There was no way she might explain and have him believe the greater truth.

"Meg and Poladouras are here," she explained, something she knew he could understand. "There would be dreadful repercussions for them if I was to leave; therefore, I cannot."

"It's more than that. I've heard it whispered about," he spat out, his fingers bruising at her arms. "I heard it in the streets as you passed by. They say that you and the bastard FitzWarren are lovers. I heard the sweetness of your laughter. I saw him touch you. Do you know how many Saxons he's killed? How could you give yourself to him?" His expression twisted in an agony of emotion.

She winced at the accusation. "Conal, please. You do not understand. I beg of you, go now before it is too late."

But it was already too late. From the street came shouts, harshly barked orders, and screams as Rorke and his soldiers began searching the vendors' stalls for her.

Behind them she heard the sounds of horses hooves on cobbled stones, the cold hiss of steel as swords were drawn from scabbards, and more shouts as other soldiers joined the hunt.

The festive mood of the marketplace erupted in screams and curses as vendors tried to protect their wares from damage and mothers grabbed their children to protect them from being trampled under the hooves of the horses.

"Please, Conal!" she cried. "It is me they're after."

When he refused to let her go, she laid her own hand over his, clamped at her arm. With a firmness of voice, she repeated, "Release me, Conal. I cannot go with you. You must go on alone."

"I will not leave you!"

When still he would not release her, Vivian gently increased the pressure of her hand, drawing on the source of the power, bending his will to her own. Against his will, his fingers loosened about her arm, releasing her. He stared at her, incredulous.

"Go now, before they find you," she told him, before he

could ask any questions. "They must not find you here. Return to Amesbury while you can."

"But what of you?"

"I will not be harmed. The Count of Anjou has already seen you before in the forest at Hastings. He suspects you of involvement with the rebellion. If you are found, I fear for your life."

Still he hesitated. "Vivian, I came for you because . . ."

She already knew what he would say. She heard the words as clearly as if he spoke them.

"No, Conal. It is impossible. I can never love as other women love. But you are a good man and have a great deal of love to give. You must find someone who deserves that love. Now, please go!" she urgently begged him.

She sensed the soldiers before she saw them. They came at them behind the row of vendors' stalls. But the men she saw were not Rorke FitzWarren's knights. They were Vachel's men!

Light glinted from steel swords as soldiers closed in on them. With the stone wall that lined the vendors' stalls directly behind them, Conal was trapped, with no hope of escape. He pulled the knife from his belt and turned to face the Norman soldiers.

Memories of the bodies that littered the battlefield at Hastings came back to her vividly. She couldn't bear the thought of Conal's death.

"No!" she insisted. "There is another way."

"I am not afraid to die!"

"There must be no more Saxon blood shed," she pleaded with him. "Conal, if ever you loved me, do this for me. I beg you."

She saw the agony of the choice she asked him to make. He loved her. She knew that. She also knew he would do as she asked.

As the soldiers tore through the stalls around them, fast closing in, she took hold of his arm and pulled him with her back toward the stone wall.

"You will have to trust me. It is the only way."

He glanced past her in the direction of the soldiers who rapidly converged from all directions. In moments, they would be seen and there would be no hope of escape. He nodded.

"I do trust you."

"Take both my hands, and no matter what happens, do not let go." Hesitantly, Conal took hold of her hands.

"Close your eyes," she told him. "No matter what happens, do not open them." What she meant to do would take all her strength—and all her powers.

Shouts were much closer now. Her hands clasped tightly over his, Vivian took a step back. Then another, and another, pulling him with her as she and Conal passed through the solid stone wall together.

Seventeen

"Vivian . . . Vivian . . ."

Her name sounded very far away, calling her, pulling her back, closer now . . .

"Vivian?"

It was Rorke. His voice was no longer harsh but filled with an unexpected gentleness of concern. His strong hands closed over her arms as though he were physically pulling her back into the physical world where he and his men existed.

The misty grayness that enveloped everything slowly disappeared. The outlines of buildings, a cart, the cobbled stones in the street, came into sharp relief once more, taking shape as her senses cleared and her strength returned as though waking from some long sleep.

She leaned against the stone wall where only moments earlier she had stood with Conal. Her sense of him was strong and undisturbed and she knew he remained hidden as she had warned him before leaving.

"I am all right," she said, in answer to Rorke's question.

"How many were there?" Rorke asked, now a sharp edge to his voice.

"I don't know," she answered carefully. Hadn't Conal said that he'd joined up with others in London? "Perhaps several," she went on hesitantly. "It was difficult to tell in all the confusion."

As soldiers swarmed around them, searching through the stalls down the length of the street, he asked, "Were they armed?"

"I saw no battle swords," she answered evasively.

He stroked disheveled hair back from her forehead in a gesture that was both rough and tender, as though he searched for the mark of a blow. She knew he sensed something amiss and did not entirely believe her.

His mouth curved a tight frown. "You're as cold as stone. Are you certain you are not harmed?"

Laughter bubbled at her throat at the comparison he chose, and she thought, if only he knew. She shook her head.

"Just frightened, is all." One certain answer in the midst of so many uncertain ones.

Two of his men returned. Their expressions were grim with their failure to find any trace of the rebels they sought. Vivian repressed a sigh of relief that Conal was still safely hidden where she'd left him.

Weak and disoriented from their journey through the stone, he'd stared at her with mute incredulity, struggling to comprehend what he'd just experienced as they emerged on the other side of the wall.

"It will pass," she had assured him. Weak from the journey at least he could not argue with her.

She infused him with some of her precious warmth through the connection of their hands so that the recovery might be quicker in the event this hiding place was discovered and he was forced to flee. He'd stared up at her in stunned bewilderment.

"It lasts only a short while," she reassured him of the oddly disembodied sensation she knew he experienced as though his body had separated into millions of tiny pieces that had passed through the stone like water through a sieve, and only now slowly and painfully, rejoined. She did not experience that same pain, merely a slight weakness because of the energy it took to pass through the stones.

"When it has passed," she hurriedly went on to tell him, "you will remember nothing of what has happened." She gently stroked her thumb across his forehead as if she was physically removing the memory.

"You will remember only this thought—you must remain hidden until the danger has passed. When the Norman soldiers have gone, then you must leave London immediately."

From beyond the wall she had heard the urgent shouts of the soldiers and knew that if she was not found soon, the search would spread beyond the market to this very street on the other side of the wall.

"Good-bye, Conal," she softly whispered, stroking her thumb once more across his forehead, leaving him with the memory of their parting. Then she stood and, focusing the power deep within her, returned through the stone.

"Did you see the direction they fled?" Rorke asked insistently.

She shook her head. "There was too much confusion in the marketplace. Then we became separated, and they were gone."

She had answered truthfully, yet she saw the questions that went unasked behind that penetrating gray gaze.

With a curt nod, he turned to order his men to continue the search down both directions of the street, then to the adjacent streets, and alleys.

"Please, Rorke!" she beseeched him, desperate to prevent it lest Conal be discovered. "Might we not return now? There is no harm done. They are fled. Surely there is no use in giving chase."

A dark brow lifted with speculation. "You beg for yet more Saxon lives, Vivian? I have already spared many for your sake."

"I ask for wisdom. The attackers are fled. You might never find them. Would you punish *innocent* Saxons?" she demanded.

The sound of approaching riders drew her attention and a new coldness of dread filled her as the bishop rode up, and behind him rode Vachel.

The bishop swung down from his mount and approached with an air of authority meant to remind everyone that he was brother to Duke William of Normandy.

"Stand aside," he commanded one of Rorke's men who blocked his way. The man stepped aside only when Rorke nodded a look in response.

"I had not thought to see you about the streets of London, milord Bishop," Rorke commented. "Of late, you seem overly occupied with affairs of state."

"I was told there had been some difficulty at the marketplace. You were attacked by Saxon rebels," the bishop explained.

"It is amazing the swiftness with which you learn these things." Rorke spoke in a coldly sarcastic tone. "One would think that you have the ear of the divine in such matters that you are able to assist so readily."

The bishop's eyes flashed anger, then his expression was carefully controlled to reveal nothing of his inner emotions. "I was nearby on another matter, milord FitzWarren. Word spreads quickly in the streets." He made an expansive gesture to the buildings that surrounded them. "I but thought to give assistance lest you be overpowered and find yourselves in some difficulty." He glanced about at Rorke's knights and his expression revealed a flash of satisfaction.

" 'Tis a pity, but it seems they have indeed eluded you." Then his gaze fell upon Vivian. A single dark brow lifted in silent speculation that was as clear as if he had said it aloud.

"My brother would be most distressed to learn that his healer perhaps conspired with Saxon rebels." He fixed Vivian with a probing gaze. "One of my men said he saw you with a man."

Vachel, of course! She began to reply, but before she could speak Rorke's fingers tightened in warning over her arm.

"She has already told me of it," he assured the bishop.

"Ah, then the rebels have been caught." He glanced skeptically from one to the other of Rorke's men, doubt spreading across his features.

"They have not," Rorke told him. "They got away. Fled into the streets and alleys where it was impossible to find them."

"Save your excuses for the king, FitzWarren," the bishop snapped.

"I make no excuses," Rorke assured him, his voice taking on a dangerous tone, "for either my men or myself. It is a statement of fact. The people of London know the city far better than we."

The bishop's features hardened. "Are you saying they vanished? Perhaps disappeared through the walls."

"I am saying that it is a simple matter to take a turn and disappear in streets unfamiliar to others. I recall your men have done the same on several occasions. You spoke of this very matter with William yestereve. And as for the skill and loyalty of my men, I would stand them against yours whenever you choose, milord Bishop."

It was said in such a way there was no attempt to disguise his contempt for the bishop. Nor did the bishop insult Rorke with any dissembling attempt on his own part. His voice was hard, almost accusing.

"I do not speak of prowess with a blade or war ax, milord FitzWarren, but of loftier ambitions."

Like a living, malevolent force, the hatred between the two men could be heard and felt. Vivian shivered at the barely restrained violence she sensed hovering between them.

"Then, milord Bishop," Rorke told him, his eyes the color of winter's death, "at least in this, we think the same." Then, his hand gentle but firm at her arm, he told the bishop, "You may continue to search, but as you can see this street is nothing but walls. A Saxon rebel would have to either become like the mist, or walk through a wall to avoid being seen. Good morn, milord Bishop."

He turned then and escorted Vivian to his horse, his men closing a protective circle at his back. He lifted her to the saddle, and then swung up behind her.

"Take care," Rorke warned the bishop in parting. "It can be dangerous in the streets of London."

As they rode back to the fortress, Vivian felt the tension of anger in every hardened muscle of his body, and the skin drawn white over those scarred hands as he firmly held the reins before her.

The ease they'd shared earlier was gone, ruined by the encounter with the bishop as much as the encounter with Saxon rebels.

His men trailed behind and alongside them as they had not when leaving the fortress earlier that morning, making her wonder which danger they guarded against.

Saxon rebels? Or the bishop's men?

"Will you tell me of it now, Vivian?" he startled her by asking. Uneasily, she realized the matter was not so easily dismissed as he had told the bishop.

She chose her words carefully, for she sensed his scrutiny even though those cold gray eyes stared fixedly ahead and betrayed none of his emotions.

"It is as I said, milord. I cannot tell you more."

"Cannot, Vivian? Or will not?" he asked, his voice low in his throat with a warning of unknown dangerous emotions.

She squeezed her eyes tightly shut in agony of the betrayal she knew he sensed. For if she told the truth, she risked Conal's life, and that she could not do.

"I cannot, milord."

He did not answer but remained stonily silent as they returned to the fortress, and she knew that he did not believe her.

It was as if the sun was now hidden behind the clouds, the

brief warmth of their relationship returned to that guarded wariness of captor and captive that made her restless, uneasy, and uncertain of what might happen next.

Once inside the fortress, she slid to the ground, eager to escape more questions, the bundles of herbs clutched under her arm. Muttering a hasty, "Thank you, milord," she returned to the kitchen through the connecting corridor at the sally port. Vivian felt a prickling of apprehension as Rorke followed her through the narrow passage to the kitchen.

"You forgot the baskets," he reminded her, setting the two baskets on a butcher's table. "It seemed of great importance to you earlier that you have the herbal mixture."

"Thank you, milord," she said hurriedly, wishing him to be gone so that she could sort through her chaotic thoughts and emotions. She could never do that in his presence, for he had far too disconcerting an effect on her.

As she reached for the baskets that contained the tansy, he commented, "It would not do to have bothersome creatures invading the royal household."

His hand remained on the handle as she tried to take it, as though they engaged in some tug-of-war. There was no mistaking the warning in his carefully chosen words.

"No, it would not," she said, needing no special sense to tell her that he was not the least fooled by her account of what had happened in the marketplace.

His expression was contemplative. "Be very careful, demoiselle," he cautioned. "Your herbs may not be enough to ward off such pestilence."

His fingers loosened and he relinquished the basket, bidding her a brusque farewell.

Rorke found Tarek al Sharif in the stables, grooming the Arabian mare. His friend was dressed in leather breeches that he'd finally given in to wearing to survive the "icy hand of the cursed English winter," and a long flowing tunic made of wool rather than the much cooler cotton he usually wore. It reached to his knees and was belted with a wide sash at his narrow waist.

With his long, dark hair sleeked back to the nape of his neck and tied, bronze skin gleaming from the workout of the grooming, the ever-present wide, curved blade hanging at his waist, he looked very much the Persian warrior. Except for startling blue eyes above the flash of white teeth as he greeted his friend.

Rorke's response was less than congenial as he strode into the stable leading the large warhorse.

The large beast had taken on Rorke's dark mood, tossing its head threateningly and curling a lip back over large teeth as Rorke smacked him across the rump to get him into the roomy end stall.

"Bite me you brainless brute," he threatened, waving a gloved fist as those teeth flashed precariously close to his shoulder, "and you will find yourself pulling a dung cart about the yard!" When the stallion was secured in the stall, he slammed a crossbar into place and turned on an oath.

"Where is my squire?" he demanded.

Undaunted by his friend's unusual temper, Tarek commented, "No doubt in hiding until the storm has passed."

Rorke glared at him, determined to vent some of his anger. "I do not understand why you insist on grooming the beast yourself, when you have a squire to do the task for you." His gray eyes narrowed. "Has the leman abandoned your bed and you've now taken to sleeping in the hay?"

As patiently and methodically as he groomed the mare, Tarek explained, "It is not the work I seek. In grooming the mare myself, I strengthen the bond between us. My life may one day depend on that bond." He gestured with a brush toward Rorke's large warhorse. "Instead of fearing that my life may one day be imperiled by the beast I ride."

"I do not fear the Frisian," Rorke informed him tightly. "I understand his strength and I trust in that strength. I need no bond to make the beast do my bidding. Methinks you spend too much time with your horse."

"And I think that yours must have thrown you into a dung heap, for you are surly enough. Although I see no stains to mark the landing place."

His grin widened as he looked over at Rorke and saw the shaggy mane of wet hair and the beads of water that glistened at the angles of hard-set features from his ablutions. "Perhaps it has already been washed. Pray tell, milord Count d'Anjou," he asked as he cleaned a brush, "what disobedient knight has put you in such foul temper?"

Rorke glared at Tarek. " 'Twas no knight, nor disobedience, and I am not fouled of temper!"

"Ah, I think I begin to see the way of the matter. If not a disobedient knight, nor a sound dumping in a dung heap, then it must be a woman. Or perhaps," he continued to speculate even at great risk if the expression of Rorke's face was any indication, "it is the lack of a woman. Although I would not have thought it so, these past empty nights when the fair Judith has withheld her presence from certain other knights." He spoke as though with some personal knowledge on the matter.

"Have you finished?" Rorke snapped.

Deliberately misinterpreting his meaning, Tarek gave the Arabian a thorough inspection, a satisfied grin barely suppressed at his mouth. He shrugged. "For now? Yes, it is finished."

"Then bring that cursed curved sword of yours and give it your undivided attention," Rorke demanded.

He unbuckled heavy mail armor, letting it lie where it fell. Clad in heavy muslin shirt and leather breeches, he unsheathed his broadsword and stalked from the stables to the practice yard.

"It is a woman!" Tarek concluded, needing no further evidence. The Arabian's ears twitched back and forth as though in answer. Tarek grinned. Unsheathing his own curved blade, he loosened his muscles with several slices through the air.

As he left the stables, he said to the mare, "You are such bewitching creatures."

They practiced until the sky grew heavy and leaden, blades flashing amidst the knife slashes of lightning that sliced the sky, steel ringing out against steel as chords of thunder rolled over them, rain pelting down until their gray, shadowy figures were like hammered silver beneath the storm-tossed sky.

They fought on, until both were physically exhausted, their clothes plastered against their bodies by sweat and rain, and tiny rivulets of crimson ran amidst the brown mud underfoot.

Unsettled and troubled by what had happened at the marketplace and the chaos of feelings she neither understood nor wanted, Vivian longed for some private moments to herself. Some hidden place, undisturbed and unseen by those who could not understand, where she might seek a vision among the flames.

But in the overcrowded royal household there was no such place. And she dared not return to Rorke's chamber for fear of encountering him there with more questions for her.

There was a small niche in the kitchen where she might work, and she found some measure of solace in preparing her powders and tisanes for the next several hours.

The syrups and precious liquids were poured into vials and sealed with wood corks. Powders and leaves were folded in parchment envelopes. All were carefully labeled so that there would be no later confusion as to the remedy.

William's cook had provided her a shelf for the vials. The dry herbs were tucked away in the leather pouches she always kept with her. Because of the lack of some necessary potions, she'd been forced to make a few substitutions from what was available at market, but she felt confident that she could take care of most complaints.

Meg had been waiting for her upon her return and even without the ability to see she sensed Vivian's distress. She waited until they were well within the passage and away from the kitchen where none might overhear.

"Something has happened," Meg said with a certainty. "I can feel it in you. Your hands are as cold as death."

Quickly, Vivian told her of her encounter with Conal and the means of his escape.

Meg shook her head. "I feared it might come to this. He was wild with grief when you were taken from Amesbury. You know of the boy's feelings for you?"

Vivian nodded sadly. "Yes, he spoke of them. I tried to dissuade him. But I fear it is not ended."

"It is not," Meg said with a certainty. "And I fear no good will come of it. What will you do?"

"I tried to convince him that he must leave London, but he would not listen." Then her gaze lifted to Meg's tense face. "Poladouras spoke of visiting friends in London. If only he were able to find Conal and convince him that he must leave."

Meg nodded. "I will speak to him of it. Certainly the bishop will give his permission. Poladouras has told me the man resents the time he spends with William." Her voice trembled with another thought.

"I fear the bishop. He is like the ones at St. Anne's, who cannot see beyond their own ambitions. I sense the bishop's ambitions are many and dangerous. You must be careful, *mo chroi.*"

Vivian kissed the wrinkled old cheek lovingly. "And have a care for yourself, dear heart." She could not let Meg know that she, too, feared the bishop.

"Bah!" Meg snorted. "These Normans cannot do any more than five hundred years have done. Did you remember the leaves for the misery of my hands?"

"Aye," Vivian laughed. " 'Tis here." She handed over the packet. "And now there are others I must see to."

Through the afternoon she treated several injuries. William's knights continuously practiced in the courtyard and sought her out with various bruises, cuts, and scrapes from their practicing war skills. Kept busy with their demands, she tried to put the events of the morning out of her thoughts.

When it seemed the last of the injuries had been tended, she looked up to find Tarek al Sharif lazily sprawled on a chair across the chamber. He rose sinuously to his feet with the lithe grace of a cat as it stretches, and strode toward her.

He possessed a virulent power that hinted at the exotic ancestry of his mother—Persian, she had been told—and contrasted sharply, fascinatingly, with the stark, bold blue of his eyes, the gift of his Norse father, a man he had never known.

Tarek al Sharif reminded her of the wild creatures in the forest—creatures of the earth, wind, and sky—living as one with other men, but at the same time always apart, aloof, solitary, and proud, like the falcon.

Yet she had never felt afraid when she was with him. On some deeper level they established that first day an unspoken understanding of one another. Vivian knew he was her friend. As he approached, her eyes widened at the wound that carved the flesh in a perfect half-moon above his left brow.

"You've been injured," she exclaimed on a note of concern.

"It is hardly more than a small cut," he said with a flash of self-deprecating smile. "But it bleeds profusely." The smile became a grimace as he tried to staunch the flow with his fingers.

"It is most bothersome. I thought you might have a curative, or perhaps the magic of your healing touch."

"Or, perhaps," she suggested with an arch of auburn brow, "you should have ducked when you stood your ground, and not been injured at all."

He shrugged as he sat at the table beside her and reached for a linen cloth to press against the cut. "It has been suggested that I have a most stubborn nature. In truth, I find it difficult to yield when victory is within my grasp."

She glanced down at his strong hands, powerfully lined with veins beneath the bronzed skin. They carried the look of the sun even in the midst of winter.

"Were you victorious?"

"My answer would be yes," he answered carelessly. "However, if you were to ask the same question of my opponent, he would claim the victory for himself."

"Fools!" she hissed under her breath, and slammed down a slender blade used for blending medicants. "Will this warring never end!"

He looked at her askance, his uninjured brow lifting with uncertainty. "It occurs to me that I would be safer in allowing the wound to bleed," he suggested, suddenly wary of her mood. "There seems to be a plague of ill humor about that might prove more dangerous than a mere cut." He made to rise.

"Sit!" she ordered. "I will mend the wound. But if next time you find your head severed from your shoulders, do not expect me to mend it." She wondered briefly who his opponent was, and then wondered no more, for the answer was a simple one. There was only one person Tarek practiced against, and that was Rorke. A tremor of fear sliced through her as she wondered if he might have been injured.

Late that afternoon long trestle tables were moved into place for the evening meal. Vivian supervised the distribution of tansy among the newly changed straw that covered the floor of the main hall. She also instructed the young Saxon servant girls to hang sprigs of tansy from overhead beams in the kitchen and the adjacent laundry.

The laundry was behind the kitchen to make use of the cook fire at the hearth for hot water. The laundress had said Vivian might use the water for bathing.

Meg's healing tisanes had been set to cool. Powders now filled vials and jars and Meg had gone to seek out Poladouras to speak with him about finding Conal in London. Mally was taking down freshly laundered garments from a line drawn across the laundry room.

"I've left the last barrel of water for you," Mally apologized. "I went ahead and bathed."

The water was barely warm and smelled strongly of lye soap. But anything at all was better than cold water.

"It will do very well. Thank you, Mally."

The girl left her then to seek out Justin, for there was no

doubt for whom she had risked the perils of bathing in mid-winter.

From among her herbal concoctions Vivian took a double handful of lavender petals and sprinkled them across the surface of the water. She shuddered at the sight of the caustic lye soap, replacing it with a vial of thick extract from glossy, dark green roots that were among the purchases she made that day.

When rubbed briskly between both hands, the extract produced a soapy lather that was far better than lye for bathing and didn't burn the skin.

It was pleasantly fragrant, scented with the essence of fresh meadows in the spring. She used it sparingly as she bathed and then lathered it through her hair, certain she would not have another opportunity to visit the market any time soon.

Some time later, as she returned to the chamber, wet hair plaited down the middle of her back, the folds of the heavy mantle held close about her against the chill of drafts found in the halls, she heard the sounds of boisterous revelry from the main hall.

The evening meal had ended and William's knights, feeling the restraint of inactivity, challenged one another to feats of marksmanship, wrestling, as well as contests to determine which man could consume the most Saxon ale.

As she crossed a passage, empty except for guards posted at each entrance and doorway, in the guttering light from torches set along the walls, she caught a glimpse of a woman.

Judith de Marque was briefly illuminated in the pool of light from a torch at the far end of the passage. She did not see Vivian, so fixed was her attention on the tall warrior whose identity was shrouded by shadows. Vivian heard the whisper of exchanged words followed by Judith's sultry laughter.

There was a brief glint as light from a torch reflected off some piece of finery the knight wore. Then they disappeared in the shadows at the end of the passage as it angled to another part of the fortress away from the main hall, no doubt seeking one of the private niches.

Vivian thought again of Rorke FitzWarren and the rumors whispered among his knights, and wondered if he sought to take his ease with the leman.

Pain twisted sharply somewhere under her breast at the thought, making it difficult to breathe. Frowning as she reached the chamber, she tried to rid herself of the unwanted feelings so unfamiliar to her. She longed for the privacy of the chamber, hoping Rorke had not returned.

Rusted from the ever-present damp and cold that coated everything inside the royal fortress with a chilled clamminess, the heavy iron latch at the stout chamber door grated uncooperatively. It usually required both strong young hands of Rorke's squire to lift it. Vivian persuaded it with but one.

It lifted easily, the metal glowing slightly as she pushed open the door to the chamber and drew aside the heavy tapestry. On a startled sound, she stopped suddenly just inside the doorway to the chamber, stunned by what she saw within.

Eighteen

With an apologetic look of innocence, Rorke FitzWarren turned from the hearth. "Please forgive me, demoiselle. When I arrived there was no one about. I did not mean to frighten you."

"You did not," she said, slowly releasing the breath that had suddenly lodged in her lungs at finding him there. She experienced a familiar alarm that she had not been able to sense his presence in the chamber before entering.

To cover her discomposure, she assured him, " 'Tis only that I thought everyone to be in the great hall. I had not expected to find you here."

Several candles had been lit, their light quivering in the sudden draft from the doorway. A trencher of food and flagon of wine sat on the table. A fire had been laid at the hearth and burned ravenously, throwing fierce golden light across the stark features of the man who sat at the table's edge.

He had poured a goblet of wine. The cracked shells of several nuts lay nearby. The small slender blade he always carried in a concealed place skewered a piece of fruit.

"Nor I," he replied with sudden seriousness of voice, the expression behind those wintry gray eyes inscrutable. It was impossible to know his mood. He drank from the goblet with great deliberateness of movement as though fortifying himself for something to come.

"Duke William deemed it necessary I seek your healer's skills," he explained.

A delicate auburn brow lifted in surprise as a surge of fear caught at her. "You have an injury?"

"Aye, and most serious," he said, his weight supported at the edge of the table.

One long leg was thrust before him and anchored the floor at the heel of his boot. His other leg hitched the edge of the table with a casual, restrained power that belied any impairment from injury.

"An encounter with a Persian blade," he went on to explain in that same grave manner.

Her brow angled even higher. Her earlier conversation with Tarek—owner of that Persian blade—left no doubt that he had considered himself to be the victor of the encounter. And yet, she had also seen Rorke's skill with a broadsword and found it difficult to believe the wound was as serious as he would have her believe.

Then, as he turned and reached for the goblet of wine at the table, she saw the large stain of blood on the sleeve of his shirt.

She crossed the chamber with a suddenness of movement that caused the flames at the candles to flutter as she passed. Quickly, she retrieved the basket of medicants and herbal potions from a niche in the wall.

"The shirt must be removed," she told him. When she turned back to him, she discovered with a start that he had already removed it.

She discovered also what she had chosen to forget from earlier encounters. Rorke FitzWarren, clad only in breeches and boots, was a sight that too easily drew the eye. She concentrated on his boots as she approached where he sat at the table with such injured grace.

There was a substantial amount of blood at his shoulder, most of it dried. She frowned as she soaked a clean linen cloth with a tincture of white willow bark extract, and then wiped away the dried blood and grime of sweat and mud from the practice yard, wondering why he had not immediately sought her skills when he received the injury.

Then, as the wound emerged under her gentle ministrations, her frown deepened. Though the wound had bled profusely, it was small. No longer than her smallest finger, and not at all deep. He bore scars on his body from wounds that had been far more severe and life-threatening.

"It must have been very painful," she said, contemplating him through narrowed gaze.

"Aye," he agreed with much sincerity. "A dreadful wound."

" 'Tis more likely a wound to your ego," she informed him, her voice tight and laced with sudden cynicism.

He gave her an amused glance. "You have a sharp tongue, mistress, hardly needed by a man so gravely injured who sits before you bleeding profusely and in need of care."

"And *you* have a lying tongue," she retorted. "The wound is hardly more than a scratch. I have suffered far more serious cuts harvesting greens in the forest."

"And yet, even the smallest wound may fester and bring on fever," he pointed out insistently. He had decided he must take a new course with her if he was to learn the truth of what happened that morning.

"You will bandage the wound now. If you please."

Vivian had no idea what game he played, or to what purpose, but she was not about to do his bidding.

"I cannot," she informed him, the blue of her eyes glittering like molten flame.

He looked at her like a cat considering a tender, succulent morsel of mouse. "Do you refuse, demoiselle?"

" 'Tis not that I refuse," she calmly replied.

"Are you incapable, then?" he challenged, eyes narrowing further, but now with the suspicion that perhaps he did not have the upper hand in this conversation.

"Not at all, milord," she assured him with a smile of deceptive innocence. " 'Tis only that before the wound may be bandaged"—her smile deepened with something that hinted at satisfaction—"it must first be *stitched.*"

"Stitched?" There was suddenly less challenge in his voice.

"Aye," she said with much seriousness. "For as you said, milord, *the smallest wound may fester and bring on fever.*"

She bit her lower lip so as not to burst out laughing at the stunned expression on his face as she removed a small wooden box the size of a square of soap from the basket.

"The wound must be properly closed," she continued, light glinting off the contents inside as she opened the box.

It contained the scarce, precious needles she had found in the physician's kit. She removed one of the needles, threading it with thick, fat thread the size of which might have been used to mend leather harness.

Under his much-narrowed gaze, she soaked it in the white willow bark solution, assuring him, "Care must be taken when stitching not to cause further infection."

Satisfied that the needle and thread were as clean as she could make them, she removed both from the solution, needle firmly grasped between thumb and forefinger.

"I must have more light," she said with a glance at the large candle on the table. "So that I do not take a wrong stitch and have to begin again."

She moved the candle closer, the flame reflecting in a suspicious glow that had appeared at her eyes. Then, with great concentration showing in the expression on her face, she proceeded to take the first stitch.

Fingers clamped her wrist firmly, bringing her gaze up in surprise.

"A simple bandage will do," Rorke informed her.

"But the risk of infection?" she protested.

"No stitches!" he insisted. "The cursed thing already throbs enough in the manner you pinch the skin together. I swear mistress, I believe you take pleasure in my discomfort."

"Very well, milord," she said solemnly. "But I cannot be held accountable for the outcome."

"I will risk the loss of the arm," he assured her sarcastically.

"I pray it will not come to that," she responded with such sincerity that he might have believed it had it not been for the mischievous gleam in her brilliant blue eyes. Nor the comment she couldn't resist making.

"And you will most certainly save great expense in the cost of garments since you will have need of only one sleeve instead of two.

"However, you may experience some impairment of movement with only one arm. It will be much more difficult," she suggested with a glance down at the table near where he sat and a smile to match the look in her eyes, ". . . to crack open walnuts."

She saw the subtle change in the look at his eyes that shifted from cool, wintry gray to some other emotion she'd glimpsed before but now recognized too late.

Before she could escape, he encircled her waist with his strong, healthy arm, roughly pulling her close and immediately making her aware that even with the use of only one arm, Rorke was still formidable and dangerous.

"You, demoiselle," he said, his face so close that she was forced to tilt her head back—so close, that her breasts were flattened against his bare chest—"are a mischievous, enchanting witch."

Her startled gaze met his.

"Nay, milord." Each hastily drawn breath only intensified the stunning sensation that spiraled through her and tingled at her breasts. Her nipples grew taut and hard so that she feared when she did free herself, he would see them through her gown.

With measured words that required a minimum of indrawn breath, she assured him, "I am not a witch."

He seemed to consider the possibility. "If not a witch, Vivian, at the very least you are bewitching." Then, so that there was no misunderstanding, he repeated, "There will be no stitches. A clean bandage will suffice."

"I cannot, milord," she pointed out, and felt a brief satisfaction at the expression on his face at her refusal, "when you hold me so close."

Satisfaction sharpened as she felt his arm loosen and lower about her. His hand shifted low on her spine and remained there, resting with faint pressure at the small of her back.

When she protested, he informed her in a tone of voice that suggested it might be unwise to argue, and that he would remove his hand no further, "Now, you will be able to bandage the wound."

With the certainty that he would more quickly release her from this disturbing closeness if she did as he asked, Vivian reached for the square pad of linen and the vial of white willow bark extract.

Blood still seeped at the wound. Dampening the cloth, she pressed it hard against the cut. Rorke glared a warning at her.

"Be warned, mistress. If it is your intention to cause an excess amount of pain, retaliation will be swift." As if to prove the promise of his threat, his arm closed once more around her. Vivian immediately became much more gentle in her ministrations.

"You did not need my skills. You might have bandaged the wound yourself," she commented as she cleaned it thoroughly.

She had so easily seen through his deception. Yet, he could not as easily see through hers.

"Perhaps I came to give a warning," he suggested.

"A warning?"

She tried to reach for the comfrey salve but found she could not, hindered as she was by the restriction of his embrace. When she glared at him, he relaxed his arm just enough to allow her to retrieve the salve, but no more. As she carefully applied the mildly sweet-smelling concoction, she felt him watching her.

"What happened this morning at the marketplace was dangerous."

So, he intended to pursue it, she thought. So be it. "Aye," she agreed solemnly. "Most dangerous. It grieved me to see those innocent people injured for no more reason than that they were in the marketplace." She looked at him with particular intent. "Will it never end until William's troops have slain every man, woman, and child in England?"

"The incident grieves me as well."

Given the sincerity in the way he said it, Vivian found that she believed him.

"But there was much more to it than that. I speak of the bishop. He is William's brother and thereby a very powerful man. He is not to be lightly dismissed for all his religious zealousness. It is that very zealousness that makes him particularly dangerous."

She could not believe it was so, yet she asked, "Do you fear him?"

"I do not fear any man," Rorke admitted truthfully. "Be he bishop, duke, or king. But I do respect the power such a man may wield. It is the power that can be dangerous. For power comes from the people, not by merely one man. One man's notions may be persuaded otherwise or set aside, but those of a multitude may not be so easily persuaded otherwise.

"William has given you his trust," he went on to explain, "a trust previously enjoyed only by a few, most particularly his brother."

"And by you, as well," she pointed out.

"Aye, but my ambitions are not the same as the bishop's." He brought his hand up, catching between thumb and forefinger a stray wisp of fiery red hair that had escaped the plait that hung at her back and curled above her ear.

"His ambitions make him dangerous. He is determined to prove you a traitor to the crown. Perhaps, then, it is more truthful to say that I came for the truth. If there is something more I should know about today, you must tell me now."

Vivian glanced at him carefully. Once before he had told her that he would have the truth from her. And once again, that promise rose like a chilling wind between them.

"I gave you the truth, milord," she said, in a voice that even to her was unconvincing.

"Aye," he answered with a faint, sardonic smile, repeating what she had told him at the time. "You *saw* nothing more."

She expected him to ask more questions. When he did not she returned to the task of bandaging the wound.

Rorke saw the uncertain look that crossed her face, the shadow of apprehension in those vivid eyes, and chose to say nothing. For the time being, he would watch her. And she was such a delightful creature to watch.

She was small and slender, fitting against his length with tantalizing, if reluctant, softness. Her head reached no further than his shoulder and as he looked down he found himself staring at the bright satin cap of fiery red hair.

Her hair was wet and smelled of recent washing, the damp, sweet fragrance reminding him of the lush, green meadows of Anjou in spring. It was the color of deep burgundy streaked through with fiery crimson, a dozen different golds, and brilliant amber, plaited down the middle of her back. He longed to loosen that restrictive braid, strand by silken strand and feel it spilling through his hands.

But not yet.

Instead, he tucked the stray wisp behind the curve of her ear, his fingers lingering against the softness of her cheek.

"What are you then, mistress?" he speculated, returning to

their earlier conversation. "If you are not a witch who casts spells?"

Her hand, always so sure and steady at this most-familiar task, suddenly hesitated at the touch of his fingers. Not looking up, as if it required some great concentration of will, she spread salve all about the wound.

"Perhaps I am a sorceress," she suggested, keeping her gaze averted from his so that he would not see otherwise.

"A sorceress? One of the Jehara as Tarek believes?" he asked. "Creatures that cast spells, a changeling, a conjurer that controls the mystical powers of the universe, and exists only between mist and reality?" He looked at her speculatively. "Perhaps—And if you were a sorceress, Vivian, what would you change yourself into?"

"A falcon," she replied without thinking, and then suggested, "Perhaps Aquila and I are one."

"Ah, but I have seen the two of you together," he answered lightly. "Therefore, I believe that you and Aquila are not one and the same. And if you are a sorceress, Vivian, why then have you not escaped in the mist?"

"It is said," she recited, as if telling an old legend, "that only those born to the mist may disappear into the mist."

"Perhaps, then," he speculated, stroking the length of her hair, "that you are a creature born in fire, for I swear that you are like fire."

"Or, perhaps," she suggested, "I am a brownie, they can be quite mischievous." This sparring of words was delightful if unnerving.

"I have heard of brownies," he said, the timbre of his voice like the stroke of rough velvet across her uncertain senses.

"As I recall they are small creatures that easily fit in the palm of a hand, with squat little bodies and spindly legs and arms, and they come out only at night."

He added, "In truth, you do not seem overly distressed by sunlight."

Vivian's head snapped up. "But you think me squat with spindly arms and legs?" she asked incredulously.

"I will admit that it was necessary for me to give the matter . . ." he paused to look her over, disconcertingly, from head to toe, "lengthy consideration."

She saw the humor that glittered in those keen gray eyes and felt his hand move low on her back.

"Perhaps not so squat or spindly," he allowed. Then as though to emphasize the other possibility, his hand opened, his thumb caressing at the base of her spine. At the same time his fingers curved downward with a faint, light pressure, proving that even if she was not as small as a brownie, she fit his hand in unexpected and thoroughly pleasing ways.

"A troll?" she suggested, hastily retrieving the strip of linen to bind the wound.

"Hmmmm, a troll," he said, as though giving it equal consideration, at the same time he struggled to keep the laughter from his voice. "I remember stories about trolls when I was a child. They are most disagreeable, and they *are* small."

He cocked his head to one side as though trying to discern whether or not there was a resemblance.

She chose to ignore him, securing a square of linen with the longer piece, which she then bound about his upper arm.

"They are also destructive creatures," he went on at great length. "They are pesty and meddlesome. It is said they have been known to demand things of people—tasks, deeds, favors— for which they offer nothing in return." He angled her a particularly long look, and conceded, "There does seem to be some resemblance there." One corner of his mouth twitched as he added, "And it is said they live under bridges."

"I do not live under a bridge," she retorted, tying off the bandage tighter than necessary.

"True enough," Rorke grunted with a slight wince of pain. "I found you in an abbey." He paused. " 'Tis also said that one always knows when a troll is about long before it is seen because they have an offensive odor much like a malodorous, rotting bog."

Once again, her head came up sharply, eyes glinting with the beginnings of anger.

"Are you now saying I smell?"

He brought his other hand up, fingers stroking across her cheek to sink into the thick satin of her loosely plaited hair.

"Aye, demoiselle." He willingly breathed in the scent of her, still damp from her bathing, a smile curving his lips at her stunned expression.

"You smell of the wind at dawn and warm spring rain." His fingers sank deeper into the thick satin cap of her hair, slowly taking possession. "And summer sun. You smell of living things, of forest pine, and sweet new meadows. Of sweet midnight dreams and even sweeter secrets." His fingers stroked back across her cheek to lightly brush her lips.

"You are no troll," he answered, caressing the curve of her bottom lip with a battle-scarred thumb, his roughened flesh scraping her tender flesh and causing unexpected sensations to tremble through her.

"Perhaps a faerie," she said in a startled whisper, her gaze lowered and shuttered lest she betray the uncertain feelings and sensations stirring within her that she dare not let him see. Her slender hand closed over his, as if she could physically stop the tender assault. She could not.

"You are no fey, ethereal creature, Vivian." The warmth of his breath bathed her, so close she could taste the heat, the dark masculine strength, and the whisper of need that moved across her senses.

"You are flesh and blood," his lips brushed hers, stunning her with the tenderness that promised all those things and more. Then he tasted her, the rough velvet of his tongue gliding along the curve of her mouth, from corner to corner, then slowly back to flick inside at the stunned, parted center.

"And fire," he whispered, as his tongue slipped past her lips to taste her more deeply and began a tender assault that began and ended, then began again, with each slow invasion allowing her to taste him as thoroughly as he tasted her.

For the first time in her life, unable to see with that inner sight, Vivian closed her eyes and experienced this wondrous pleasure with all her other senses.

"You taste of sweet wine," she said in a stunned whisper as he withdrew to graze his teeth across her lower lip and she experienced an unexpected pang of desire, first glimpsed in a vision long ago when she had seen the phoenix rising from the flames, "and spices," she whispered on a shuddering breath. And some other dark, alluring essence she could not name but needed to taste again as she opened her mouth to his, and drew the velvet of his tongue deep inside in an elemental, primal joining.

"Old Meg warned me at Amesbury that first day," Rorke said on a harsh guttural sound, as his hand glided down the curve of her throat to the silken place where her blood stirred beneath her skin.

"She said I had no notion of your power. Ah, but I do, demoiselle," he whispered as his head bent low and his lips followed his hand to that soft, vulnerable pulse place that lay exposed above the laces at her kirtle. His tongue stroked into the soft indentation of flesh, startling her anew. Hands that raised to stop him, curled over the hard contour of muscle across his chest, the tips of her fingers gently digging in.

It might have been an oath, so harsh was the sound of his voice as if forced from his throat. "You have the power to bewitch and beguile."

The flickering strokes of his tongue were like the velvet beat of a butterfly's wing at her flesh, making her breath shudder from her lungs.

A long-ago memory flashed through her stunned thoughts— of Bronwyn and Ham that day in the glade . . . of hasty, hurried kisses . . . the frantic tearing of clothing . . . then the even more frantic joining of their bodies as they thrust at one another.

There was no hurry nor haste in Rorke's kisses. It was as though each was deliberate, lingered over, and savored completely before the next was begun, filling her with a sensual madness that she wanted neither to understand nor end even as she felt the gentle tugging of laces at her bodice and then the downward, stroking journey of his lips to other needy places.

"My God," he whispered. "Your skin is so warm and sweet." His tongue stroked over a dusky nipple. "You are like sweet fire."

Vivian gasped at the reaction of her body. Her breasts tingled with each plucking stroke, her nipples taut and hard like berries as he nibbled with his teeth. Then his lips closed over her possessively, and she experienced a gentle, rhythmic tugging as she was drawn more deeply into the dark, wet heat of his mouth in a tender, relentless assault.

Abandoning herself to her newly awakening senses, her head fell back until she was supported only by his arm about her waist, neck arched, nails leaving small pale half-moons in the skin at his shoulders as she held on to him, her breath caught in her lungs as her body betrayed her. Her breast taken more deeply into his mouth as each tugging, suckling stroke echoed in some dark, deeply hidden place within her. Vivian whispered with a fear that came from that deeply hidden place, "Rorke, I cannot . . . I must not . . . Please . . ."

His hand at her back moved lower, fingers closing over one soft swell of rounded flesh to gently squeeze. His own need whispered at her other breast as a new and equally tender assault began, "There is nothing to fear . . ."

"Please!" Tears of need, uncertainty, and anguish quivered in her throat as her hands found their way into the thick mane of his hair, twisting in the long dark strands. "You do not understand . . . I cannot . . ." The words broke on a soft sob. "I do not know how . . . to please a man."

He had waited for her refusal, certain it would come, so firmly had she held herself against him, even as he repeatedly exposed the need within her.

There was no guile or deceit, only an honesty far more alluring than he could have hoped. That honesty of innocence sharpened the need deep inside Rorke, hardening even more the flesh that already ached for her.

"Do not be afraid." His mouth returned to hers, fingers tenderly framing her face, his voice low and thick with the pleasure of a truth far more than any he had expected. "For you please me very well . . ."

Her guileless eyes, like twin flames that reflected the brilliance of the clear blue stone that hung between her breasts, stared back at him with an open wonder of desire.

His fingers caressed down the length of her neck with an agony of slowness, as if he was learning her all over again. Then, fanning out along the silken curve of skin to her shoulders, hard, callused thumbs grazed silken flesh across the swell of each breast, until those strong, battle-scarred hands clasped her shoulders. Then he turned her so that her back was to him.

"Your honesty pleases me."

His fingers glided back across the top of her shoulders, caressed the back of her neck, creating entirely new sensations. She could not see, only feel and imagine with a breathless anticipation that there must be so much more. His hands firmly held her in place as they moved to the thick plait of her hair.

"Your softness pleases me," he whispered as a slow-twisting agony of the desire spiraled through him.

Vivian was aware of the gentle tugging of the thick, damp strands from the plaited braid that hung down the length of her back. She imagined his fingers uncoiling one heavy strand after another. Then she felt the damp mass heavy against her back, and she waited in breathless anticipation.

With a startled sound, she felt the heat of his mouth at the back of her shoulder, tongue flicking across her skin. Her nipples tingled as they once more grew taut as though with a memory, yearning to be taken captive once more in the dark possessive heat of his mouth.

Those hard, scarred hands, capable of wielding death and destruction, tenderly held her entire body captive as he brushed the heavy fall of hair forward over one shoulder, exposing the column of her back, then swept down her arms, taking with them the sleeves and then the bodice of her gown to her waist, the laces parting as if they conspired with him. The gown tumbled to her feet.

Other memories of that day in the glade flashed through her stunned thoughts. But this was not the same. There was no frantic tearing of clothes or the eagerness that became almost an animal frenzy to be joined. Instead, he had slowly, deliberately, undressed her, rousing her further with each touch that smoothed across her skin.

Vivian gasped at her sudden nakedness, then gasped again as his hands closed over both her breasts and she was pulled back against the stunning, hard length of him. His head angled down beside hers, his beard-roughened cheek grazing hers as his teeth grazed down the side of her neck, drawing forth startled breaths with each tender bite.

"Your innocence pleases me," he said with such fierceness that she trembled.

"Please . . ." she whispered, certain that she must do something, but with no idea what it was.

"Be still." He barely controlled the agony threading his voice. "Soon you will know," he murmured, as his hands glided slowly down the length of each arm to slender hands that he imagined touching him as he was about to touch her.

Then, feeling the anticipation that quivered through her, sensing the deep burning desire within her for things she did not know, he stepped back a half pace and went down on one knee at her feet.

The breathless sound of his name at her lips was like a slender hand closing over his aching flesh. Whatever else she might have said died at her throat as he pressed his mouth low on her back at the place where slender straight spine flared gently to softer, fuller flesh, and began a different assault of her senses.

"The sweet taste of you pleases me."

In countless places, she felt the warm heat of his mouth in tender kisses, hands locked over her hips and holding her so that she could not flee from this new sensual assault. She would not, even if she could have.

Visions of that long-ago day in the glade swept over her. As a young girl on the brink of womanhood she had watched that fierce, frenzied coupling, knowing that such a thing was forbidden to her even as she experienced a strange sensual awareness that hinted at some deeply hidden desires that marked her of mortal flesh and blood.

Rorke FitzWarren had awakened those desires, unleashing within her a longing for things forbidden. This once, she silently bargained, no matter the cost, she wanted to experience what caused Bronwyn such pleasure that she laughed in the midst of it.

She wanted to know the desire that sent Judith de Marque down darkened passageways to seek out a man she could not marry but would lie with.

She wanted to feel the awakening of her other senses in a longing of fulfillment that had joined her mother and father, and created her of mortal flesh and blood, and passion.

"And your heat pleases me . . ." Rorke's hand fanned down across the taut flatness of her belly, fingers stroking through the fiery silk below, as his teeth gently sank into that tender swell of flesh below her spine.

Her skin quivered beneath his lips and those nibbling teeth that she imagined sinking into her flesh, arching her back like a sleek cat that begs for more. He delved deeper, fingers stroking down over the silk-shrouded mound at the juncture of her thighs, then gliding back through twin folds of satin flesh.

It began subtly. This new assault that created a sort of breathless agony which Vivian was certain she could not bear. The gentle, warm bites nibbling at flesh that rapidly became too sensitive to his touch, the gliding downward stroke of his tongue below her spine that made her wet. And the rhythmic alternating stroke of those long fingers, slipping inside her, caressing, gently stretching, preparing her as he drew forth from her body a sweet, slick rain as she wept with both joy and a sort of aching sorrow at the sensations he created.

She softly cried ancient Celtic words. The sound of his name shattered on a desperate sob as her body shuddered beneath his hands and mouth, and the sweet fiery wine of her body drenched him.

When he stood once more and turned her toward him, he was stunned by the wild, passionate look of her. He had said she was no fey, ethereal creature, but at that moment, with desire burning like blue fire in the depths of her eyes, matched by the gleaming blue crystal that was all she now wore, she seemed somehow unearthly. As though, with the brilliant crown of her hair—laced through with colors of deep burgundy, shimmering red, richest amber, and molten gold, and the flames at the hearth framing her—she was a creature born in fire.

This one night, Vivian thought, as she laid both her hands against his chest. *I will have this one night, for it must last an eternity.*

"I want to touch you as you have touched me," she whispered.

The sweet innocence and fiery passion of her words almost drove him to his knees. He kissed her fiercely, hands thrust back through the thick satin of her hair. It cascaded in fiery ribbons through his fingers as she breathlessly broke the kiss to begin another, pressing her mouth against his chest, tasting him. As he had aroused her, she now aroused him with sweetness, innocence, and fire.

Her small tongue stroked across all the hard, scarred contours of him. The pale ribbon of a sword's deadly kiss at his side, the strange wide path as if he had been burned, to then nibble and suckle a flat, male nipple as he had suckled her.

He swore softly. "You are like sweet fire, burning me." But instead of stopping her, the words encouraged and pleaded for more. A plea she heard in the harsh sound of air leaving his lungs as her fingers sought the laces of his breeches, then felt the taut flesh at his belly that quivered and leapt beneath her seeking fingers. Engorged flesh sprang into her hand.

"I can feel life pulsing within you," she whispered, with that passionate innocence of wonder as she held the weight of him in slender hands. With that same innocence of things only half-known and longed for with the instinctive yearning of her mortal soul, she closed a hand around him, fingers barely encircling his veined flesh to glide from warm satin tip down the length of him to that dark thicket and back again, a glistening droplet beading at the tip of the engorged flesh.

He groaned. "You make me weep with need for you."

She could not imagine that this magnificent part of him wept actual tears. She touched a finger to him as he had touched her so intimately, the *tear* of his desire glistening at her fingertip. Then she tasted him again. Stunned she looked up at him.

"You are sweet," she whispered in awe, "like the first honey of spring." The sound he made was primeval, feral, like the cry of some ancient creature in agony as he stepped out of breeches and boots. He felt control slip away as he swept her into his arms, no longer certain who was the seducer or who had been seduced.

He had no patience for the extra time it would take to have borne her to the bed, and, so, lowered her to the thick carpet of furs spread before the hearth.

It was as if the fire worshiped her, bathing across her naked flesh, glowing in all the soft, satin hollows to set aflame the silken mound that glistened with her own sweet wetness and in the satin of her hair fanned across the thick, dark furs.

"Now let me please you," he whispered, moving low over her, his breath whispering at her belly, stirring the fiery silk that shrouded the center of her body. "Let me taste you as you have tasted me."

Certain she could not bear more than she already had, Vivian watched as he bent lower still, the heat of his whispers felt at her thighs as he rained kisses across her startled flesh, his lips following where his words led in yet another assault on her senses.

He parted her with the velvet heat of his tongue, slipping past aroused swollen flesh to penetrate her dark magic, the sweetness of her like none other. She was as intoxicating and stirring as warm wine that moved through his veins like molten fire.

Fire burned through her. It began at the place where his lips and tongue made love to her, then spread through her like a firefall tumbling out of control. Her hips rose to meet each thrust of his tongue, seeking a deeper joining. Her eyes were closed as she abandoned herself to the pure physical sensation of his pleasuring of her.

This one night.

The prophecy had warned she must never love as a mortal woman. What might the price be for this night of pleasure? She did not know. She knew only that she could not go back to her lonely existence, comforted only by the magical fire that burned within her. Not after having experienced the greater magic of the fire of Rorke's passion. Tears of both sadness and joy glistened in her eyes.

Just once she would be a mortal woman, even if it meant the loss of her powers. To know what it was to be loved and physically joined with a man. One night to last all of eternity. Whatever the loss, it would be worth it.

The image of a young woman and man in a sheltered glade became nothing more than a distant memory as the fire bathed her soul in flaming heat while her bold warrior bathed her body with love. Her skin shivered with heat and the need to experience that deeper love as his fingers closed over her knees, parting her.

She shivered with an anticipation of pleasure she could only imagine and, it seemed, had waited half an eternity to experience as Rorke slowly moved over her. His hardened, scarred warrior's body was magnificent in the gleaming light from the hearth as if the flames paid homage to every curve of hardened muscle and every seam of torn flesh.

"Touch me," his voice ached in his throat.

Her slender hand moved between them, stroking over him, as his hands closed over her hips, lifting her.

"Sheath me in your sweet fire."

Her answer was like the freeborn cry of the falcon as Rorke thrust inside her.

Smooth and sleek she molded him, her sweet fire easing his passage until he lay full and heavy within her.

Sweat glistened across his body at restraint that became almost a painful agony as he braced himself over her to keep from hurting her further.

"Forgive me," he whispered against the hollow of her throat. "I cannot bear to cause you pain."

He made to ease from her, but she stopped him, slender hands moving low at his back to clasp him within her.

"Nay, milord," she whispered fiercely. "You bring me no pain. You are magnificent," she whispered. "As if you are not real, but some beautiful creature born in fire and blood."

Rorke shuddered at the words.

Never had he—battle-scarred from a score of blows, hardened by torture, the cruelties of his bastard life, and the harsh realities of war—ever been called beautiful.

It was a word for mystical, unearthly things not of this world, seen but once, and then never again except in a dream. Never had he known such a passion of innocence.

"Then burn with me, sweet fire," Rorke told her as their bodies began to move together, taking, giving, in a fierce joining until neither was certain where one ended and the other began.

Head thrown back upon the furs, Vivian's eyes glistened as the magical creature became earthbound, mesmerized by the man whose love filled her repeatedly. She sought the sky, flew, and soared on the strength of his passion, like the creature whose fiery image spread across the tapestry wall—a creature born in fire and blood.

Rorke felt as if the very fabric of his life was being torn asunder, consumed by the sweet fire of her body, until, like that mythical creature that leapt from the flames of desolation, with a harsh, fierce cry, he felt himself reborn in her passion.

* * *

The chamber was cold, the fire having long ago burned low on the hearth. Vivian rose from the bed, wrapping a thick, warm fur about her. Rorke stirred at the sudden loss of her warmth, in that half-sleep awareness an arm moving across the empty place as though to gather her close once more.

She wanted only to return to that place, to feel his strong arms about her, his body stealing the heat from hers and then giving it back in the fiery passion as their bodies joined. But she could not.

A restlessness drove her from his bed to the hearth, the stones at the floor icy beneath her bare feet. Satisfied that he slept on, she went to the hearth to lay more wood on the fire.

Embers still glowed amid the ash, casting a feeble warmth as she passed her hand over. The embers suddenly flared as the flame within stirred to life, bursting forth like the newly opened petals of a flower.

She fed the fire small bits and pieces of pine twigs and tree bark, a sudden pungence filling the air as the fire found droplets of sap. As the fire grew she laid a larger log across.

Flames leapt hungrily about the log, golden light leaping onto the cold stones, creating deep shadows just beyond. For a long time she sat before the hearth, feeding it more logs until it burned brightly; the shadows receded to the edges of the chamber, and the stones became less icy.

This one night . . .

Against everything that she was, against a destiny that had been written long ago, and a prophecy that she must not deny, she had risked all, abandoned the warnings of her very special gift, and crossed over into the mortal world to join with a man seen in her vision.

For the first time in her life, she didn't understand, and the Voice that always guided her, speaking to her through visions and dreams, had been unusually silent.

"You're there. I know you are," she whispered, one hand closing around the dark blue crystal, the other reaching toward the fire now burning brightly at the hearth.

The flames curled and danced about the logs in colors of soft yellow, bright orange, fiery red, and blue as brilliant as the shimmering heart of the crystal.

She stared into the flames, casting her thoughts far beyond stone walls and wood fortress. Beyond the inns, taverns, and marketplaces of London. Beyond the veil of night and the boundaries of time and place, to another place of hope, dreams, and ancient legend found in that lingering time just before dawn. In those few, brief moments when night is no longer night and day is not yet day—a place found only in the mist.

"Please, come to me," Vivian implored as she held her hand before the fire. "You must help me understand."

The fire calmed and burned steadily with a soothing, lambent glow as a hand reached out to her from the flames. Though gnarled with age, there was both a powerful strength and a gentleness of love as it beckoned to her.

Vivian reached out, fingers extended into the flames. She laid her hand in that outstretched one. Strength and calm flowed through and about her. A vision appeared, surrounding that outstretched hand that offered love and comfort, of a forest clearing covered with freshly fallen snow, and a single standing stone.

Then that gentle, comforting grasp was broken, the fingers slipped from hers, disappearing into the flames. All that was left was the vision of the standing stone at the edge of the clearing in the forest. Then it, too, slowly faded, until all that remained was the fire burning at the hearth.

Nineteen

Torches burned low along the walls of the passage as Vivian left Rorke's chamber.

At the main hall, she could make out the humped shapes of

William's men slumped across long trestle tables or head-to-foot across the floor in rushes that reeked of spilt ale and stale food, and littered with bones from the evening meal that had been thrown to William's hounds.

She pressed the folds of the mantle flat against her body to prevent any movement that would betray her as she carefully stepped over the sleeping knights.

The fire at the hearth had long since burned to embers, wisps of smoke trailing lazily upward. As she passed by, the embers flared to life, glowing bright once more as though sensing her presence.

There was a brief stir among the slumbering bodies as one man turned over, disturbing another. She stood frozen as there was much reshuffling and resettling. Then it was once more quiet except for the snores that began anew, indicating they all slept once more.

The hounds were chained to the wall. One caught her scent and raised its head, threatening to rouse the others. Conveying an unspoken command, Vivian, unafraid, reached out and laid a hand on the hound's sleek head.

It immediately calmed, lowered its head to paws, and once more slept with the other hounds. She adjusted the hood of the heavy mantle lower over her face as she crossed to the heavily fortified entrance. At a niche beside the door a guard had been posted, and stepped from the shadows at her approach.

Leaving by way of the sally port might have been more discreet, but it would also have taken a great deal of time, for it was beyond the kitchen, buttery, and pantry, at the far side of the compound. The front entrance was more heavily guarded, but it was closer to the small forest that bordered the fortress.

The guard's name was Sevien. He was a large man whose size rivaled that of Duke William himself and any of his knights, including Rorke FitzWarren.

He maintained his post with a formidable prowess that could easily have bested any six men and left no doubt as to the reason he'd been entrusted with such an important position. He recognized her immediately, an expression of surprise obvious on his broad, flat features.

She saw the suspicion that immediately replaced his first puzzlement. She reached out, laying a hand on his mail-clad arm.

"Good morn, Sevien," she said in a gently, hypnotic tone. "All is well with you, I pray."

Suspicion was immediately replaced with confusion in the guard's eyes, then a bewilderment of uncertainty as he stared at her as though he had never seen her before.

"You will unbolt the door," she said, keeping her voice low and even in rhythmic, pleasing tones. He hesitated and she gently increased the pressure of her fingers at his arm. His wide, flat brow furrowed. Then, he nodded.

"I will unbolt the door," he repeated woodenly and moved to do as she asked.

Still holding on to his arm, she instructed him, "You will allow me to pass without trying to stop me."

"I will let you pass. I will not try to stop you." He stood aside, no longer blocking her path.

"You will tell no one that you have seen me," she reminded him, her fingers still conveying that message of warmth through the sleeve of his mail hauberk.

He nodded. "I will tell no one."

"And you will remember nothing of what has happened."

Again he repeated after her, "I will remember nothing."

"You will remain at your post as before," Vivian told him, slowly releasing the pressure of her fingers. Then as he released the mechanism that lifted the heavy crossbar, she bid him, "Good morn, Sevien."

She slipped out, down the steps, and into the inner courtyard.

There were four guards at the gatehouse, many more positioned at intervals along the inner wall. She might slip past one or two, possibly even a third using the same persuasion she had with Sevien. But there were far too many others for her to simply walk past all of them, through the gate, and then past the guards she knew were positioned outside the wall.

Clouds gathered across the moon, a portent of the storm whose chill bite could be felt on the air. The moon sank low at the horizon with the coming dawn. Time was very short.

As the clouds rolled across the moon, the courtyard was, for a time, thrown into darkness as deep as night. Vivian seized her opportunity and cut across the courtyard away from the gate-house.

She passed the kennels, vacant now, with William's hounds kept in the main hall. Just beyond the kennels were the mews where William's hunting birds, brought all the way from Normandy, now resided. She slipped inside.

The sounds inside the mews were soothingly familiar. The sudden rustling of feathers, the nervous movement of talons on a perch as her presence was sensed, the scratching sound of a rodent in the straw underfoot as it fled danger, unaware that the predators were all, for the moment, tethered.

The small falcon, Aquila, had been given a perch apart from the larger birds at the end of the mews. Even though she was hooded, as were the other birds, to keep her calm, she caught Vivian's scent and sound, and called out with a short, chirping sound.

Vivian whistled back softly, the familiar four-note signal of greeting. Aquila stepped carefully onto Vivian's unprotected arm. Once they were outside the mews Vivian removed the hood.

In the gathering gray of the fast-approaching dawn Aquila cocked her sleek dark head first in one direction then another, and flared her powerful wings.

"Are you feeling restless, my pet?" Vivian cooed softly, her lips a scant few millimeters from that deadly beak as she let her breath wash over the falcon. Aquila sat perfectly still, yellow eyes blinking as though she answered on some primal level only they two understood.

"You must fly for me. I have need of your eyes, my beauty." Holding her arm wide, she sent the falcon aloft.

Aquila rose swiftly into the gray predawn sky, easily escaping the high stone walls. She circled once and then seemed to disappear, but Vivian was not alarmed. The falcon would seek a perch beyond the walls and wait for her.

"Now to my own freedom," Vivian whispered with growing anticipation as she moved along the wall that ran behind the mews and separated the royal household from the hunters' wood that lay beyond the moated embankment.

She had glimpsed it many times from inside the fortress. Driven by the images of her vision, the wood was now her destination.

There were no breaches in the wall by which she might escape. All had been repaired and fortified before William's arrival in the city. Every precaution had been taken against any surprise attack.

Even now, a massive stone tower of Norman design was being built within the royal compound by William's brother the bishop, count de Bayeau, to replace the crumbling Roman fortress.

When completed, the Tower of London, as it was already being called, would be an impregnable fortress built to stand for a thousand years. A monument and reminder of the Norman conquest of Britain. But the future was yet to be seen. Only time would reveal if the tower would still be standing a thousand years hence.

She heard the sound of voices very near and though the words were spoken in French, she understood the conversation that passed between the guards. Very soon they would pass along this portion of the wall. There was no time to look for a more secluded place. She must leave now or risk being discovered.

Yet, Vivian hesitated. For the first time since learning the true depth and scope of her powers, she was uncertain, the prophecy that old Meg had revealed to her filling her with doubt.

She was not like other women, and yet for a few precious hours she had turned from her powers to become a woman. What if her powers had now turned from her?

Her hands trembled slightly as she flattened them against the cold stones of the wall before her. Seeking help and guidance, she had reached out to the flames. She'd had a vision, even sensed the powerful presence of the one who reached out to her in return. Surely not all her powers were forfeit because of what had passed between her and Rorke.

She took a deep, cleansing breath and let it out, releasing all the doubt and fear. With the sound of voices very near, she closed her eyes and pressed firmly against the stones at the wall.

They were cold and wet with mist, yet she felt only warmth as she turned inward to that hidden place of dreams, secrets, and magic where the power of the flame burned brightly.

Vivian imagined the wall, visualizing it in her thoughts as if it existed in her mind—every coarse grain that made up the stone, each crevice, seam, and joint, and the thick mortar between.

Then she allowed herself to feel the cold and wet, seeing it, too, in the moisture that seeped from each flat surface and the frost that glistened at each jagged edge. Then, still turned inward, she imagined herself stepping through the wall.

First her hands, then her arms, reaching through the mass of stone. A step, then two, and as the power gathered and focused within her on the single point of that golden blue flame, she passed through the wall as if she were no more than the mist, or a single droplet of water that seeped out of the stones. And on a single, ragged breath she emerged on the other side.

Her first awareness was the bone-aching cold of having passed through the wall, as if for those few brief moments as she passed from one side to the other, she had become stone and mortar, glazed by ice, seeped through with an aching dampness.

She felt weak, as if the life had been drained from her and now only slowly returned in the tingling of warmth that spread through her arms and legs to settle once more within her. Gradually, she realized that at least this ability had not been taken from her.

It took her a few moments more to recover fully, reminding her of another reason she had never cared for passing through solid barriers. She didn't like the unbearable coldness afterward. She heard a soft, skreeling cry overhead. Aquila sat atop the western bastion, waiting for her.

"You, my fine winged friend," Vivian told her, "are far too smug. Just you try passing through stone and see how you like it." In answer, Aquila swept from the top of the bastion, winging circles and spirals overhead against a leaden sky.

On a silent airborne thought, Vivian sent her toward the wood. There was no time to waste as the sky grew lighter in that time between darkness and light when night is no longer night, and day is not yet day. . . .

Vivian crossed the dry moat bed, and entered the edge of the wood, casting her thoughts far and wide with those of the falcon, searching with her special gift for a clearing in the wood, in which stood an ancient stone.

In the wood, the snow had not been trodden under foot or cart and lay like a white mantle across the ground, reflecting the growing light. A sense of urgency now filled her. She must find the clearing before the sun rose. Then she heard the falcon's cry, the same cry as when prey had been sighted.

She plunged through heavy tree cover and thick underbrush, following that sound, until she emerged at a small clearing. The snow glistened as it grew lighter all about. A feeble golden light splintered the thick sea of clouds at the horizon and penetrated the glade. Mist rose at the warmth that slowly invaded the clearing. It was then she saw the stone.

It was tall, a large obelisk that seemed to be etched with the eons of time. It rose out of the earth and snow like an outthrust hand, or possibly the blade of an ancient stone sword. She slowly walked toward it.

The stone did not sit on the ground but hovered just above it, surrounded by a faint, shimmering light. At first she thought the light was the dawn that slowly broke behind the stone. Then she realized that the dawn had not yet broken but seemed to be suspended and the light came from within the stone.

This was the stone of her vision, suspended in time, the source of her power drawn to the shimmering light that radiated from the stone. With a sudden inner calm, she laid her hands against the front of the stone as she had the stones at the wall.

This time, there was no bone-aching cold, no sensation of being fragmented or slowly torn apart as she passed through the stone. This time there was no pain or weakness. It was like a curtain parting, passing through incredible velvet warmth from darkness into the light.

As she emerged into the light, she felt a hand touching hers, then closing more firmly over hers, conveying such unconditional love and strength, as if she was being reborn, slipping from the womb of the mortal world into the spiritual world of her soul.

Vivian felt the folds of the mantle settle quietly about her and a soothing warmth, as though bathed by a radiant sun. She slowly opened her eyes to look into the eyes of the one whose hand held hers with comforting warmth, the one who waited for her.

"Father!" she cried out, stepping into his protective embrace.

"My daughter," he said, folding her close.

For long moments he simply held her as he had when she was a little girl and he comforted some hurt. His words were as tender and soothing as the hand at her hair. Tears glistened at her eyes.

"I thought you had abandoned me," she said with cheek pressed against his strong shoulder.

"Never, daughter." His voice was filled with unexpected emotion. His arms tightened about her as if he was afraid to let her go. Finally, he did let her go. Just enough to hold her a ways apart, laying his hand against her cheek.

"It is all right, my child. You are safe here."

The sun was warm at her back. A soft breeze bathed her face.

Here there was only light and sunshine. The fortress and all of London that lay beyond it were gone. Only the stone remained, the monolith shimmering in the light. Then it, too, slowly faded until she could not see it clearly if she looked directly at it, but could see it at the edge of her vision.

"Come, daughter," he said, gathering her to his side as he kept his arm about her shoulders. "Your mother waits. And I have wisely learned not to keep her waiting. Especially when it comes to her daughters."

They walked together from the wood which was not a wood at all but an orchard, filled with trees heavily laden with peaches and other golden fruit that ripened in the sun. She cast a sideways glance to her father's patrician profile, little changed in all these years.

He was still handsome, regal of bearing, the son of a king according to some ancient legends, sprung from the joining of even more ancient gods according to still others. To her, he was teacher, mentor, guardian of her soul, keeper of the wisdom of the universe, and above all her father whose love was unconditional and never-ending.

"The garden is so bountiful," she said in awe as they approached the simple cottage. It never failed to amaze her the abundance with which everything here grew while everything on the other side lay shivering beneath winter's frozen mantle and would for some months to come. It was her mother's touch.

"Larkspur!" she cried out with delight, some of her urgency and fear easing. "I have had no larkspur for months. And look how beautiful it is. And anise, foxglove, lily of the valley, angelica."

He chuckled softly, for a time the fear around his own heart easing. Perhaps, he thought, he could persuade her to stay.

"There will be plenty of time to wander about the gardens. But I fear if we keep your mother waiting any longer you will need to prepare a curative for the tongue-lashing she will give me for keeping you from her overlong."

Her mother, not content to wait for them to come to her, was running down the garden path toward them.

"Mother." Vivian's voice broke softly as slender arms went around her. With her father she could be as strong as the falcon that flies the heavens, but with her mother there was no need of it. She could be vulnerable and very human, with mortal doubts and uncertainties. For it was that mortal bond that they shared as she shared a very different sort of bond with her father. And it was Ninian who now sensed something in *her*.

She held Vivian a ways apart, studying her with a woman's eyes, needing only the insight of a woman who has loved deeply to see it in another.

Ninian stroked her daughter's face. "Come, dear heart. I have brewed a special tea. Then we will eat."

Her mother pulled Vivian between them and they walked back toward the cottage where wonderful aromas emanated through the open windows.

As they reached the cottage, Vivian was aware of a void of loneliness, its presence only recently lifted, and the equal strong awareness that it was her presence that filled the void for a time. As she turned to ask the question, her father sensed it.

"Your sisters are not here," he answered. "It has been some time since they visited us." He frowned slightly, as though troubled by a thought. "I had hoped that you might all come back here."

"Father?"

Something in his tone alarmed her. But he said nothing more of what was bothering him and prevented her from knowing his thoughts. She knew he would not allow her to know until he was ready to speak of them.

Only one had ever managed to make him reveal something against his will, and that was her mother. He always said that his love for Ninian made him vulnerable to her.

"Let us eat," he said.

Her mother had prepared all her favorite foods—bread with rosemary, fresh spring carrots in honey, and garden stew subtly flavored with hints of herbs that were rare in summer, some which, in the natural order of things in the real world, had not been present in summer or any season for several hundred years.

There was the pungence of star leaf, the subtle taste of lister, which lingered at the back of the throat, and the hint of cassin seed. All of which could no longer be found in any wooded thicket or glade, and had equal curative powers.

There was also her father's favorite wine, made from whatever fruit was in season. The essence of peaches mingled with the other aromas, to fill her senses with a longing of memory.

They spoke of memories in the way that all families do when brought back together after a long absence. And yet her mother and father seemed hardly older than when she was first allowed to return for a visit after her first vision in the flames. Everything here remained constant, unchanging. Here Vivian felt renewed. Here she gained her strength. She knew that on the other side, beyond the portal, barely any time would have passed at all. A few seconds, minutes perhaps.

Vivian helped her mother clear the kitchen after the evening meal. The fragrance of floral candles permeated the air as shadows filled the room. Beyond the small cottage, the sun sank low over the orchard. Again Vivian felt an urgency of something looming on the horizon. That same urgency that had brought her through the portal.

"Father, I must speak with you."

The special magic of the shared memories was broken. She felt it in the sudden silence between her parents. A look passed between them and she was aware of a sadness in her father's face that she had first glimpsed when stepping through the portal.

He sighed heavily. "Walk with me, daughter."

They left the cottage together, walking through the gardens to the orchard and beyond, climbing the footpath of the ancient verdant hillside. Vivian paused frequently to glance back, with a sense that things had already changed and she was only just becoming aware of it. Something had been set in motion and even now changed the course of their lives, or perhaps fulfilled the course of their lives.

Far below, she caught a glimpse of her mother in the garden, gathering herbs. She stopped and looked toward them on the hillside, shading her gaze with her hand against the glare of the setting sun at their backs. She sensed Ninian's love as though the words were carried to her on the wind, and sensed something else.

"I know you must follow your destiny, my child of passion, my daughter of fire. Know that I will always be with you."

As they walked on, the sun turned the verdant hills to burnished gold in the setting sun, then to deep purple as the sun slowly slipped below the horizon and shadows fell across the ancient place where he took her.

It had not changed in all the years since he had first brought her here, and each of her sisters in turn. Legend said that after the great conflict Merlin was buried in the hollow hills, in a chamber with luminous golden walls that gleamed from the light of a single candle set in a niche in the wall.

It was also said that a beautiful young maid with powers of her own joined him, leaving the mortal world for this immortal place.

As Merlin lay on his funeral bier made of white stone, she gave him the gift of herself. And a once-mighty sword, ravaged and scarred, that she brought from a place called the Water of Time. The sword was called Excalibur.

"Father?"

He turned from the niche and smiled at her, not quite dispelling that sense of sadness about him. Crossing the chamber, he sat on a gleaming white stone bench in the middle of the chamber. Overhead, the chamber was open to the night sky where dozens of stars winked in a twilight heaven. The bench had once been the place where he lay waiting for death.

It was Ninian who brought him the sword, who had a hole cut in the top of the chamber open to the sky so that he might see the stars and had a bench cut from the large lying stone.

He always returned to this place that had once been intended for his death, to think and contemplate the world that lay beyond.

"I have seen something, father. Something powerful and terrifying. A great darkness in the world."

He shook his head sadly. She sensed that he still tried to shield his thoughts from her but was seized by a weakness so strong and powerful that it seemed to drain the strength from him, so that he seemed physically changed. No longer a vital, powerful man, but bereft of his powers and standing before her suddenly much older than only moments before.

"Father!" she went to him, with a growing alarm for things she still could not see but sensed, even with his increasingly feeble efforts to keep them from her. She took hold of him by the shoulders and she almost cried out at how feeble he suddenly felt beneath her hands.

"What is it? You must tell me," she demanded. "What is this darkness that I've seen? What does it mean?"

"Sweet child." His gaze, when he finally looked up at her was filled with unshed tears. "I hoped it would never find you. I prayed it would not happen."

Then some of his strength seemed to return in the fierce emotions that crossed his features. Vivian felt the sudden tension of his arms beneath her hands, as though he was seized with an impotent rage.

"I vowed it would not touch any of you. I shielded you from it! It is the reason I sent you and your sisters into the mortal world. I hoped you would be safe. And now . . ." The rage remained, but tempered once more by a growing sense of hopelessness.

"Now," he repeated, as though gathering himself, "I fear it has found you. Forgive me, daughter, that I could not prevent it."

She had never seen him like this. Her father, who was all-knowing and all-powerful, always so strong and sure of himself, the wise counselor, teacher, and mentor she and her sisters had always looked to for guidance. Now he was consumed by some overwhelming grief that she could not fathom.

"You must tell me everything, Father. From the beginning so that I may understand."

There in the golden chamber, with darkness lowering over them, and a canopy of stars glistening above, Merlin told her of the great Darkness.

In all the great patterns of the galaxies, there was a balance of forces that kept the planets aligned. It created order out of chaos. But always there was the threat that chaos would overpower order—with wars, famine, pestilence, and death.

The great Darkness that existed in the world of Beyond was the ruler of chaos, kept at bay only by the power of the Light. But always there was struggle for domination.

In the years of her father's youth, the Darkness had grown stronger, emboldened by the lack of a strong king to sit on the throne of England and rule the kingdom.

The Darkness grew, reaching out, seizing and destroying all that it could in a quest to rule the kingdom.

With Merlin to guide him, a powerful young king defied the Darkness and for a time ruled over the kingdom. That king was Arthur, and the kingdom prospered. But Arthur was betrayed by those he loved and trusted. Not even Merlin could protect him from betrayals of the heart. Arthur was struck down in battle and died.

It was said by those who believed, that after Arthur's death, Merlin was hunted into the hollow hills and slain, his powers of Light banished from the kingdom forever.

The kingdom was lost and once again the great Darkness swept over the land, bringing five hundred years of war, famine, and death in the form of one usurper after another who invaded, conquered, and laid waste to the land.

There was none to oppose or stop it. Merlin was gone. And so the Darkness rested, retreating to the far recesses of memory, confident in its power over the kingdom.

From time to time there were faint stirrings of hope in the

kingdom. And from hope, legends grew—that Merlin was not dead. As the legend grew, so too were there malevolent stirrings. For the Darkness sensed that its hold on the shattered kingdom might not be secure.

"I am the cause of it," her father said softly, hands cradling her face. "I should have foreseen that it would happen. But I could not. Your mother made me so happy. She brought me life and I loved her as any mortal man would. You and your sisters are the blessings of that love." His expression grew somber.

"But from the moment you were born, I felt the presence of the Darkness gathering once more. Watching. Waiting, as before."

She closed her hands over his, unable to stand the torment she saw in his gentle face. "How could you be the cause of it?"

The gentleness faded, replaced by a fierceness she had never seen before. "It wasn't enough that I was banished to this place, trapped in the mists of time where my powers were rendered useless except in what I might see. It wasn't enough that your mother was forced to give up everything to live with me here because I could not be part of her world. Now, the Darkness wants my daughters!"

In sudden fear Vivian held her father and felt his torment. It was as if the places they had lived in all these years were suddenly changed and she was the parent and he was the child in need of comforting.

"What of William of Normandy?" she asked. "I saw great change that would come over all of England in my vision and knew he would defeat King Harold. Is he the king that England has waited for all this time?"

"It is not William," he answered hesitantly. "He will be king for a while, but as before there will be much strife."

"If not William, then who? A son perhaps, by right of succession? Is that what the Darkness has come to prevent?" She sensed that he knew, but refused to tell her.

"Father, you must tell me! What has it to do with me? Why have I seen it in my visions?"

"It has nothing to do with you!" He rose of a sudden and, as though filled with torment, stalked across the chamber where there was no wall. It opened out onto the small valley below, where the light at a cottage window could be seen and Ninian waited.

Merlin sensed the power within this daughter, Vivian of the fire, and knew that it was strong, much stronger than he had ever imagined. He protected his thoughts from her because it was the only way to protect *her*. But in the end her power was much stronger than his.

"I have seen other visions, Father." She told him then of her vision of a creature born in fire and blood—the image carried on Rorke FitzWarren's battle shield; of the warning about a faith that has no heart, and the sword that has no soul; and finally, of her recurring vision of the tapestry.

His expression was tormented. He suddenly looked very old; sadness and grief etched his handsome features.

Vivian felt his anguish and pain, sensed, too, the thoughts he was no longer powerful enough to keep from her.

"The tapestry is a prophecy," he said with a great weariness of spirit. "What you see in the design are the things that will come to pass."

She thought of the figures of the man and woman, the threads forming their images in brilliant, glorious detail as they came together in a profusion of color, light, and texture that seemed real. And she knew that even before she had given herself to Rorke FitzWarren, it had already been written that she would.

"Whose prophecy?" she demanded. "The force of Light? Or the forces of Darkness?"

"You are a child of the Light. The vision is yours; therefore, it is a prophecy of the Light."

"But it is not yet finished. How may I know the prophecy if parts of it are not yet woven?"

"You cannot know it," Merlin said insistently, turning his tortured gaze from her.

As clearly as if he had already confessed it, Vivian knew that he lied.

"I have seen myself in the tapestry," she said with quiet voice, sensing many other things that before were closed to her.

He shrugged. "It is common enough. After all, it is your vision."

"You're trying to protect me, Father." She saw his shoulders stiffen and she dreaded that she must search his thoughts to know the truth. It was there, along with such unbearable pain and regret that she thought she could not bear it.

"I am part of it." She read his thoughts and knew it of a certainty. "What I have seen woven in the tapestry is a prophecy of what was destined to happen. But that which cannot be seen, which is not yet woven, has not yet been written."

"No! It has nothing to do with you."

"The weaver who weaves the tapestry." She spoke aloud of the image that came so clearly to her now in this place of magic and light. An image that had been hidden from her before. Of a young woman sitting before a loom, feeding through the threads that would create the images in the tapestry.

As clearly as if she saw the young woman before her, she watched as the young woman's head lifted from her weaving, as though summoned by some unknown voice. As she slowly turned, the hood fell away from her head, revealing brilliant red hair. The face that turned toward her was her own.

She was the weaver of the tapestry. And suddenly, Vivian knew beyond any doubt what it was that tormented Merlin, and that he had tried to prevent her from seeing.

"The tapestry is not yet woven," she said softly. "The future is not yet decided. I am the weaver at the loom. I will determine the design. I—and I alone—must face the Darkness."

Merlin stood at the opening of the chamber, hands braced to either side, his head hanging between.

"I tried to keep if from you."

She nodded with a new clarity of understanding. "I know that, Father. But I also now know that perhaps I can change the design of the tapestry. It is in my hands. I must face the Darkness."

"You need not," he said with quiet voice. Then he slowly turned. His face was lined with weariness and suddenly he seemed very old. "Do not go back. Stay here with us."

She went to him then, filled with a new awareness and, because of it, a new power. She held his hands in hers and brought them to her cheek.

"You know as well as I that I cannot stay."

With grief deep in his heart, he said, "Aye," pulling his hands free only long enough to wrap his arms about her and hold her close. "I knew it would be your answer, but I had hoped that I might change your mind."

"What of my powers, Father? For I have loved a mortal man."

"The answer, my daughter, is to be found in his heart. If his heart is true, then your powers will be the stronger for it. But if his heart is false . . ."

"I cannot see his true heart, Father."

"You cannot because he must open it to you. You will know only when he surrenders both his heart and soul to you."

They stood together beneath the canopy of the sky, father and daughter, bound by the common threads of destiny. Much time had passed since they had come to the chamber of light in the hollow hills. The night sky faded and became silvery with the coming of the dawn.

"Do you have the crystal?"

She removed it from about her neck and handed it to him. He held it aloft, the shimmering dark blue crystal clasped between thumb and fingers. He began to recite the words of the ancient ones.

Slowly, across the heavens, the last of the night stars began to glimmer and brighten as though in answer. The crystal seemed to absorb all the light of the stars, then cast it back again in a blinding flash that streaked the sky in a shimmering blue arc as if the crystal had become a blue star that streaked the sky—a dragon's eye to see beyond the mists of time.

The stars rested once more in their heaven, slowly winking out until only one remained. Her father handed the crystal back to her.

"Do not part with the crystal. As long as you possess it, we are joined. What powers I have will also be joined with yours on this journey." He held her at arm's length and looked into her eyes.

"Is there nothing I can say to stop you?"

She hugged him fiercely. "There is nothing, Father."

After a while she moved out of his arms, knowing that if he could physically keep her in his world, he would.

"It is late, Father. I must be going."

He did not argue with her, but instead nodded. There were tears in his eyes.

"I will walk with you."

They returned along the footpath together, down from the hollow hills, and the ancient place of legend where her life began.

At the edge of the orchard Ninian was waiting for them. She was wrapped in the ethereal light that still glowed from the eastern horizon, seeming to set her hair and clothes afire, and for a moment Vivian was given to question whether or not her mother was mortal. For in that moment, she seemed other-worldly.

She had wrapped many of the ancient herbs that grew in such profusion in her garden and handed them to Vivian, along with a special packet for Meg.

"It is a special brew that will ease the aching in her bones and rejuvenate her as none of your earthly herbs can."

Vivian tucked them inside the mantle that Merlin wrapped about her shoulders. The three of them returned to the small clearing in the middle of the orchard.

"May the powers of Light be with you, my daughter," Ninian said in parting, and Vivian knew that Ninian was aware of what had passed between father and daughter.

"I love you, Mother," Vivian replied.

Merlin walked with her across the clearing to the obelisk which was almost visible now in that place between night and day when time stands still in the mist.

There was such sadness in his expression and she knew he did not want to let her go.

"I did not foresee that you must take my place, Vivian. Forgive me."

"There is nothing to forgive." She touched the blue crystal. "I am not afraid, Father. I know that you will be with me."

Then she stepped away from him and bade them both goodbye. She turned and slowly walked toward the obelisk that seemed as if it was suspended in the mist, hovering just above the earth.

With her hand clutched about the crystal, she turned all her thoughts inward. She focused all her powers and the force of the Light that burned within her on that inner place where memory and dream were interwoven like threads of a tapestry, and then stepped into the portal.

But this time it was much different. It was as if everything about her exploded in a painful, searing profusion of light and sound.

Cruel, painful images bombarded her thoughts, attempting to break her concentration in a profusion of ghastly visions that seemed not her own, as though controlled by some other force.

She saw her mother and father on the ground where she had left them, covered in blood, and unmoving. She saw her beautiful sisters horribly tortured and maimed, then left for dead.

Everything about her was laid to waste in some dreadful cataclysm that focused itself in the pain that tore through her as she was being pushed back away from the other side of the portal. As though some malevolent force was trying to prevent her from entering the real world.

She could feel it tearing at her flesh, burning into her soul, trying to destroy her, and knew it was the Darkness.

She saw it, just as she had before. It hovered just beyond the edges of awareness, in some vague, dark, shifting shape that resembled a man shrouded in darkness, whose image came at her, pushing, shoving, denying her entrance. A gatekeeper whose horrible laughter rang at her ears.

Vivian clung to the stone. She drew on its ancient powers, reaching back through the fiery Light of the stone to draw on the strength her father had promised, joining it with her own.

It burned as bright as the ancient light of a billion stars, escaping her fingers, piercing the darkness, holding it at bay. It bent and writhed, shielding malevolent, evil eyes from the Light, then retreated once more to the edges of reality, no longer able to stop her.

In a blinding flash of light, as if a star had exploded, Vivian was flung through the portal to the other side, collapsing into the freshly fallen snow in the clearing of the wood.

She lay there, utterly still, unmoving. To all appearances, dead.

Twenty

Flames at the torches fluttered wildly and cast fierce, angry images along the walls of the entrance to the royal hall as Rorke angrily confronted the guard.

"She must have passed this way!" Rorke insisted, questioning the guard for the third time, uneasiness sharpening his anger to a dangerous edge since first waking to find Vivian gone from his bed, then by turns gone from the chamber, and, apparently, gone from the fortress.

"No, milord," the guard, Sevien, replied carefully and with absolute certainty. "I was at my post all night. Mistress Vivian did not pass this way, nor anyone else."

"Are you certain?" Rorke again asked. "She can be most persuasive. Perhaps someone disguised that you did not recognize," he suggested, frustration adding to the anger and rising fear.

How was it possible? he thought for the dozenth time, for a maid to leave and not be seen, in a place where people crowded the halls and passageways all times of the day and night! She would have had to step over people to go to the necessary, for God's sake! Adding to the anger was the underlying uncertainty of what had passed between them.

Sweet Jesu! he had never known a woman of such passion. Nothing they shared had in the least conveyed any grievance of unhappiness or distress on her part, though he had anticipated it, for he had sensed by her innocence that she had never lain with a man. Then, upon discovering that what he suspected was true, he had taken care not to hurt or frighten her. But it was he who was stunned and dismayed by the depth of her passion and uninhibited responses. And now she was gone.

But Sevien replied without any hesitancy or apprehension, "Milord, I saw no one," and he insisted again, "No one passed this way."

Frustration mounted. It was nearly dawn. Soon everyone would know she was gone, including the bishop, and he already looked for reasons to discredit her with William.

Tarek abruptly returned, for Rorke had immediately told him of Vivian's disappearance. With a silent shake of his head, Tarek indicated a thorough search of the royal household had yielded nothing. Somehow she had gotten past the guards and fled. But where? Rorke thought furiously. How? . . . Why?

"Have the entire yard searched," he ordered Sevien. "Along both sides of the wall, and each building." Then he turned to Tarek.

"Come with me," he snapped, anger raw like a festering wound.

They first checked the stables. Then, as the sky lightened, crossed the yard to the mews. At the far end, where the small falcon was usually tethered, he found the old woman, Meg.

"She has gone," Meg said, without surprise, and turning to-

ward him though he made no sound as he entered, as if she had
seen him in spite of her blindness. "And taken the falcon with
her."

"What do you know of this?" he demanded, suspecting that
she knew a great deal. But the expression on the old woman's
face was as blind as her sightless eyes. Or perhaps she chose it
to be.

"She did not confide in me. She was with you, milord." Then
her tone sharpened. "She knew she must not stay with you!"

He crossed the mews in furious strides, his anger communicating itself to the birds, who flared their wings with sudden
alarm and cried out. He seized Meg by her frail, thin shoulders
and shook her.

"Do not lecture me, old crone! Nor point that bony finger
in blame. There were no chains to bind her. She stayed with me
of her own free will. I would never force her to do anything,
even if I could." He shook her again.

"No chains, perhaps," she defiantly spat at him, "but bound
as surely as any chain! I told her she should flee. She could
have at any time." Those sightless eyes narrowed.

"Do you truly believe that any bonds you place on her could
hold her?" she asked, and then said with a grave certainty, "Milord, you know not what you deal with!"

"Silence, you old fool! She would not leave you behind.
Wherever she has gone, she means to return. Surely, even you
know that! Surely, too, you must see the danger to her. If you
know where she has gone, then say it, or trouble me no more!"

"You have your conquest," she said contemptuously. "You
have bedded her. I dreamed of it last night. I saw her virgin's
blood on your body. And yet having conquered, you still seek
the vanquished." Then enlightenment spread across the wrinkled features in something almost akin to a smile.

"Could it be," she asked with a particular pleasure edging
her words, "that the conqueror now finds himself to be the one
conquered?" She laughed, a low mocking sound.

Rorke shook her again. "I have no time for your riddles nor

your dreams, old woman. She has said that you see many things in spite of your blindness. Can you see where she has gone?"

Meg turned toward the open door of the mews as if she could see the light there. Her gaze saw far beyond and in ways that he could not begin to understand. She saw in the way of one with the knowledge of secrets and too many years of life. She saw as one who has lost the child she has nurtured and now feared for her as deeply as did the warrior who stood over her.

No longer defiant, her voice thready with that fear, she replied. "She has gone to seek the truth where no man may find her." She turned back and looked at him, the milky opaque film across her eyes giving the disquieting appearance of white on white, as if she had no eyes.

"Give me an answer that I may understand!" Rorke demanded.

"She has gone into the wood and taken Aquila with her. You must find her." She shivered as though taken by a sudden chill.

"Aye," she agreed. "You know well, bold warrior. There is much danger. My mistress has seen it as well." She went on, in a seemingly rambling tone. "It is no longer here, but waits for her." Her bony hand closed over his arm with surprising strength. "You must find her!"

Outside the mews, Rorke's gaze scanned the sky overhead to the crown of trees at the wood that could be seen beyond the fortress walls.

Doubt ate at him. Had she deliberately fled to get away from him as the old woman had said? Try as he might, he could not recall anything in Vivian's manner the evening before to indicate distress over what had passed between them.

She had been passionate beyond his wildest dreams. Responsive, curious, inventive to the point of bringing him to his knees. She was sweet and tender one moment in her discoveries of his body, filled with a fiery abandonment the next. They had made love repeatedly.

Sensing her uncertainty, then discovering her virginity, he had gently initiated most encounters. But several she had initiated, boldly touching him as he had touched her, until near dawn they had finally fallen asleep with exhaustion. At least he thought they both had slept.

Now, she was gone. And what danger was it that the old woman had spoken of? Was it the nonsensical ravings of an old madwoman, as the crone would have everyone believe? Or was it something else?

Encountering his squire, he shouted an order, "Saddle my horse. Only saddle and bridle. No battle armor."

Tarek strode toward him. "You've had word?"

"Aye, the old crone. Vivian has gone to the wood."

"I'm going with you," Tarek announced. Within moments both their mounts were saddled and they left the courtyard gate nearest the wood.

"There will be a storm soon," he told Rorke on a grimace. "More cursed snow. I hate this cold, forbidding scrabble heap. Is there ever a spring in this place called England?"

Rorke allowed himself a small twist of smile. "I have heard it spoken of, though I cannot promise it."

Tarek grunted as he wrapped the thick folds of his robe more tightly about him. "Perhaps, then, I shall be able to feel the blood in my veins again. For now, I fear it is frozen and has been since Hastings."

"You might try wearing more clothes, my friend," Rorke suggested. "Those robes of yours hardly protect against the cold and wet."

Tarek grinned wickedly. "Ah, but they have their function, my friend. Especially for quick encounters in dark passageways. With those cumbersome breeches you prefer you might find yourself caught with some Saxon maid, by her husband."

Rorke shook his head in warning. "Beware my friend, there are some *passageways* one would be advised not to enter."

"Ah, but that is why I carry a *stout blade* into all dark passageways." His grin deepened. "When I wield it, there are none who defy, or deny, me."

"Do not turn your back, my friend," Rorke warned. "Or you might find a Saxon blade between your shoulders."

Tarek roared with laughter. "I think, my friend, that we speak of very different weapons. I have always found my own true sword to be very persuasive in such matters."

They rode swiftly along the outside wall of the fortress. It was not long before Rorke found what he had been searching for—small, softly made footprints. A maid's slipper, and leading into the wood.

Tarek cursed. "I hate the forest. I *much* prefer a darkened passageway. At least then I might meet the enemy face-to-face."

As the forest closed around them, Rorke commented, "You may get your wish."

How long had she been gone? he wondered. One hour? Two? Longer? And how had she done it without anyone seeing her leave? As though she had vanished into thin air.

At the moment, it didn't matter. The important thing was to find her. There were too many dangers for a woman, alone and unprotected. Fear sharpened the anger and gave it a lethal edge. He swore heavily in French, against the unwanted feelings that surfaced and made him wish for the blood of any who might have harmed her.

He had fought for wealth, lands, and the promise of more wealth and land at the side of Duke William of Normandy, sharpening his warrior's skills to a deadly edge. He had seen horrors and atrocities on countless battlefields, many of them attributed to his own sword.

Cold-blooded. Ruthless.

He had heard those words and more whispered behind his back by his enemies, and friends who envied the wealth he'd acquired. He denied none of it. He had always fought for himself, and feared nothing.

If lands were lost, he fought to regain them and claimed thrice in recompense. If fortunes were lost, he hunted down the thieves and made them pay tenfold.

But what of a bewitchingly beautiful Saxon maid with eyes

like blue fire, hair the color of flame, and the power to make him want to laugh, rage at her in anger, and make love to her until they both burned?

What price might assuage that loss?

Soon it became impossible to follow her tracks in the wood. "We will part here and each search a portion of the wood," Rorke announced, feeling the urgency to find her more than ever now that they knew she had come this way.

Tarek nodded and set off through the trees. Rorke wheeled the warhorse about and moved off in the opposite direction.

How long had she been gone? An hour? Two? Or was it longer? And what had brought her into the wood?

He sent the warhorse through heavy thickets and over fallen trees, searching for some sign that she'd passed this way. Occasionally he picked up the impressions of tracks in the light mantle of snow, but then they disappeared altogether or turned out to be those of an animal. He was about to turn back and redouble his efforts in a different direction when he heard the cry of a falcon.

The falcon was high, skimming the treetops overhead, unmistakable in the easily recognized four-note call that Vivian had taught her. It was the small peregrine, Aquila. Trained by Vivian's own hand. If the falcon was nearby, then she was also nearby.

Then the falcon's call sounded again. But this time it was not the familiar four-note greeting by which the falcon and her mistress might easily recognize one another. The call now was a single, high-pitched, piercing cry of alarm. He sent the warhorse plunging in the direction of the falcon's cry.

Vivian tried to move only to discover that even the smallest movement sent pain shooting through every muscle and joint in her body, and required great concentration of physical and inner strength.

She had no idea what it was that had roused her, nor for

several moments, where she was or what had happened. Then, she gradually became aware of the cold beneath her and the gray dawn above her filtering through the crowned treetops overhead. Then it all came back in a sudden rush of memory and physical awareness—the vision in the flames, her trip to the wood, and her journey through the stone portal.

Her body ached at even the least movement, as if she had been beaten. It brought back as well the vivid memory of the vast difference between her journey to the other world and her return. Almost as if something had been trying to prevent her returning.

She tried to move, but she was still very weak. The sound came again. Like that of something moving rapidly through the forest. She cast her thoughts afar but could not discern what it was. As the sound drew nearer, she turned her head on the pillow of cold snow beneath her cheek in the direction of the sound.

When it stopped, Vivian thought she might have imagined it, for her thoughts were confused and disoriented. She could control them no more than she could control the pain. She closed her eyes and fell back in exhaustion. The frantic warning of a falcon's alarmed cry overhead pierced through the wall of pain and mind-numbing lethargy.

It was Aquila's repeated warning cry that pulled her from her stupor. Something was wrong. There was danger, and very close by.

Then the silence was suddenly shattered by a thrashing through heavy brush and fallen timber, followed by the staccato crunch of hooves and the agitated snorting of an animal as it plunged into the clearing. Vivian now sensed the danger as well as heard it in the falcon's alarmed cry.

Moving slowly, as much from pain as the instinct not to frighten whatever it was that had entered the clearing, Vivian levered herself up on one elbow. As her senses continued to clear and focus, she knew the danger even before she saw it.

A large, shaggy boar had entered the clearing from the other

side of the forest. It would not have been easily seen, its spiky
matted hair blending with the muted browns of the surrounding
forest. But a plume of breath jetted into the chill morning air
from that tusked snout, a faint grunting sound was heard with
each exhaled breath.

Vivian went absolutely motionless

Cloven hooves impatiently pawed the snow. The beast's long
hair stood straight up along the bony ridge of spine, curved
tusks stained yellow like golden hooks. It was a seasoned warrior, its thick hide marred by the scars of many encounters. One
ear was torn, the split hide having healed with the tear intact.
One of the tusks was broken off and much shorter than the
other, but no less lethal.

Highly intelligent, hampered only by weak eyesight, its other
senses easily found her. That broad head swung in her direction
with almost casual recognition. Beady eyes fixed on her with
unusual perception, the piggy snout twitching as it gathered her
scent.

The creature stared as though contemplating her. A tremor
of uneasiness swept through her at some vague memory of the
return journey through the portal.

The memory expanded and sharpened like the facets of a
perfect blue crystal, of a vast darkness that shifted and took on
many forms. First, the shape of a man. Then some hideous
misshapen, otherworld creature charging at her, forcing her
back, as though it was trying to prevent her returning to the
real world, trapping her in the mist.

It seemed impossible and yet as she stared at the beast, those
piggy eyes black as midnight, devoid of any pinkish outer rim
and fathomless as the great, waiting Darkness, she knew the
creature had come to finish what it had failed to do in the portal.

Overhead a falcon's call pierced the morning air, urgent and
bleak as the storm that quickly gathered. Then Rorke saw the
small huntress, swooping the treetops.

He urged the warhorse through the trees, following her

winged flight toward a clearing. The urgency of her cry made his blood run cold through his veins.

Amid the stark white, cold gray, and barren green of the forest, he spotted the fiery crown of Vivian's red-gold hair as she lay at the base of what appeared to be a large, standing stone. Then he saw the boar.

It stomped and snorted, its breath jetting on the bitter cold air, layers of frozen mucous gleaming at its vicious tusked snout as it prepared to charge.

He had only one chance and that was to distract the creature before it charged. With a piercing battle cry, he sent the warhorse crashing into the clearing. He vaulted to the ground, with both broadsword and the smaller blade in hand, using the stallion as a diversion.

Having caught the boar's scent, the stallion charged across the clearing, eyes rolling wildly as it ground to a halt. Amazingly the boar was only mildly distracted. Then, as if dismissing this new threat, it swung its head once more toward Vivian.

"Do not move," Rorke told her. "I will draw the beast away. Take my horse and flee."

The wind shifted, easily carrying his scent to the creature. Its head swung about, and for a moment it seemed that it considered this new target with a keen awareness, the look in its eyes sharpening as if it contemplated him with profound interest that hinted at cognitive thought.

"No," Vivian whispered desperately, for she too had seen the subtle change in the beast's stance. As if it measured Rorke, gauging his strengths, searching for weaknesses with an unusual intelligence.

She could almost hear the beast's thoughts and knew the creature was otherworldly. Knew, too, that it would kill Rorke. There was only one chance that he might live.

Then the beast's thoughts were closed to her, like a shroud of darkness closing over them. Pushing unsteadily to her feet, Vivian took a step toward the beast, drawing its attention back to her as that ugly, misshapen head swung toward her.

It snorted, spewing a stream of phlegm and saliva as it pawed at the snow. Eyes as black as the waiting Darkness gleamed with an evil light, and something very near a deadly grin curved the beast's mouth.

With a piercing, blood-chilling scream that recalled the terrifying noises Vivian had heard on her journey through the portal—like the souls of the ancient dead being torn asunder—the beast plunged across the clearing, head down, dark eyes fixed on her.

The blow drove her to the ground. Amidst the beast's grunting and bloodthirsty squeals, she felt those deadly tusks tearing through her flesh. The pain was intense, driving the air from her startled lungs, burning through her.

As though she had stepped out of herself she saw the attack from afar and at the same time from within her body. She stared out across the stark beauty of the glistening snow and then turned her thoughts inward toward survival.

She disconnected from the physical pain of the mortal world, as though it was someone else who endured the attack. She concentrated instead on the Darkness of the beast that sought to destroy her. Her hand fiercely clasped over the blue crystal as her soul reached through the fiery blue heart of the stone to the power of the hand that reached out to her.

"Live, daughter!" the words pierced through the pain tearing at her soul. *"You must fight the Darkness! Draw upon the power of the Light!"*

Brilliant dots of color spun before her, then gradually separated and coalesced so that the colors beaded together and became strands of color—dark forest green, glistening white like the snow, silvery gray of the leaden sky overhead, rich woody browns, and brilliant crimson blood—all interwoven in the vision of the tapestry.

She caught only a fleeting glimpse of the images that had begun to emerge as threads joined with others as though some invisible hand carefully wove them—a man and woman whose bodies slowly came together in a burst of fiery, blazing color that shifted sensuously, erotically in an intense intimate joining as the threads of destiny were joined.

Then she no longer felt or saw anything as she heard Rorke's fierce war cry.

He attacked, carving dozens of wounds until at last the beast swung that grisly head toward him. Blood streamed from those lethal tusks—her blood—to mingle with the blood of the creature.

"Come, you bloodthirsty spawn of Satan!" Rorke's curses filled the clearing as he stood in battle stance, the broadsword held before him in both hands.

Rorke saw what seemed to be a smile at the beast's leering mouth, as if it mocked him and the gleaming blade that had already tasted the creature's blood.

"Come and meet your death!" he challenged.

As if it understood, the beast pivoted, lowering its ugly, misshapen head, grunting and rutting at the snow-covered ground with its bloody tusks. That head swung slowly back and forth. The creature screamed its bloodlust, pivoted, and charged.

With broadsword raised, Rorke waited for the beast to strike. The creature launched itself with amazing power, aiming for Rorke's legs with the intent of crippling him with those deadly tusks and then driving him to the ground for the kill.

The broadsword was a clumsy weapon for hunting. He would have only one chance to disable the creature. When the beast was only a few feet away, Rorke dropped down on both knees, notching the butt of the sword handle in the hard-packed, ground before him, the blade held at an angle on a level with the boar's chest.

The creature struck, the force of the blow almost driving Rorke into the ground. But he held fast, bracing all his weight behind the blade as the deadly tip finally drove through coarse hide and heavy muscle, skittered along bone, then sank deeper still into the soft, yielding flesh of vulnerable organs.

The blade bowed at the impact of the boar's headlong charge, sinking deep, taking with it a two-foot length of the blade.

Squealing in pain and fury, stunned by the blow, the boar rolled to its side and clawed to regain its footing.

In those few seconds, Rorke retrieved the smaller blade from the ground where it lay within easy reach should he need it.

With both hands clasped around the handle of the blade, he drove it deep into that vulnerable place between those thrusting shoulder blades, severing the creature's spine. Then, removing the blade, he ended the creature's squealing frenzy with a quick slash across the twin veins at its throat.

It grunted, thrashed once more with its front legs, back legs dangling helplessly, then gave one last dying shudder as its life-blood pumped from the massive, brutish body.

With a fierce cry of anguish Rorke threw himself off the vile creature and vaulted across the clearing to the slender girl who lay crumpled and motionless in the bloodstained snow.

The coldness of her body as he reached for her stunned Rorke. It seeped into him through his fingers, pouring through him to clasp around his heart. He turned her over, cradling her in his arms as he frantically searched through the thick folds of the torn mantle for the bloodied wounds.

A gasp of air escaped her lips. Her eyelids fluttered open, exposing the startled blue-gray color of her eyes, a stark look that reminded him of the sightless eyes of the dead in the aftermath of battle. Her skin was deathly pale, almost bloodless.

"Rorke?" she whispered through frozen, gray lips.

"Do not try to move!" he ordered, the fierceness of the battle just fought and a new seeping terror, sharply edging his words.

"The creature . . . ?"

"Dead!" he said, flinging the word away with a feral, harsh sound.

She shuddered violently. "I was afraid . . ."

"There is nothing to fear." He gentled his voice. "It is over, *ma chère petite.*" The endearment was like a caress, taking away her pain. He gathered her close. "I must get you back to the fortress, if you think you are strong enough to ride." She nodded weakly as his hand came away bloodied beneath her.

Overhead, the falcon called frantically. Very close by there was another movement in the trees. Not the frantic, crazed thrashing of another beast on the hunt, but the barely discernible whispered movement of one who moves powerfully, silently, at one with the wind.

Tarek emerged from the cover of the trees, the deadly curved blade clutched in both hands and held before him as he moved with the silent stealth of a cat.

A sweeping glance took in the clearing, the boar's lifeless body, and his friend bending over the beautiful, magical woman.

His voice filled with remnants of fierce anger from the battle past, and a new anger at the bleeding that he could not stop, Rorke shouted to his friend, "Bring my horse!"

Moments later, as Rorke sat astride the warhorse, Tarek gently lifted Vivian up to him. She was pale, her slender body fragile as glass and wrapped in the voluminous folds of his heavy mantle.

A long, jagged wound ran the length of her leg from ankle to above her knee. As a warrior, Tarek knew that a single wound such as this one was could be deadly in the loss of blood. Vivian had several such wounds. If a person survived a single wound such as this, the limb was left horribly crippled. Tarek said nothing as, grim-faced, he tucked the edges of the mantle about her legs and feet, the heavy dark fabric darker still with her blood.

A grim expression etched his hardened features as Rorke cradled her against the warmth of his own body, which was covered with her blood. At the scent of the boar's blood mingled with other blood, the stallion shifted nervously. But he was held in check by a powerful hand at the reins.

"I will bring your weapons," Tarek assured his friend as Rorke whirled the warhorse about and sent him plunging through the trees at the edge of the clearing and toward the fortress.

Vivian's wavering gaze fixed one last time on the clearing. The stone portal was gone, vanished in the mist. Her blood and that of the dead boar, mingled in a stark pattern, staining the snow.

The creature was dead. She had seen it slain by Rorke's sword, its body lying motionless.

Yet, as Vivian's eyes closed and she turned her powers inward toward the weakness of her torn flesh, she sensed something more terrifying than her blinding pain. The creature of Darkness still lived. It moved steadily through the forest, stalking them from behind each tree and rock and the cover of each thicket.

A shout went out along the top of the wall as they approached the fortress. Rorke and Tarek were recognized, and guards scurried to throw open the large gates for them. Without breaking stride, Rorke sent the warhorse plunging across the dry moat bed, up the opposite embankment, and through the gates.

The stallion slid to a bone-jarring halt, sending mud flying before its large hooves. Grim-faced, Rorke hooked a leg over the front of the saddle and slid to the ground, holding her close. His squire immediately appeared.

"Find the old crone and have her sent to me!" He vaulted past the stunned squire, who immediately ran to do as he was ordered.

Rorke quickly carried her through the front entrance to the royal compound, across the great hall and down the passage to his private chamber. He kicked it open and carried her inside. Laying her gently on the bed, he caught sight of his squire.

"Where is the crone!" he shouted.

"I am here," Meg informed him, pushing her way past Tarek and Rorke's squire to the side of the bed.

His voice was tight. "You have knowledge of healing." It was more of a command than any appreciation for her skills.

"Aye," she said, staring in the direction of his voice. "I taught the girl everything she knows of healing things. Her knowledge is mine. In most things."

"Do you possess the same knowledge that mends broken bones and seals the flesh with the touch of a hand?" he demanded.

Though sightless, her gaze fastened on him with a new awareness. She had not realized until this moment that her mistress had revealed her very special gift to him. Yet, knowing of it, there was no ridicule of doubt in his voice, but an acceptance of what he had obviously seen with his own eyes, even though such things went beyond accepted belief of things in the real world.

"Sadly, milord, that gift is hers alone," she admitted with great heaviness of heart. "But I will do what I can."

"You will do *all* you can, and more," he ordered, his voice breaking. "She will not die!"

At the desperation in his voice, Meg looked toward him with new insight. Was it possible that this bold Norman warrior was the *one* told of in ancient legend?

"I will do what I can," she repeated. "The rest is up to her."

She approached the bed, bending over Vivian and *seeing* her with the sight of her fingers as she touched her mistress' face, her arms, hands, and the length of her body to the rent and blood-soaked hem of her gown.

A deep, sad sigh escaped her thin lips and her frail, old shoulders sagged as though what she found was almost more than she could bear.

"Eist le, mo chroi," she whispered the ancient Celtic words of endearment as she stroked Vivian's face, as though comforting a beloved child. Her voice trembled with uncertainty when she spoke again as though she reassured her mistress, who lay as if in a deep sleep where no one could reach her. "I will do all that I can."

Rorke issued orders to his squire. "I will have Mally sent to you," he told Meg.

"No!" the old woman said sharply. "No one is to be allowed near her. I will do it. I have everything I need. Send the others away."

She sensed the warrior's fierce gaze on her, and in it the mistrust. She sensed something else as well—a powerful emotion as raw and anguished as those he had felt in any battle.

Was it possible? she wondered again, that this Norman knight, a mortal man with human frailties, might love her mistress?

She had heard the whisperings when he returned with her mistress. A great battle had been fought in the forest. With only sword in hand, Rorke FitzWarren had faced a boar, a huge, fierce creature. Even now he had the smell of the creature's death about him.

It was an evil smell, far different than the usual lingering odor after the hunt. She shivered again, sensing that in the clearing far more than merely a creature of the wood had been vanquished.

Was it possible? Meg continued to wonder, that this man who carried the creature rising from the flames on his shield, whose thoughts her mistress could not discern or bend to her own will as she could others, had a destiny as great as that of her mistress?

A creature born in fire and blood that would spread its wings across the land, as her mistress had seen in her vision. War was already upon England then, with the duke of Normandy's army at Hastings. With no clear meaning to the vision, her mistress had assumed the creature to be the creature of war and destruction. But what if the creature was a man—a warrior tested in the fire and blood of battle, whose purpose was not to destroy but to save the kingdom?

With a new awareness of insight, Meg said, gentling her voice, "When she slipped into this world, it was my hands that first held her. She is like my own. If you want her to live, you must leave her to me. It is the only way."

On a harshly whispered oath, Rorke ordered everyone from the chamber. Then his gaze fastened on Vivian in the bed they had shared only scant hours earlier.

How was it possible? he wondered, that he had been the cause of so many countless deaths on the battlefield and never felt remorse. And yet at the possibility of this sweet creature's death he experienced such an intense anguish as if it was his life that ebbed and flowed with each fragile beat of her heart. For the first time in his life he felt fear.

A fear that he might lose her light and laughter. Fear that if he left that chamber, he might never see her in this world again.

"I give her over into your care, old woman," he agreed. "But I shall remain." When she would have protested, he cut her off.

"Whatever you must do to save her, do it! But I will not leave."

Meg heard the steeliness in his voice, like that of a warrior's blade, uncompromising, lethal, certain unto death.

"Aye, warrior," she said, "I sense that you are brave enough to confront any foe in battle, including death. But are you brave enough to confront the truth? No matter what that truth might be?"

With a finality, Rorke told her, "You already have my answer."

"So be it, then." Meg resigned herself that she could not change his mind. "I ask only one thing of you."

"And that is?"

"That no matter what happens, no matter what you see, you must say and do nothing."

"Agreed."

"Then bar the doors so that none may enter," Meg instructed. "Once it has begun, there must be no distractions or interruptions. Build up the fire at the hearth and light every candle, placing several near the bed. I will do the rest."

When he told her everything was done as she asked, Meg approached the bed where her mistress lay.

She removed the torn mantle and the kirtle beneath. Rorke's agonized hiss of breath very close by told her of the severity of the wounds even before she touched them. He refused to be banished to some far corner of the chamber. She accepted it, because there was no time to argue and she knew he would not listen.

Within the folds of the mantle, she found the packet of ancient herbs. Their strange, pungent essence—not experienced for hundreds of years in this world—told her who had sent them.

Ah, Ninian, she thought, *first child whom I brought into this world and mother of this child who now lies so near death. Did*

*you somehow sense the special potions you sent might be used
to prevent her death?*

Meg longed for the world in the mist, left so many years ago
with a tender babe in her arms. Sent into the mortal world, as
her master believed, to escape the dreaded Darkness.

There was no answer to her silent questions, for she had not
the power to send her thoughts into that other world. There were
only the precious leaves that might work the magic she herself
could not, if she could not summon the flame of life.

"Perhaps there is hope," she whispered, pausing only once
more as her fingers brushed torn flesh. She steeled herself and
began crooning an ancient Celtic song of enchantment while
she bathed her mistress with fragrant herbal water, cleansing
away the blood from the torn flesh.

Then she bound the wounds, using potions mixed from the
ancient leaves, and covered her mistress with warm furs. Lastly,
she removed the blue crystal that lay dull and dark, and almost
colorless against Vivian's pale skin as if it, too, lay dying.

Meg had heard the words countless times. Still, she was filled
with doubt. The power was not with her as it was with her
mistress. It never had been.

Her fate was that of those born from the union of a changeling
and a mortal, with only the random chance of fate determining
if she would be born with the gift of enchantment. She had not.

Her powers were meager and merely compensated for the
sight she had been born without. But this time it must be enough
to summon the Light. Her voice quavered slightly, then grew
stronger as she held the crystal before a candle and recited the
ancient Celtic words.

*"Element of fire, spirit of light, essence of life, awaken the
night.*

*"Fire of the soul, flame of life, as light reveals truth, burn
golden bright."*

There was only silence. Feeling the helplessness of her blindness that prevented her seeing the crystal as she held it before
the candle's flame, she began again.

"Element of fire, spirit of light, essence of life, awaken the night!" Her voice caught on a sob.

"Fire of the soul, flame of life, as light reveals truth . . ."

But it was another who murmured the last words of the enchantment, as Vivian whispered, *"Burn golden bright."*

Rorke watched as Meg's old face lit up with inexplicable joy. She clasped her hands together over the blue crystal.

"Dear child! I thought you were lost to me."

Vivian sighed with a bone-aching weariness. It took almost more strength than she had left, but she concentrated on the crystal Meg clasped in her hands, and the ancient words that had awakened her.

"Dear Meg," she whispered, as though she had not seen him. "Bring the candle very close."

Meg did as she asked, and from the shadows at the side of the bed, Rorke watched as Vivian focused her gaze on the flame of the candle, reflected in the depths of the blue crystal.

Vivian clasped the crystal, feeling its fiery heat burn through her as the fire became her own, rekindling the flame that lived within her as surely as the flame that lived in the heart of the stone.

Meg's sightless gaze fastened on Rorke where he stood in the shadows at the edge of the bed. In her expression, he saw the silent warning that he must say and do nothing.

Vivian extended one hand toward the flame of the candle while the other remained clasped about the blue crystal. Then she closed her eyes, lips forming ancient words in the same cadence of ritual that Meg had spoken only moments before.

"Element of fire, spirit of light, essence of life, awaken the night.

"Fire of the soul, flame of life, as light reveals truth, burn golden bright."

He watched in fascination as the flame of the candle expanded and grew. A current of air, he reasoned. Nothing more. Then he watched, stunned, as Vivian extended her hand into the flame.

Meg sensed his movement when he would have stopped her. Her bony hand, strong as the finest steel, clamped over his arm.

"You wanted truth, warrior," she hissed. "Now you will have it. But you must do nothing. Or it will mean her death!"

Rorke watched as the ancient ceremony began. Watched and said nothing, filled with pain as if a blade had been thrust deep inside him, as if the flames leapt down the length of his own arm.

Watched and still said nothing even as he felt as if his own life blood seeped out of his body as those flames engulfed her. Continued to watch in silent agony as if it was his own death, as the flames seemed to consume her, until he was certain he could watch no more.

When he would have turned away, Meg refused to allow it.

"You are part of it now," she whispered, for though she could not see, she could feel everything that happened. "This is her truth. She risks much in revealing it. If you now turn away, you will be the cause of her death as surely as if you plunged a blade into her."

Rorke continued to watch, until he was certain he might go mad. There was no logic in what he saw—no logic that existed in the real world. Then, he forced himself past the madness.

He felt the heat of the fire that burned around her. With head thrown back, a radiant expression on her beautiful face, the brilliant cascade of her hair becoming one with the fire, it was as if she was some fire-born creature. Not destroyed by the flames, but drawing life from them. And he knew she was not of this world.

Rising from the bed, Vivian gently laid a hand on Rorke's arm where he stood as though stunned in shadows at the wall beside the bed.

He still wore the bloodstained leather breeches and tunic, and she shivered slightly at the contact. For it was not her blood but that of the evil creature he had slain. Then it passed.

Through the layer of leather at his arm, she felt his lifeblood pounding through his veins. It was rapid and fierce as though a battle had just been fought. And she sensed something more beneath her fingers, an anguish so great that she could scarcely bear it. But in this new awareness she sensed far more. A joining far deeper than the physical joining of their bodies as they made love.

He had risked his life for her and slain the beast, a creature of such Darkness he did not yet understand. In the mingling of his warrior's blood with hers, there had been a joining of far more than the flesh. There had been a joining of the soul. The mortal joined with the immortal.

He was now part of her, and she was part of him. But he did not yet have an understanding of that either.

He had just seen such as few mortals ever see, and she knew that part of his anguish came from his struggle to comprehend it. She saw it in his fierce gray gaze as he looked at her, the rest of his features concealed in the shadows.

She tried to sense his other thoughts, but the bond between them was still too new and fragile. Vivian found she did not want to take hold of his thoughts as she could so easily do with others. For he was not like others. Whatever they shared, it must be because he willingly allowed it and opened to her.

She felt the muscles of his arm tense beneath her hand and for a moment she experienced a doubt so painful she thought she could not bear it, that he might refuse to accept what he had seen. If he refused it, he refused her as well.

That tiny fragment of doubt sliced through her like no pain she had ever experienced, not even the pain of death in the clearing. When she would have removed her hand, his hand closed over hers with a fierce strength. She sensed the turmoil of uncertainty mixed with relief in his touch, and knew the silent battle he had fought, not knowing what he might find beneath his hand after what he had seen.

"You are not burned?"

"Nay, milord," she said on a tentative breath, knowing the battle he still fought—the battle to believe.

"And the wounds?"

"They are healed. You may see for yourself."

But he did not wish to see for himself. Instead, his gaze remained fastened on hers.

"And you are real? You are no spirit that I may not touch?" As though only touching her would convince him, his fingers tightened over her wrist in a desperate, fierce grasp that would have been painful to anyone else.

She smiled softly. "You may touch me." Behind her, she heard the latch set at the chamber door as it closed and knew they were now alone.

As if he still was not convinced of it, he pulled her roughly into his arms. He felt warm flesh and blood beneath his hands, saw it standing embodied before him.

He crushed her fiercely to him, hands plunging back through the fiery cascade of her hair, holding her as if he thought she might transform to smoke and disappear on the air. Then his mouth plunged down over hers in a kiss that was both tender and powerful, gentle and fierce with the need to banish any doubt that remained.

He invaded her senses, the heat of his mouth creating a new fire that joined with hers and burned bright.

"Aye," he whispered with harsh and profound wonder. "You are very real."

Twenty-one

"Tell me," Rorke said from the chair where he sat before the hearth.

His features were less harsh, etched now with the lingering

traces of another sort of fierceness from their recent lovemaking.

It sheened his powerful body, glistening at the scars of old wounds, covering the hard angles and contours of him with a fine patina as though he were carved from stone that glimmered with the fine mist of dawn.

After her near brush with death, they had come together with an urgency and fire that threatened to consume them both, as if he would sooner perish in her flames than exist without her. And then, having assuaged the last traces of doubt, his loving of her had taken on a new tenderness, as he caressed and stroked every part of her body with a need to touch the places that had been torn and bleeding and then lay once more whole and sleek beneath him.

And finally, he needed to understand, to be able to reconcile what he had seen that was not of this world, with the very real woman who lay with him, bringing him a passion that was equally real. A passion that left him in awe of her ability to feel and experience every essence of their joining with a pleasure that was beyond his wildest dreams.

"Tell me all of it," he said again as she turned and walked back from the table, with a goblet in one hand.

A pale, slender leg showed at the opening of the fur, void of even the smallest scar. The healing touch that had repaired William's wounds and saved his life had served her well.

Her hair framed her face and shoulders in a brilliant fiery nimbus, while the fire at the hearth glowed golden behind her, seeming a part of her still.

The doors were barred. The old woman was gone. It was midday, or perhaps it was midnight. It didn't matter. Not even William of Normandy would have received an answer had he summoned his knight.

She handed him the goblet of wine, their fingers brushing in a rediscovery of the fiery warmth that leapt so easily between them. When she would have moved a distance away to sit in the other chair, his fingers closed over hers, tenderly forbidding it.

With a fluid, flamelike grace that he now realized was so inherently a part of her, she knelt and then sat amid the thick furs at his feet, untouching except for the unbroken bond of their intertwined fingers.

Vivian wondered how much he believed of ancient legends. How much would he allow himself to believe?

"My mother's name is Ninian. She was born in a place called Tintagel in the far west of the kingdom."

He nodded. "I have heard of it."

When he sipped his wine and said no more, Vivian continued. "She was born in the year 572."

The goblet stopped in midair and remained suspended for several moments. Then Rorke finally brought it all the way to his lips and took a sip, silently contemplating her over the rim of the goblet as she went on.

"My father was born in the year 558 in the north of Wales." She took a deeper breath. "His name is Merlin."

Rorke took a much deeper drink of wine. He set the goblet back to the arm of the chair. His other hand remained clasped over hers. The expression at his face was intense yet contemplative.

Finally, he said, "Go on."

The fire burned low on the hearth. He built it high twice more, and again it burned almost to embers with the telling of the legend.

Vivian told him of the time of Merlin's youth, his discovery of his very special powers—a bequest from the keepers of the Light. Of his guardianship of the young boy who would one day be king of England—Arthur. Of the forces of the Darkness that conspired against the forces of the Light for dominion over the kingdom.

She refilled his goblet and built the fire high once more, and told him of Arthur's betrayal and death as the powers of Darkness swept through the kingdom. Of Merlin's banishment to the world between the worlds, where there is no time.

Then she told him of Ninian, a changeling born of a sorceress and a mortal, who found the lost sword Excalibur and braved the evil Darkness to take the sword to Merlin. She found him in his tomb and thought to lay the sword at his feet and leave. But Merlin was not dead. He slept deeply from the near-mortal wounds inflicted by the Darkness.

Ninian healed his wounds and his broken heart at the death of Arthur and the loss of the kingdom. But Merlin could not leave the mist, so Ninian chose to remain with him. They became devoted to each other and built a life together.

In time some of Merlin's great powers were restored with good health. His gift of inner vision, the power of fire which he shared with Vivian, and always his great intellect, which was a powerful weapon against the Darkness.

Three daughters were born, bringing great joy and happiness. Each was endowed with special powers, but they were also mortal. Because they were mortal, they were sent to live in the mortal world.

"The Jehara that Tarek believes in," Rorke murmured thoughtfully, pulling her across his lap and holding her close, as though she might somehow escape, this ephemeral, magical creature who was born of fire and light.

She nodded, the loose fall of her hair tumbling over his arm and falling to the floor in a brilliant firefall.

"What of the old crone?" he asked, his lips grazing a bare shoulder. "Is she gifted as well?" He heard the sound of her breath, catching on something that might have been a sigh of pleasure or desire, or both, and need raced through his veins again. His arms closed about her more tightly.

"Meg was born to a changeling and a mortal," she explained, the top of her head nestling at the curve of his throat. "She has limited powers. But what she lacks she more than makes up for in loyalty." The warmth of her breath stirred the hair at his chest, recalling how her lips had pleasured him over the length of his body.

"It was Meg who cared for me when I was born," she continued, "and then carried me across the whole of England until she found Poladouras."

"How did she accomplish this great journey without your gift of sight, or even mortal sight to guide her?" he asked, frowning with a mixture of curiosity and the extreme effort of keeping his growing desire for her under control.

"She was guided by a silver falcon. The falcon provided her with food and led her through the forests and countryside to her destination. Only the falcon could be entrusted with the location, for she was pure of heart."

"Aquila?"

"Aquila is a descendant of the falcon who guided us so long ago. It is why she is protective and a fine hunter."

He nodded. "The falcon guided me to you, this morn," his voice filled with unexpected emotion, "or I would not have found you in time."

Then, he became thoughtful once more.

"What of the standing stone I saw in the clearing?"

"It is a portal into the other world. It is possible for some to pass through the stone."

"And fortress walls as well?"

She shrugged and gave him a small smile. "At the time it seemed the most expedient means to leave without being seen."

With a growing huskiness of voice, he asked, "What other powers do you possess?" he asked.

She told him of the other powers she had slowly discovered and gradually learned how to use, including the unusual healing power that had saved William's life, and her own hours earlier. And the power of fire.

"Fire is one of the elements of nature. My mother calls me her daughter of passion, daughter of fire. It is as if the fire burns within me."

"Aye," Rorke acknowledged, his gray gaze fixed on her, his

voice once more low in his throat with remembered passion. "I have tasted your fire. It is, I think, the only way I should wish to die."

"No!" she said passionately. "Not die, but live! The fire is the power of life within me. So, too, is it with you, now that we are joined. It happened in that moment when your blood joined with mine in the clearing when you slew the creature."

"A fierce beast," he remarked with a frown, his thoughts churning with everything she had told him. "I was not certain it would die."

"It has not," she answered gravely. Her gaze met his, a troubled expression on her lovely features. "It lives still."

"Go on," he urged, sensing her fear. "Tell me of it."

"Like the changeling, the Darkness takes many forms. For Arthur it came in the form of his friend's betrayal that brought his downfall. I saw it in the form of a man who attempted to attack me as I passed through the portal. When I escaped, it became the boar. I saw it in the beast's eyes."

"What form did it take with Merlin?"

"It was a battle of power. First it destroyed Arthur, for Arthur was like a son to Merlin and possessed the true heart to be a powerful king who might have destroyed the Darkness once and for all. When the Darkness could not destroy Merlin, it imprisoned him, preventing him from returning to the mortal world and using his powers of the Light."

"But the Darkness did not know that there were others with Merlin's powers," Rorke concluded. "His daughter."

Like the great warrior and tactician he was, Rorke saw the logic of everything she had told him. It explained so much of what he knew of legend, myth, and fact. "Then the legend of Arthur and Merlin is true," Rorke said with simple acceptance. He had seen too much of her unusual powers not to believe it.

"Aye," she said softly. " 'Tis true."

Then she told him of her power of inner sight, and of the visions that came to her, beginning with the first vision at Amesbury. Of a creature born in fire and blood—the phoenix rising from a bed of flames—and the warning of the prophecy, *"Beware the faith that has no heart, the sword that has no soul."*

He looked at her with a new understanding. "You knew William would be victorious at Hastings."

She nodded. "I saw it and other things."

He lifted a hand and touched her cheek. "What other visions have you seen?"

With all her powers, it was the power of *his* touch that had the ability to unnerve her as no other, sending shivers across her skin as he stroked a thumb across the curve of her lower lip, recalling in an instant the taste and textures of him.

"I have seen a weaver at a tapestry," she said, her breath catching on a sigh of pleasure. "But the design is not yet finished. I do not know what it means."

"Can you see my thoughts?" he asked.

She confessed, "Unlike others, your thoughts are closed to me."

"And it disturbs you."

"It is only that I have always been capable of seeing a person's true thoughts and emotions." She remembered Merlin's warning, that she would only truly know him if he allowed it.

"Then you have reason to doubt me. You may even believe that I am a creature of the Darkness?"

"Nay," she said with a growing huskiness of voice as his hand wandered lower and stroked over a breast. "I would know it. The creature of my vision—the phoenix rising from the flames—is a creature of fire and light, not a creature of Darkness."

"And yet, you can not be certain."

"There is a way."

He nodded. "Say it and I will prove myself."

"It is not that simple. In order for me to truly know your heart, you must open your thoughts to me."

He shrugged. " 'Tis not a great thing you ask." With a crooked smile he took another drink of wine. "I have been told that my head is full of hay. Perhaps you will find only grazing for horses when you look inside."

" 'Tis not a matter to be taken lightly," she protested. "It is not just your thoughts I will know, but your hopes, memories, and emotions. Your very soul will be laid bare to me."

"I would bare it to no one else, mistress. You may steal my thoughts, in truth you already have. And you already have my heart. I knew it this morn when I discovered you gone." Though he had made a jest, the gently restrained power in his hand as it stroked through her hair to clasp the back of her head spoke of deadly earnest.

"I feared that I had lost you, and then relived it twice over when I saw that damnable creature attack you. You drew it away from me."

"To give you time," she answered softly. "A chance, perhaps, that you might live."

"With no thought to your own life?"

"The creature would have destroyed you and then returned for me. That was its purpose all along. I was weakened from my passage through the portal, I had no strength to fight it a second time."

"A second time?"

She nodded. "The first was in the portal. I saw the image of a man . . ." She closed her eyes, instantly recalling the image. "It was as if he was blocking the opening to the other side. He kept trying to push me back, to prevent my return."

"A man? What did he look like?"

She slipped from his lap, moving with an uneasy restlessness that conveyed the fear she still felt. "It was only an image. The Darkness had taken a form to strike at me. It is part of the deceit and trickery that it uses."

He leaned forward in the chair. "Can you sense its thoughts?"

She shook her head. "It is very careful to keep its thoughts protected from me. For then I might find a way to destroy it."

"Just as my thoughts are closed to you. I will do this thing that you ask so that you may know I tell the truth."

"No!"

"I do not fear it."

"I do!" Vivian cried out. "It is dangerous. If a person is not strong he or she may be destroyed."

"Do you think me not strong enough to endure it?"

" 'Tis not that. You are more than strong." She felt color burn wildly across her skin at the remembered strength of his body joining hers.

"The pain is intense with such a joining. Every part of you will be laid open to me, like a wound. Your natural instinct will be to fight it and in the fighting there will be a pain so intense that you may not survive it. I will not risk you in that way. I could not bear to be the cause of your death."

"You will not risk *me?*" Rorke vaulted from the chair, the fur mantle flowing about his powerful naked body, like skin, making him seem even more a feral, untamed creature framed by the fire at the hearth. He was angry. She needed no gift to understand that. It was there in the hard lines etched on his fierce, handsome features, in the ridges of veins that patterned his heavily muscled forearm as he made a fist, in the fire and ice in that gray gaze.

"I must accept all that you have told me. For I have seen your power with my own eyes and there is no other explanation. I have seen the portal in the mist. I have seen your healing way unlike any in the mortal world. And I have known your fire until I was certain I would perish from it, and it would not have mattered to me.

"Now you tell me of a great Darkness that seeks to sweep away everything before it with but one hope. That it may be vanquished. You have said that in this learning of me you will know all about me and my true heart. But is it not true that I will also learn of you. And in the learning might there not be something to be gained to vanquish this Darkness?"

He walked back toward her, on the furs before the chair where he had sat only moments before. Each movement was like that of a powerful hunting beast, spare, perfectly balanced, barely restrained. He did not return to the chair but crouched before her at the earthen floor strewn with furs, all of his virile, naked glory displayed with as much ease of confidence as though he wore battle armor.

"You fear for my soul, mistress. But in truth you have already laid claim to it," he said, laying a hand alongside her cheek. "And my heart, my every thought, every breath I take. I would die for you on any field of battle. It is not for you to say yea or nay. 'Tis for me to risk it if I am willing."

He assured her, "It will be done."

Vivian knew there was nothing she could say or do that would dissuade him. Not everyone was strong enough to survive what she must do. What if he was not strong enough to endure the pain that was both physical and mental? What if she was the cause of his death? As if he sensed her fear and doubt, he lowered his mouth to hers and lightly brushed his lips across hers.

"It must be done, my lovely Jehara. There is no other way."

She nodded sadly, her eyes closing as she breathed in the powerful, passionate heat of him, drawing it deep inside her and feeling his power become one with hers.

"Aye," she whispered." Then taking another deep breath, she moved away from him. "I must draw on the powers of the Light. The fire must be built high. Every candle and torch must be lit."

He nodded. When it was done he returned to stand before her.

"You must be completely relaxed," she told him, drawing him back to the chair before the hearth. When he sat reclined in the chair, the fur robe draped about him, she encouraged him to drink more of the wine.

"I have blended an herbal powder in the wine. It will aid in relaxing you. You must not fight what you will feel. You must give in to it."

He gave the goblet a long look, as if contemplating the true nature of what she might have placed there. Then, abruptly, he downed the entire contents. He set the goblet aside, his lips curving a smile.

"I can think of other ways to relax me, for you have a power beyond any wine or potions, mistress." He reached out to her, taking a silken tendril of her hair between his fingers and stroking it. With a shudder, she felt that simple contact and knew it was a trick of her own mind, recalling the pleasure of his touch on her body.

"Perhaps for you, milord. But I must have my wits about me, and in truth I have little control over them when you touch me."

"A witch bewitched?" he suggested, the expression behind his gray eyes filled with myriad possibilities.

"By God, mistress, you threaten to undo me with no more than words."

"I would not undo you at all, milord," she said gravely, thinking of what was to come.

His hand gently twisted in her hair, wrapping it about his hand as he slowly drew her close. The warmth of his breath mingled with hers. His mouth brushed hers in an agony of tenderness. But the words were hardly tender.

They were filled with the raw, naked power of a man who surrenders nothing as he whispered against her lips, "I surrender to you, mistress of fire."

Please, she thought, whispering a silent prayer to Poladouras' God, *let his heart be true. For I could not bear to be the cause of his death.*

She brought a candle from the table closer and held it between them.

"Look into the flame," she instructed, deliberately lowering her voice so that the words were wrapped in soft musical tones as she began the bonding spell that would bring their thoughts together.

"Concentrate on the flame, and nothing else. See its shape, the way it gently breathes and moves, all the colors—pale yellow at the tip so that you can almost see through it," the words became rhythmic, "then bright yellow, soft gold, and finally blue at the heart of the flame.

"Look into the flame," she said softly, concentrating her own gaze into the heart of it. "See the colors. Feel its warmth. Hear the guttering sound it makes.

"Thinking only of the flame, close your eyes and see it still—pale yellow, bright yellow, soft gold, deepest blue, and hear the words it whispers."

He did as she bade, sitting before her with eyes closed, head bent slightly forward, arms resting on the chair's arms. His warrior's body was completely relaxed, the powerful, heavy muscles at ease on his long frame. His features were in repose, eased of their fierce emotions and the equally fierce mask he kept over them.

He had surrendered his will to her, but she felt no satisfaction in it. She felt only uncertainty at the outcome, at the truth that might be learned. And for the first time in her life, she hated the gifts she had been born with that she now realized with a certainty of clarity was both gift and curse.

She might end it here, bring him back from the place of gentle repose where his thoughts now lay. But he would demand the truth. And she would be forced to tell it. Another gift that was equal curse. There was no other choice but to find the greater truth that lay within his heart and soul.

Still holding the candle between them, the fragile bond of the flame now their connection to one another, she passed the fingers of her right hand through the tip of the flame, strengthening the bond, reaching out, opening a portal to his soul.

She felt the strength of the flame burning through her veins, reaching out, seeking and finding the flame of life that dwelt within her. She set the candle aside.

Turning back to Rorke, the fire burning within her, she laid one hand along side his head, fingers gently pressing in until she felt the sharp ridge of bones beneath her fingertips. The other she laid over his heart, then closed her eyes, and whispered the ancient words.

"*Element of fire, spirit of light, essence of life, awaken the night. Fire of the soul, flame of life, as light reveals truth, burn golden bright.*"

Her consciousness joined with his in a burst of fiery color. She felt the struggle within him to push her away, the layers of years of protectiveness like a shield over his heart and soul, closing everything out.

She sent him a thought—a memory of their shared moments recently past, the image of their bodies joining; his tender assault of her body as she now tenderly assaulted the barrier that surrounded his heart; opening herself physically to him as she now persuaded him to open to her; the fiery power of their bodies meeting as one as her thoughts sought to join with his.

Then word by enchanted word, as the power flowed from her through him with gentle persuasion and gentle force, layer upon layer was stripped away. She felt the last of his struggle as his powerful body ceased the physical struggle, and the complete surrender as his soul opened to hers.

It was like being thrown into a vortex of sight, sound, and color of every experience, thought, and emotion he had ever possessed. It was overwhelming, the images sweeping past her consciousness in a blinding blur that was out of control with the torment of emotion at surrendering himself to her.

The colors were chaotic, brilliant, multihued rainbows that were as chaotic as his emotions. Images of faces flashed before her. Tarek al Sharif, Duke William, Stephen of Valois, Queen Matilda, the count, and more she vaguely recognized, countless more that she did not.

Then the images slowed their chaotic bombardment and settled into some vague order, passing from his lower consciousness of memory to her own as she learned him.

She saw images of a fierce battle and knew that it was the Battle of Hastings, and in experiencing it as he had she also experienced his emotions during the battle—methodical, cold calculation, exhilaration as the battle was met, a moment of uncertainty followed by the fierceness of spirit that allowed nothing but victory.

She saw everything as he had seen it that day, including the bloody aftermath and his own aftermath of grief and senselessness of waste. Then she was catapulted back through his memory of his own past to Normandy; the council of the nobility as William made his decision to seize the throne of England; countless encounters with his men, his feeling for Stephen of Valois like that of a brother, his lack of feeling for Judith de Marque as he took her to his bed.

Farther back through countless military campaigns; the events of his long friendship with William of Normandy; the military campaign to the Byzantine Empire; more battles; his unique friendship with Tarek al Sharif and the encounter that had brought them together—a life spared for a life saved and a blood oath of loyalty.

Then back farther still past the events of his early knighthood, several bloody encounters and deaths as a young man proved his warrior's prowess; back to the shadowy days of his youth. It was here that she felt such a devastating ache of loss and pain.

She saw a man she knew through Rorke's memory to be his father, the Count de Anjou. Saw, too, Rorke with a young man she knew to be his younger brother, Philip. She experienced his shame and pain at his bastard birth to the count's mistress, his longing to be loved as his younger half brother and his father's heir was loved, and his undying love and devotion for Philip in spite of it all.

She felt his joy at the gift of a mongrel pup, the only thing in this world that he might love. Then felt the sting of tears at her own eyes at his pain when his father had the animal cruelly taken from him.

There were countless other childhood experiences—the bastard child who could never be claimed by his father, who grew strong and tall in his father's own image, stronger and taller than his brother, quicker of mind with the regal bearing of his royal forebears while Philip languished and was sickly. She felt his unconditional love for his brother that never wavered or turned to bitterness for the cruelties of fate that had him born a bastard.

Then she experienced the wrenching pain of separation as Rorke was sent from the only home he had ever known, fostered out to a soldier's life, the black shield he carried that heralded his bastardy, the hard years that followed, the countless campaigns as he grew in stature and prowess. Then the pivotal battle at Antioch, where brother was reunited with brother on the battlefield.

She experienced his joy and genuine pleasure at being with Philip once more, the camaraderie as brother fought alongside brother, the protection Rorke gave his brother who was ill suited to the rigors of war. The horrors of a battle met against overwhelming numbers, their position overrun, the fierce fighting.

Rorke reacted like a man possessed, striking down all those about him until the battlefield around him was littered with bodies piled upon bodies, and the earth ran red with their blood as he fought to reach his brother. But he was too late. In shame, Philip had plunged his own knife deep, taking his own life. He died a slow, agonizing death.

"I could not bear to have our father know that I was a coward." Philip spoke haltingly, death bubbling his own blood at his lips. *"I thought I could be like you. It's all I ever wanted. Please do not be angry with me, brother."*

Philip died in Rorke's arms. But the greater tragedy lay at the end of the long journey when Rorke took his brother's body home to Anjou and his father's cruel accusation that it was Rorke who had taken his own brother's life so that Anjou might be his. And Rorke, to hide the shame of his brother's death, refused to tell the truth.

Vivian relived all the pain and emotion of Rorke's painful reunion with the father he hated as if he was living it once more. The hard, cruel words that could never be taken back, the accusations, his father's contempt and hatred that were like a battle sword hacking away at him, and finally banishment.

"Take yourself from my presence!" his father swore at him. *"What cursed fate is it that the bastard lives while my true son lies cold and dead? Leave Anjou and never return, for you are no son of mine!"*

The pain was intense, greater than any blade thrust deep. Vivian felt the tears that streamed down her cheeks at the same time she experienced his pain and loss, all the hopes and dreams of a small boy shattered and frozen in the heart of a mighty warrior whose only fault had been to love his brother too well.

Rorke left Anjou, vowing that one day he would return and claim it for his own, even if the only means was to spill more blood.

Everything that came after, came from the pain and loss at his brother's death, and his hardened heart at his father's accusations and final rejection. Any lingering, feeble childhood hope of one day winning his father's love died as surely as his brother died at Antioch.

Vivian didn't think that she could go on. And yet, she knew that to sever the connection between them now, would mean almost certain death for Rorke. She had to endure all of it, until she knew everything of the past and could then take the journey into the future of what was yet to be.

She learned everything that came after his brother's death, returning once more to the events at Hastings, the journey to London, through the sensual experiences of their discovery of one another, the fiery passion of their lovemaking, and finally the boar that was slain in the forest.

Tears streamed her face at the pain he had endured with so little joy. She had asked him to open his soul, and he had. His heart and soul were true. Now, she felt herself turning irrevocably from the past of what had been to the future of what was yet to be.

Visions appeared. Images filled her consciousness—a creature born in fire and blood, the phoenix rising from the flames;

of great danger and strife, the rising Darkness, a cataclysmic battle met in which the future of the kingdom was at stake, the fall of ancient kingdoms, the crowning of an all-powerful king, fierce twin lions born on a soldier's crest.

And, finally, the echoes of old truths that Rorke had never known and which she could see only now that she had learned all the things that had shaped his life.

She cried out softly as the truth unfolded within her own thoughts.

She saw once more the battlefield at Antioch and Philip's careless disregard for his own safety, the shield that he cast away, and his final thoughts during the battle willing to risk death rather than return to Anjou and the father he had learned to hate. Then Vivian saw a second and more profound truth.

Rorke had been born the rightful, firstborn son and rightful heir, to the Count de Anjou and his young countess. But it was a loveless marriage. The fiery, high-spirited young countess hated her husband. Upon her deathbed from childbed fever, she contrived her own son's *death* rather than have him raised by a cold, despotic father.

The child was replaced with the body of the count's own bastard child who had died that same night in childbirth. The Count de Anjou buried his wife and his child, never knowing the truth until many years later after he had banished his first-born son forever and lost the younger son born of his second marriage.

Rorke had given his heart and soul to Vivian. Now, she gave them back, melding her thoughts once more with his so that he saw what she had seen in her visions.

She sensed his pain in the powerful clenching of his jaw beneath her hand at his cheek and at the wild beating of his heart beneath her other hand, then saw it in the tears that streamed his face. Gently, very gently, she released her hold on him, retreating from his memories and thoughts. His eyes slowly opened.

He stared back at her with such a torment of old pain and

new truths. She sensed his turmoil and anguish, as she had never been able to sense him before. Every emotion lay open to her like a newly opened wound that must be allowed to heal.

"I never knew!" he whispered, his body suddenly taut and tense as though he tried physically to fight off the pain. "I was my father's true son!"

And for a moment, Vivian sensed that she should not have entered his thoughts nor his past. That any lie he believed was better than the pain of this sad truth.

"Forgive me!" she said, eyes brimming with tears. "I should not have shared it with you. I did not wish to cause you pain." He pressed a finger against her lips, tenderly silencing her.

"Nay!" he whispered, equally fierce. "The truth is the sweetest pain. At least now I know that I was not the cause of my brother's death. He was the cause of it himself. And as for my father . . ." His clear gray gaze bore into hers, lit with a golden fire of its own.

"The truth would not have changed him. He was the man he was long before I was born. Even my mother chose the sweet release of death rather than go on living with him. Your powers have given me that solace, when all I had before was lies."

"Nay!" he repeated, both hands closing about her face to cradle it with a barely restrained power.

"I would have only the truth." His thumbs gently stroked down across her cheeks, feeling the wetness of tears that spilled from her eyes and slipped down her cheeks.

"Your sweet truth," he whispered, his lips closing over hers in a kiss that spoke of all the fierce emotions they had just shared.

There was no gentleness in him. It was as if the torment he had just experienced through the joining with her vision power now ached for release. She felt it in the barely restrained power of his hands as he pulled her to him in the chair and pushed back the edges of her mantle.

She tasted it in the urgency of his mouth at hers, stealing her breath away as one kiss ended and another began. She sensed the physical need that raged through him, and saw the proof of it in the gleaming swollen flesh that thrust between their naked bodies as fur mantles fell away.

Her slender hand stroked low between them, nails tenderly raking down over pouches of heavy male flesh as her other hand closed over him, stroking, coaxing the breadth and length of him until he was near to bursting.

A fierce sound came low from his throat. Rorke's hand twisted in the heavy silk of her hair, holding her for his kiss. It was a sensual joining as his tongue thrust between her lips, gently stroked them apart, and then plunged deeper to mate with her tongue. She gasped as the kiss ended, then gasped again at the heat of his mouth at the base of her throat.

Vivian released her precious bounty as her hands stroked up across the hard ridges of muscle and scars patterned across his chest and the taut corded muscles at his neck, then buried in the thick mane of dark sable hair. On a soft moan, she brought him to her breast as the urgency flowed from one to the other.

His teeth grazed a swollen nipple, puckering it until it stood hard, erect, tingling, and eager for his mouth. Then, before her fascinated gaze in the brightly lit chamber with a hundred candles casting their glow across their bodies, she watched as he drew her flesh into his mouth, the tingling spreading to become a sharp ache of need at the center of her, and creating a fiery wetness between her thighs.

She clasped him to her, and when her flesh ached from the fierce hunger of his mouth, she drew him to her other breast.

"Rorke," she gasped on a throttled sound. "I cannot bear this emptiness any longer." Her voice ached to a whisper as his teeth closed over the taut, hard nipple.

"I must have you inside me."

"Soon," he whispered against her flesh, dark lashes lying against sharp ridges of cheekbones as he savored her. He guided a slender knee along each hip so that she straddled him, naked, exposed, and vulnerable.

His fingers lovingly caressed down over the silken folds of

flesh at the center of her, returning to deftly stroke them apart and flick over the taut button of flesh that was like a hidden jewel.

She shuddered at the intense pleasure of his teasing fingers, the need raging out of control so that she thought she might burn to cinders and die if she wasn't joined with him soon.

"Please," she whispered urgently, her slender hands closing over his proud warrior's flesh and guiding him to her. She felt the thrusting probe of his blunt flesh, then her own flesh parting, yielding, then gliding over his as the deep center of her ached for all of him.

His hands clamped over her hips as if he would stop her, his thumbs gently bruising.

"Now," she said, breathlessly, and realized that he but held her as he thrust inside her.

Her hands clasped his shoulders, eyes half-closed as she watched their bodies coming together, retreating, then coming together again with even more urgency, his dark, gleaming flesh heavily veined as it withdrew from her pale body, then glided deep once more in an increasingly powerful rhythm.

She held that image in her mind as, with eyes closed, she arched her back to take him deeper.

His hands were no longer gentle, but stroked and caressed her with a longing of desperation.

"Give me your fire," he whispered as his mouth closed once more over her breast with an aching need almost like that of a child that drew the fluid of life from her. "Bathe me in your fire."

Ripples of pure pleasure swept through her. The fire burned through her, igniting a thousand other fires that pulsed over him.

She turned her thoughts inward on a sensual journey and took him with her. With visions of pure pleasure they *saw* his engorged flesh with its hard ridges and pulsing veins slicked with her wetness, saw the length of him moving deep inside her, and saw too the glistening pearls of his seed cast into her womb.

The fire of their passion engulfed them. He was like the phoenix reborn in the flames of her love, the inferno burning about them until they lay spent in each other's arms like dying embers at the hearth.

Vivian moved tentatively, luxuriating in the wonder of his flesh still snugged deep within her. Their bodies glowed. His was like liquid amber, hers pale and golden, like the different hues of a resting flame.

She felt complete, the ache of longing eased with the joining of their bodies, her soul complete with the truth of his past that he had let her see.

Rorke rose from the chair on a single powerful move that astonished her when she felt as if her arms and legs had turned to water. He took her with him as if she weighed no more than air, his flesh still nestled in hers.

She stretched luxuriously like a contented cat, clasping him tight about the waist with her legs and with stunning results as with each movement as he carried her she felt him grow hard in her once more. Her head came up in surprise to find those wintry gray eyes that she had once thought cold and forbidding watching her with something that could only be interpreted as a wicked pleasure.

"Is it possible so soon after?" she said with breathless wonder, for he had not seemed so quickly recovered the night before when they had first come together.

" 'Tis possible," he assured her, sinking on bended knee in the thick furs to lay her across the width of the bed, his body moving with hers to fill her even more deeply.

"Oh, aye," she said on a note that was half surprise, half wonder, and all pleasure. " 'Tis more than possible."

They came together and the room glowed with the fire of a thousand flames.

So great was their need of one another that neither saw the flames bend and quiver. Nor did they see the shadow that lifted its dark head to gaze at the entwined lovers before receding into the far corners, where it lay watching and waiting.

Twenty-two

It was almost three weeks since the boar's attack in the forest. All who had seen Rorke carrying her into his private chamber knew of the life-threatening wounds she had received.

As far as anyone other than Rorke or Meg knew, her *recovery* was slow and measured as it should be after receiving such terrible wounds.

Meg and Rorke knew her wounds had in fact been healed that same night after the attack by her own mystical powers. When she eventually did emerge from Rorke's chamber it was to walk slowly and carefully about, with assistance. Only the bishop seemed unconvinced by the game they played, constantly watching her as though he knew the wounds no longer plagued her. But how might he know?

For several days after the attack, she had remained abed. Rorke insisted on taking care of her himself. Meg was only allowed in the chamber for the sake of royal gossips and always emerged with a progress report of her slight improvement.

Until she finally emerged from her convalescence to limp about, with Rorke complaining—good-naturedly and with an occasional wink—that he would much rather have her abed.

Now he stood beside the chair where she sat in William's chamber, his hand resting lightly on her shoulder. She wore the new mauve gown he had given her. Mally had made it from a length of fine woven wool he'd purchased at market the day she encountered Conal.

He'd given it to her during her recovery though he had refused to let her wear it or any other clothes. As he explained, she could not be seen at William's coronation wearing her old, much-mended kirtle. In all that time, though Poladouras had inquired of his friends in London, there had been no word of Conal.

"The coronation will take place on Christmas Day!" William insisted as he met with Rorke and his trusted knights in his private chamber. "I will not delay longer, and it shall be done at Westminster Abbey!"

" 'Tis dangerous," Rorke replied with the caution of one who knew the temper and determination of the man who sat before him, and also knew the risks involved. "It is beyond the fortress walls. The journey through the streets long. It would be difficult to protect you. And God knows any of the Saxon archbishops would gladly see you run through on a holy scepter and then proclaim your death the work of God."

"What say you, monk?" William demanded of Poladouras. "You know the temperament of your brethren."

"Aye," Poladouras remarked with a deep sigh, filled with old pain. "I know it well. They do not confide in me, milord. They consider me fallen away, and now a traitor. But my sense of it is the same for I know well their ambitions. They are capable of such as milord FitzWarren has said. They would name it a just cause, even though the cause serves themselves for they know well that you will have them replaced."

"I would give my support to waiting as well, brother," the bishop added his voice to the argument. "London is already yours. You need no official proclamation for this. Our army is spread across the whole of England. Why this impatience to see yourself crowned so quickly? Wait until summer," he urged smoothly.

"Secure the countryside against the rebels and outside usurpers who will no doubt also attempt to lay claim to the throne. Then, when England sees how you defend her against others they will be reconciled, yea even supportive of their new king."

William seemed to consider his words, and indeed, Vivian knew he had good reason. There had been constant rumors of skirmishes in the far north country, adding to other rumors that the Danes intended to send an offensive strike against England with the intent of laying claim to the English throne.

Because of those rumors, immediately after their arrival in London, William had sent his son, Stephen of Valois, and his knights, along with Sir Galant and his men to secure the north country against the threat of invasion.

"You pose convincing arguments," William now told his brother with a half smile on his face. "But there is another I would ask. Mistress Vivian."

William turned to her from his chair before the hearth where he sat encircled by his advisors, all except his brother, who stood slightly behind and to his side. The bishop's expression was concealed in shadow as William sought her opinion of his decision. But Vivian saw it.

The eyes narrowed as the bishop watched her. Rorke had spoken of his ambitions and she wondered how they were best served by postponing the coronation.

"I must caution you, brother," the bishop interceded, "against seeking the counsel of this woman. She is Saxon and her loyalties are obvious. She has made no secret of them. Surely you jest in this folly."

"I do not jest, brother," William replied in an even manner that in itself was silken with warning that his younger brother had perhaps overstepped himself.

"Because she is Saxon, she may perhaps offer a unique perspective. Mistress Vivian?"

She felt Rorke's reassurance in the warmth of his hand at her shoulder, and that physical awareness that seemed to spring so easily between them. She also felt a subtle warning. She understood it well—blood was thicker than water, and while William might rebuke the bishop for his intemperance, he was still William's brother and that was a loyalty that ran deep. Therefore she tempered her reply with logic, for William was above all a logical, thinking man.

"The people of England will more readily serve a king they

are bound to by oath, be he Saxon or Norman," she said after much consideration, aware of all who listened and judged every word. Some of whom would readily see her cast in a dungeon or her head on a pike and the fortress wall.

"Your oath of kingship to the people, milord, would also assure them of your intention to end the chaos. They grow weary of it and would in time set aside their blame of who is the cause of it, if they have their families, their homes, and England once more thrives."

William nodded. "And of the ceremony?"

Again she felt Rorke's silent warning. "It should be no less than Harold's coronation in the eyes of all Saxons," she suggested, then she added, "and Normans, and any foreign usurpers as a clear sign of your intention to rule well and strong."

"There are dangers," William reminded her. "If I am slain, I can hardly rule at all."

As a warrior, she sensed William had little fear of dying. A soldier would have long ago accepted such a fate. Indeed, she had sensed it in him that long-ago day at Hastings when she had first seen the devastating wounds that slowly drained the life from him. If he had died, he would have accepted it as a soldier's due. But as a king, it hardly suited his ambitions.

"If milord FitzWarren can defend you in the streets of London," she suggested, "then surely he can protect you within the abbey."

"Armed knights in the abbey," William contemplated. "It would be highly unusual." His keen gaze took in the number of loyal armed guards posted inside his anteroom, hundreds more filling the halls and passages of the royal fortress.

"I protest!" the bishop spoke out. "Armed soldiers in the abbey? It is sacrilege! The Pope would be horrified at such drastic measures. He might even withdraw his support should it be thought you represent his name by such action. It is outrageous. I will not abide it!"

"It is outrageous." William agreed. Then a slow smile began

at one corner of his mouth and spread to the other. He turned to Rorke. "Can it be done?"

Rorke's bemused expression lifted from Vivian's and met that of his commander. He, too, saw her wisdom. "It can, milord," he said hesitantly. "The guards would conceal their swords so that none are aware of it. But it might open the door for censure from the Pope."

"The Pope is in Rome," William pointed out coolly. "It will work! The coronation will take place at Westminster Abbey on Christmas Day." He turned to Rorke, "You will take every precaution that there be no bloodshed."

"Aye, milord."

William turned to Vivian. "Thank you for your wise counsel, demoiselle. I find myself relying more and more on your wisdom as to the ways to most fairly deal with the Saxons.

"Then let the preparations begin."

"I must protest strongly. It is not safe . . ." The count de Bayeau was cut off.

"It will be Christmas Day, brother," William told him in a tone that brooked no further discussion or argument.

"Send for the archbishop of York. Tell that pious toad that I will be crowned at Westminster Abbey."

"He may refuse," the bishop warned. "He has already spoken of it."

"Then make certain he does not!"

Afterward, Vivian returned to the chamber she now shared with Rorke. Her mood was uneasy and restless, having grown more so as she sat through William's council meeting.

Sensing her mood, Meg had followed. She built up the fire at the heart as Vivian continued to pace restlessly, driven by an almost wild, uncontrollable energy. Something was about to happen. She sensed it.

When the flames were high, she looked deeply within them as she recited the ancient words. The vision came slowly, stirring from the heart of the flames.

She saw a strange, cold land, craggy and windswept, and

knew it to be the far north country. She saw horsemen and soldiers under Duke William's banner, and other soldiers she did not recognize. She saw a battle with Stephen of Valois and Sir Galant at the forefront of it. Then she saw blood and death, a gallant knight falling from his horse, having been struck through with a lance.

The knight slumped to the ground, Duke William's banner clutched precariously in his dying fingers. As the battle continued around him, his comrades ran to his side, seized the banner and sought to raise it high once more. The knight who raised the banner was Stephen of Valois.

Her heart constricted with a pain of loss and grief, for she knew many had fallen and among those, men she knew, though she could not see their faces. She sensed their loss deeply.

Rorke found her kneeling before the hearth, tears streaming down her cheeks, fists clenched in a powerless rage at the gift that allowed her to see but couldn't prevent what she had seen.

"What is it? What have you seen?" Rorke was immediately beside her, his arms closing around her with a fierce urgency. "What has happened? Are you unwell?" She heard the fear steeling his voice, making the tender words harsh with his own fear, and love welled inside her for this Norman warrior who was her enemy.

She turned into his embrace, clinging to his strength that somehow renewed and comforted her as none of her immortal powers could. She clung to him as if she were dying and he was life itself. For in a sense a part of her had died with the knights who had been slain. It was always so. She was diminished by the loss of those she cared for.

She told Rorke of her vision, of the battle and the deaths of his men. His own emotions had reached out to hers in that unique way that now connected and bonded them so deeply. She felt his grief, experienced all the shared memories with the three brothers, and knew his grief was deep. Along with the grief, she sensed his depth of concern for Stephen of Valois.

He cared deeply for the young man, as for a younger brother.

Now that she had shared his own memories, she understood where the deep affection came from.

"Stephen is safe," she assured him, sensing his apprehension.

Rorke nodded, accepting her truth, dealing with his own grief as he comforted hers, his hard, callused hand tender on her cheek.

"This magical gift of yours can be most burdensome, when the truth is grievous."

Her eyes filled with tears once more as she looked up at him, feeling such an overwhelming ache of love for this fierce warrior who understood as few others were capable.

"There are times when I would cast it away, even cut it out with a blade, if I could," she admitted. "Sometimes the pain of what I see is almost too much to bear. But I cannot cast it away. Such is my fate."

"You will not bear it alone any longer," he told her, tenderly stroking her hair as he held her close against him, the solid beat of his heart beneath her cheek a litany of physical strength and power that replenished her.

"Whatever comes, whatever visions you see in the flames," Rorke told her fiercely, "be they good fortune, or pain and sorrow, we will share them together."

Afterward, she tried several times to see more in the flames, so that Rorke might know the fate of the rest of his men. But each time was without success.

It was as if something blocked her ability to see and a fear had grown within her for she sensed the Darkness very near, and she remembered Merlin's warning that it would try at every turn to destroy her. But where or when it would choose to reveal itself she did not know.

"So," Rorke said with grim expression, "we must wait until we receive word."

"Forgive me," Vivian whispered. "I wish I could tell you more."

"Nay, demoiselle," he said with such deep tenderness, as he brushed his lips against hers, "do not ask for forgiveness. At least I know that it is imperative that William be crowned as soon as possible so that the crown is secure. To wait until summer," he thought aloud, remembering the bishop's words, "would be a grave misjudgment."

Later, when meeting with William, Rorke told him there had been rumors of an encounter in the north country. More than that he could not say, for though William had come to trust in Vivian's advice, Rorke was wary of the bishop, and therefore chose to say nothing of Vivian's visions.

Matilda, duchess of Normandy and William's wife, arrived three days before the coronation. She was heavy with child and the Channel crossing had been difficult. Still, she was a strong-willed, captivating woman and from the moment Vivian saw them together, she understood why William had banished Judith de Marque from his chambers.

Beneath the swelling of her pregnancy, Matilda was slender and fine-boned, with fair features and gentle blue eyes, her belly now distended and her pace slow and measured with the heaviness of the child she carried. Born to a noble Flemish family, she had the regal bearing and studied graces of a queen.

But Vivian immediately sensed that the regal bearing and grace was part of a carefully constructed facade that balanced a quick wit, a sharp intellect, and perfect grasp of her position in the world and the methods by which that position—and her husband's—was best served.

Like many of royal birth, she was a woman for whom there had been few options. Well educated, headstrong, there were but two—the Church or an advantageous marriage. She refused to enter the Church, or, as she honestly confessed to Vivian, "The Church refused to have me."

William—for whom the alliance of the Church was most critical—had colored at her comment. He whispered a comment to her. She smiled in that secret way of lovers.

"Let us just say," Matilda added with that same smile, "that all parties involved suggested an advantageous marriage might be the best arrangement.'"

And that advantageous marriage had presented itself very quickly in an alliance with Normandy.

"It is said," Matilda confided to her when they retired to William's chamber so that the queen might rest before being presented to her husband's new court, "that William married me for my title, my dowry, and an alliance that would guarantee support against the king of France."

She gave Vivian a knowing look. "I am aware that Judith de Marque travels with his household. But he sends for me, not her, in the midst of war," she said proudly, "and sleeps at my side rather than taking his mistress to his bed as he might easily choose to do."

Her slender hand smoothed the brocade satin down over the curve of her belly. "He plants his seed within me, even though I have already borne him two fine, healthy sons and guaranteed the line of succession. Nor is it out of duty, for a woman knows these things. When I am with him, even swollen as I am," her smile softened and she glowed, "we still take our pleasure of one another."

"Three strong sons," Vivian commented as she stirred the fire at the hearth in William's chamber.

"What did you say?" Matilda asked, more than a little startled.

"You will have another son," Vivian repeated what she had seen so clearly the moment Matilda reached out and touched her hand in gratitude for saving her husband's life.

"You are certain of this?"

Vivian nodded. "It is a gift. My mother had it as well. And you need have no fear," she responded to the emotion she sensed in the woman. "The child is strong and healthy."

"William has said he would have you attend the birth," Matilda said. "You saved his life. He spoke of it, his wounds so grievous that he should not have lived. Yet he lives, and he walks. I would have no other at my side when my time is at hand."

Christmas Day dawned bright and clear.

Those who believed in such things proclaimed it an omen, a blessing from God no doubt invoked by the Pope in Rome for his loyal servant who had seized the English throne in his name.

The coronation had been announced far in advance and word had gone out across the whole of England. The nave of Westminster Abbey was filled to overflowing with both Saxons and Normans.

For the Saxons, who had prayed for divine deliverance from the Norman scourge, it was a mournful occasion, signifying the end of England. But they were no less determined to attend the ceremony at Westminster Abbey. The Saxon barons lined the walls, resplendent in all their finery, for many of them now were aligned by marriage or pending marriage with the houses of Normandy, Burgundy, and other Norman allies. Behind them, William's knights stood a half dozen deep and spilling out into the street.

William and Matilda knelt before the huge altar. Hundreds of candles had been lit, their pale light glowing across stone walls that Edward had built in the reign of years before the hapless Harold who had died at Hastings.

To the casual observer, oblivious of the cataclysmic changes taking place, the ceremony no doubt seemed grand and auspicious, with all the noblemen wearing their finest tunics and braces, the Norman costumes all worn with their finest mantles in spite of the warmth inside the nave with so many crowded into such a small space amid the smothering, acrid stench of tallow candles.

But the Normans knew, and perhaps a few others sensed, that the mantles concealed far more than mere finery. Occasionally there was glimpsed a glint of steel of broadswords and battle-axes carried low at their sides, unsheathed and at the ready should there be any sign of trouble from the Saxon barons or their knights.

Tarek made no pretense of hiding the curved blade that was always carried at his side. After all, he was a True Believer and not an infidel Christian. He felt no sense of sacrilege at carrying a blade into what he considered another cold, stone building.

Matilda was aware of the great risk as she cast many sidelong glances among her husband's men, as if to guess which carried a weapon and which did not. And then found her gaze seeking the same among the Saxons. A dozen Norman knights surrounded her.

"There will be blood shed before this is done," the duchess of Normandy had fretted to Vivian as they left the royal apartments. Vivian had calmed her fears as best she could.

"No one will be harmed this day," she told Matilda with certainty. For she had seen this vision long ago, even at the loss of her beloved Saxon England.

Matilda looked at her with an expression of keen interest. "The way you speak of it, one would think you have a special knowledge of such things."

"Oh, aye," Vivian said with a faint smile. "I cast ancient stones in a circle and read them for messages. It is common among the Celtic people."

"We must speak of this gift of yours one day, mistress," Matilda told her. "I would like very much to know how it is done."

There was no time to speak of it then, for which Vivian was grateful. She sensed a strong, willful spirit in William's wife and knew the lady would not let the matter rest until she had the truth. Though she sensed she could trust Matilda, the lady was surrounded by people who might not so easily be trusted.

At Westminster Abbey, the words of the coronation ceremony were recited twice—once in Saxon English and the second in French before the assembled congregation.

"Blessed by God, in keeping with his Holy Covenant, and in the name of his Son, Jesus Christ," the Archbishop of York's voice intoned the ancient English rites that William had insisted upon, ringing out clear if a bit thready with nervousness through the nave of former King Edward's Abbey at Westminster.

His voice quavered noticeably and Vivian sensed his refusal to recite the critical words that would follow. Rorke stood beside him and with a gentle prod, the archbishop hurriedly proclaimed, "I crown thee William I, King of England, in the name of the Pope, by God's grace and his holy ordinance." His hands shook as badly as his voice as he lowered the ornate gold crown onto William's head.

Vivian shivered as a sudden chill swept through the nave in spite of the hundreds of people pressed tightly together. The candles at the altar fluttered wildly, threatening to extinguish themselves and cast the nave into complete darkness.

Her thoughts moved through the room, sensing moods, emotions, and ambitions. Not surprising, there was anger, bitterness, sadness, and also jubilation and triumph.

She focused her power on the flames, steadying their quivering light as surely as if she laid a calming hand on them, using their fiery warmth to see like hundreds of eyes at a hundred different vantage points throughout the nave.

There were shadows at each corner and angle of stone, but still she could not see the true Darkness.

The crown wobbled and would have slipped off—a portent of misfortune to those who chose to believe in bad omens. She felt the forces of Darkness at work and turned her thoughts inward. Closing her eyes, she thought only of William and the crown, steadying it upon his head as surely as if she had reached out a hand and done it herself.

With her inner sight, she saw the crown snug on his head, even as she felt the buffeting currents of evil that would have tumbled it.

"Yield, mistress. For you cannot win," the Voice of Darkness whispered through her senses. *"You will be destroyed as your father was."*

"Yield, for the kingdom is mine."

Vivian cast her thoughts out across the nave, with but a single word, filled with brilliant, glowing radiant light as she closed her hand over the blue crystal and drew on ancient powers endowed by the promise of the Light.

"Never."

The light in the nave wavered. The shadows grew long and threatening, as if they would sweep over everyone, and Vivian sensed that Stephen of Valois had returned to London. Then just as suddenly they were gone, receding to hide under the edges of the stones at the walls.

Once more, she heard the words of the ancient ceremony, as they were spoken again for Matilda, and a smaller crown was placed on her head.

Next, the assembled congregation, comprised of the most powerful men in all of England and Normandy, was asked in French to declare their approval.

The Saxon barons and earls who understood only English remained silent, at a loss to comprehend what was being asked of them and failed to respond. There was a rustling of uncertainty among the Norman knights as hands closed over broadswords hidden at their sides in suspicion.

If there was a moment when the rebels would strike, it would have been then. A simple mistake that could so easily end in bloodshed. Poladouras quickly spoke up, translating the request into English. Approval was given as the Saxon earls, if somewhat reluctantly and with great resentment, added their assent to the Norman congregation.

The archbishop of York declared with grave reluctance of voice, "Rise William I, King of England."

Cheers went up among the Norman congregation. Over all, relief swept through the abbey. Whatever else followed, William was now king of England.

William turned to escort his queen from the abbey. Even against the counsel of his knights, he was determined to make a proper exit as befit the king, rather than escaping to safety out a side entrance.

At a signal, Rorke and William's men formed an armed phalanx around the king and queen, to all outward appearances a finely dressed royal escort that but made way for their monarch. More soldiers lined the steps outside the abbey. As they turned to follow, Vivian laid a hand over Rorke's arm.

"What is it?" Rorke sensed the urgency that flowed through her. "Have you sensed something? Is there danger?"

"Aye," she nodded. "But not here." Her sad blue gaze met his. "Stephen of Valois has returned to London."

Rorke turned to Tarek. "There has been trouble in the north country. Word awaits our immediate return." A look passed between the two men. Then Tarek looked at Vivian. He nodded. His expression rigid, Rorke gave orders to his men to escort William back to the fortress without delay.

Still the processional took almost an hour to reach the fortress. People filled the streets in an atmosphere of guarded celebration that was barely controlled and threatened to become violent at any moment.

Just as Vivian had foreseen, Stephen of Valois was waiting for Rorke at the gates of the fortress wall.

"Two score dead! A score more injured, many so badly they could not ride," Stephen quickly reported to William. Beyond the royal anteroom, the coronation celebration had begun. Inside the anteroom, faces were grim. "But that is not the worst of it." He lowered his voice, sadness filling his handsome young features.

"Sir Galant is dead."

"Tell me everything," Rorke ordered him as Gavin stood beside him with rigid expression and listened of his brother's death.

"There was no warning," Stephen explained. "My men found no sign of an enemy presence. Then they were upon us. They came out of nowhere."

William listened with grim expression. "Their banner?"

"None was seen."

"Were captives taken?"

"They are all dead." Stephen's expression turned even more grim. "They died by their own hand."

William's fist slammed down on the table before him. "By God, boy! Do you know anything of these attacks, except that you have near two hundred men who either lie maimed or dead?"

The words were harsh, with the underlying tension of a father berating a son who he felt had failed him. Vivian cringed at the turbulent emotions she sensed in both men that bordered on becoming violent.

The father was burdened by the conflict of his own bastard birth as he confronted his bastard son. There was a need to love, a need that must be denied. It manifested itself in an expectation of performance and duty far and above that of any of his other knights. The son had lived his entire life with the pain of his bastardy. It was compounded by an ambitious father who could never acknowledge him, yet still expected perfection.

"I have this, milord!" Unwise as it may have been, before the man who was not only his father, but especially now, his king, Stephen walked boldly forward and flung an object down onto the table with a gesture that bordered on contempt. It was a war ax, but of an unusual design.

"They carried no banner!" he spat out angrily. "My men will vouch for that. Any who were able-bodied enough fled. They left behind this war ax. It bears the mark of the Dane, Canute." Rage burned in Stephen's eyes, so like his father's, and Vivian feared they might come to blows.

She held her breath until Rorke stepped between them and with a calmness of experience of many such encounters, ignored both his young knight and his king as if nothing was amiss.

"Canute of Denmark," he said thoughtfully. "The weapon is Danish." He turned the blade over and over, examining it carefully. "And new from the forge. A young warrior's blade perhaps."

He turned to Stephen, "Do you remember anything else of the attack? How did they come at you? From several directions, or only one? Were they mounted or afoot? Were other weapons retrieved?" And countless more questions in that even inquiring manner that had the power to defuse at the same time he gleaned valuable information about the attack.

The anger left William's face. He made much ceremony of pouring a goblet of wine, then sat at the head of the table to listen thoughtfully, his gaze constantly returning to his son.

Squires brought food and drink, for neither Stephen nor those who had returned with him had eaten anything but dried bread and water on the long ride back. Though exhaustion was etched in every line of his handsome young face, his armor caked with dried blood and mud, Stephen refused to seek his bed though he dismissed his men to theirs.

Vivian observed much in his manner that reminded her of Rorke. His spare movements that wasted nothing, his concern for his men over himself and their obvious loyalty to him, a pride of honor that refused to cower before his father and king, and a singular stubbornness that reminded her very much of that father.

"I would have your counsel as well, mistress," William said to Vivian when she asked his permission to leave, for it had grown late.

"I have come to value your words," he told her, making no excuses to any of his knights or the bishop as he asked, "What say you of these Danish invaders?"

The Danes from the north had long coveted the English throne. From the history which Poladouras had taught her, she knew well of their countless attempts to invade England over the past several hundred years. And Canute had boldly announced that the English throne would be his.

" 'Tis no secret that Canute would seek to expand his claim-hold over all of England. There were rumors of invaders before the Battle of Hastings."

"Then you believe the words my young knight brings me."

She did not have to look at Stephen of Valois to sense his pain at having his word questioned by a Saxon woman, and one that was considered a prisoner at that.

"The ax Stephen of Valois has so ably brought you, at the

risk of his own life, would seem to bear that out. You do not need my counsel, milord, for I think you have already made your decision."

He nodded, "Thank you, mistress. You remind me that I can be intemperate in some matters.

"Aye, milord," she answered with the utmost diplomacy and a brief sideways glance to Stephen. "As can we all be at times."

"Then see to your own comforts, mistress. And when you see my queen bid her kindest thoughts, for I fear it shall be many hours before I may give them to her myself."

It was nearly dawn when Rorke finally returned to their chamber. The fire at the hearth had long since cooled. He moved about in the muted shadows, removing his garments, kneeling before the fire as he fed it fresh wood, the soft golden glow of the fire gleaming across his naked flesh, then bursting to fiery crimson, making him seem even more a creature born in fire and blood.

She went to him, clutching a fur about her against the chill in the chamber, a chill that ached deep at her bones with a foreboding of what was to come and unknown things she could not see.

"William has ordered that we leave for the north country at first light," he said with a grimness of voice and without looking up, but with a sense of her nearness. Then he turned to look at her.

"You have foreseen it," he speculated.

"Aye," she said with a deep trembling of foreboding. "But it took no magical powers. Once the gauntlet was thrown down there was naught else that William could do."

"Have you seen more in the flames, Jehara?" he asked.

Her gaze left his, seeking the fire that was so much a part of her, seeing again as she had that very first time and again only moments before, embodied in the man as he knelt before the flames.

"I would know all that you can tell me, mistress. No matter what it might be."

Tears glistened at her eyes as she saw the fierce winged bird at the flames. "I see a creature born in fire and blood. I fear there will be more death, but whose I cannot see. And that is the greatest fear."

Her tortured gaze returned to his and she laid her hand alongside his face, the muscles of his jaw leaping beneath the slash of a pale scar on his skin that only made him seem more fiercely handsome.

"Beware the faith that has no heart, the sword that has no soul." She repeated the prophetic words whispered that day at Amesbury when she had first seen the creature in the flames.

Laying his hand over hers, Rorke turned his head, lips grazing the palm of her hand.

"You are my faith and heart, mistress. With your sweet vision to guide me I shall not fail."

Tears stung at her eyes as she moved into his arms with a restless urgency, the fur falling away as her fingers went back through the thick silk of his hair, and her mouth sought his with a desperate hunger to taste and feel his strength and warmth.

She was like fire in his hands, burning everywhere he touched, tears like glistening diamonds at her cheeks as he pressed her back into the furs, all wet heat and urgent demand as they came together in a violent claiming that spoke of all the uncertainty that lay just beyond the coming dawn.

William's knights and soldiers filled the yard amid the noise of shouted orders, jangling harness, and the dull glint of swords and lances under a leaden sky. Hundreds more waited beyond the walls, preparations made throughout the night in the armed encampments that lined the river Thames.

The king was determined to lead his army. No amount of argument from Rorke or any of his knights could dissuade him. Some knights were already mounted, making the final adjustments to their armor. Squires hurried about, delivering pouches of provisions for the journey, four days' ride to the north.

Among the horses, Vivian saw Tarek's Arabian mare, as she moved with a purposeful urgency, darting out of the path of a cart, wending her way through mounted riders. Tarek al Sharif caught her as she almost went down in the mud that sucked at each step before the path of another cart.

"This is no place for you, mistress," he said with a glint of amusement in his sky blue eyes that she always found so disconcerting. He grinned wickedly at her.

"Unless you have it in your mind to take another form and steal away in Rorke's saddlebag, and accompany us north."

"I am not a changeling," she reminded him, as though with great regret.

"Ah, but for the Jehara there is always a way. And I am not looking forward to sleeping on the hard, cold ground and listening to my friend complain of it as well and grow surly for lack of your warmth beside him at night."

Color flared at her cheeks. "I would ask a favor of you, Tarek al Sharif." He, who usually had great disdain for all knightly manner, struck a knightly pose.

"Your wish is my command, mistress. For I would not wish you to turn me into some low-form creature."

She laid a hand at his arm. "The favor I would ask is that you guard your friend's back well. There is great danger."

He nodded. "There is always danger, mistress, and I have always guarded his back."

"Danger may take many forms," she cautioned. "It is the danger you cannot see that will strike the deadliest."

His expression grew somber. "Have you seen something in your visions, mistress?"

She shook her head. "The visions are unclear. There is much darkness."

"And cold, no doubt," Tarek snorted disgustedly. "I have heard the north country is a cold and forbidding place. I pray to your god and mine that we could find a war in a warm place."

Then he became serious once more. "You have my promise unto death."

"What promises do you make my friend, that will be impossible to keep?" Rorke asked as he led his warhorse over to where they stood. "Especially to beautiful young women."

"I keep all of my promises," Tarek corrected him. "I have never promised myself to a young lady because I have not yet met one with a true heart. Perhaps only the Jehara possess true hearts. I shall have to look for one."

Stephen of Valois walked with Rorke, his features rigid with anger and frustration.

"I would ride with you, milord," Stephen pleaded with him as Rorke swung astride his warhorse. "Be damned what my father says! He thinks me a coward!"

Rorke leaned over to lay a hand on the young knight's shoulder. "He is also your king," he reminded Stephen. "And cowardice was never spoken of."

"But he thinks it," Stephen glared. " 'Tis worse. If it was plainly spoken, I would challenge him on it."

"He thinks of your safety, Stephen," Rorke gently explained. "You were injured in the battle," he gestured to the layer of linen bandage barely visible at the neck opening of Stephen's armor. Vivian had bandaged a deep sword cut that had almost severed his arm from his shoulder. He had ridden three days with the almost-useless arm bound to his side with a strip of leather harness.

"I have another good hand," Stephen argued with the recklessness of youth. "I can still wield a battle-ax."

"While you hold your horse's reins in your teeth?" Rorke suggested, and continued before Stephen could argue further, "You must recover and hold the fortress for your king."

"He leaves my uncle to protect his throne," Stephen spat with contempt.

"The bishop thinks himself a capable warrior," Rorke dared to speak aloud. "But he wields fear of the holy cross more effectively. If there is trouble in London, there must be one who remains to meet the challenge," he said with hidden meaning, then added, "and there is a favor I would ask no other."

"Anything, milord," Stephen replied without hesitation.

"I would ask that you protect Mistress Vivian."

Her startled gaze searched his, but he looked only at Stephen, many myriad more messages conveyed in that steely look. "I would entrust her safety to no one else."

"Aye, milord," Stephen agreed. "With my life."

"I pray it shall not come to that."

She and Stephen exchanged a look. She sensed his inner turmoil, yet knew he would keep his word to Rorke, even before he obeyed his king.

The order went out along the column of mounted knights and soldiers, seeming much as they had that day a Amesbury— fierce, ominous in the drizzling rain that had begun to fall. They were followed by a long line of creaking carts filled with supplies they would need on the ride north. Rorke leaned down from astride the stallion, his hand slipping through her hair. He plucked a mauve satin ribbon from the plaited braid amid the firefall of Vivian's bright hair.

"I would carry a part of you with me, mistress."

She removed the thin silver chain from about her neck and placed it about his, the blue crystal glinting with hidden light on such a dreary day.

"Unknown dangers await," she said, her voice breaking softly over what they had already spoken of. "Keep the stone with you at all times. As long as you wear it, there is a bond between us, my phoenix, that cannot be broken."

Rorke's fingers closed over the crystal as if it were the most precious jewel on earth.

"Until I return, I will keep it close to my heart, mistress, as I hold you close in my heart."

Vivian ran into the royal fortress and climbed the stairs to the highest watchtower. There, with rain streaming across her cheeks to mingle with her tears, she watched that dark column, like a long ribbon as it wended its way through the streets of London.

It stretched all the way through the city, until the darkness of the storm closed around them and she could no longer see them.

"May all the power of the Light go with you, my love," she whispered.

Twenty-three

They rode north for four days, following a different but parallel route to the one Stephen and his men had traveled, as a precaution against attack by raiders. Horsemen, stripped of the cumbersome armor that would have readily given away their presence, rode far afield to seek out any sign of the Danish invaders.

At night they made cold camps with no fires that would give away their position. By day they rode hard to reach the north coast location of the attack. Stephen had been forced to leave two dozen badly injured men. Rorke's squire carried pouches of medicines that Vivian had prepared. There was no question that she could accompany them with the queen's time so near.

The fourth night out, their camp was once again cold, their meal consisting of days' old bread, cheese, apples, and watered-down wine—just enough to warm against the forbidding north country cold.

"By the gods," Tarek swore, "I had not thought it could be any colder than the bone-aching dampness of London. But London pales in comparison to this frozen land."

"You would not have been so cold in London had dame Judith been well pleased," Rorke commented, pulling his fur mantle more closely about him as they sheltered for the night in the lee of a craggy outcropping of rock.

"She seems to have been pleased enough," Tarek snorted. "I'll wager her bed is warm for she is most quarrelsome when it is not. Although it is difficult to say who warms it now. She was most disagreeable over the loss of her place in William's bed and then yours. Knowing her ambition, she no doubt hopes to regain that coveted place."

"I promised Judith nothing. She has always known how I felt about the camp women."

"Until the Jehara, my friend?"

"Vivian is unlike any woman I have ever known."

Tarek looked through the narrow slit of his fur mantle at his friend, barely visible in the fading light. There was something changed in his voice, something that spoke of more than mere ambitions of Anjou and new conquests.

"Can it be that the conqueror has been conquered?"

"That is William's ambition. It was never mine. All I ever wanted was Anjou." His voice had lost the steeliness which was always present whenever he mentioned his childhood home.

"And now, my friend?"

"I grow weary of fighting, of cold camps, and the ever-present threat of the kiss of cold steel. Bone-achingly weary."

"Perhaps you find yourself thinking of evenings spent before a warm hearth, good food, drink, and a remarkably beautiful woman."

"A fire before a hearth," Rorke repeated, thinking also of the woman he had shared it with only days earlier, her silken body spread with fiery splendor beneath his, her soft cries of need, the sweet gasps of surprise he startled from her lips over and over, and then their impassioned, fierce joining that made him weep with joy at her breast as his body wept its seed within hers.

"Aye, a fire," he murmured, aching for her.

The following morning they rose before first light, driven by the cold, unyielding stone that had been their pallets, certain the backbreaking hours ahead atop their horses could be no worse.

If possible, the day dawned even more bleak than the previous one, with a portent of snow across the Scottish moors. By all calculations they should find Stephen's camp by midday.

They found what was left of the camp less than two hours later.

There were no fires lit for warmth, only the charred remains of a several days' old fire and several humped shapes beneath the mantle of snow. Otherwise the camp was completely empty and silent, except for the howl of the wind, that carried the sting of the nearby ocean.

With curved blade drawn, Tarek was one of the first to dismount. He gently prodded one of the humped shapes with the toe of his boot. Firmer prodding overturned the object to reveal the body of a soldier. The others were turned over as well to reveal all the soldiers Stephen had left behind now all dead.

"This fire has been cold for days," Tarek said angrily. "They must have been attacked almost as soon as Stephen left."

William stared at the camp with disgust, his features etched with fury. "If he had true courage, he would never have left them!"

"It took far more courage to do what he did," Rorke said with grim certainty as he kicked the snow from a large humped shape—a warhorse that had died beneath its rider. William stared at him hard. Rorke ignored his look as he gestured to the fallen steed, and at least three dozen more that had been scavenged by carrions.

"The hardest choice a commander must make is to choose those who will go and those who will stay. This place is well sheltered," he pointed out. "With ample food and weapons." With a frown, he watched as others were found.

"Your son, milord, made the only decision he could make. They should have been safe until our return."

The dead were buried, the carcasses of the dead horses left where they had fallen. It was a grim task. William watched stone-faced, his gaze fixed toward the coast. He moved with much stiffness in his leg, from the past four days astride a horse, but there was hesitation in his orders.

"I want the coastal region searched, every villager, crofter, and farmer questioned. The men who did this will pay."

"It shouldn't be too difficult," Rorke interjected, rising from a crouched position where two dead Norman soldiers had been found. He held a long-bladed knife in his hand, the handle elaborately decorated with intricate carvings. He handed it to Tarek.

"What think you of this?"

Tarek needed no more than a brief glance. "It is of the Danes also."

"Aye," Rorke said thoughtfully, sheathing the blade at his own belt. "There is no mistaking it."

Unwilling to risk being caught as Stephen had been with his men all in one command, William split his army into three and each to follow a set course that would take them along the coastline, north, south, and the third further inland in the event the Danish raiders had done the same. Riders were to keep the three contingents within constant communication with each other in the event there was an attack.

Rorke and Tarek sat about the fire that night. The encampment was heavily guarded, with Rorke's men positioned along the perimeter, and then another perimeter of guards beyond. It was something he had learned from Tarek al Sharif—always expected the unexpected.

"You are thoughtful, my friend," Tarek said as they ate roast fowl, their first warm meal in over four days. "Something troubles you."

"Horses," Rorke commented, separating a portion of meat from the bone with his teeth.

Tarek looked at him askance. "You think of horses, when you could be thinking of a very beautiful red-haired Saxon? There are times, my friend, when the workings of your mind worry me."

"How many sets of tracks did you see at Stephen's encampment?" Rorke asked.

Tarek shrugged, cleaning off the last of meat on a roasted leg of fowl. "Many, and even more partially concealed by the snow. No doubt there were far more we could no longer see."

"How many men rode with Stephen?"

"They were your own men," Tarek replied as if he should

know the answer and have no need to ask it. "A full fourscore rode north."

"Aye," Rorke said thoughtfully, stirring the flames of the fire with a stick as though hoping to see something there. "Half that number returned to London. The tracks we saw were at least twice that many and made after those of Stephen's men."

Tarek's gaze narrowed as he began to see the direction Rorke's thoughts took. "The attackers were astride."

"Horses brought in ships?"

"William brought horses from Normandy." Tarek gestured to their own mounts tethered nearby.

"Across the narrow channel. These raiders had to come across hundreds of miles of open sea. Yet no boats were seen by Stephen's men."

"He is young. He might have been mistaken."

"He is young, but I would ride with him sooner than any hundred other men I could name except for yourself," Rorke answered, and then said with certainty, "No, he missed nothing. Everything was done as it should be. These attackers were astride, yet the Danes are not known for their horsemanship nor for mounted soldiers. And then there is this." He seized the blade from his belt and threw it to the ground near where Tarek sat.

It embedded in the ground, the ornately carved handle gleaming in the firelight. Tarek retrieved the blade and turned it over in his fingers.

"A fine blade."

Rorke nodded. "What soldier leaves behind his weapons? Especially one so finely made. And the war ax that Stephen found as well?"

"No soldier leaves his weapons as long as he draws breath, for they may mean the difference between life and death another day."

Rorke answered on a single word, "Aye."

Tarek studied the blade. "What do you want me to do?"

Rorke frowned. "An army this size is too easily seen. Leave before first light. You will have to trade in those flowing robes for simple leather garments that are not easily seen. Take only Sir Guy with you. He was here with Stephen; he knows this forbidding land.

"My sense of it is that we are being watched even now. You must find the watchers. Only then may we know the truth of Danes with horses, Danes who do not ride and are so careless with their weapons that they leave them behind like a guidepost."

Across the fire, Tarek grinned, teeth flashing in the golden bronze of his features. "I will do anything if it means we may leave this cold, forbidding place sooner. I will be one with the wind. I will find them, before they me."

Tarek left long before first light following Sir Guy. Rorke said nothing to William. Two men missing, one of whom traveled at will, was not likely to raise questions that for the time Rorke didn't want asked among the rest of the men, or by King William.

Tarek discovered that Stephen and his men had learned much of this cold northern land. Sir Guy was a capable guide who rode through craggy rock outcroppings, glens, and deep glades one would not even have known existed. And which would have hidden anyone who chose to be hidden. The small glades and valleys never failed to amaze him.

He had thought this a cold, forbidding land and in many places it was, but like the desert, which yields the pleasure of an occasional oasis, the north country too had its verdant secrets. The morning of the second day, he discovered just such a place after he and Sir Guy separated, each to follow a split in the mountain trail.

At midday he still had found no sign of the Danish raiders. If they had taken shelter in this valley he had not yet found them. He stopped to water his horse at a small lake.

The valley was sheltered from the bite of the wind up on the slopes. Thirsty, Tarek waited until the mare had drunk her fill, then sprawled at the water's edge after first removing the smaller knife he carried at his boot and laying it just under his right hand. If anyone approached him, the mare would immediately sense it.

It was late afternoon and the sun had broken through the clouds. The water was smooth as glass, broken by only the ripples made by the mare as she drank. The warmth of the sun on the cool surface of the water caused a mist to rise. It spread across the water and up the embankment.

She came from out of nowhere, slender and graceful as a doe, and just as startled to find him there. If she had sprung from an opening in the earth, he could not have been more surprised.

His first instinct was the blade and it was immediately in his hand. His second was that the mare had not sensed her. Now the Arabian's ears merely flicked back and forth as she recognized a creature that posed no immediate threat. Just as immediately Tarek was on his feet, the blade gripped firmly in hand and leveled at his lovely intruder. And she was indeed lovely.

Her face was heart-shaped with flawless skin flushed pink across the faint angle of cheekbones. Her nose was small and slender above the surprised O of a deliciously full, ruby-lipped mouth. Her chin was also small but firm, and above all was the startling green of her eyes. As green as the velvet moss that clung to the water-splashed rocks.

At first she seemed no more than a child, small, pale, and slender. But she turned and glanced back up the slope and in her profile, Tarek saw the high thrust of firm, full breasts beneath the folds of the fine woolen mantle.

The hood of her mantle had fallen back to her shoulders, revealing a green satin lining as rich as the wool and startling as her eyes, and also revealing a thick cascade of hair the color of sunlight through mist. It was all spun gold threaded through with pale silvery light and even from the distance that separated them, beckoned a man's hand.

Wild, improbable thoughts filled his head, as he wondered if the rest of her was as luminous, pale, and perfect as the features of her face and the slender hands that clutched the folds of the mantle. And more improbably what it might take to possess such a creature, who seemed as if she were no earthbound creature at all, but made of sunlight and mist, and the verdant green of nature itself.

Still more improbable, if he did possess such a creature, what would it be like to feel her slender body beneath his, to watch her pale, slender hands at his darker flesh, to discover if there were other colors in those emerald eyes as he discovered all her passions.

She would be as elusive as sunlight and mist he decided, and took a step toward her, for the first time in his life experiencing the need of the Persian and Norse blood as it hammered through his veins, to abduct her, throw her over the saddle before him, and be willing to spill the blood of all in the name of the Prophet to make her his own.

A slender hand came up in warning. Again she glanced over her shoulder.

"You must leave this place at once. It is not safe."

Her voice was as light as the mist, almost breathless with fear. The words were oddly accented yet spoken in English. Tarek took another step toward her.

"Who are you?"

"There is no time. They will be here soon."

"Who will be here?"

That emerald gaze swung back to his. He saw none of the natural fear that a maid alone in a glen with a strange warrior should have felt. Instead he saw a mixture of curiosity and fascination as she made as thorough an assessment of him as he had of her.

There was no coyness about her, only a faint shyness like the startled creature he had first imagined her to be. Then she stunned him as she answered his question.

"The men you seek. They are very close by and there is grave danger. You must warn the others or they will all be killed."

He looked at her with more than a little surprise. "How do you know of this?"

"They are on the trail above. They have been waiting for you. If you do not leave now, you will be trapped and unable to escape."

"If they wait above, I cannot leave by way of the trail."

"There is another way, through those rocks." She gestured across the small pool to a cluster of steep, craggy rocks over which the water spilled in a tumbling water fall.

"There is a way behind the water and through the rocks. You cannot ride through it, you must walk through it, but it is wide enough."

With another glance up the hill, Tarek asked, "What do you know of these men?"

"They were the ones who attacked and murdered the soldiers." Her gaze fastened on the hillside above. "You must go quickly."

"What about you?"

"These hills are my home. I know them well. They will not find me."

"Shouldn't you come this way as well? If these men are as you say, I wouldn't want you to remain behind."

"You fear for my safety?"

"As I would any rare jewel that is beyond price."

That green gaze darkened until it was the blue-green of the water. "You have a strange way about you, and your words are strange. You are not like the others."

"I am called Tarek al Sharif. My home is very far away. What are you called?"

She seemed about to tell him, when a sound came from the hillside above. The Danes, having tired of waiting for his return, had decided to take matters into their own hands.

"Please! My dark warrior, you must go quickly!"

Tarek swung astride the Arabian mare. Leaning over from the saddle, he seized the maid's slender hand. As he knew it would, her skin was like the finest pale satin against his and stirred an ache of longing unlike any he had ever experienced for a woman, to touch other hidden places until she cried out beneath him.

She stared at his deeply bronzed hand closed possessively over hers, her fingers curled against the palm of his hand like the cool, pale petals of a rare blossom. Her expression was stunned.

"Go! Now!" And she jerked free of his grasp, as easily as if she was a slender, silken reed. "Behind the falls, and through the rocks," she repeated, slapping the mare hard across the flanks.

The mare leapt into the shallow pool and stopped only as Tarek hauled back on the reins. But when he twisted in the saddle, the maid was gone.

There was no trace of her at the water's edge, the embankment, nor on the slope of the hillside above. She was gone, the air shimmering where she had stood only moments before, as if she was no more than sunshine and mist. Then a shout from the hillside drew his attention.

With a curse at his misfortune at having found such a beauty only to lose her just as quickly, Tarek sent the mare plunging through the shallow pool toward the waterfall.

It was just where she had said it would be, an opening through the rocks just wide and tall enough for a man to lead a horse. Through the silvery veil of tumbling water, Tarek glanced back once more at the pool. The water from the falls spilled into a separate pool that fed the larger one.

The surface was once more calm, except for faint ripples of water that moved steadily away from the rocks, not toward them as it would if he had caused them. Then he saw what had caused them. A graceful bird glided slowly across the water.

It had a sleek, long neck, and pale silvery feathers that made it seem as if it floated on the mist. It turned its head this way and that, and for a moment he would have sworn on the book of the Prophet that it looked back toward the rocks almost as if it knew he was there, watching.

He glanced once more to the hillside. Riders quickly descended to the pool. And when he glanced back to the silver bird, it was gone. He glanced skyward, but there was no sign of it. With a new urgency as the riders reached the water's edge, Tarek led the mare through the rocks.

It was a steep climb over slippery, water-slicked rocks, but he eventually emerged at the end to discover that he was now above the pool and the riders who had hoped to trap him there. Mounting the mare, he thought of the beautiful maid he had seen there and hoped she was safe.

He was late in returning to the appointed meeting place, but Sir Guy had waited for him.

"There are riders no more than half a kilometer from here," Tarek informed him. "And more ride to attack William's column."

"How do you know this?"

"I met a highland dweller who spoke of it."

"What manner of highland dweller?"

Sir Guy would not have believed it if Tarek told him the truth of it. "An old crone in the hills. She warned me of the riders, and spoke of the attack. She saw the attack on Stephen's men. William and his men ride into a trap."

"Then we must find them with all possible haste."

Rorke spun the warhorse about hard as he rode to meet one of his men who had just ridden in. Still there was no word of Tarek or Sir Guy. Four other men had failed to return. And William had split his men into three columns too far apart to be of any good to one another in the event of a surprise attack by a large force. He was beginning to feel very uneasy about this.

"What have you to report?" he snapped.

The soldier's face was grim. He had been with Rorke many years and was a seasoned veteran of many campaigns.

"Champlain and Dulonges."

Rorke knew the men well. They were two of the four he had sent out the previous afternoon.

"They are dead, milord. Just outside yesterday's encampment. We found them in the brush, with their throats cut."

Rorke swore. "They never even made it beyond camp! By

God, I will have answers, and no more dead men! Rejoin the others. You will remain with us."

"What of Tarek al Sharif and Sir Guy?"

"They will have to find us. We cannot stay here." Rorke glanced around and felt a tingling of uneasiness at something his friend was wont to complain about frequently. They were spread out in the forest, an easy target for an attack.

Tarek found them at the edge of the forest. He cursed as he cut through the trees to reach them, finally finding his friend near William's column.

"Soldiers lie in wait just ahead at a place called Brecon. They are the same ones who attacked Stephen's men."

"You're certain of this?" Rorke asked.

Tarek thought again of the lovely maid and vowed that if he lived through this, he would find her. "I am certain my friend. I encountered soldiers very near here."

The battle came on a lowland just beyond the forest. The warning had given them enough time to arm and prepare, dividing their forces to surround and encircle the raiders.

It was fiercely fought. Steel rang out against steel. Horses screamed and fell, taking their riders with them. The hard, cold, unforgiving ground ran with blood. Twice the raiders rallied, both times striking against the armed contingent that fought beside William. Both times they were beaten back greatly weakened, until the last man fell beneath Rorke's blade.

With a savage war cry, he leapt from the back of the warhorse and descended on the fallen Dane. The heavy woolen hood that concealed the man's features was pulled back to reveal a familiar face.

Rorke didn't want to believe it. Had refused to believe it even as he sensed something familiar in the way the man fought. Now he saw what he had not wanted to believe. The dead soldier was not a Dane at all. It was Vachel de Marque.

"By God! What is the meaning of this!" William demanded.

"The meaning of this," Rorke said, his heart turning as cold as stone, "was to be your death, milord. And I fear this may not be the worst of it."

William's expression was contorted with rage and the effort to control it. "Go on."

"Betrayal. This man owes his loyalty to only one man."

"My brother," William's voice strangled over the word.

"I fear the threat may not end here, milord." Rorke went onto explain the fear that took hold of his heart.

It was William who spoke the words. "The queen and my unborn son!"

But Rorke sensed the danger was far greater still. Vivian had spoken of her fears of the Darkness. Twice before, it had tried to destroy her. And she had given him the crystal for protection. Leaving herself dangerously vulnerable.

It was she who now needed that protection. Needed it urgently. But even if they rode without stopping and the horses lasted the journey, it would still take them two full days and nights to return to London.

Twenty-four

Vivian stirred the fire at the hearth against a pervasive cold that no amount of wood seemed able to dispel. She shivered as she drew the edges of the shawl more tightly about her shoulders.

She had left the queen's chamber a short while earlier after giving her a soothing tisane so that she might rest after a sleepless night with the child so large within her.

Over the past several days, since Rorke left with the king for the north country, Vivian had also experienced a restlessness, but of a far different nature.

"I do not like this infernal cold," Meg said uneasily from the chair beside the hearth, where she sat spinning yarn, her old gnarled fingers moving with the ease of memory back and forth between the wheel and the spindle.

"It grows worse each day." The old woman's fingers fell idle at the wheel. Her head was turned toward the sound of Vivian's movement at the hearth, but her head was cocked as if she listened for some other sound. Her voice whispered low as though to keep others from hearing.

" 'Tis unnatural."

"Aye," Vivian said softly. "I have felt it as well."

"Will they return soon?" Meg asked as Vivian knelt before the hearth.

Vivian smiled faintly at the old woman's undisguised eagerness. "Why, Meg," she remarked. "Can it be that you miss milord FitzWarren"

"Bah!" Meg scoffed. "I do not miss him. But I will warrant it was not so cold when he was about. I do not like it!"

Vivian knew that Meg referred to the shadows that seemed to be everywhere with Rorke and William absent from the fortress. But she found herself thinking of far different aches of coldness that she found eased by the fire that filled their bed at night.

"Aye," she agreed, gathering the shawl more tightly about her shoulders. "It was not so cold." Or dark, she thought to herself with a shiver of apprehension. As though to warm herself, she extended her fingers toward the flames as she silently whispered the ancient words, calling upon the powers of the Light for a vision in the flames.

The flames leapt wildly, the brilliant golden, orange, and red hues smothering almost to nothingness in the darkness of shadows at the hearth, then flaring suddenly and fluttering violently, an uncertain image forming briefly before it disappeared in the chaos of the fire. Fear welled inside Vivian as she rose suddenly from the hearth.

"Stay here where you may hear if the queen should need you," she told Meg, taking her mantle from the peg near the door. She closed the stout door behind her and hesitated only a moment in the passage before turning her steps toward the great hall

It was oddly deserted. Even the Saxon earls and barons who hovered about daily for an audience with the count in the king's absence were strangely missing. Missing, too, were the guards usually posted in the passageways and at each entrance as she made her way toward the chapel. Relief swept through her at sight of Poladouras. He looked up with surprise at seeing her so soon again after morning prayers.

"What is it? Has there been word from the north country?"

She shook her head. "Nay, there has been no word. But I fear something is amiss." With much effort, he pushed from bent knee to his feet and walked toward her with grave expression.

"Have you sensed something?"

"Yes . . . No . . . It is not clear. I know only that something very grave has happened." She laid a hand at the sleeve of his cassock. "The guards are nowhere about."

His silvery eyebrows lifted in the round moon of his face. "That is most unusual. Young Stephen of Valois was left in charge of the household. He would not dismiss the guards with so much unrest about London."

"There is more," Vivian explained. "Something I glimpsed in the flames."

Poladouras sensed her urgency and nodded. "I will come with you."

They left the royal compound by way of the passage near the kitchen. At least the cook was where she should be, ordering her serving girls about as she labored over the evening meal. The woman seemed to think nothing was amiss, lifting a shoulder with little concern when Vivian questioned her about the guards.

"No doubt they are in the practice yard or the armory."

With some measure of relief, they encountered a guard outside the sally port. He gave no acknowledgment of greeting and Vivian realized that he was not the usual guard.

There were soldiers in the practice yard, others could be seen in the armory. Many more armed guards walked the bastion walls and stood guard at the main entrance.

"It seems the cook was right," Poladouras commented as they crossed the yard toward the kennels and the mews beyond. "There are ample guards about."

"Aye," Vivian said, her feeling of apprehension growing. "But they are not William's guards. They have all been replaced." As they passed the kennels, William's hounds set up a chorus of barking.

"And the hounds are kept confined." She quickened her pace as she turned toward the mews.

She needed no special sense to tell her what she had feared. She heard it in the unusual silence of William's birds as they sat at their perches, their feathers roughened at their sleek bodies as though they, too, sensed it. And she smelled it in the heaviness of the air that usually smelled of fresh straw. She smelled death.

Even though she sensed it, still she cried out when she found the small falcon. No sleek, golden head turned with a familiar chirped greeting. No special bond of communication flowed magically between them.

Blood stained the straw beneath the perch. The small falcon's lifeless body hung limp from the leather jesses that had bound her to the perch. Her once glossy feathers of such an unusual gold color were now dull with death and the blood that seeped the bludgeoned body.

Vivian felt Poladouras' gentle hand at her shoulder. "I am so sorry, child," he whispered with heaviness of grief, for the girl and falcon had been raised together and he knew the special bond that existed between them. He looked about the mews and drew the natural conclusion.

"The other birds, no doubt would not accept her."

"Nay!" Vivian whispered, her heart aching. " 'Twas not the

other birds for they are firmly tied, nor are the wounds what another bird would draw." Her voice broke softly. "She was beaten to death while tethered and hooded, unable to defend herself or flee." Tears coursed down her cheeks at the loss of a beloved, gentle friend.

Poladouras sighed heavily. "I will see to the creature," he said, moving to step past Vivian. But she stopped him with a hand at his sleeve.

"I will do it."

She cut the leather jesses with her small gathering knife, cradling the lifeless falcon in her arms. She had no sense of life that she could call back with her powers remaining in the broken, bloodied body. With Poladouras following, she carried Aquila from the mews.

She climbed to the highest bastion until she found a place apart, where no soldiers watched. Huffing and puffing up the stone steps, Poladouras had followed. His expression was grim with Vivian's own unspoken thoughts.

Focusing on the ancient power of the Light within her, Vivian closed her eyes and spoke the ancient words that reached beyond time and memory into the mist of the world beyond. When the words had been spoken, she opened her eyes, and, on a single thought cast into the overcast sky above, she opened her arms.

A man of faith, caught between the immortal powers that he knew existed and that faith that he believed in, Poladouras watched the ancient ceremony with a mixture of sadness and inspiration. He had no explanation for her powers, other than what they were. He accepted them because he had learned long ago there were far more things in the world and beyond than man could explain merely by faith in God. So he accepted and embraced both.

There was a sudden fluttering of movement, a disturbance in the air. From her arms the falcon rose seemingly alive once more, unfurled its glossy wings that were caught with sudden light as if the sun had come out, and in a single motion leapt into flight. She circled once, majestic wings dipping faintly. Then, on a slow arc, she circled away, disappearing into the mist that rose beyond the fortress walls.

No amount of Vivian's powers could call it back to earthly life. And so she had released its spirit to the skies it had once flown.

"We must return quickly," Vivian said, moving past Poladouras with a new urgency. "Aquila's death is part of something more." As they descended the bastion, they passed the guards once more.

Vivian stopped and approached the guard they had passed only moments before. Only it was not the same guard.

"Where is the man who was here only a few minutes ago?"

The guard looked at her uncertainly. "Forgive me, mistress. I do not understand. There has been no other guard here since I relieved the previous guard at midday."

"What are you saying?" Poladouras demanded. " 'Tis just midday now."

"You are wrong, monk," the guard informed him. "It is well two hours past midday. I have been here for two hours."

"But that is impossible!" Poladouras' round face became red with anger. "We passed the other guard only moments ago. What trickery is this?" he demanded. "Lying is a sin! You had best repent for the sake of your mortal soul!"

She laid a restraining hand on the monk's arm. "Please, Poladouras, there is no time to waste."

"What is it?" he asked between puffed breaths as he followed her across the yard.

"He was not lying," Vivian told him. "He had been at his post for two hours. But to us it was only moments."

As they reached the sally port, Poladouras held up a hand that he must have a moment to catch his breath. "It makes no sense, child."

"Nay," she agreed. "Not in the mortal world. But what has happened is not of the mortal world."

"What are you saying?"

She pulled the door open and quickly ran up the steps to the passage. Poladouras was forced to follow or be left behind. "The vision of Aquila that I saw in the flames was a deception."

"But the falcon is dead," he protested, and then asked, "Is she not?"

"Aye," she said sadly. "She is dead. Her death was a lure to draw me away. Once I left the royal tower, time as we know it was altered. What we were certain could only have been a few minutes was in fact more than two hours."

"But why? Who has done this?" Poladouras sputtered, gasped a breath, and then asked, "To what purpose?"

"To give enough time to accomplish what might not be accomplished in a few minutes, but required more time and cunning," she told him. "It is not *who* has done this, but *what* has done it." Her somber blue gaze met his briefly in the flickering of torchlight as they approached the main hall.

Her pace quickened as with a new urgency she ran for the queen's chamber. In the passage she tripped, almost falling over a slumped body.

"Stephen!" she cried out, as she recognized the young knight. She knelt beside him. Blood covered the side of his face and matted his hair from a deadly blow. But he was not dead. She felt the life pulse that beat beneath her fingers at his neck. With no time to waste, she channeled her power through her touch to the life force deep within him.

His eyes slowly opened. Recognition came a moment later and he struggled to sit up.

"I tried to stop her," he protested. "I told her no one was to enter the king's chamber except for you and the old woman. Especially not her. But she would not hear of it." He struggled to say the next words.

"When I tried to stop her . . ." he shuddered at the remembered memory. "It was dreadful. I have never seen such a creature . . ." And then he cried a warning, "The queen is in danger!"

"Stay with him," Vivian told Poladouras as she moved past

Stephen's prostrate body to the door of the queen's chamber, which stood ajar. She slowly pushed it open. For a moment, she was surprised by what she saw.

"Mally?" And for a moment she could not grasp why Stephen was so anxious about the girl being in the chamber for she often attended Matilda. Then Mally turned toward her at the edge of the large bed. The queen stirred weakly on the bed.

"The child has but brought me a tisane," she said with great lethargy that sent a ribbon of fear knifing through Vivian for she sensed not only Matilda's increased weakness but distress in the child that lay within her womb. Her gaze fastened on Mally, and she saw a glimmer of what Stephen had seen.

They were not Mally's eyes that looked back at her, but the vacant, dark eyes of someone—or something—else. Vivian glanced to the vessel held in the young woman's hands and knew that what was left of it contained poison.

There was a brief flicker of challenge in those flat dark eyes as Vivian slowly walked toward her, then it wavered. In that moment of weakness, Vivian reached out and seized her by the wrist. The young woman jerked and spasmed, crying out painfully, then falling to the floor.

As she fell she transformed, Mally's features disappearing to reveal Judith de Marque.

"You cannot stop it. You cannot win!" she spat out at Vivian. "You will lose all, including Rorke FitzWarren, for you are no match for him."

"Who, Judith?" Vivian demanded. "Who is it that you have sold your soul to? And where is Mally? What have you done with her?"

"I have sold my soul to no one. He loves me. He vowed it. Even now, he has given me some of his powers. He has taken the girl."

"Taken her where?"

"Into the ancient catacombs where she will die."

"You fool!" Vivian told her. "The power cannot be given.

What he has given you is death! Now tell me, who is it that promised so much!"

Judith stared up at her. "You're wrong. I will live forever now. He promised it. And I will have great riches. And I will have Rorke FitzWarren." But even as she spoke it, she faltered as though short of breath.

"What is happening?"

Vivian released her, for it was not her own power that gripped the woman, but the power of another. Judith gasped, her face suddenly contorted in pain. She stared down at her hands. Both were suddenly heavily wrinkled and twisted with age. When Vivian looked at her face, she saw the same.

"What is happening?" Judith cried out, her voice no longer young, but the rasping wheeze of a dying old woman.

It was brutal to watch, as she slowly withered and died, her body no longer beautiful but unrecognizable with the passage of decades in only moments, until she lay curled on the floor, nothing more than a dried wisp of herself, horribly misshapen and bent with the cruel punishment of the price she paid for her own ambitions. And then she crumbled to dust, scattered into the rushes at the floor.

The adjoining door slowly opened and Meg stood in the doorway.

"Quickly," Vivian told her, "bring my healing potions. Judith is dead and I fear the queen may be very near death as well."

She worked quickly, throwing back the bedcovers, giving instructions for Poladouras to build up the fire at the hearth and light every candle. By the time he had finished, Meg had brought her medicines.

"She has been given a poison. Even now the child within her dies and she will surely die as well if I cannot stop it."

There was no time to waste. She sat beside Matilda at the bed. Turning her thoughts inward once more she focused on the power of the Light as she placed one hand over the queen's heart and another at her swollen womb.

Drawing on the power, she quickly found the darkness of

poison that flowed through the queen to her unborn child. As if it were a tangible thing, Vivian seized it, closing her thoughts around it, then drawing the poison within herself.

On a painful gasp, she released her connection with Matilda. She felt the poison within her. Its killing potential was gone, leaving only a lethargy that she fought to control. She must not give in to it, for Mally was in grave danger.

"You must give her a cleansing tea," she instructed Meg. "Then she will sleep."

"And the child?"

"Both will live." But her unspoken thoughts were less certain. None of them would live if she was unable to stop the evil of Darkness that had caused this.

"What will you do now?" Meg asked worriedly.

"The queen must be protected against any further harm." Going to the fire on the hearth that now burned bright and steady, she passed her hand through the flames, building the energy drained by the purging bond that had removed the poison from the queen's body.

She spoke the words in the ancient Celtic language of her ancestors, drawing on their power to join hers. Then when the power was once more strong within her, she returned to the bed where the queen lay.

In the way of the ancient ones, handed down through generations of sorcerers and their daughters, she touched her fingers to five points, forming a protective star about the queen, enclosing her in an invisible protective shroud that no darkness could reach. As long as Vivian lived, the queen would be safe.

"You must remain here," she told Meg and Poladouras. "I need your strength to protect the queen."

Poladouras shook his head."I will not let you go alone."

Vivian laid a restraining hand gently at his shoulder. "Dear teacher, where I go, you cannot. For there are things that will pass that are not of this world nor of your God. I must do this. It is me that the Darkness waits for. If you are here, then I know the queen will be safe, for not even the powers of the Darkness can match my power combined with your true faith."

"Do not, my child!" Meg cried out, her blind eyes filling with tears. "Send me in your place. You can do it. Transform me as the Darkness transformed that miserable creature."

"It would do no good. The deception would be found out and the consequences unthinkable. I need you to remain with Poladouras, for I rely on your strength as well."

Meg knew there was no dissuading her and when Vivian had gone, wept bitterly. No amount of comfort Poladouras might offer eased her pain.

"You do not understand," she cried. "She cannot protect herself and the queen at the same time. If she protects the queen with her spell, she will be destroyed. She goes to her death to save us."

The catacombs were the ruins of the Roman fortress that had once stood in London over five hundred years ago. Succeeding generations of invaders and their kings had built over the catacombs, until now the opening lay beneath the royal chapel at the far end of the courtyard.

William's soldiers had spoken of it. Some said perhaps King Arthur's own soldiers were buried there, for over the succeeding centuries the catacombs had become burial crypts. She took a torch with her as she began the downward descent from behind the chapel altar into the ancient Roman ruins.

The torch cast fingers of light across dark, damp walls like threads of gold in the darkness of a vision at a tapestry loom.

She was the weaver she had envisioned in her dreams. The threads were not yet woven, the future had not yet been decided. Only she could alter what would be. The kingdom and the fate of all those she held dear depended on her doing this.

Other torches had been set into the brackets at the walls, lighting the way.

She found Mally in a dark, crumbling chamber, her hands clasped before her and bound. With a quick glance around, Vivian sensed the ancient dead souls that surrounded them and knew this place must have been used for a burial crypt. And more.

"He's dead, mistress!" Mally cried. "He's dead."

Turning, Vivian saw. It was Conal.

He'd been horribly beaten, no doubt caught that day in the market by the bishop's men. But why? Sadly she sensed the cause of his death. The bishop had been after the truth about her, and Conal had died protecting her.

"Dear friend," she whispered. "I am sorry."

Encountering no resistance, she untied Mally. It did not surprise her. Mally had served her purpose, that of a lure to bring her down here. Once that was accomplished, the girl was no longer needed. Mally wept with relief and clung to Vivian.

"He brought me down here. He said you had sent for me. That your healer's skills were needed in this dreadful place." The girl shivered. "Then he left me here. What is happening, mistress?"

Lies woven into yet more lies. Deception and death. Handmaidens of the Darkness. There was no need to ask of whom she spoke.

As though a portent of the battle that was to come, she felt the poison moving through her with increased heaviness in her arms and legs, her thoughts coming less quickly, and knew this, too, was all part of his plan.

"You must go, now," she told Mally. "Follow the stairs, the torches will light the way. Whatever happens, do not look back."

Mally looked at her incredulously. "You can't stay here, mistress. You must come with me."

"I will follow," Vivian assured her, pulling the girl to her feet. With a comforting touch at Mally's shoulder, she sensed the girl well, as was the child she carried. She gently shoved Mally toward the entrance of the chamber, sensing as well the Darkness that but waited beyond, but not for Mally. She no longer served a purpose.

"Go now!" she told Mally. "And do not turn back. Concentrate only on the flames at the torches until you reach the top.

Then go to Meg." Mally hesitated, glancing fearfully about the chamber.

"Go!" Vivian repeated fiercely and Mally turned and fled. Vivian could hear the girl's slippers making frantic whispering sounds over the stone steps and knew she would be safe.

As soon as Mally had gone, Vivian felt the Darkness closing in, seeping from the corners of the chamber, spilling through the doorway. Even if she attempted it, she knew she would not escape. As soon as Mally was through the opening Vivian felt an invisible portal close.

"I knew you would come."

Vivian slowly turned around, recognizing the voice.

"Milord Bishop," she acknowledged. "You were correct. I had to come, of course. To stop you."

He stood before her, dressed from head to foot in black, darkness upon darkness of his embodied evil. Even his eyes were as black as night with the darkness of his soul. He no longer wore the silver cross, for it would have burned him at a single touch. Instead, his tunic and mantle glistened with myriad black stones that seemed to absorb and drain the light from the torch.

"You cannot stop me," he told her, the Darkness now embodied in the ambitions of the bishop, Count de Bayeau. William's brother.

"Merlin tried over five hundred years ago and I destroyed him. Now I will destroy you and the kingdom will be mine."

"I cannot allow it." But even as she spoke it, Vivian felt the poison working through her, robbing her of much-needed strength and concentration. She sensed as well that any weakness gave him access to her thoughts. And so she closed her thoughts to him, concentrating her conscious thought on emotions and images his Darkness could not penetrate—memories of Rorke.

The bishop's expression sharpened. "Very clever, mistress. More clever than your father. Having never experienced the mortal pleasures of which you have partaken, he could not shield his intentions with thoughts of happiness and love as you have. But it will do you no good. In time, the poison will weaken your thoughts. And the time is already at hand in the north country, even as we speak."

With sudden clarity, she realized the full extent of his treachery. He had planned all of it. And beyond any doubt she knew that the treachery in the north country was not from Danish raiders, but the count's own men, no doubt led by Vachel.

"Ah, you see the way of it," he acknowledged. "Then you know there is nothing that can prevent it. It is already done."

It wasn't. She couldn't believe it, she refused to believe it. For she had no sense of Rorke's death. And that she would surely have known. She concentrated her ability to close her thoughts to the Darkness.

The Darkness had altered time to its own purpose. It was also possible it might serve hers. But only if Rorke lived.

"You cannot stop the Darkness," the count told her as he raised a dark, gloved hand and swept it before him. "No more than your father could stop it."

The meager light in the chamber seemed to be swallowed up within the bishop's grasp. Vivian hesitated when she would have countered his move.

The Darkness knew her powers and would, naturally, anticipate them. That must not happen. Instead of countering his move by focusing her power in the flames at the torch, she pulled the fiery light deep within her, channeling it into the very soul of her being, and plunging the chamber into complete darkness. Then she quickly turned and fled to the back wall of the chamber.

There was no door by which she might escape. Instead, she fled through the stone, deeper into the catacombs. Weakened as she was by the poison, if her powers were no match for the powers of the Darkness, then she would become like the darkness.

She collapsed on the other side of the ancient stone wall into another chamber that seeped water. Guided by inner sight, she saw the pattern of chambers like the cells of a honeycomb. Even as she fought to gather her strength once more, she felt the Darkness closing in again.

"You are no match for me, mistress of the Light. You cannot stop me, for to do so you must release the spell that protects the queen."

She heard his thoughts whispering through the stones as the Darkness pursued her.

"And that you will not do for you cannot bear to risk another's life for your own. Your mortal compassion for others is your weakness. I am not hindered by such meaningless human frailties. You will be destroyed as your father was destroyed."

She sent a single thought into the gathering darkness that smothered about her.

"Never."

Twenty-five

Rorke took his most trusted knights with him. They removed all battle armor and the heavy shields that might weight them down, carrying only their battle swords and lances. Though William was determined to ride with them, he was too weak from their ride into the north country to ride at the pace Rorke intended to set. With grim-faced expression he bade his knights farewell, leaving them to follow with the remainder of his army.

"My brother has betrayed me," William solemnly told Rorke. "He would have me slain to fulfill his ambitions. I should have seen it. I should have known that he would not be content with what he had. He wanted England. And it may have cost me my queen and my child."

Rorke knew, but did not say, it might have cost far more than that.

"I pray we will be in time," he responded grimly.

"If you are in time and the queen still lives, then I shall deal with my brother," William told him in a tone that allowed no argument. "You will not deny me this!"

"Aye, milord," Rorke acknowledged, grateful that William had not bound him with any promises in the event the queen had not survived the bishop's plan.

If she had not, it could only mean that Vivian was dead as well, for he knew in his heart that she would do all to protect the queen. And in that event neither the bishop's God nor his treachery would save him.

With a shouted order to his men, they set off at a killing pace, trailing extra horses taken from Vachel's men.

They stopped only long enough to change from their exhausted mounts to the fresh ones they had with them and then continued the bone-wearying pace. In the last hours before dawn the morning of the third day, the fires of London could be seen on the horizon. Though both horses and men were exhausted, they pressed on.

Word was sent out as they rode through the city. His own soldiers were gathered so that by the time they reached the fortress, three hundred strong rode with him. He saw the surprise on the faces of the guards at the gates and knew that those loyal to the bishop were stunned to see him and his men alive.

A skirmish at the gate quickly ended, Rorke's soldiers swarming into the fortress to subdue any others loyal to the bishop. Rorke vaulted from the back of his trembling mount, his own warhorse left along the journey from the north country. With battle sword drawn and flanked by Tarek and Gavin, he kicked open the doors of the hall.

In the passage outside the royal chambers he encountered an armed soldier. It was Stephen of Valois. He clutched a battle sword in one hand, his wounded arm hanging all but useless at his side.

He had a new wound at the side of his head but it was bandaged. His back was to the chamber door, his stance balanced with blade at the ready, as if he would make his last stand here against the enemy.

"Hold!" Rorke called out and as he reached the young knight and was finally recognized in the flickering light of the torches. Stephen collapsed against the wall.

"I tried to stop him."

"Aye, I know. Rest easy for you have served your father well."

"The queen is safe within," Stephen assured him. "The old woman and the monk protect her."

"Vivian?" Rorke asked anxiously, for Stephen had not spoken of her.

"She saved my life," Stephen said incredulously. "Death was upon me, I felt it, and your lady gave me back my life."

"Where is she?"

"She has gone after him." The young knight fought to return to his feet, but the cumbersome broadsword would not be lifted again with but one hand. He swore angrily. "Give me a smaller blade and I will fight by your side, milord. And when we have the traitor, I will slit his throat."

Rorke eased Stephen to his feet and handed him over into Gavin's care. "You have done all that anyone could ask, my young friend. William's brother has betrayed him and be will feel the loss sorely. He will have need of his son. There is no need of more of your blood. You have spilled enough this day."

Rorke turned and pounded at the door with the handle of his sword, calling to those within. Old Meg opened the chamber door, sliding back the heavy bolt to peer at him through the narrow opening with those opaque sightless eyes that still had the power to see truth.

"I feared you would not return, milord," she said with quavering voice that spoke of a fear he had never known the old woman to possess.

"I am returned. Where is the queen?"

Matilda called out weakly from her bed and Meg stood aside to let him enter. The queen sat up in the bed propped against thick pillows. At the foot of the bed, positioned between her and any who might try to enter was the monk, a large silver crucifix, gleaming in his hand. The girl, Mally, cringed at the side of the bed.

"Milord," he sighed with relief. "I was not certain which end of this thing I might be forced to use. God forgive me, I would have run the bastard through if he had come through the door."

"Where has Vivian gone?"

"She was lured to the catacombs to free the girl," Meg informed him. "He knew she would follow."

A coldness of rage filled him, closing around his heart. "How long ago?" he asked with in voice as cold as death.

"Not long," Meg replied, wringing her hands. "She made us swear that we would not leave the queen. The bishop's power is useless against her protective spell as long as my mistress lives."

"He threatens women and children to feed his ambition," Rorke said, eyes glittering like frozen shards of ice. "Now, the bishop will deal with me."

"Nay!" Meg cried out, running after and grabbing as his arm. "You are mortal. You cannot stop him for in truth it is not the bishop that has done this, but the Darkness that has claimed his soul."

Whirling around, Rorke demanded, "What nonsense is this? Stephen of Valois spoke his name as traitor. His men manned the gates against us. It was the bishop's men who attacked us in the north country and sought to murder King William."

"The body is that of the bishop, but the soul is not!" she repeated. "It is the great Darkness and it seeks the power of the Light. Once the forces of light and dark are joined as they were five hundred years ago, the Darkness will rule the kingdom."

" 'Tis true, my son." Poladouras added his voice to the old woman's. "Meg has said that you know the truth of Vivian's powers. You know as well that she is a daughter of the Light. Merlin's own true daughter, who possesses great power. The bishop is but a vessel for the Darkness. He has embraced it in his quest for power. But it rules him for its own purposes. And its purpose is to destroy the keepers of the Light." With a great aching of sadness, he said, "He will destroy her."

"There must be a way to stop it," Rorke insisted. "I will not accept that she is lost to me." He seized old Meg by the shoulders. "By God, there must be a way!"

"There is only one who might know how you may free her from the Darkness," Meg said with trembling voice. "Her father." Those pale, keen eyes glowed with a sudden slyness of speculation.

"How great is your courage, warrior?" she asked. "Is it enough to confront the power of the Light and challenge the Darkness for the love of a sorcerer's daughter?"

Without hesitation, he said, "Tell me how it may be done."

Staring at him with those vague, blind eyes, Meg finally nodded. "Merlin may not enter this world. Such was his fate at the hands of the Darkness in the days of Arthur. You do not possess the gift of inner sight so that he might tell you of it, even if he were inclined. There is only one way, warrior." That opaque gaze shifted with a sort of curious speculation.

"You must travel through the stone portal to the world between the worlds."

It was almost dawn as Rorke stood in the forest clearing. Snow had fallen, blanketing the ground with a pristine whiteness beneath the gathering gray in those last moments before the sun rose.

"You have the means to enter into the other world," Meg told him, her gnarled arthritic hand clamped over his forearm. "But do you have the faith? Do you believe strongly enough that it exists? For only if you truly believe may you pass through the portal as few mortals ever have." As she spoke, the first golden rays of sunlight spilled into the clearing.

A strange, ethereal mist slowly formed as sunlight warmed the cold snow, and in that vague, shimmering, gray mist, if he looked very carefully, he saw the wavering image of a stone obelisk. The portal from this world into the next, if one believed.

"The blue crystal." Meg gestured to the odd stone that hung about his neck as it had since the day he'd left London. Vivian had given him the stone for protection and he felt a wrenching helplessness. For hers was the greater need. She had known of the dangers of the Darkness and yet she had given him the crystal.

"The crystal possesses the flame of the Light," she went on to explain. "So as it protects it may also guide you through the cold darkness of the stone. But," she cautioned, "only if you believe."

With a wariness, Rorke asked, "What is on the other side?"

"Truth."

"Will he be there?"

Meg nodded. "But he may refuse to see you."

"He would refuse, knowing that I want only to save his daughter?" Anger poured through Rorke. He was a warrior, who saw everything in the context of battles fought and won. There was no acceptable loss. Especially this one.

"It is not enough to want it," Meg cautioned. "You must prove that you are worthy of what you seek." She looked past him to the stone.

"Time grows short. You must go now." Even as she spoke the light grew brighter in the clearing. As soon as the sun climbed over the treetops and filled the clearing, the portal would be closed once more.

With his hand at the sword that hung by his side, Rorke stepped up to the shimmering image of the stone obelisk. Tarek was immediately beside him.

"Think only of the Jehara, for such a love is rare," Tarek told him, thinking fleetingly of the beautiful creature that had warned him of the attack and saved all their lives. If he found love as his friend had, he would hold on to it with his last dying breath.

Rorke nodded. "Thank you, my friend."

Tarek smiled grimly. "I will wait for you on this side."

"You must believe, warrior," Meg's last words cautioned as his other hand closed over the blue crystal, holding on to it as if he were holding on to Vivian. He stepped up to the stone. Closing his eyes, he thought only of her as he took the next step.

It was like being hurtled down a deep, dark hole. He felt himself tumbling and rolling, thrown against hard surfaces that he guessed must be the stone, and then the searing, tearing sensation as if he were being torn apart by the cold stone. Then he felt the coldness seeping inside him, invading his thoughts, breaking his concentration.

He had no idea whether or not he still had his battle sword or even if he was still alive. His only awareness was the stone clutched in his hand and his thoughts of Vivian.

Threading vaguely through his consciousness as he continued to be hurled down the dark chasm, he became aware of a pinpoint of light.

He seemed to be falling toward it, for it grew steadily larger, like an opening at the end of a tunnel. Then, in a sudden burst of pain and light, as if everything had exploded about him, Rorke was thrown free of the darkness and into a grassy clearing.

Battered and bruised, stunned by the experience, his senses slowly cleared as he remembered stepping up to the stone portal. Yet there were no outward signs of the horrendous journey he'd just made.

There was no blood, nor were his garments torn. The sword was still clutched in one hand, his other closed around the blue crystal, as if he had but casually stepped from one room into another.

He rolled slowly to his feet, coming up in a crouched stance. The clearing was the same, only now it was void of the cold and snow, appearing no doubt as it might in spring with but a light mist slowly rising from the earth as the sun poured down.

A few feet away he could barely make out the shape of the stone.

"Stand and fight, warrior!"

Rorke leapt to his feet, both hands clasped around the handle of his battle sword as he spun around to meet this new challenge.

The man he faced was tall and broad-shouldered, with imposing strength in the hardened muscles at his arms as he clutched a sword before him. There was no mistake; he was a warrior. It was in his stance, the way he held his weapon, and the fierce expression on his face.

He was not a young man, nor was he old, but in the prime of his years and with a cunning that could be seen in the gaze leveled at Rorke. But it was his battle raiment that gave Rorke pause. This man was not Vivian's father.

He wore no chain mail, but a thick, gold breastplate reinforced with panels of polished metal. It was worn over a skirted garment that ended just above the knees, rather than breeches, and was richly edged with gold braid trim. Armor-plated boots, glinting golden encased his heavily muscled legs.

A mantle hung from his shoulders, held in place by twin gold medallions at the breastplate. On his head he wore a steel-domed helm with a magnificent plumage of horsehair that had been died brilliant crimson to match the bloodred color of his mantle. By contrast, the battle sword he carried was remarkably void of adornment, although it appeared to be of stout strength and a fine sharpness.

His raiment was finer than that of any common soldier and his bearing bore it out as well. This man was no common warrior, but a leader of warriors.

"Fight or die!" the warrior challenged, lunging toward Rorke on the attack.

Rorke met the blow and turned it aside, then swung about to meet a new attack.

"I do not seek to battle with you, stranger. I come seeking the one called Merlin." His answer was another blow of steel against steel.

The warrior was strong, a formidable opponent in any world. It took all of Rorke's strength and cunning to parry each thrust and meet each blow, then turn it away, and take a new stance. And all the while he was aware that time was slipping away. Valuable time that might mean the difference between life and death for Vivian.

He wanted to be done with this. Where was Merlin? if he truly existed.

"I have no time for this!" he spat out furiously.

"You have time for nothing else, warrior," his opponent taunted. Another blow rang out in the clearing.

The rage of battle filled Rorke. He studied his opponent, turning his thoughts toward the outcome. He noticed each tiny flaw of movement, a momentary hesitation, the weakness of a side left unprotected.

Slowly, surely he began to turn the attack on the offensive, driving with unrelenting blows, taking every advantage learned in countless other battles. There were no distractions, there was only the outcome. An outcome of which he was certain for he would accept no other. He was relentless, until he felt his opponent waver under the barrage of blows and knew victory was within his grasp. Still, he rained blows, driven by a bloodlust to see it ended.

You must prove yourself worthy. Old Meg's words whispered through the heat of the battle.

It is not enough to want it. You must believe.

A blow stunned him with his concentration broken, and he fought back all the harder.

How must he prove himself? A test? What test might a sorcerer ask of a mortal?

With each blow he received, he instinctively struck back with two.

What might the true test of a warrior be?

He felt his opponent weaken, and as he faltered Rorke struck another blow. And another. Until he had driven his foe to his knees. Another blow drove the blade from his opponent's hands, and he stood over him with blade poised to strike the death blow.

Was there death in the immortal world?

He hesitated. Was anything real? Was this proud, fierce warrior real?

A test of worthiness. A warrior was as worthy as his sword. In the mortal world.

You must believe.

"I will not kill you!"

On a fierce war cry, Rorke flung his battle sword away. In that instant he saw the gleam of satisfaction in the other warrior's gaze. If he caused his own death by his choice, Rorke thought with an aching of regret—not for himself but for Vivian—then so be it. The warrior rose to his feet, undaunted, still as proud, and undefeated. He grabbed a small blade from the sheath at his belt.

"I have seen enough," a voice called out.

A man stepped from the cover of trees that surrounded the clearing and slowly walked toward them.

He was older than the warrior, silver streaking the hair at his temples. He was tall and just as regal as the warrior, but with a faint weariness in his bearing that might have been from some old injury or the infirmities of age.

He was a handsome man, with lean features and a thoughtfulness about his mouth. A neatly trimmed silver beard covered his face.

As he drew closer, his gaze lifted and met Rorke's. The eyes that looked back at him, though lined with the passage of years and much sadness of life, were as blue as the heart of a flame. They were Vivian's eyes. This was her father.

The warrior greeted him, not with the obeisance of a servant to his master, but as friend to friend that spoke of deep, unbreakable bond.

"He fought well," the warrior commented with grave amusement. "I thought myself beaten until he cast aside his blade."

Merlin said nothing but continued to watch Rorke carefully.

Rorke sensed the keenness of mind that lay behind that contemplative gaze and a fierceness of power that still burned within the sorcerer. For he had seen such fire of the Light that burned within the sorceror's daughter.

He had joined with her in ways that transcended a physical joining. They had become one in the sharing of their souls. He had touched the fire within her and he recognized that same power that still burned within the sorcerer, though he might be trapped in this immortal place.

"Why did you throw your battle sword away, warrior?" Merlin asked, his eyes narrowing, not with curiosity but with scrutiny. "It is your strength. With it you kill, vanquish your enemies, and conquer kingdoms. You might easily have been killed for such foolishness."

Rorke sensed that scrutiny and realized that this was the test old Meg had spoken of. Merlin didn't seek answers, he sought wisdom.

"Because," Rorke speculated, "it is precisely what you expected of me."

Merlin's expression eased as did the tension that seemed to radiate from him. He nodded as though something pleased him.

"She said you were of true heart. I had to know if you possessed great wisdom. For only with wisdom can you have any hope of accomplishing what you seek." He looked to the warrior who stood beside Rorke.

"There may yet be hope." A look passed between the two men and then the warrior stepped back. He bowed his head slightly. Again not in obeisance but in salute to the sorcerer.

Then the warrior looked at Rorke. His fierce gaze seemed to burn through Rorke as if he tried to see something more.

"We have waited five hundred years for the warrior who could carry the sword back to the mortal world." He nodded and resheathed his own sword. Then before Rorke could respond or question his strange meaning, the warrior disappeared as if he had never existed.

"Trickery and conjuring?" Rorke asked with sudden anger

as he turned back to Merlin, whom he half expected to vaporize into the air as the warrior had.

"I did not come here for this. I have met your test. Now I want answers. How may I fight the Darkness?"

But Merlin's only response was a contemplative smile as he said, "Walk with me." Then he turned and, without waiting for Rorke, began climbing the footpath into the hills.

He hadn't come for early morning strolls in the hills. He had come for answers. Rorke hesitated, angry and frustrated by what he could not understand and sorcerers who would not make themselves understood. All the while time was running out and Vivian was in danger.

"Go with him," a gentle voice pleaded. He turned and saw a woman standing at the edge of the clearing. She was beautiful, with soft green eyes, wearing a pale blue gown, and fiery red-gold hair that flowed past her shoulders.

Rorke need not know her name to know who she was. The resemblance was there in the perfect angles of her face, softened now with age, but nonetheless beautiful. In legend she was called the Lady of the Lake.

"Please," she begged. "He has waited so long for you and his heart is heavy. But he will not beg. You must go freely because of what lies in your heart."

Rorke glanced to the footpath. Merlin had not looked back, but continued a slow, steady climb. There was nothing to do but follow.

"I will find her, dear lady."

She nodded. "You must, for you are our only hope."

He turned and followed Merlin up the path into the hills.

It was an easy climb and not far, but all the while Rorke worried about the passage of time. It was not the same here, he knew that, for Vivian had spoken of spending a day and night with Merlin when it seemed she had been gone no more than an hour.

But how much time had passed in the catacombs of the fortress? Was she still alive?

Yes! the answer came from his heart, for he could not believe otherwise.

He followed Merlin to a niche that had been cut into the top of the hill. Within the niche was a chamber made of white stone.

It seemed to be some sort of observatory, with a portion of the roof open to the sky. One entire wall opened out onto the little valley below. It seemed a place above the world below, as if it might somehow touch both the mortal and immortal worlds.

"Do not be impatient," Merlin spoke, sensing his thoughts. "For now, she is alive. There is something I must show you." He moved to the back of the chamber and touched the wall low at one corner. It opened, the stones separating and moving back on themselves to reveal an inner chamber. Merlin beckoned for him to follow.

In the center of the inner chamber was a small pool of water. Though the chamber was dark except for the light that spilled through the entrance, the pool glowed with an iridescent shimmering of light as though from within. Again Merlin beckoned to him to stand beside the pool of water.

"Tell me what you see."

"What game is this?"

"It is no game."

"A test then?" His patience was worn thin.

Merlin nodded. "A test of the ancient ones. For only a warrior who is true of heart may stand at the water's edge and see beneath its surface to the treasure that lies within."

"I did not come seeking treasures, old man."

"You came seeking the means to save my daughter. Is that not a treasure worth dying for?"

"Aye, old man, it is."

"Then look into the water and tell me what you see, for only a warrior true of heart will see the warrior's treasure."

Rorke turned and peered into the water. It was pale and shimmering, milky white, and impossible to see anything. Then, as if a hand had passed through the water, sweeping aside the cloudiness, the water cleared. And at the bottom of the shimmering depths he saw a magnificent sword.

Knowing his thoughts, Merlin told him, "You have seen the sword. You are a warrior of true heart, and wisdom. Such a warrior must have a blade that is also of true heart. Raise the sword from the water, warrior. You have the power."

When he looked at Merlin with uncertainty, the sorcerer explained, "You have always had it, for it is in the blue stone. The jewel from the hilt of the sword Excalibur."

At the sound of that name, told and retold through countless legends, the waters of the pool began to bubble and churn. Rorke's fingers closed over the stone that Vivian had placed about his neck.

He immediately felt the warmth of the stone, the fire in its shimmering blue depths that burned with the power of the Light. Then he looked to the pool. The sword slowly began to rise from the water.

It was a magnificent blade, a legendary sword, Arthur's sword—Excalibur.

Now Rorke knew who the warrior was who had challenged him as he emerged from the stone.

"Aye," Merlin acknowledged, sensing his thoughts. "Arthur."

The sword lifted clear of the churning water, turned slowly and then moved toward him. When it reached him, it hovered, suspended in air as if held by some invisible thread.

"Take it," Merlin told him. "For only with the sword of Light can you hope to free her."

Rorke reached out and the sword moved of its own accord, the handle slipping into his sword hand as if it had been precisely shaped to it. Merlin slowly walked toward him.

"The stone."

Rorke nodded, reluctant to part with this last connection to Vivian. The sorcerer removed the fiery blue stone from about his neck. Then he placed it in the hilt of the sword. Like the sword to his hand, the stone fit as if held by a loving hand that had but waited for its return.

"I gave the stone from the sword to my firstborn daughter, to protect her, when I sent her from this place. I always hoped that it might one day be returned when a warrior had need of it." He wrapped his hands around Rorke's, clasped over the handle.

"For five centuries the sword was thought to be lost. Vivian's mother brought it to me, and I have kept it hidden since. The sword has the power of the Light—the power to see and know— but the true power lies in the man who wields it. Only with great wisdom and a true heart, can you truly see."

"But Arthur was a great warrior," Rorke protested, needing something more to tell him how it must be done if he was to have any hope of vanquishing the Darkness.

"Arthur's heart was filled with bitterness of betrayal. The bitterness became a weapon that was turned against him. You must close your eyes and see with your true heart, warrior. Then you will be victorious."

They returned together to the clearing in the orchard. The Lady of the Lake was waiting for them. Tears welled in her eyes as she saw the sword in Rorke's hands. But she said nothing. It was not necessary. Everything she felt was there in her eyes, filled with her love for her daughter.

"You must return now," Merlin told him. "Time passes and the Darkness grows ever more bold in its quest to destroy her."

It was like dawn in the clearing as if no time had passed at all, and yet in his memory it seemed much time must have passed. Rorke stepped over to the stone, shimmering faintly in the early morning light, and for the first time Merlin's implacable facade wavered. He placed both hands at Rorke's shoulders.

"Do not let her perish. You are her only hope."

Rorke nodded and, with one more glance to the lady who stood watching, turned and stepped through the stone portal.

This time there was no searing torment of pain, no ordeal of falling down a long, dark passage. And he realized that, too, had been a test.

He felt no anger or resentment toward Merlin for his tests. He had only one thought as he stepped out into the snow-covered clearing with the legendary sword Excalibur clutched in his hands.

Vivian.

Twenty-six

"I feared you might not return, my friend," Tarek greeted him, a look of concern etching his features. "Did you find what you sought?"

"I found Merlin," Rorke said tersely.

"Then the legend is true?"

Rorke held the sword before him and Tarek's eyes gleamed as blue as the stone in the hilt of the sword.

But it was old Meg who breathed the legendary name with a mixture of awe and disbelief, "Excalibur!" as if she had seen the sword in his hands.

"He has given you Arthur's sword," she said in awe. "I had prayed that your heart might be true, milord."

"By the heavens," Poladouras said almost with reverence. "I believed, by God, I have always believed, for her powers were undeniable. And the legend is carried in every Englishman's heart. But to see the sword and to know it is real, that Arthur was real . . . It restores a man's faith that there is more to this world than we can see. It gives hope."

"He did not give it easily," Rorke admitted. "Merlin is as cunning as his legend. I had to win the sword."

"A contest?" Tarek exclaimed with stunned voice and his gaze traveled over his friend for signs of injury.

"Aye," Rorke said softly, without bravado or boastfulness, "I was forced to battle a king for the right to the sword. Arthur lives in that world between the worlds. I pray I am worthy of their trust."

His gaze was as bleak as the leaden sky behind him. The portal vanished with the dawn that was shrouded behind clouds like a portent of a great darkness that loomed.

"How much time has passed?" he asked with a new urgency as he secured the sword in the leather sheath at his back, and quickly left the clearing.

"No more than moments, my friend," Tarek assured him as they returned to their horses for the ride back to the fortress. The gates were once more secured by Rorke's men. The armory was also secured by Rorke's men—with the count's men imprisoned inside until William's return.

There was no time to waste, nor could he wait for William's return. Vaulting from his horse, Rorke strode to the corner of the courtyard where ancient stones stood at the entrance to the catacombs that had once housed a Roman army.

Perhaps even Arthur and his men had dwelled within those ancient walls five hundred years earlier—before Tintagel, before the Darkness betrayed a young king, before the Battle of Camlann, where Arthur was mortally wounded, then carried off to a place called Avalon in legend and the mythical sword with the power of the Light was plunged into the deep waters of a hidden pool.

Beside him, Tarek readied his own curved blade, securing a second one at his belt. Rorke stayed him with a hand at his shoulder.

"This battle I must fight alone."

"I have fought by your side since Antioch," Tarek protested. "A life owed for a life saved. By all that is holy before your god and mine, I have the right."

"Aye, my friend," Rorke acknowledged, "You have the right. I am asking you to set it aside this one time." He saw the refusal in Tarek's sky blue eyes and he sought to dissuade him.

"What I seek is not of this earth, my friend. I may well fail. I do not fear death, but I would not be the cause of yours against these forces of Darkness. If I fail and die, Stephen will have need of you." He did not ask it for William, for no matter what passed from this day forward, William of Normandy's future was already written. But he asked it for the young man who was like a brother to him, and whose fate was still unwritten.

"I cannot forbid you to go." He spoke what they both knew to be true. "But I ask it as my friend whose blood I share by the bond of our blood shed on a battlefield."

"Do you believe that sword will protect you?" Tarek asked, needing to be reassured of the decision his friend made.

"I believe the Jehara will protect me, for she is my life."

Finally, Tarek nodded. "For this you owe me a great favor, which I fully intend to ask upon your return, and which you cannot deny me."

Rorke smiled. "Agreed."

Poladouras stepped forward and laid a gentle hand at Rorke's shoulder. "Take this," he said, handing Rorke the crucifix that usually hung from his substantial waist. "I have great faith in it. It has a power of its own." The monk's voice wobbled and his eyes glistened.

"Bring her back and I will say the words over your union in this world or any of your choosing."

Meg was the last, holding back until everyone else had bid him farewell. He looked over at her, standing apart, her sightless eyes devoid of color except for that unsettling whiteness upon white. She was old and bent, her life spent in service to the masters of the Light, and her mistress.

"There is no magic I can give you, warrior," she said with whispery voice, somehow sensing that he stood before her.

"I can only give you words and pray to the forces of the Light that you will remember them." Then she recited the prophecy of Vivian's vision that long ago day at Amesbury.

"Beware the faith that has no heart, milord. And the sword that has no soul."

Lastly, she reminded him, "The Darkness may take many forms. It will try to deceive you. You cannot rely on what you see or hear. As Merlin tested you, so shall the Darkness test you, for all is at stake." She stepped closer then and extending her frail, gnarled hand, laid it over his heart.

"Be of true heart, warrior. Believe in the power of the Light." Then she stepped back.

"I will bring her back, old woman."

"See that you do."

Rorke could have sworn a faint smile played at one corner of the old woman's mouth, revealing a hint of the beauty she had once possessed decades or perhaps centuries ago. He stepped to the entrance of the catacombs.

With but a single thought, he removed Excalibur from the leather sheath at his back.

Hear me, sweet daughter of fire. Know my thoughts, know what is in my heart, and know my love for you.

He heard no answering reply, nor had he expected one. For the gift was not with him. But she possessed the power to know another's thoughts. He sent his to her and prayed she still lived to hear them. Then, holding the sword in one hand and a torch in the other, he began the descent into the ancient ruins.

The urgency to reach Vivian made him want to hasten his steps, but Meg's words and his own warrior's caution for danger tempered that urgency. He might well lose all by acting hastily or rashly.

Patience and care, he thought, making his way carefully down the timeworn stone steps.

The way was lit by torches that had been set into brackets, both a lure and a warning that there was another who waited for him. He moved silently, training his gaze ahead from one pool of light to the next, aware of the shifting shadows at the edge of his vision and remembering Meg's other warning—that the Darkness might take any form.

Then he cleared his thoughts, steeling them to think of nothing that might betray him. For if Vivian could know his thoughts, so, too, could the Darkness know of them. As Arthur had been betrayed, so could he be betrayed with his own thoughts.

The moment he stepped into the chamber he knew Vivian had been here. He felt the essence of her presence—a lingering of warmth within the coldness of the stone walls. He closed his eyes and could feel it even more strongly, a memory of that same warmth that surrounded them as he joined his body with hers and felt himself completed in ways he could not begin to explain or understand as his flesh became one with hers.

Here in the muted shadows of the chamber, able to see only within the pool of light from the torch, his other senses grew stronger and compensated for what he could not see.

He heard the subtle muted drip of water as it seeped from the ancient stones, felt the dampness of centuries in the air as it eddied and shifted across his skin on subtle, unseen currents of movement. He slowly opened his eyes once more and searched for some means by which she had fled. He found it at the back wall of the chamber, where the wall had caved into another open space.

Stone and debris blocked any escape, but he saw that she had passed that way, escaping through the stone in the faint, glowing traces of light that glistened on several of the stones.

He ran from the chamber, down the passage, and into the next, and the next, until he found a connecting passage. Several paces into the passage he found what he was looking for—the crumbled stones at the back wall of the first chamber and more faint glowing points along the stones. She had passed that way.

It was like a maze, an underground warren of chambers and subchambers that had once been a military post of barracks that housed the ancient army of Rome as long as a thousand years ago.

The sounds of water and stale air moving about in the chambers were like whispered voices as he ran down one passage after another with a sense that he was being drawn deeper and deeper below the fortress, guided by a flicker of glowing light at a stone here, another there. Until he made a turn and discovered another wall.

He doubled back, looking for other traces that she had passed that way as she, too, was driven deeper and deeper within the catacombs with a purpose that made itself increasingly clear. Here there was only the light of the torch he carried.

The Light was her source of strength and power. She was renewed and replenished by it. Without it . . . she would die.

If the Light was life, then the Darkness—robbed of all light—would be as death to her. He continued to search for some other trace that she had passed some other way, but there were none and with growing frustration found himself returning to the stone wall that blocked the passage he had originally come down.

Iridescent traces glimmered on the sidewall and then suddenly disappeared. Perhaps she had passed through the back wall as she had in the first chamber. But there was no trace of her presence at the back wall. With sword in hand, Rorke cursed as he searched for some other sign of her. As he searched first one wall then the next, the light from the torch caught at the blue stone in the hilt of Excalibur and reflected off tiny fragments in the stones of the walls—except for the wall that blocked the passage.

Rorke passed the hilt of the sword before the wall several times, angling it so that it caught the light of the torch. There was no reflection of light. On a sudden thought he thrust one hand against the wall. To his amazement it passed through the wall.

Vivian possessed the power to move through stone walls. It was the means by which she had escaped the fortress that morning she had gone into the forest. But he possessed no such powers. Still his hand passed freely through the wall into a clear space beyond. Uncertain what he might find on the other side or even if he would arrive there, Rorke took a deep breath and walked through the wall.

Unlike his journey through the stone portal, he experienced

nothing at all. It was if he had merely walked a pace further down the passage. It was an illusion!

"The Darkness will try to deceive you," Old Meg's words came back to him. At the wall he saw fleeting traces that Vivian had passed that way. The illusion of the wall was meant to deceive him into turning back. The Darkness knew he followed. Holding Excalibur before him, Rorke continued down the passage, moving with no more sound than the air and water.

"You will never find her, warrior," the walls seemed to whisper as he passed by. "She is beyond your meager mortal emotions. She will be entombed in the darkness, her powers banished forever."

As the words seeped from the walls, taunting him, attempting to undermine him, Rorke realized that the Darkness indeed knew his thoughts. He must guard them against the Darkness.

It must not know what he was thinking even if it could sense his presence. And so he closed out all thought and fought to conceal his emotions as he moved deeper into the catacombs. Then he heard other voices very nearby, mingled with the sound of feminine laughter that he recognized.

The sound caressed the walls of the passage, drawing him on with a breathlessness of passion that echoed the desire as she lay beneath him before the hearth in his chamber. He rounded the corner in a passage and suddenly stopped. There in a chamber he saw her as beautiful as she had ever been.

She lay on a pallet, head thrown back, her body naked and spread beneath a man as they coupled with a violence of passion that tore through him like a blade. A rage of jealously welled within him. His hands clasped over the blade as he raised it high over his head to strike.

Then the man turned his head toward Rorke and the face he saw was his own. And with a sudden awareness Rorke realized that had he brought the blade down he would have caused his own death.

Vivian turned her head as well to stare at him. But in spite of the naked perfection of her body, the eyes that looked back at him were not filled with brilliant blue fire, but were as bleak and dark as death.

He swore an oath, lowering Excalibur abruptly as he realized the trap of the deadly illusion. Light from a torch at the wall, glinted off the stone in the hilt and the illusion shattered and disappeared in a burst of ear-piercing sound that could only be described as an explosion of rage.

Dark shadows crawled the walls and scattered to the far corners, seeming to seep out of the chamber as the light from the stone in the hilt of the sword played across the walls as if it chased them.

"The Light of the sword!" Rorke whispered with a new awareness as he realized the Darkness fled before the Light of Excalibur. "You are not invincible."

He left the chamber with a new confidence. There was a way to fight the Darkness. But to find where it had taken Vivian before it was too late, he had to be as cunning as the Darkness.

He moved on relentlessly even as the flame at the torch began to gutter and die out. Still he moved on, following the glimmers of light at the wall, knowing that the Darkness could not deceive him with traces of light. Only Vivian could have left them.

"Rorke, I am here!" the sound of her voice stopped him. He turned and saw her standing in an adjoining passage only a few feet away from him. Wary at first, he glanced to the walls and saw the traces of light that she had passed this way.

"It is over," she said, as she slowly walked toward him. "He was no match for me."

"Where is the bishop?" Rorke asked, skeptically, doubting that it was over so easily after Merlin and Meg's warnings, yet with an enormous, almost overwhelming relief that she was safe.

"Nearby," she answered as she reached a hand to him. "He realized that he was no match for me. It is over now. The Darkness is gone," she moved into his arms, her body soft and yielding.

"I was afraid," she whispered, pressing close so that her

breasts thrust against him. Rorke frowned. He had never known her to fear anything. And yet she felt like magic against his body, his own fear mingling with a growing desire for her.

His hand moved through her hair as hers stroked the muscles of his sword arm. She raised her face to his, so close that he could taste the sweetness of her waiting kiss. His hand closed over the thickness of her hair that hung loose at her back, angling her head back for the hunger of his mouth. Her hand closed over his wrist, then glided downward to his fingers clasped around the handle of the sword.

"It is over," she breathed again, her mouth so close to his that he could taste the blatant sexual arousal. But where was her sweet fire of innocence? he wondered, frowning.

"There is no more need of the sword." Her fingers loosened his from the handle of Excalibur.

Just as her lips met his, Rorke's fingers twisted brutally in her hair, imprisoning her, at the same time his other hand tightened over the handle of Excalibur and swung the sword beyond her grasp. The eyes that looked back at him were dark and bleak.

"Do you wish the sword?" Rorke asked with a fierce growl, hurling the creature away from him. She fell to the stone floor, shimmered, and then disappeared as surely as the other illusions had disappeared.

"You may not have it," he shouted to the Darkness. "For I will not be betrayed with your illusions. I will find her, no matter what form you take. I will find her!"

Once more the shadows ran the walls of the passage, like dark, ghostly figures fleeing before the light. This time, Rorke pursued it, sensing that it was not yet finished. It was drawing him onward to a final confrontation.

The passage ended, opening onto what might have once been some sort of arena. Here there were several torches set in brackets along the stone walls, revealing the dark openings of several other passageways, all meeting here like the spokes of a wheel.

The arena was large with shelves of stone seating fanning out from the center between those passage openings like the

424	*Quinn Taylor Evans*

concentric ripples in a pool of water. Here the spectators would sit, watching whatever event might have taken place for their enjoyment so far from Rome. Feats of wrestling perhaps, jousting, and swordplay, as ancient combatants met to test their prowess and ability much as his knights practiced with lance and sword.

He knew he had been deliberately drawn to this place. When the Darkness discovered that he could not be easily deceived, it had brought him here.

"Let it begin," Rorke said to himself. For he much preferred the open battlefield for which he'd trained his entire life. His fingers flexed about the handle of the sword as his gaze slowly scanned each entrance.

"So it shall begin and end, warrior," came the voice in answer. And as Rorke spun about in the direction of that voice, his gaze rested on his opponent.

He was a formidable opponent, standing as tall as Rorke and dressed in the finest chain mail raiment. His tunic was jet black as were his leggings. Even his mail-covered armor was black, as was the sword he carried, his gloved hands that closed over it, and the visored helm that enclosed his head.

He bore no crest, nor would any have been discernible, for his colors were black on black. The Darkness was his crest. He struck the first blow, swinging at Rorke's head. Rorke ducked and lunged out of reach of the second blow he knew would follow, striking a blow against a mail-covered arm.

Parry, lunge, thrust. Blows rained down as they both struck, quickly repositioned themselves, and then struck again. The sound of steel on steel rang out across the arena.

Rorke returned blow after blow, the steel of Excalibur as solid in his hands as the steeliness of purpose that drove each blow, until his blows began to take their toll. A return blow came a few seconds slower, his opponent's stance not quite adjusted to fend off the next, until he began to give ground, fighting on the defensive. Still, Rorke drove him back.

He drove past the point of exhaustion, past muscles that

cramped and burned with fatigue, then lifted for another blow as a darkness of purpose took hold and drove him onward, consuming every thought, giving him strength for another blow and another when he was certain none remained.

Soon there were no returned blows. His opponent could only muster the strength to block Excalibur. Then even those weak efforts began to falter, his opponent's blade barely raised as Excalibur sliced closer to the warrior's helm with each driving blow. His opponent's sword fell from stunned fingers.

The dark warrior fell back against the stone half wall that encircled the arena, his weapon gone, vulnerable, the visor of his helm thrown back. Rorke raised Excalibur for the death blow.

Kill! the thought rose like a dark specter, blinding him to everything except the need to destroy.

In that moment as he raised Excalibur to strike the final blow, Rorke looked down at his opponent. He wanted to see death in the face of the dark warrior. He wanted to feel it beneath his blade and know the exact moment when his life ended.

But the gaze that looked back at him from the visor was not the bleak, black visage of the Darkness that he'd seen before. The gaze that looked back at him now was brilliant blue, with the last dying color found at the heart of a golden flame.

Not the black of the Darkness, but the fiery blue gaze of a daughter of the Light.

He sensed the Darkness all around him, invading his thoughts, wrapping around his heart, whispering at his shoulder, closing over his hands as though it stood behind him, driving the blade down. He felt it, as real as living flesh and blood.

"Never!" he swore with a fierce battle cry. He pulled free of that evil grasp, pivoted, and though he could not clearly see its shape, he knew it was there. With all his strength, Rorke brought Excalibur down through the shifting Darkness that hovered where he had stood only moments before.

A cry of agony filled the air.

Rorke felt the blade slicing through thick garments, then the soft-as-butter yielding of flesh, the dull scrape of bone, and finally the dragging weight that pulled the tip of the blade down.

Leaning heavily on the blade, he forced himself back to his feet. Staring down at the body that lay before him, blood seeping through the bishop's fine raiment, Rorke withdrew the tip of the blade. The bishop moaned, but did not rise. Rorke staggered with exhaustion as he turned about.

The pervading Darkness was gone. Gone too was the illusion of the warrior Rorke had battled. Instead, Vivian lay against the bottom of the wall where the warrior had stood. Her long hair fell forward about her shoulders and face as she slowly pushed herself up with her hands. Her head turned toward him, the light from a nearby torch falling across pale features, glowing brilliantly in fiery red hair and gleaming like a blue flame at her eyes.

He went to her, pulling her into his arms as he went down on both knees.

"Rorke," she cried out, slender arms closing around his neck. She sobbed as tears spilled from her eyes and she clung to him. "You came for me."

His hands framed her face, looking into the shimmering depths of her eyes as if finding himself again in the fiery light of her gaze. His hands stroked back through her hair, down the length of her body, and then back to cradle her face, as if reassuring himself that she was flesh and blood, and not some illusion of his mind.

"How could I not?" he asked, tears melting the icy gray of his eyes.

Her breath was sweet and at the same time tasted of tears. Her skin glowed golden with the warmth of life, her eyes with the fire that burned within them both.

The shadows fled before the radiant light of the fierce warrior and his lady of fire, protected by a legendary sword.

His lips closed over hers as he kissed her fiercely.

"I would die for you."

Epilogue

"Waes hael!"

The toast rang out across the great hall of William's royal court. It was the last night of the year, on the morrow a new year began.

Then toasts were made to the health of William's newborn son, and for peace. Then Poladouras offered a blessing.

At least for this night, the court was alive with laughter and celebration, mingled with the music of lutes, tabors, and shawms.

A huge fire roared at the hearth. Flames of the torches along the wall burned brightly. Hundreds of candles burned at long tables set for the feasting. Acrobats performed in the center of the hall before the raised dais and William's table.

William's knights sat about him, goblets raised in countless other toasts to good health, a long reign now that the treachery had been put down, and a more somber one to the knight Sir Galant and the others that had fallen by the bishop's treachery in the north country.

Rorke FitzWarren sat at William's right hand, with Vivian beside him, and Tarek al Sharif at her other side. William's other knights, a loyal dozen, sat along both sides of the long table.

The queen rested in her chamber with her newborn son. In her place—a place of honor and recognition for having risked his life for the queen—sat Stephen of Valois. Seeing father and son together, Vivian thought their resemblance all the more striking and she desperately hoped this might be the beginning of a bond between the two men.

Poladouras had been given a place of prominence in the position formerly occupied by William's brother, the bishop, Count de Bayeau.

The bishop would survive his wounds, though he would carry the infirmity of a badly maimed shoulder for the rest of his life. William had not ordered his death, but instead banished him from the court in disgrace. As soon as his wounds were sufficiently healed, he was to return to Normandy, where he was to remain in monastic seclusion for the rest of his life—a fate deemed worse than death by those who knew the ambitious man.

The powers of the Darkness, which had used the bishop's ambitions to seize the kingdom, were gone for now. For a while there was a fragile balance in the universe. But Vivian's sense of it was that it was not yet ended.

With the sword Excalibur, Rorke had faced down the Darkness, but it was not destroyed. And therein lay Vivian's fear, for Merlin had warned that it must be destroyed in order for the kingdom to be safe.

But this night, William was in a benevolent mood. A new year loomed only moments away. His throne and his queen were safe. He had given his newborn son a Saxon name to signify the bond between Saxon England and her Norman king.

Civil strife remained. Vivian knew that much turmoil lay ahead as she had seen in her vision. William would not easily rule England, but as Rorke had once said, his legacy was already woven into the tapestry of history. There were other threads not yet woven, and as she sat beside Rorke, she knew that only time would see the threads woven in that unfolding pattern. As for the threads of her own future—they had not revealed themselves to her yet.

Wine, brought over from Normandy, flowed in abundance, and William called for his seneschal and scribe to take down his words and make an official record of them. He had pledged land and titles to his knights and noblemen in exchange for men, arms, and horses for his army. Now was the time for the granting of those promises.

* * *

William's voice rang out as he called to his knights, bestowing various titles and landholds to most according to rank and importance of loyalty. A favored few he allowed to name the landhold they desired, always mindful of the Saxon barons and widows who sat in their midst. One by one these favored few made their requests, mindful as well not to overstep the bounds of William's generosity lest they be publicly rebuked before their fellow knights.

Vivian was both fascinated at the means by which William secured both Norman and Saxon loyalty—as it was apparent he had taken her advice on the matter—and at the same time deeply saddened by the cataclysmic changes that lay ahead for all of Saxon England. It was as painfully real as her vision had revealed to her—change, sweeping away all that was before.

Beside her, Rorke listened with a quiet contemplation. He had ridden ahead of William to return to London from the north country. When he had found her in the catacombs and fought against the Darkness with Excalibur, she had known he was of true heart. And she had allowed herself to believe that his love for her was as great as hers for him. But after William's return, there had been little time for words between them.

There were still many of the bishop's men to be dealt with. Once London was once more securely in William's control, there had been countless meetings, long hours spent with William determining the best course for handling the complicated details of dealing with some of the bishop's men who were of prominent Norman families. She had rarely seen Rorke, and then only when he returned to their chamber at night.

For a few hours then, it was possible to close out the rest of the turmoil and strife, and pretend the world existed no further than those four walls. Their lovemaking had taken on a deeper meaning, with a poignancy—even in their most urgent, hastily taken joinings—of having very nearly lost something that each was still yet discovering the wonder of. And yet, no words were spoken of the future.

Now she sat and listened as these men named their future, including Tarek al Sharif.

"What bounty would you have, Tarek al Sharif, for your loyalty to King William?" the seneschal's voice rang out amid the raucous laughter of celebration.

Tarek sat back in his chair at the end of the table, the curved steel blade winking from the light of a dozen nearby candles, his body like that blade, with a tensile, dangerous strength and power, both deadly and beautiful. And Vivian was struck again by the unusual handsomeness of this dark warrior who had returned from the north country somehow changed.

In the aftermath of the bishop's betrayal, he had spoken to her of an encounter with a beautiful young woman who warned him of the traitors' attack.

"She was like the mist, her hair pale gold and eyes that a man might lose himself in. And then she was gone, as if she had not been there at all." Tarek had looked at Vivian then, with a thoughtful expression on his darkly handsome face. "She reminded me of someone, though I cannot remember who."

"Perhaps it was a dream," Vivian suggested, keeping her other thoughts about his strange encounter to herself, for she had heard of this place called Brecon.

Tarek nodded. "Yes, a dream—of flesh and blood—and I swear I shall find her."

Now, his fellow warriors only half listened as he made his request known, for the Persian's desires were well-known. A bounty in gold to continue his search for his father, and his wish to be anywhere but this forbiddingly cold place called England.

"The north country is not yet secure," Tarek said, as memories of an ethereal, golden creature filled his thoughts. "I should like a landhold there and men of my own to defend it in your name," he told William.

It had suddenly grown very quiet around the table and across the entire hall as word spread of his request. Knights and soldiers stared at him in disbelief.

"And," he added, with a sudden smile, as if his thoughts had suddenly returned, "fur-lined breeches." This met with bursts of laughter and raucous, ribald comments of other means by which he might warm himself between the thighs of wenches.

"Done!" William slammed his fist down with satisfaction. "I do not know what has changed your mind, Tarek al Sharif, but I welcome you as a loyal warrior. You will have your landhold, with men and arms, and my name to carry to the north country. What landhold do you desire?"

"It is near a place called Brecon, where your knights died."

"Aye," William said somberly. "They claimed it with their blood. Pray you will not be forced to yield yours in order to hold it." Then, instead of asking Rorke what his request might be, William's gaze fastened on Vivian.

"Mistress Vivian," he said with good spirit, "I am not in the habit of granting bounties to ladies, but I find I am indebted to you for both my kingdom and the life of my queen. I once asked you to name a boon for having saved my life," he reminded her. "I ask that you name it now, for I would bind you to me as I bind the others. I find I am in great need of your wisdom."

Vivian was startled. Around the table she saw the speculative glances of William's knights, some of them now betrothed to Saxon brides.

Since that day long ago at Amesbury, there had been only one thing Vivian had wanted—that the villagers would come to no harm because of her. Now, she thought, the opportunity was at hand if William was of a mind to grant it. And surely he would, he had promised.

"I would have the village of Amesbury, the abbey, and the surrounding fields and forest," she said, and at the surprise that leapt across William's face, she hastily explained, " 'Tis not a great deal, milord. The villagers are poor, the abbey is almost tumbled to ruins. It would not deprive you of great riches, but to me it is of great value, for they are my people."

"Aye," William acknowledged, his mouth pulling down at the corners as he contemplated his wineglass. Then his gaze met hers. "I cannot grant what you ask, mistress," he said, and seemingly with regret in his voice. "You must chose another boon."

"I want no other, milord," she insisted.

"You may return to Amesbury, of course," William told her. "At any time you so chose. But I find I would keep my wise counselor close at hand for there are many things you may help me to understand. Choose another boon while I am in a generous mood. And," he continued, "at my lady Matilda's suggestion, I would give you the title of Lady Vivian. Is that acceptable?"

She dare not refuse it any more than any of the other Saxon women—daughters and widows—dared to refuse the arrangements for their titles. She saw how neatly she had stepped into a trap of her own making in the advice she had given him.

"Thank you, milord."

Vivian did not want to hear any more. She was too disappointed that he had refused her. She only vaguely heard him ask Rorke what he would name for his reward for faithful service to his king.

Anjou, she thought with growing misery, for she had seen what was in his heart and soul in the vision they had shared.

"We have spoken of it, milord," Rorke reminded William.

"Ah, so we have," William nodded. "You have not changed your mind then."

Vivian felt Rorke's gaze on her, but she couldn't bear to look at him. For she knew what he had asked. She knew as well that the world could not be kept beyond the four walls they had shared. His world was Anjou. He had spent half his life for it.

"I have not changed my mind," Rorke said beside her, reaching to take her hand. But suddenly, she couldn't bear to stay there any longer.

Vivian rose suddenly from the table, drawing Meg's startled

attention where she sat at a table behind William's. Mally sat with her, and beside her was Justin, who had spoken to Sir Gavin about marrying the girl, for he cared deeply for her and would make her a fine husband.

"Are you unwell?" her old nurse asked, an expression of concern lining her face as she reached a hand to Vivian.

"Nay," she hurriedly assured Meg, even as her hand lay protectively over her waist and the fragile light of new life that glowed even now at her womb. She was not unwell, she was with child. Rorke's child.

Vivian gave a careful excuse, not wishing the woman to know just now, although it would be impossible to keep it from her.

" 'Tis only that it is uncommonly warm. I must have some fresh air."

"I will come with you," Meg told her, rising from the bench at the table.

"Nay," Vivian said gently. " 'Tis much too cold for you." She knew how the winter cold made the old woman's bones ache, but she especially wanted to be alone. She couldn't bear to remain and hear Rorke talk of what lay in his heart, as the others spoke of their good fortunes.

With the excuse of seeing to the queen, Vivian left the main hall. Once she was past the main doors of the hall, she sought the stairs that led to the topmost battlements and watchtowers, where she had watched Rorke and his men ride off to the north country, uncertain whether or not he would return.

Rorke watched her leave and saw the direction she took outside the main hall. Not in the direction of the queen's chamber, but the opposite direction. Giving his own excuse to William, he left Tarek to explain his choice to Rorke's knights, for they all thought him mad. Young Stephen basked in his father's recognition, though Rorke knew all was not easily resolved between fathers and sons.

As he rose from his chair, he laid a hand on old Meg's shoulder. "Stay old woman, have some wine, and do not follow, for I wish to speak with your mistress alone. Where has she gone?

And do not give me that look, old woman, or I shall deny you the pleasure of attending the birth of my firstborn child. Where has she gone?" he repeated.

Meg considered for several moments and then decided. "She spoke of the need for fresh air. She was sorely vexed that William denied her Amesbury."

"Aye," he acknowledged, and then asked, "Did she say which direction she was going?"

"Nay," Meg said, reading his thoughts, "she is not of a mind to travel through stone walls, though I would not blame her. She should leave this place."

"That is precisely what I have in mind, old woman." Then he demanded. "Where has she gone?" For he could see already that keeping track of his lovely witch was going to prove no small task.

"When you left for the north country, she spent many long hours on the battlements," Meg finally told him.

That was where Rorke found her.

It was crisp and clear after snowing the night before. The courtyard lay white and pristine beneath the silvery glow of the moon high in the sky. Stars glittered in a midnight sky.

High on the bastion parapet of the king's new tower, she stood on her toes and reached out over the edge as if she sought to pluck the stars from the sky.

Vivian gasped as a strong arm swept around her waist, pulling her back against a lean muscular body. Another arm closed over her breasts holding her very tight.

"Do you think perhaps to fly into the night sky, sweet witch?" Rorke's breath warmed her cheek, sending tiny rivers of fire shooting beneath the surface of her skin. Sweet, sad fire even now, when she knew he would be leaving. He still had the power to fill her with longing and a desire of passion so strong that she wanted to turn in his arms and beg him not to leave England.

But she did not. Instead Vivian leaned back against him, closing her eyes as she rested her head against the curve of his shoulder, letting her senses fill with the essence of him, as if she could absorb him into her very soul, for it would have to last an eternity.

"I have never learned to fly," she confessed in a most serious voice, and then added, "It was never necessary." She heard the thickness of her own voice, filled with tears, and said no more.

"Perhaps not," he agreed. "For one who has the power to walk through stone walls, see another's thoughts, and draw on the power of the flame, I suppose flying is a trivial matter."

He continued to hold her, refusing to release her when she tried to step away, turning her instead to close her within the folds of his mantle and drawing her against his body so that every part of them touched in subtle ways that teased the senses. He tilted her face up, frowning at the tears that streaked her beautiful, pale cheeks.

" 'Tis a night for celebration and yet you weep, mistress. Why is that so? You should be pleased. William has honored you with a fine title, *Lady* Vivian."

"He was most generous," she told him, directing her gaze away from his. "I am pleased."

"Aye," he said in a cynical tone, his head moving down beside hers, so that the spicy sweetness of his breath filled her senses, turning her head, drawing her mouth to his even against her will.

"You are so pleased that your tears would turn both of us to ice." He gently angled her gaze up to his. "And for one who can never tell lies, you are a dreadful liar." He looked keenly into her brilliant blue eyes.

"I had thought you would want to return to Amesbury."

So, all the arrangements had been made. She was to be sent to Amesbury. Perhaps her child would be born there. "Yes, of course."

"But you shall have to wait of course, until a proper keep has been built, for I do not fancy living in a pigsty or a tumbledown abbey, although it is doubtful any invader would want to lay siege to a pigsty or a pile of rocks. Still, I would not have my son born there."

Her startled gaze met his. His son? How was it possible that he knew?

As if he sensed her thoughts, or perhaps guessed them, he smiled, "I have spoken with an old woman regarding the matter. Did you think you could keep it from me for very long?"

Meg, she thought, realizing that her old nurse would have known almost as soon as she had. "But what do you mean by a proper keep?" she asked, for that she could not understand.

"Aye, for the lord and lady of Amesbury." At her confusion he smiled tenderly and shook his head. "For one so gifted, mistress, you are quite blind. William could not grant you Amesbury, because I have claimed it for my landhold. William has need of strong keeps to house his knights and soldiers."

"But that cannot be!" she protested, disbelieving. "What of Anjou?" She asked incredulously. "It is all you wanted all these years since your childhood. I saw it within you."

"You saw the anger of lost dreams and vengeance, sweet mistress." Rorke lifted a finger to stroke back a tendril of hair that the icy wind stirred at her cheek. Her skin was as warm as fire gently at rest.

"You released me from the anger of the past with the gift of your vision."

"I would not bind you with magic or sorcery, or the burden of a child," she told him, her throat suddenly tight with all the emotion that welled inside her.

"Only by what lies in your heart."

Rorke took her hand in his and placed it against his chest. "Then know my heart, mistress."

Vivian opened her senses to him and felt the love that beat fierce and powerful, a true heart, a true love that had challenged the Darkness and driven it back.

His hand moved low at her belly and he said with a fierce tenderness. "My future lies here." And she felt such a completeness, as if his hand moved deep inside her and cradled their unborn child so completely were they bound one to the other.

Rorke kissed her then, taking her fiery warmth deep within him and then giving it back in the breathless wonder of discovery as his senses opened to her, and they became one.

From remote fortress castle, from fields tending their flocks, from boats with lines cast into gleaming dark waters, and blazing forges, men looked into the winter sky and saw a bright blue star high in the midnight sky like a brilliant jewel suspended between heaven and earth.

A sign, some said, as the star streaked the sky, a fiery beacon that lights a path, a dragon's eye that sees beyond the mists of time . . . a promise on the cold night wind.

Don't miss *Merlin's Legacy: Daughter of the Mist,*
the second book in Quinn Taylor Evans's wonderful,
mystical series. Here is a taste of the passion
and adventure to come.

Daughter of the Mist

"There!" the young Scots lad called out, pointing at the fierce battle at the bottom of the hill as the riders reached the crest. Wasting no more time, he let loose a battle cry and ran down the hill to join his kinsmen.

The knights he led were fourscore strong, their battle armor glinting in the hazy sun that broke through the fabled highland mist.

Stephen of Valois' battle horse reared at the fierce, bloodcurdling cry. He tried to stop the lad in his headlong plunge down the hill, but failed. He whirled the stallion back around, looking to the man who commanded them for their orders.

Tarek al Sharif, now master of the landhold of Inverness by the grace of William of Normandy, king of England, sharply surveyed the land surrounding them.

Startling blue eyes set in the dark bronze of handsome features narrowed, searching for deadly traps behind each rock and craggy outcropping—eyes that had gazed across a hundred battlefields across the width and breadth of Europe, eyes that spoke of the fierce Norse blood that flowed beneath golden Persian skin and claimed him bastard. It was a trait of brotherhood he shared with Stephen of Valois, bastard son of William of Normandy, the Conqueror.

But here the land was gently rolling, reminiscent of the lush, rolling hills of Normandy except for the mist that claimed it most hours of the day and night.

It swirled around both men and horses, making them seem

like ghostly creatures not of this world. Visible one moment, then gone the next, only to reappear again as the gray veil shifted once more on the eddying currents of air.

It had been bitter cold all morning, the dampness seeping through layers of garments and beneath battle armor to chill the soul. But the mist here was warm, gently caressing, almost like a lover's whisper if he closed his eyes.

The vision returned then, part dream, part memory, of a beautiful golden creature who had come to him once before through the mist.

"Milord?" Stephen inquired as young Duncan disappeared into the melee below, the sounds of battle and dying reaching them at the top of the hill. "They will be slaughtered if we do not joined the battle soon."

"Patience, my young friend," Tarek cautioned, forcing his thoughts back to the battle at hand.

Stephen of Valois had been given over into his care as they left London by King William himself. He would not jeopardize the young man, though Tarek well understood he and his other men longed to join the battle in this cold, damp land they now claimed.

He nodded to Gavin de Marte, trusted knight of many campaigns who had come to this cold northern clime to avenge the death of his brother.

With a sharply angled glance to each flank, Tarek gave the orders. Half would follow, the other half of his men, led by Gavin, were to split and close in from two sides like a pincer.

Gavin nodded and sent twenty heavily armed men to each flank. At a signal, Tarek then led the rest of his men in a sweeping charge down the hill toward that joined battle. Their horses plunged into the thickest part of the melee, scattering embattled warriors who were afoot.

The Scots warriors fought with long, crudely made swords, shields made of animal skins, and short narrow blades they called dirks. They were dressed in homespun linen shirts and woolen trews, their distinctive plaid tartan mantles belted at their waists and hanging to their knees in pleated folds.

They had been attacked by a horde of Norse raiders, distinguished by their fur-lined vestments and wrapped fur leggings, their dome-shaped helms worn over wild manes of tawny and golden hair, gleaming war axes and metal battle shields covered with blood as they hacked and slashed their way through the Scots warriors.

Tarek's men speared through the heart of the battle at the same time his other men closed the pincer blades from both sides, surrounding and attacking.

Tarek and Stephen fought back to back, wielding their battle swords, slashing first to one side and then the other. Over and over, one name filled Tarek al Sharif's thoughts. Mardigan. It was rumored these Norse raiders were his men. He wanted at least one live captive to question when the battle was over.

Stephen called a warning and Tarek blunted a blow that would have severed his leg from his body and cut his horse from beneath him. The Norseman who swung the blow was covered in blood, but it wasn't his own. He had cut his way through several Scots. He swung again and again Tarek blocked the blow.

He vaulted to the ground and took up the attack there against the Norseman. A fierce cry went up in the midst of battle and the raiders began to retreat toward the forest while escape was still possible.

Tarek became separated from the rest of his men as he battled into the rocks. There was danger there. He sensed it in the sudden raising of the hair at the back of his neck like hackles going up.

He fought into the sun and realized too late the Norseman had maneuvered him so that he was momentarily blinded. It was a cunning trick that he'd used often himself and it might have worked had not the sun betrayed the other warrior who now made it two against one as sun glinted off his raised blade.

He went down on one knee as he struck toward that glint of steel with a slicing arc, felt the sudden shudder of the blade, then the dragging weight as it sliced through flesh and sinew, the dull scrape against bone, and finally the stunned hiss of air from his attacker's dying lungs.

As he drove back to his feet, kicking away the body of the Norse warrior, and then whirled around to face the man he'd chased into the rocks, a bloodcurdling scream rent the air.

Through the gently swirling mist that seeped over the ground and swirled the rocks, he saw the other Norseman sprawled on the ground. His tunic was bloodied, his sword arm lying slack and equally bloodied. The features of his face amidst the bloodied hair were slashed. Beside him crouched a large, slender, tawny cat.

It was a magnificent animal, its golden fur tipped with silver that seemed to hold and spin the mist into a silvery mantle that gathered about it. But the perfect tawny coat was marred with blood that streaked its left shoulder. The Norse warrior had wounded the animal before he died.

Tarek had seen such creatures in the middle empire. They were wild, exotic animals. Some with sleek black fur, others with spotted markings or stripes. They were elegant, fierce creatures that feared nothing, displayed for man's pleasure in palaces, but with such regal bearing that no man could ever own them. But he knew of none in this cold, forbidding place called Britain.

The creature caught his scent, that sleek, golden head turning toward him. Its gaze was curious, measuring, not the least afraid. Then the mist shifted and swirled again like a curtain drawn back between him and the cat, and before the animal fled he saw something that startled him. The cat's eyes glowed cool and green, like a highland glade. Then the creature suddenly turned and loped into the swirling mist.

Run, the Voice whispered. *Flee, my child. You are in grave danger.*

Again Tarek experienced that sensual awareness along the back of his neck, and down his spine. But this awareness was not fear. It was a memory of another time in a different place but in much the same way with the mist closing around him.

He followed the footpath up through the rocks where the cat had disappeared, then continued down the other side as the path descended the hill. The way was difficult but not impassable. It had been traveled before, the soft grass flattened underfoot. Someone had come this way recently.

The cursed mist blinded him, disoriented him, muffled the sound around him so that it was impossible to tell from which direction he had come, or which he should follow. Then it began to lift in that strange way that often occurred in these highland places. Rocks to his left reappeared as the sun pierced the gray shroud that lay over the land. The path once more lay clear before him.

He followed it, darting through pockets of lingering mist that washed warmly against his face, rather than the cold clamminess of misty glens. Then, through the haze that gradually retreated, he saw something on the path just ahead.

Behind him the sounds of battle had ceased. In the distance, he heard horses and knew his men followed. It was risky to venture further afoot. But a huddled shape on the path ahead drew him closer, curved blade held before him in both hands as he slowly made his way closer.

In the trailing mist the huddled shape was tawny-colored. As it had before, a frisson of warning moved across his skin, every muscle tensed, lest the creature suddenly turn on him. But it made no movement to either attack or flee as he approached. Nor did it respond even at the sound of approaching riders, the horses nearing on the path behind him.

Then as he approached closer, Tarek saw that it was not the tawny-coated creature at all, but a slender boy.

With the tip of his curved blade he prodded the boy, dressed in fawn-colored breeks and tunic made of soft animal skin. It was neither the costume of the highland Scots, nor the Norse barbarians, but did not assure that he was not enemy.

There was no movement. Yet Tarek was wary, mindful of trickery. The lad might well have a blade concealed beneath him, waiting only to strike as he drew closer. He cautiously nudged the lad with the toe of his boot. Still, there was no movement. With blade held poised to strike, Tarek nudged the lad over with his booted foot.

Pale sunlight bathed silken skin over fragile bones and delicate features. Slender brows arched over the crescents of downcast dark gold lashes. Full curved lips were softly parted, the curve of equally delicate, slender throat exposed, head thrown back amidst a torrent of silver-gold hair. The lad was not a lad at all, but a girl.

Blade sheathed, Tarek knelt beside the girl. As he reached for her the hazy sun disappeared and the mist returned.

It shimmered in the thick, pale gold of her hair and bathed delicate features, making her suddenly seem like some fey, ethereal creature of the netherworld. Amidst the sounds of the approaching riders, Tarek heard a desperate warning.

"Do not touch her! Leave this place!"

He glanced about, his sharp blue gaze searching the rocks, the path ahead, and behind. The warning seemed to come from nowhere and everywhere, yet he saw nothing. He glanced back down at the girl. A stain seeped through the soft leather tunic at her shoulder. He jerked open the tunic and discovered the bloodied wound that carved her shoulder, discovered too that she was no girl, but a woman in the high full curve of breast that now ran with the blood from the wound at her left shoulder.

As he touched his fingers to the wound, the silvery mist retreated and fell away like a silver veil. Dark gold lashes quivered against her pale cheek and slowly lifted to reveal eyes the color of a highland glade.

They were soft green, the irises as dark as slate as she stared back at him with pain and confusion, and for a moment the illusion returned—of a slender, tawny cat glancing back at him through that veil of mist, blood smeared across its left shoulder as it stood over the slain Norseman.

"There is danger . . ." she whispered, the words stirring another memory of another time and a slender, golden creature who emerged at the edge of a highland pool and led him to safety. Then thick gold lashes fluttered down over those green eyes, like the mist closing out the sun.

"A captive, milord?" Stephen inquired as he pulled his horse to an abrupt stop.

Tarek slipped one arm beneath her legs, the other beneath her shoulders. Her silver-gold hair fell over his arm and brushed his thigh like a mantle of mist and sunlight as her head lay against his shoulder. Her bloodied hand—slender and delicate, hardly the lethal claws of some wild cat—lay curled against his chest. As he lifted her, he again heard that voice that seemed to come from the rocks, the sky, the very earth beneath his feet. Only this time it was the sound of mournful weeping.

"Aye, a captive," he nodded as he carried her to his horse. But at that moment he couldn't be certain who the captive was. The beautiful creature he held in his arms, or himself. Nor could he say for certain what it was he had seen in the mist at the edge of the battlefield.